A. L. White, a Yorkshireman, researched *The Homeward Tide* and its predecessor, *Ravenswyke*, while living in Robin Hood's Bay on the Yorkshire coast. A former journalist and BBC correspondent, he is the author of many novels – including *The Long Day's Dying*, *The Long Drop*, and *The Long Summer*.

By the same author

The Long Day's Dying
The Long Drop
The Long Summer
Ravenswyke

A. L. White

The Homeward Tide

A MAYFLOWER BOOK

GRANADA

London Toronto Sydney New York

Published in paperback by Granada Publishing Limited in 1982

ISBN 0 583 13295 2

First published in Great Britain by
Granada Publishing 1981

Granada Publishing Limited
Frogmore, St Albans, Herts AL2 2NF
and
36 Golden Square, London W1R 4AH
866 United Nations Plaza, New York, NY 10017, USA
117 York Street, Sydney, NSW 2000, Australia
100 Skyway Avenue, Rexdale, Ontario, M9W 3A6, Canada
61 Beach Road, Auckland, New Zealand

Printed and bound in Great Britain by
Cox & Wyman Ltd, Reading

The Homeward Tide

BOOK ONE

September 1939

CHAPTER ONE

John Godson sat in the stern of the coble, the *Hope of Ravenswyke*, the tiller clasped tight in his hand, a sweat of fear on his forehead despite the coolness of the post-dawn morning. His pullover had felt damp and sticky when he'd yanked it over his head this morning; he could taste the salt spray on it as he used its sleeve to wipe his nose and forehead. The coble bucked as a wave ran catercorners beneath its bow; he corrected its motion swiftly with the tiller the way his father, Reuben, had taught him, breasting the wave straight on, seeing the bow lift up and over, heading away from the Cut out into the open sea. He'd toyed with the idea of starting the engine to pull him safely away from the land but, remembering the warning that diesel fuel was going to become scarce now the war had started, he'd hoisted the lug sail and, taking his courage in both hands, had trusted it to pull him away from the slip. The wind was streaming off the land and he could feel it on his neck, lifting a spray of salt droplets that ran down the back of his head. He cursed himself for having left his cap behind, and his jacket, but he'd been over-confident that the dawn would bring the sun with it this late September of 1939.

His mam would shout blue bloody murder at him when he came back in – he knew that – but he'd been determined to go out this morning; he'd been promising himself all week that, come Saturday, he'd get into the coble and take it out. Bugger school, anyway! What was the good of school to him, a Godson of Ravenswyke, the only Godson left in Ravenswyke on the male side now that his dad, Reuben, had gone away and his brothers, Wilfred and Arthur, were in the Navy. Funny the way things happened! His dad had volunteered for the Navy, to teach the new recruits about boats, and had been sent to the Army. His two brothers had volunteered for the Army and had wound up in the Navy at Gosport! It boded ill for the war if they didn't know from the start how to use their people to best advantage; the thought of his dad, who'd spent his lifetime at sea, footslogging with the rest of the landlubbers was a silly joke.

His dad had never done much at school, so John had heard. Of course, Wilfred and Arthur had both done much better than could be expected, considering their background, but John, at thirteen, was bored with school, bored with the maths and the geography, the English and the history. He held the tiller of the coble with affection. This was what he liked. This was all he cared about. He'd swap everything to do with the school for the chance to take out the coble, to drop the hooks out of a couple of baskets the way his dad had taught him. And what did it matter if back there he was consistently bottom of the class?

Mr Redfern, Sly Silas as they all called him behind his back, had been to the Godson cottage only yesterday, rabbiting on about John not having any interest in schooling, never seeming to pay attention or putting up his hand to answer questions. And he was right! John could understand anything Silas Redfern said about the growth of cocoa in West Africa, the Napoleonic Wars, the way to multiply fractions, the sonnets of Shakespeare, but none of it would stay inside. None of it had any meaning, any reality, when the wind was streaming off the land and the smell of seawrack and salt spray heavy and unmistakeable told him there were fish about, that herrings were running, mackerel streaming off the bottom of the beck, and no sign of the bad weather warning of a Black Cap on Tockett Top.

He glanced up at the cliffs now, an instinctive sailor's gesture. No clouds above the big house inhabited by the Tocketts, and no trace of a black one coming slowly over the moors, a certain indication of a storm ahead. The morning had broken, throwing rays of light the colour of eggs over the purple morning sky that now had thinned to a delicate blue. One or two puffs of white hung in the air high up, hardly moving despite the cold morning blow across the surface of the water that creamed every wave top with swirling spume. The boat sat the water, its nose nicely down under the pressure of the wind in the sail that John was holding almost fully open, too timid to let it out the full way so that it sat on the stays, remembering the swing of the Chinaman that had swept his uncle Lewis off the side of the boat.

Strange how his dad, Reuben, always remembered the death of his brother shortly after he came back gassed from the 1914-18 war, as if he blamed himself for it. Winds and waves are deceptive buggers and can combine all too easily to get under a spread sail and lift it murderously across the boat, the boom swinging heavy across the deck at head height, sweeping everything before it. John had been caught a time or two in that way and once, even with Reuben at the helm, had been swept overboard. That had been one July, and Arthur had come out after him quick as a flash, a rope tied round his waist. Since then, he'd never let the sail bag and belly on the stays, but had kept it half pulled in, even though that meant a loss of speed.

What the hell, he was in no hurry this morning since there was no school on Saturday, though Sly Silas had given him an armful of homework he'd have to tackle by the fire on Sunday evening, when he'd rather be out with the lads hanging round the back door of the Raven where Ephraim Hardcastle, the new owner, had installed tables and chairs for the summer season and now sold the new bottled cider that was all he would let the underage lads drink. Of course, it wasn't like being inside the Snug itself with the few fishermen still left in Ravenswyke, and the sailors who came on leave from their shore camps before joining a vessel. Ephraim had known nothing of the old tradition and had permitted the men from Newquay Town, the part of Ravenswyke built by the Tocketts on the other side of the Cut, to drink at the Raven pub in the Snug that had been reserved for as long as anyone could remember to the fishermen of Old Quaytown, the older part of Ravenswyke that dated back to the fifteenth century. The tables and chairs outside were another innovation, occupying the flat space between the pub and the slip where formerly the horses, and in recent years the tractor, had stood waiting to drag the boats out of the water when the fishermen came in on the tide.

John Godson always felt grand, really grand, lolling on one of the chairs, wearing his fisherman's pullover and his high boots, knowing the pasty-faced visitors from inland were looking enviously at him.

The *Hope* was pulling well, riding the waves easy without the vicious roll of some cobles. His eye ran over the baskets of line, hooked and baited, ready to stream out when he reached the fishing ground. He nodded to himself, satisfied that even if his dad, Reuben, were on board, he'd find no fault. The decks were stoned until they gleamed almost white. Every night after school John went down to the slip in all weathers to look after the boat, getting it ready for his Saturday foray. Now they were starting to talk about the shortage of food, happen his mum would let him out on a Sunday. Hadn't they said on the wireless Reuben had bought for them before he'd left that everybody should save as much food as he could, since it could be in short supply. Happen, he thought, his eyes gleaming with the anticipation of it, happen they'd reckon that catching fish for food was more important than schooling. Maybe he could pack school in, and start fishing full time? It was an unbelievably delicious thought, a speculation that carried him happily the two miles or so away from the land.

Tom Clewson had brought out the *Marguerite*, using the engine. 'Lazy sod,' John Godson thought, listening to the slow thump thump of the diesel that laid a mist of smoke across the water's surface. Walter Bredford was out in the *Nelson*, the sail filling well. John had spent a couple of evenings helping Walter rig it ready, now that all his brothers and his dad had gone to the war. The new mainsail, dark brown coloured, sat well in its gunter rig. As John looked back at the mouth of the Cut to the slip, he saw them launch the *Rose*, with George-Willie Mountjoy at the helm and his brother Phil up in the bows with the pole, ready to fend them off the rocks should a wave turn them side on. They'd hoisted sail but George-Willie seemed to be having trouble with the sheets. It had always been George-Willie's way to go off half-cocked instead of settling down and sorting out all his sheets before the launching. He chuckled as he remembered the time George-Willie had been working on his anchor and had left it on the dock hooked into a crack in the cobble-stones when they launched him. The anchor warp had streamed out behind the boat without George-Willie even noticing it, until the *Rose* had been stopped dead in her tracks. The sea had been running out, and the anchor warp had stretched astern as tight as a fiddle string, until George-Willie had woken to the danger and had cut it. It had been a month before he dared show his face in the Raven, after that!

He felt a glow of satisfaction that, once again, a Godson had been first off the mooring in the *Hope of Ravenswyke* – happen some might think it a foolish family pride but it was there, in the blood. When Reuben had been at home, more and more the other fishermen had waited for him, watching him read the weather, taking their cue from him before deciding to launch. If Reuben went, they'd all go, no matter what the weather. But on the rare occasions that Reuben looked up at Tockett Top and said, 'not today', not a man would venture out, no matter how short of brass he might be and how much he might need the shillings he'd earn with his fish. How well they all remembered the day last October when the Brawnham lads had gone out against Reuben's suggestion, and the storm that blew up within minutes had knocked the boat over within sight of the crowds lining the edge of the Cut. Reuben and the others had launched the lifeboat through the tumultuous waves and had rowed out in peril, looking desperately to find the Brawnham lads, but by then they'd gone under in their heavy fishermen's clothing, and Ravenswyke waited until one by one, over a period of days and nights, their bodies were washed up among the shingle at the bottom of the beck, adding yet another name to the long list of fishermen whose families had been decimated by tragedy at sea.

Emily Godson walked slowly back up the cobbled street when she had watched her son John safely take out the family boat, the *Hope of Ravenswyke*, from the flat paved area between the two houses overlooking the broad sweep of the bay below. Her apprehension was only partly assuaged by the evident skill with which the young lad had handled the craft; all fishermen's wives know that danger can come at any time on that severe coastline when sudden freak storms can blow up in seconds and placid waves can leap to twenty-feet-high monsters on the turn of a tide, when thick blanketing fogs can descend and sea-mists that reduce visibility to an arm's length in front of your nose. Was she wrong to permit the young lad to take out the boat? Her husband, Reuben, had trained him ever since he was old enough to clasp the tiller in his tiny hands; he'd taught him about weather and tides, about the movement of winds and waters, but would the lad be man enough to cope with any sudden emergency that might arise?

Of one thing, however, she was quite sure. Nothing she could have done or said would have kept the lad back in; the sea was deep in his blood, as deep as in the blood of any lad with an unbroken line of seafaring ancestors dating back to the fifteenth century. John was a Godson, and that's all there was to it. And now that his dad had gone away to the war, and his two elder brothers were in it, she knew John felt an obligation to take out the boat, to do *something* to prove himself. She couldn't blame him for that!

Though it was early, the houses of Old Quaytown were already bustling with life, and she was greeted from all sides with hellos as the women shook bedding out of windows, stood in the doorways despatching kids to school, walked down the street with their purses in their hands to do a bit of shopping. She greeted them all with the old familiarity of a close-knit community – 'how's that leg of yours today? – Willie getting over his cold, then? – was that bit of cloth long enough for Sarah's skirt?' The replies were comforting, helping to dispel the gloom that had descended on her when the boat had sailed on its inevitable way. The visible living proof that life goes on, no matter what happens, that days follow each other as sure as the tides, helped to comfort her and by the time she reached the Godson cottage, she was quite her normal, imperturbable, phlegmatic self again. She poured herself a cup of tea from the pot on the hob; it was thick and dark the way she liked it and she poured in two large spoonsful of sugar, her one act of self-indulgence. She liked her tea strong and sweet! The girls had gone to work; Eleanor, Reuben's older sister who lived with them when she was on leave, was away in York on her ambulance driving, and the day stretched before Emily in reassuring comfort. She had her mental list of jobs to be done, the cosy routine she could wrap round herself to keep out disturbing thoughts. She'd been promising herself to strip down John's bed and give the blankets a day's airing in the back yard, to give his carpet a thorough going over. She had a basket of mending but that would come later, when she could sit down at peace. She was going to give Eleanor's two rooms a good clean today, and black her stove again. The table needed a good polishing, and the whole place was due to be dusted through.

She thought over each of the jobs she needed to do in turn, trying to decide which one she would tackle first, but delaying the start in the luxury of drinking a cup of tea by the warm fire. These days, she greatly appreciated these moments when she could be alone – it seemed that most of her married life she'd had people about her, fulfilling their needs, their constant demands on her time and energies. Now, suddenly, she felt drained by them all. She excused herself for what seemed like a disloyal thought, mentally chiding herself for self-indulgence – they were her *family*, after all, a part of the necessary and unquestionable endless progression of childhood, youth, marriage, children, old age, renewing itself without question or reproach.

She heard the foot on the step and the knock on the door and got up to open it, pleased of the chance of a bit of a gossip with one of the neighbours. She opened the door to find Silas Redfern standing there, his shoulders pinched forward, hunched in the cold morning air. 'Mr Redfern,' she said, 'what brings you down here? Come in and have a cup of tea?'

The schoolmaster came in willingly. 'I'll not say no!' he said. 'It's nippy this morning, with the wind blowing through the Backs.'

She sat him at the table, brought him a tray with a cup of tea on a saucer, a biscuit on a plate by the side. She'd embroidered the tray-cloth herself in coloured Sylko with a pretty pattern of flowers on a design drawn out for her by Eleanor; her rough hands had made hard work of the delicate embroidery but she'd stuck at it and was proud now of her achievement.

'I've come about your lad, John,' Silas Redfern said when he'd drunk half his tea and had eaten his biscuit.

'I thought you might. I reckon you must have seen him going off . . .?'

Redfern nodded.

'He doesn't like schooling, you know,' Emily said.

Redfern nodded again.

'He won't learn, if we force him . . .'

Redfern smiled but it was a wintry effort without humour or warmth. 'That's where you're wrong, Emily,' he said. 'You don't mind me calling you that . . .?'

'It's my name, isn't it?' she said defiantly.

'An education isn't a privilege, you know, Emily. It's our *right*. It's your *right* to see your children educated, their *right* to be taught as well as can be! Folks have fought for that right, Emily, aye, and died for it or been put in prison. If we don't do the best we can by our young ones, the sacrifices that were made to give us all an education which is our *right* will all have been in vain.'

Emily sighed. 'I don't know about that, Mr Redfern,' she said. 'I'm not one much for that sort of thinking. The lad feels he's learned as much as he's going to, and that's about it . . .'

'John has a good enough brain, Emily,' Redfern said, 'but he lacks interest. I had hoped that we could talk about ways and means of giving him that interest. That's why I came down here when I knew you'd be alone, to see if we couldn't work out some way to give the lad a bit of interest in his education. It's for the future, Emily, it's important for his future . . . Surely you can see that?'

Emily was in a dilemma. Of course, education had helped her other two sons because Wilfred and Arthur had both wanted it. They'd both buried their noses in books from the earliest days and time spent away from studying had been begrudged. But John had none of that, and any time not spent on his beloved fishing was, to him, a waste.

'I don't see how we can force him to take an interest, Mr Redfern, honest I don't. I make him sit down and do his homework, at least, that's what he's supposed to be doing, but I can see he isn't thinking about sums or essays, but about fishing tackle, bait, hooks, lines, taking the *Hope* out, bringing it back. Let's face it, Mr Redfern, there's many a man out on the ocean who had nowt of an education . . .'

Including her own Reuben, she thought to herself. He'd been no more interested in schooling than John was . . .

Redfern's voice had a hard edge to it. 'Trouble with so many of you,' he said, his voice rasping in her ears, 'you've got an easy life. Own boat, fetch in the fish that earns more than enough to live off . . . That's the trouble with the bourgeoisie . . . they've already got enough to make them happy, and therefore they don't strive for the other people, the truly deprived . . .'

Emily didn't, frankly, know what he was talking about, but it sounded offensive, and an attack on her and her family. 'Nay, Mr Redfern,' she protested. 'Tha'll not say that! The Godsons have never been indifferent to other people, never refused to give a helping hand to anybody in need . . .'

'I know the Godson type of charity,' he snapped. 'I'm talking about men's rights and you're talking to me about giving a helping hand. The tragedy is that you'll never know the difference, never realise how much of it depends on the under-privileged being given an education as of *right*, not by the Godsons' and the Tocketts' charity!'

He stood up to go, and Emily stood up with him. 'I could report your John and send the Truancy Officer running after him. But I shan't bother. I've more to do with my time than waste it on somebody who doesn't know, doesn't appreciate, what a benefit a good education could be . . .'

She watched him leave without saying good-bye. He'd come with a bee in his bonnet, that she knew. He was one of the new breed of young men who always seemed to be arguing about something or other. Mercifully he hadn't realised that if he hadn't left when he did, he'd have seen a different Emily. 'I'd have told him,' she said as she washed the cup and saucer he'd used. 'I'd have *told* him!'

Nobody, simply nobody, could attack the Godsons like that and get away with it! Even though, Emily had to admit ruefully, she hadn't fully understood what the attack had been all about.

John slipped the looped end of rope round the handle of the tiller and went forward to the two baskets, lashed to the bottom of the mast, nervously checking them. He fingered the knot that secured the end of the second line to the cleat at the bottom of the mast, remembering the times he'd cast the line without securing its end. Once he'd lost a whole basketful of line with all its bait and hooks and Reuben had tanned his arse for it. Old Bill Clewson, who'd had to give up fishing on account of his rheumatism, had cackled when he'd seen John sitting outside the pub. 'Even a Godson can do it,' he'd said. 'Your dad had his arse skelped a time or two for that!' he'd said. 'It's the only way to learn!'

To be safe, John untied then retied the securing rope. He checked the tiller was still holding central, keeping the

Hope on course, then went forward into the bows, looking at the spume and spray through which the boat was carving its steady progress, eyeing the differences in texture and colour that wouldn't mean anything to anyone not brought up on the sea. If anyone asked, as frequently they did when he was sitting outside the Raven, how he knew where in this vast ocean to drop his hooks to pull out fish, he wouldn't be able to tell them. The common legend was that a fisherman could 'smell' the fish. But fish are like all God's creatures. They seek somewhere the atmosphere is pleasant. Just as a dog will curl up on a piece of ground some would find uncomfortable, because there it can loll in the sun out of the wind, so fish will look for a patch of water that's a bit warmer, a bit better stocked with whatever food the fish likes to eat. Some fish like the light; some dive to the deeps to shun it. Some feed off the creatures that live on the bottom of the ocean, some like to come nearer to the surface. Some fish are vegetarians, some eat other fish.

During the short years of his life John had listened to everything his dad, Reuben, had told him, acquiring a constant but unknown education in the ways of the sea. His two brothers, Wilfred and Arthur, both of whom had had good schooling, had asked the questions, trying to turn everything into logical facts. But John, four years younger than Arthur, knowing no questions to ask, had sifted his dad's answers through his mind, quietly observing and listening, absorbing unconsciously all the instinctive lore his brothers had sought to explain in terms they could understand. John remembered one time Reuben had told them the ocean can be hot or cold in streams. That a cold current can run through a hot patch of water and not be heated by it. Wilfred couldn't understand that. 'If you mix hot and cold water,' he'd insisted, 'they both turn out to be the same temperature in the end.' John hadn't even tried to explain it; he'd merely accepted it as fact, since his dad, Reuben, had said it.

Dead ahead, he sensed, was a warmer current. Cod isn't overfond of warm water and he'd waste time shooting lines in that part of the ocean. He didn't know how he knew, but he was so certain of it he went to the stern of the boat, disengaged the tie, and turned the boat so that the wind was on his beam, bringing the sail half in, running across the wave tops. Now the boat was rolling but not enough to bother him. He looked at the colour of the water, saw the faint blueish shade begin to turn a little greener, differences no landlubber would have noticed but infinitesimal changes that read the temperature of the water as accurately to John Godson as if he'd thrown in a thermometer. He looked back towards the other boats. They were heading straight west, against his northwesterly direction. He smiled to himself. They'd get nothing that way. Not today!

As he sailed along he felt the air temperature drop when the cliff top obscured the early sun and once again his blood quickened with that well-known feeling. He stood up, jamming the tiller between his knees and looked westwards past the sail with his knees bending to the rise and fall of the deck as the *Hope* rode each wave-top gracefully. The air had that keen iodine smell and something else, too, a very faint odour of marine decay. He moved his knee to bring the nose of the *Hope* slowly round, letting the main sheet run out between his fingers. *Now* he could head west. Now he could follow the cold stream away from the land, the green water spray falling away on each side of the bow, lapping against the varnished timber of the hull with a soothing ripple. He centred the rudder, drew in the main sheet to keep the sail off the stay, feeling the wind on his neck, judging its reliability. It was a good, firm, strong, even blow. The waves were long and even-topped. He was well away from the land and any stray currents and back-winds. Was it safe to shoot the line? Was it safe to secure the tiller, go forward and stand by the mast, shooting the line over the side? He badly needed a second pair of hands in the boat, but the Godsons were choosey about taking out a crew and, anyway, John would always rather be out on his own.

He eased the tiller a few degrees over, bringing the *Hope* more northerly, and the wind abeam. When he was making west-nor'west he slipped the loop on to the tiller and brought the slip-knot tight around the hand-rubbed oak of the tiller handle, knowing it would hold but checking, always checking, as his dad, Reuben, had constantly taught him. He let go of the tiller but stood where he was, feeling the *Hope* settle on its new direction. Now he let out the main sheet until it was on the stay, the boom tight up. The *Hope*, he knew, would hold that direction for ever, provided there was no wind change, no backing force to gybe the boom over.

He went forward and lifted the first basket to the gunwales, bracing his right foot so that he could stand facing the stern. He bent down and ran his fingers lightly over the top of the basket in which he himself had curled the line, trailers and hooks, so exactly. He checked the position of the second basket, close to his left hand, and then he began to shoot. First over went the cork float buoy. The sea took it, whipped it astern, line streaming from the *Hope* as it made progress through the water, hissing quietly as it whirled from the basket. John's hand was already on the first hook which he flipped upwards as the line lifted, seeing the hook dragged clear of the gunwale. Already his hand was on the second hook, deftly finding it on the basket rim, freeing it, flipping it just sufficiently far upwards to clear the gunwales. The main line stretched for fifty fathoms with a ten-fathom leader. The hooks were attached to smaller lengths of line, each about two yards long. Any one of those hooks could catch round a loop of line in the basket and entangle the lot. Or any one of them could snag John's hand, its barb driving deeper and deeper into his flesh until the sheer pull of the line in the water would yank out a chunk of his hand. It was a feat of deftness any conjuror or juggler would have envied until he'd looked closely at John's hands, or the hands of any fisherman, and seen the multitude of cuts.

John didn't think of these things. His eyes were everywhere, looking into the basket, at the gunwales, the run of the line into the ocean, the sail bellied on to the stay, the set of the tiller in its collar, the way the *Hope* was taking the waves, the steady direction it was maintaining so that the line streamed smoothly astern. The first basket gone, he changed his position swiftly to the other basket, tossed the centre cork float over the gunwales, pushed the basket to his right, and had his hand ready on the first hook when the leader came to its end. Now he was safe. Even if something went wrong with shooting the second basket, the first one was out, hanging like a giant necklace between its two cork floats.

The second basket ran smoothly out, a tribute to the way he'd laid the line the previous evening with its loops neat around the basket's inside.

When the last hook had gone and the twenty fathoms of line after it were taut, secured to the mast, John slipped the securing knot, throwing over the cast iron pig that would carry the second basket of line down through the water. That way, the hooks would be hanging at descending depths though the pressure of the tide on the cork floats would prevent the line standing too vertical.

John looked back to where the first cork float was marked by a yardstick with a white pennant fluttering from it, clearly visible from a mile. He turned the boat around so that he was sailing parallel with the line, the wind now coming over the starboard beam, and put the lashing back on the tiller. Now was the time he enjoyed the most, with his lines shot and nothing to do but to sail the *Hope* and wait. He took out the thermos of tea he'd made for himself, creeping quietly round the kitchen so as not to waken his mam, who'd start nagging him about school homework, and bit into the first dripping sandwich. They said bread was going to be scarce during the brief months the war would last, and maybe even meat, but it was hard to believe the government scaremongers. How could meat become scarce, with all the sheep that ran about the moors? Even Monty Neckridge, who'd sold his dad's boat and bought the renting of High Tor farm, was said to be running well over a thousand head. And kept four cows for the milk. Anyroad, John thought to himself, if meat was all that scarce, they'd just have to let him off school to catch fish. They'd have to bring more of the boats out and send the lads to sea again instead of so many of them going into the Army and the Navy.

He was going steady along his lines, the thermos-cup to his lips and a dripping sandwich in his hand, when he saw the object in the water.

At first, he thought it was a floating oil-drum, a black, forty-gallon drum, but then it wallowed in the waves and he saw that it was round as a ball, three feet in diameter. From the way it righted itself, he could see it had some kind of weight hanging beneath it, keeping it stable in the water as it moved slowly with the waves of the tide, which was now running out from the land.

It seemed to have studs sticking out of it, a bit like hedgehog spines, but spread wider apart, about an inch thick, and three inches long.

He gulped down his tea, took an enormous bite of the dripping sandwich, then hastily stuffed it and the thermos back into his snap-bag.

'Yon bugger's a *mine*!' he said out loud. 'It's a sodding *mine*!'

The mine was ahead of him, moving slowly across his path.

He pulled the tiller towards himself, putting the wind behind his back, turning the boat before the wind. The bow swung quickly in response to his direction and the *Hope* went past the mine with only fifty feet separating them.

When he was safely past, he brought the *Hope* round so that its bow was into the wind, the boom holding central, the boat stalled but slipping slowly back under the run of the falling tide.

He stared, fascinated, at the black sphere floating through the water twenty yards from his bow, twenty yards to the starboard. Once, when it tipped more violently in a heavy wave, he saw the chain that dangled from a ring at the bottom of it and doubtless had been used to anchor it, with others, across the line of the sea-ways. God, what a devastation the thing would have made if it had been washed up the slip!

The Navy lieutenant who'd turned up in Ravenswyke one day had brought a poster on which details of some of the mines had been printed. They'd all read it with interest and had even pinned it on the wall of the Snug of the Raven. This one, he remembered, was capable of sinking any vessel that wasn't compartmented below decks, by blowing a hole in its hull over six feet in diameter. It would destroy a small fishing boat completely if it banged against the side!

Somehow, he had to immobilise the damn thing!

But how?

He looked speculatively at its smooth black-painted metal surface, and those fearsome-looking prongs that jutted aggressively from it. Obviously, it would take a bit of a hit to cause them to explode the mine, but how much of a hit? If, by any chance, he could get near enough to grab one with his hands, would that fire it? And anyway, how would he get that close without risk of the damned thing smashing against his gunwales with the next wave. He had the gaff pole, about three yards long. Could he get to within three yards, and snag that chain with the gaff pole? But then, if he did, how could he hold the mine away from his boat? And, with the mine at the end of the gaff pole, what else could he do? Sit on the ocean and wait for the Royal Navy to arrive from Grimsby?

One thing was certain; he couldn't just leave the damned thing there! Quite apart from any thoughts of danger to shipping, his canny Yorkshire mind reminded him he had two baskets of line in that ocean, and he'd be damned if he'd just lose them! He couldn't thoil to abandon a couple of hundred fathoms of line, with a hundred baited hooks on it!

He looked round the boat, wondering what he could find to help him; his eyes lit on the third basket with its line neatly coiled and hooked, but not baited. His mind made up, he went to the mast, and quickly dropped the sail, tying it deftly round the boom and stowing it amidships. That done, he opened the engine box lid, put in the handle of the diesel engine, lifted the valve lifter, and wound the handle round until he felt the heavy flywheel take over the momentum. He dropped the valve lifter and let the engine turn a couple of times. Then he lifted out the plug, squirted a thimbleful of oil into the cylinder head, and whirled the handle round again. When it was moving the flywheel he used his spare hand to push down the plug on the cylinder head and the valve lifter; the engine gave a long, slow thud, then another, then started its rapidly increasing rhythmic motion. He throttled it back and waited until it settled down into steady motion, his eyes looking constantly back at the black ball of the mine, noting that it was maintaining its distance from the boat, rising and falling with each run of the wave tops.

But keeping its distance, thank God!

He swiftly uncoiled the line from the basket until he had all the leader, the float, and the first two hooks. He dropped the end of the line with the float over the side, kicked in the gear lever, then motored the *Hope* in a circle round the mine, slowly paying his line over the gunwales in a ring with that round, black mine at its centre. It took him five minutes to get all the way round the mine, back to where the float bobbed on the water. He untied the float and then slowly steamed past the mine back in the direction of the land, the ring of line round the mine slowly flattening as he worked it carefully round and through his hand, trying to leave the two hooks at its far end. He knew he ought to attach more line so that he could get further away but was scared that if he lost sight of the mine he might not be able to find it again in those swelling waves. He'd gone about a hundred yards when he kicked out the gear lever and felt the boat check. The line was almost straight now, and he began to draw it in, as slowly as if he had a prized hake on the end of it. He felt it in his fingers, moving against the tension of the sea. How deep did the chain, fixed to the bottom of the mine, extend? How well attached to the mine was it? The mine was low in the water, which seemed to indicate there was a heavy weight dragging it down, but how buoyant such a sphere would be John had no way of knowing. What would happen if his thin cotton line snagged one of the rods sticking out of its surface? How far did the blast extend, when the mine blew? Were John and the *Hope* safe at a hundred yards?

These thoughts ran through his mind as he drew the line through his hand, easing it forward and coiling the surplus automatically at his feet.

He knew immediately the line touched though, of course, he couldn't see which part of the mine the line was against. Slowly again, he pulled the left line, letting the right hand line run, but keeping the tension on both cords. Somewhere along that line were two hooks, with barbs. John was counting on them. The line ran smoothly though the motion of the waves made the tension jerky, especially since the *Hope* and the mine were both bobbing up and down at separate intervals. John hoped the six feet of leader on each hook would take care of the effects of the swell.

Suddenly he felt the resistance in the left hand line, a resistance that didn't communicate itself to the right hand line.

The *Hope* was wallowing from side to side up and down the troughs of the waves but he dare not bring its bows up, since the line might snag round any one of the fixings on the boat and he would lose his fingertip control. He kicked in the gear lever, and then carefully, with his chin, opened the throttle a mite. The *Hope* started to move slowly, heading at an angle but back towards the land. The stink of oil and diesel filled John's nostrils, and he realised he was sweating profusely in the warm morning. The line in his left hand was holding firm; both lines were slipping slowly through his fingers, the right hand line completely without tension, as the distance between the *Hope* and the mine slowly increased. As soon as he felt the tension start on the right hand line, he kicked the *Hope* out of gear. Now he had the mine attached to him, snagged by one of the two fish-hooks.

He belayed the line round one of the posts amidships, sat in the stern wiping his forehead on the sleeve of his pullover, and stared about him. He *had* the mine, certainly, but *what the hell was he going to do with it*?

One thing was damned certain – they wouldn't say thank you if he towed the mine into Ravenswyke!

He made up his mind quickly, and tied the ends of the line to the six-feet square canvas he used as an emergency sheet anchor, attaching a cork float, carrying a pole and a flag, to the line. With that dragging behind it as a tail, the mine wouldn't wander very far. He could report it to the Navy authorities, and they could damned well deal with it in their own way. He cast the sheet anchor over the side, with the cork float marker, and sat back on the stern of the coble, his knees suddenly wobbling like custard with the delayed shock. It took him five minutes to recover, during which time he drank all the tea he'd brought out with him in an attempt to settle his nerves.

Then he went back to the fishing ground, about a mile away, and one by one picked up his hooks and lines. It almost seemed as if there was a Divine compensation – he took out forty codling, all good sizes, half a dozen good soles, three haddock, and a dog-fish that'd make good bait. He couldn't remember having a catch like that, in September!

'Bloody hell,' he said, indulging in the luxury of swearing since his mam couldn't hear him. 'We should get a few more of these bloody mines, if that's what they bring with 'em!'

Eliza and Anne Godson were waiting at the top of the slip when John brought the *Hope of Ravenswyke* back to the dock.

'Our mam's going to give you such a braying,' Eliza said. At seventeen, with her older brothers and her father away to war, she assumed moral responsibility both for her sister and brother. 'You were supposed to do your homework this morning.'

'Look after t' fish,' John said grimly. 'I've found a bloody great mine.'

'And when I tell her you've been swearing . . . !'

'Look after t' bloody fish and never mind about t' swearing,' he said. 'I tell you, I've found a mine!'

It was obvious that neither of them had the faintest idea of what he was saying, but old Bill Clewson, bent almost double with his rheumatism, heard him. 'Found a mine, lad? Where is it? Haven't brought it in, have you?'

'No, you daft old bugger!' John said, exasperated. He pushed his way past the small knot of people who'd gathered to watch him in, and raced into the Snug. Three of the old-timers were sitting in there, sipping beer, but John ignored them as he walked quickly up to the bar where Ephraim Hardcastle was standing, polishing a pint pot.

'Can't come in here, young John,' Ephraim said firmly.

'I've found a mine!' John said. 'Honest!'

Ephraim put down the pot and came round the counter. 'A mine? What sort of mine?'

'Happen it's a gold-mine!' Bill Bredford said, cackling. They all ignored him; he'd been dotty since the winter's day in 1938 when the boom had knocked him out of the *Nelson* and it had taken them twenty minutes to get him up out of the icy water back into the coble, on account of the weight of stones in his pocket, the stones that should have taken him down to a quick watery grave and would have, if a line hadn't tangled itself around his shoulders.

John was standing in front of the poster. 'It's like yon bugger,' he said, pointing at one of the pictures, 'only a lot bigger.'

'You're sure?' Ephraim said, looking intently at him. 'I know your mam was after you for not doing your homework. It isn't a tale, is it?'

'Bloody hell, I'm telling you, I found a mine. One of them buggers!'

Ephraim went back towards the steps. 'Tha'd better come upstairs. That's if you've done swearing. I'll not have swearing upstairs!'

It took Ephraim only a minute to get through to the exchange on the top of the bank. 'Eva,' he said, 'young

John Godson's been and found a mine. Who should we talk to?'

'I reckon the police will know,' she said. 'Likely as anybody, any road!'

Ephraim cupped his hand round the mouthpiece. 'She's calling the police,' he said to John.

Despite the mine, John was looking round him in awe. This was the first time he'd penetrated the inside of the pub. At once, he loved its smell, the rich comfortable odour of the beer, the warmth of the rooms, the gleaming copper everywhere, the glint of the bottles on the shelves, the red plush lampshades, the deep pile of the carpet on the floor. They said Hardcastle made a mint out of the pub, with people coming to stay all through the summer, paying as much as fifteen bob a night for bed and breakfast. They said he even had them sleeping in the attics and happy to get a place.

'Aye, well, it's Ephraim Hardcastle here, from the Raven at Ravenswyke. Aye, and young John Godson's just come in from fishing, and he says he's found a mine! Where? I don't know where. You'd better ask him direct.'

He pushed the ear-piece across to John. 'You listen to this,' he said, 'and you'll hear them talking. And when you talk, you talk into here,' he said, pointing at the daffodil shaped mouthpiece. 'Only speak up. She's put us through to Whitby.'

John cleared his throat, then bellowed into the mouthpiece. 'I've found a mine,' he said. 'Honest! In t' water off Ravenswyke, you know, by Sear Point ten minutes west.'

'You don't have to shout,' Ephraim said. 'Just talk up, that's all.'

John had taken the ear-piece away from his ear, but Ephraim pushed it back. 'Hold on to it, lad,' he said, 'else you'll never catch what they're saying.'

John heard the faint voice. 'What did you do with it? You didn't touch it, did you?'

'Touch it . . . ? I'm not that daft! I put a line round it, wi' a marker, so's you'd be able to find it. Aye, and a sheet anchor at t'other end of t'line. Mind you, I want that sheet anchor back. That bit of canvas is worth a bob or two.'

He heard the voice again. 'When did you spot the mine?' It wasn't a local voice, but then they took policemen from anywhere these days, didn't they?

'Spot it? I didn't spot it . . .'

'When did you find it . . .?'

'I found it a couple of hours ago . . .?'

'What took so long to get back in and tell us . . .?'

'I had to pick up my lines, didn't I? I had twenty stone of fish to pick up and bring in . . .' Bloody daft questions, John thought.

'In the ocean, off Sear Point, and marked with a buoy. What colour?'

'It's a stick, with a white flag on it. That was all I had with me.'

The line clicked at the other end, and he heard a *brrr* noise. 'I reckon they've gone away,' he said to Ephraim, handing him the ear-piece.

John was astounded when they went back downstairs; word had run round Old Quaytown, and it seemed as if the whole village had assembled. John was the hero of the moment. Even his mam had taken off her pinny and had come down.

'What's this you've done, our John?' she asked anxiously, as if he'd committed some monstrous sin.

'I found a mine, Mam!' he said proudly. '*And* talked on the telephone to Whitby!'

'If only you'd done as I told you and stayed in to do your homework . . .'

'It's all right, Mam,' he said. 'I've been talking to Whitby, to the police. *On the telephone*.'

'Oh dear,' she said, 'whatever next . . .?'

'It's all right, Emily,' Ephraim said. 'They'll be right pleased he's found it and snagged a line on it. The damned Germans are putting mines right across the sea-lanes, so that our lads'll run into 'em. Well, thanks to your John, this is one that'll do no harm to nobody. I reckon he's done a good thing, finding it and tagging it. Wouldn't be surprised if they don't give him a pat on the back for that!'

John had been sucked into the crowd. 'What's it like? How big is it? What colour? What's it look like? How did you snag it? Were you afraid it'd explode right in your face?' The questions came at him, thick and fast. Emily Godson, though somewhat mollified by what Ephraim had said, clutched her son's arm protectively. 'You ought to have left it alone,' she said, 'a lad your age! You've no call to go round finding mines at your age!' But he could tell from the tone of her voice that she was proud of him, like the time about two months ago when he'd got Eliza and Anne safely out of one of Monty Neckridge's fields where they'd been trapped by a bull. He'd thrown stones at the bull, going closer and closer to it, until one of the stones smacked it between its eyes and the bull had taken off with a bellow! He'd never told the girls, nor his mam, that the 'bull' had, in fact, been a cow!

He told the story of snagging the mine, sailing round it with his lines, hoping to snag one of the fish-hooks into a coil of the chain. It started off simply, but by the third telling, he began to embroider it to make it a bit more interesting.

He was on his fifth telling when the police arrived in their bull-nosed Morris motor car with its canvas hood flapping at the back. A naval officer was sitting next to the driver, and John told *him* the story without embellishment. The naval officer listened intently, not interrupting.

Then he asked one question. 'How strong is the line?' he said.

John took him to the *Hope*, which had been winched to the top of the slip.

'Is the line in good condition?' the officer asked, as he examined a similar piece.

'All our line is in good condition,' John said proudly. 'We're the Godsons!'

'Aye, the Godsons of Ravenswyke,' the officer said. 'I knew your dad. A real modest man he was, too!'

John coloured – he hadn't meant it to come out like that. He felt his mam's hand on his shoulder. 'Lad meant no harm,' she said, 'only that he takes a pride in looking after everything, now his dad's away. It wasn't his fault he found the mine . . . '

The officer laughed. 'Nobody's blaming him, missis,' he said. 'I reckon it was a right brave thing he did, snagging it like that so's we could find it easy. But, knowing his dad, I'd have expected nothing less from his lad. Right, we'd better get away and do summat about it.'

'What'll you do?' John asked eagerly.

'We'll happen drag it a bit away from the shore-line, if your line holds, and then we'll blow it up . . . That's one mine that won't be harming any of our lads . . . !' He held out his hand. 'Thanks to you, lad. I reckon your dad would be proud.'

It seemed as if everybody who'd been on the slip managed the cliff path to Sear Point, even Old Bill Clewson, who could hardly walk sometimes. They followed noisily in the wake of John Godson, with Eliza and Anne, and even Emily Godson, behind him. By the time they'd all arrived, the gunboat from Whitby was standing to, about half a mile from the mine, and they'd launched a motorboat which was inching its way across the wild surface of the sea. The waves had begun to swell since the fishermen had come in, and were now cracking ten feet to the crest, spuming violently as they ran. The late morning sun, September low, caught the wave tops and spread rainbows in the sparkling droplets, making visibility well-nigh impossible. Several times people shouted – there it is, there it is – and pointed, but each time John shook his head. He knew he'd recognise his own marker when he saw it. At last, it hove into view on the crest of one of the waves and, a short distance from it, he saw the ugly black mine rear at the end of its anchor through the next wave crest.

'There it is,' he said authoritatively, pointing.

They all saw it, and watched silently as the navy boat drew near to it.

They saw the sailor lean over the stern of the boat, and hook the sheet anchor out of the water before attaching a line to John's line.

The navy boat slowly pulled away, circling the mine in a wide angle, moving at its slowest speed though that was quite fast in the ebbing tide.

It was John who first saw what happened. The navy boat and the mine began to draw further apart. 'I reckon that line of ours has broken,' he said quietly to his mam.

'It were too much to expect of it,' she said.

The navy boat took off with a roar they could all hear, heading back to the gunboat. The questions buzzed around the cliff-top, but no-one had any correct answers.

'They ought to have left your sheet anchor down,' Old Bill Clewson said, 'and paid you compensation for it!' but beyond giving him a withering look, John Godson didn't answer. Clewson's missis had made him a nice business before she'd died of TB, and he'd buried her in the cheapest coffin he could find, with a potted meat tea for the mourners! If his sons hadn't forced him to buy the *Marguerite*, he'd have lost every penny of her legacy.

Lots of folk believed the rheumatism was an Act of God! It was just like him to think of compensation at a moment like this!

When the navy boat returned, they saw the sailors lean over the side as the boat circled the mine closer, John told himself, than he would have dared to go. They dropped six canisters into the water, one at a time, all on cork floats and short lengths of line. Fewster's son had brought his brass telescope and handed it to John, who adjusted it and saw the cork floats surrounding the mine. The navy boat took off again at full speed, heading back to the gunboat.

Nothing seemed to be happening.

Again the questions buzzed around the cliff-top.

'What's happening?'

'What on earth are they waiting for?'

'What are they doing?'

The wind was blowing fiercely off the land, and people began stamping their feet on the grass of the cliff-top, feeling the chill of waiting when nothing, apparently, was happening.

Then they saw the bubble in the water and the first puff of smoke as the first of the grenades the sailors had hung in the water round the mine, each with its delayed time fuse, exploded. It seemed to take the thump of the underwater explosion a long time to reach them after they'd seen the puff of smoke. The second grenade exploded, and then there was silence.

'Bloody hell,' Walter Bredford said. 'They've made a mess of it.'

The *Marguerite*, the *Nelson*, and the *Rose*, had all come back in from fishing, following the *Hope of Ravenswyke*, but their combined catch didn't weigh as much as his. 'We were going to shoot again,' George-Willie Mountjoy had said, 'but we saw Tockett Top begin to blacken, and thought that was why you'd come home.'

'Us never guessed as you'd caught ought like yon bugger!' Walter Bredford had said, laughing. 'If you could have sunk it, happen it'd hit one of them submarines they've seen off Scarborough.'

The third grenade exploded and, almost immediately after it, the fourth.

Still the mine bobbed up and down insolently, it seemed to John, on the crest of each wave.

It was inevitable that one of the metal fragments, whirling at high velocity from the exploding grenades, would hit one of the mine's detonators. The fifth grenade and the mine seemed to explode together, and they all saw the giant gush of water shoot up into the air before they heard the ear-shattering bang. The water spouted upwards in a column fifty feet high, then lazily turned over as it fell back. The flash of light had lasted only a fraction of a second, burning its way through the rainbow to a bright, flaring white before it, too, disappeared into the engulfing sea. When the water-spout settled, nothing remained on that foaming ocean but the timeless spuming surging waves that, since the dawn of time, had consumed man's puny malevolence.

CHAPTER TWO

Mark Tockett sat at his desk in the declining light of the afternoon, reluctant to kill the glow of the fire by turning on the harsh electric lamps, though he could barely read the letter his daughter, Felicity Mildred, had sent him from Philadelphia, where she had gone in late August. There'd been much talk of bombardment of the coastal towns from the air, and shelling from the sea, once the German Air Force and Navy found their targets. Already they'd laid mines along the North Sea shipping lanes and several fishing boats out of Hull, Scarborough and Whitby had been sunk with all hands.

There was talk of giving young John Godson some kind of award for his bravery in tackling the mine that he had been lucky enough to find last week off Ravenswyke. It would surely have come ashore on the next high tide and God alone knows what devastation it would have caused if it had followed the run of water up into the Cut that separated Old Quaytown from Newquay Town, the two halves of Ravenswyke nestling below Tockett Top.

Mark marvelled at the way the two sections of the village had been brought together once war had been declared. Old Quaytown had been built into the sheer cliff and there wasn't a street that didn't climb at angles impossible for vehicles. The early-fifteenth-century cottages were still intact but now completely surrounded by cottages built to accommodate the large families born over the years to the fishing community. Mark could remember when he was a lad that the Godsons had led a fishing fleet of more than twenty boats; he could still smell the horses they'd used to drag the boats in and out of the water on their lumbering cradles. Of course, in those days the Cut had a clean deep bottom and on an easy day at high tide, a vessel could come right up as far as the bridge.

He chuckled as he remembered the stories his grandfather had told him of the smugglers who used to come up the Cut, carrying tea and gin from Holland, cognac from France. Legend had it that from the Cut to the high moor above the village, a continuous passage ran through the old houses. They said that when you took a case of tea off the boats, it never saw the light of day again until it was stored on the back of a pony taking it inland to Pickering or Malton across the bleak North Yorkshire moors. Many an Excise officer had known for sure that smuggled goods were being stored in a certain cottage, but by the time they'd got the door open, the goods had been miles away. Old Quaytown, they said, was still a rabbit warren of passages, and well it might be with the roofs of the lower habitations at a level with the ground floors of the ones higher up, and cobbled streets that twisted round and through the Backs, up steps and steep slopes that defied even an Excise man's horse to climb.

The people of Old Quaytown traditionally had been fishermen, boat-builders, riggers, sail-makers, weavers of lobster-pots. Over the ages their wives had baited their lines, taken them to the slip, seen their men off, and waited for them to return. Not one family in Old Quaytown had survived intact as the men had battled, all too frequently unsuccessfully, with the raging North Sea storms, and the hazards of launching and berthing a boat on that perilous slip at the mouth of the Cut. Any one of them could have sailed with greater success and ease out of Whitby with its calm inner harbour. But their ancestors had chosen Ravenswyke for whatever illogical reason, and there they meant to stay.

Not even the building of Newquay Town on the other side of the Cut by the Tockett family had deterred them; they'd seen the modern constructed houses go up, all in straight lines, each with its strip of garden front and back and its lavatories at the bottom of the yard, and had ignored the people who'd taken jobs with the Tocketts, either in the boat-yard or the potash mine, and had been given a tied cottage at an economic rent.

During his lifetime, Mark Tockett had seen a steady decline in the local Tockett enterprises. His family had been farming stock who'd slowly acquired, sometimes by dubious methods he had to admit, most of the land at the top of the cliffs into which Old Quaytown had been built. One of his ancestors had built Tockett House, a vast construction to which members of the family had added generation after generation, until it became a sprawling mansion with a varied assortment of styles. Mark didn't mind the local decline; his father, James Henry, had foreseen that large fortunes could best be serviced in the City of London and had been active on the Baltic Exchange.

Now Mark was more at home in London, it sometimes seemed to him, than in the vast sprawling mansion of the family seat. He'd bought a house in Brook Street, Mayfair, where he could entertain his London business partners in style and elegance; more and more he'd been spending his time there ignoring his North Yorkshire origins. And, old Thrummell had said to him only this lunch-time in the Philosophical Club in Whitby, his Yorkshire responsibilities. Old Thrummell, the last surviving founder-member of the law partnership of Thrummell and Slade, must be at least ninety years old and spent his days in the corner of the lounge at the Philosophical Club, hectoring the younger members about times past. Still, every Club had to have its Club Bore, Mark Tockett told himself, if only to drive away the people who might otherwise be tempted to spend too much time within its convivial walls!

He got up and crossed to the fireplace, staring in the gloaming at the clock on the mantelpiece. God, it was moving slowly today. He took the poker and stirred the coals, brightening the room with the flickering flames. Elsie was late, and that wasn't like her! He walked over to the window and looked out across the lawn and the rose-beds to the drive and the road beyond. Why wouldn't she use the car? Why did she insist on walking up from her own cottage in Old Quaytown? Why wouldn't she push the date of their marriage forward? Why wouldn't she travel down to London and take some of the money he'd put into an account for her in Coutts Bank to buy herself some jewellery and clothes, the way he'd pleaded?

Of course, he recognised she had a fierce independence of spirit and he'd no desire to conquer that. His marriage to Hester Gramond had shown him clearly that two people have to recognise each other for what they are, not try to change them, to mould them into new ways of thinking. Elsie Milner had made her own way in life, had even started a prosperous little business for herself. It was her independence that had first attracted him; she had seemed such a wild young thing when she'd been working here for his father, so different from all the other *yes sir, no sir, three bags full sir* servants they'd had around them.

He didn't hear the tap on the door, and the cough startled him so that he turned suddenly around to see Netta, his housekeeper, standing in the doorway.

'Shall I draw the curtains and light the lamps, Mr Mark?' she asked quietly. 'And then I'll bring your tea, if you're ready for it?'

He could see from the thin line of her pursed lips that she was in one of what Elsie called her disapproving moods, again.

He'd have to have a word with Elsie, though he'd no

idea what she'd say, other than that she'd laugh. Elsie was late, and he usually took tea with her, so tea was late. Netta liked everything to be on time, everyone in his place at the right time. If Mark said he'd like dinner at eight, though Netta didn't approve of his London habits of eating dinner at such a late hour, having been brought up on the idea of High Tea and Supper with *dinner* as the midday meal, she'd bring the first dish through the door of the dining-room promptly at eight o'clock come hell and high water. She didn't approve of tea at five; Mark had deliberately set the hour back so that Elsie, who closed her shop at half-past four in winter, could be there. Four o'clock was teatime to Netta, not five, and anyone who wasn't there didn't deserve or get any! 'Could we perhaps wait, just a few minutes, Netta?' he asked.

'Very *well*, Mr Mark,' she said, 'though you mustn't blame me if I'm busy with the black-out curtains when you ring the bell.'

Mark had no desire to start old arguments. When the government had imposed the black-out at the start of the war, and all the windows had been fitted with heavy material, Netta had insisted on taking upon her own shoulders the responsibility of drawing them. 'If the police come and see a chink of light,' she'd maintained, 'it'll be *me* they blame!'

Now that Felicity Mildred had gone to America, and Mark was alone in the house, and would be until his marriage to Elsie Milner, they had reduced the staff to five indoors with only two gardeners and a chauffeur. Mark's butler, Fossett, stayed in London to look after the Brook Street household. Any one of the three maids in Tockett House could have looked after closing the curtains at black-out time, but Netta insisted on making a martyr of herself.

'If you're busy with the curtains, then we shall just have to wait on tea, shan't we?' Mark said.

He went and stood by the fire, ending the conversation. Netta glared, walked across to the windows and swished the curtains shut, one by one, then turned on all the lamps, and the overhead light, so that the room was ablaze with illumination.

Mark sighed when she left the room, and walked round, switching all but two lamps off. Netta was so damned efficient – what a pity she was such a pain to have around. Still, he'd been lucky to get anyone after the death of his father had made him the head of the household, and people had started drifting into well-paid jobs with the approach of the war.

He wished Elsie would come!

Elsie was walking the streets of Old Quaytown, her mind a seething pit of indecision. Slowly she climbed the cobbled streets, purposelessly going from one alleyway to the next, up the backs, round the Square where Wesley had preached, down the Lane past Fewster's butcher's shop, along past the Chapel where Captain Walham held sway, despite his advanced years, as lay preacher. Up and around, down and about, with the same thoughts pressing into her mind – was she doing the right thing to marry Mark Adam Tockett, to leave the Old Quaytown where she'd lived most of her life, to become the Lady of the Manor.

She knew the people were talking about her, averting their glances as she passed their houses, hurrying past her along the cobbled streets with a muttered 'evening' that was all they could permit themselves. Elsie knew she'd always held a special place in their thinking; ever since her mother, Margaret (Meg) Milner, had given birth to her without, as the local saying went, the benefit of matrimony, she'd been someone apart. When she'd taken a job at Tockett House during the time of James Henry Tockett, Mark's father, the tongues had begun to wag.

James Henry, they said, made free with any young lass who went to work in his house – it confirmed all their suspicions when Meg Milner's 'love-child' took a job up there. Elsie had trembled with fear the first time she was alone with 'the Master', but beyond a keen look of appraisal, nothing untoward had happened; she'd quickly grown to enjoy her hours of work since the House was so silent, so dignified, it seemed to her, so peaceful in contrast to the hustle and bustle of the busy clattering streets in which she was born, where no cottage was more than a hand's width from any other, and everybody seemed to know his neighbour's innermost thoughts. Elsie had always been a strange mixture, she realised. Though she seemed free and easy on the outside, and many people believed she hadn't a thought in her head or a care in the world, she had somehow erected a façade of frivolous spontaneity behind which she kept her secret self. When she'd tried to leave Old Quaytown and had travelled the world with a rich man whose fancy she'd taken, she'd shown him only that devil-may-care exterior, since it had been the only aspect of her that interested him. He'd been a restless soul, continually on the move from one gaiety to the next, eating, drinking, travelling, spending money like water. It hadn't surprised her when, finally, he'd killed himself rather than face the inevitable bankruptcy of his spendthrift way of life.

And now, here she was, planning to take up with another rich man!

Of course, she told herself, Mark Tockett is *different*. For a start, he was one of the few men who'd ever taken her seriously, had bothered to find out what she thought, what she believed. And, unlike her former companion, he wasn't a spendthrift, though he'd already shown that he intended to treat her generously.

Would she sacrifice her independence if she married him and went to live up there, in that splendid mansion?

Could she match up to his life in Mayfair? She knew she could shine on whatever social level fate cast her, but could she remain a *thoughtful* companion in a world of investments, of Stock Exchange dealings, and Commodity Markets? As soon as Mark had used one of these terms, she'd insisted he explain it to her since she didn't want him to have a language she couldn't understand. But could she contribute anything to that level of his life?

She saw Eliza Godson walking along the street from the butcher's, a shopping creel on her arm and a woefully small package inside it. Eliza looked shyly at her. 'Hello, Elsie,' she said and hesitated.

'Hello, Eliza! Or is it true, as I've heard, you like to be called Liz now?'

'Eliza sounds awful,' *Liz* said, 'but my mam goes on calling me it. She skelped me when she knew I'd asked Tommy Thompson to call me Liz!'

Elsie laughed. 'Happen that's not so much because of the Liz, as because he comes from Newquay Town. You mustn't expect your mam to change overnight – for a long time the folks at this side of the Cut have been downright suspicious of anybody from the other side, as if they came from a foreign land. Your mam was lucky; she came from the top of the bank and was acceptable!'

'Tommy Thompson was born in Leeds,' Liz said ruefully. 'His folks *own* that house they live in.'

It made no difference to the folks of Old Quaytown. The houses had all been built by the Tocketts and kept as tied cottages on rent. After the First World War and the decline of the Tockett local interests, some of the houses had been sold to holiday-makers coming mostly from the West Riding of Yorkshire. Many of them were quite well-to-do people with good businesses inland, but that made no difference to the fishing community – they were foreigners and would be for generations to come.

Liz shuffled her feet and looked up at Elsie, a cheeky

grin on her face. 'Happen *you'll* be moving up the bank, Elsie,' she said. 'They're saying you're going to be very grand! It'll be a penny to talk to you!'

Elsie grinned back. 'If you believe that, Liz, you'll believe owt!'

'It's true, then? You're getting wed? With Mr Tockett . . . ?'

'You'll know when you get an invitation . . . '

'You're going to invite us . . . ? Honest . . . ?'

'If I make up my mind to get wed, I shall invite you. Believe me, I shall invite everybody!'

Liz laughed out loud with the excitement. 'There'll be some green eyes on that day, Elsie, you can bet!'

'Green eyes, and long faces. But they'll take a slice of the wedding cake, all the same!'

'Shall you wear white . . . ? White weddings are lovely . . .'

'And carry orange blossoms . . . ? Now that would really put the cat among the pigeons, wouldn't it?' Elsie looked at the young girl, so immature, so fresh and, presumably, unspoiled. She knew she'd have no doubts if she could go to Mark Tockett the same way, with innocence fresh as the apples in Liz's cheeks. She laid her hand gently on Liz's arm. 'When your dad comes home on leave,' she said, 'I'll have a word with him about Tommy Thompson, if you like?'

'Would you? Dad'll listen to you, I know.'

'He'll see great changes when he comes back from France. I'd like to see his face the first time he walks into the Snug at the Raven and finds it full of Newquay Town folk. Aye, and married women wearing trousers to go to work in Whitby, with their hair all tied up in scarves . . .'

People seemed to think the changes were temporary and would last only as long as the war itself, but Elsie knew differently. Reuben Godson, like all the Godsons before him, had controlled his family rigidly. Just a few years ago it would have been unthinkable for one of his daughters to think of keeping company with a lad from Newquay Town.

'When your dad started courting your mam,' she said to Liz, remembering the day as vividly as if it had been yesterday, 'he thought Phil Naseby was showing a bit too much interest, and laid into him, out there on the scaurs. He got a fright, too! He knocked Phil Naseby cold and nearly drowned him. Phil Naseby was living in Newquay Town. All the Nasebys lived there – a right bad lot they were!'

She didn't tell Liz about the time the Nasebys had lain in wait for her, had dragged her down, and one by one had raped her. That had been *her* introduction to the whole grown-up world of sex.

'You have to understand, it's folks like that who gave Newquay Town a bad name in the old days, and a bad name takes a lot of living down. Believe me, I know!'

She watched Connie Cathcart walk past as she spoke, and pitched her voice a little louder so that Connie couldn't help overhearing. Connie shot her a glance of pure venom, tightened her thin lips, and said nothing.

'Your dad will have to come to terms with the changes that have taken place,' she said. 'Perhaps I can persuade him that not all changes are bad, especially if we have young lads like Tommy Thompson bringing a bit of new blood into the place.'

Liz went even redder in the cheeks. 'Just so he knows,' she said, 'that some of us aren't babies any more . . . '

The brief encounter with Liz had reassured Elsie; she walked down Godson Street to Liz's door then carried on to the dock and up alongside the Cut, climbing the hill that led to the vast gaunt Tockett House on the top of the cliff. Once again, as she neared the house, she chided herself for her uncertainties – here she was, a woman going on forty with all the experience of travel in foreign parts behind her, and she was dithering like a lass of Liz's tender years. Mark Tockett was a fine honest man who loved her. She loved him.

'Let's get married quickly,' she said after he'd drawn her beside the study fire and had kissed her, before settling her down in the armchair. 'Let's get the date settled right away.'

CHAPTER THREE

They all stood up when the captain walked into the room. He looked at their faces, noting their young eager eyes, their expressions which ranged from overt self-confidence to blatant anxiety, then told them all to sit down, calling them by the collective name they'd use all through officer training, *gentlemen*. For some, he could see, it was the first time they'd ever been called gentlemen. Others accepted it with an arrogant certainty, as of right.

'My name is Nesbitt,' he said, 'and I suppose by now you're all aware that these three pips on my shoulder entitle me to be called Captain, whatever other title you might have for me when you come to know me better. I shall endeavour to learn all your surnames and call you by them. It would help if, in the beginning, each of you would state his name first whenever you speak to me.'

He seated himself in an armchair on the low raised platform that ran across one end of the hut. The twelve officer cadets wore identical serge uniforms with a white ribbon across the ends of the epaulettes of their battle-dress blouses; he'd read all their records and wondered which faces connected with which names. Which one, for example, was Willoughby, son of Sir Percival Willoughby, Bart, barrister? Which was Lionel Bailey, son of Marguerite Bailey the well-known actress? Which were the Godson brothers, whose father's profession had been listed in the space provided simply as 'fisherman'? And who could be Peregrine Montgomery d'Arcy, whose father was MP for Stoke Newington? Which was

Cameron, surely a Scotsman, and which Davies, presumably Welsh?

'While you are here,' he said, 'we shall call you *gentlemen*, and try to make *officers* of you. Various members of the staff will report on your individual and particular abilities in each section of the training. I shall watch you all the time, and it'll be my task to try to assess your overall suitability for the great responsibility that being an officer, a man who leads other men often into danger, can bring. And, just so that we understand each other perfectly, I'm not interested in your successes – you can be a wonderful instructor, a brilliant tactician, an outstanding athlete, but if you haven't got the stuff of leadership in you, I won't permit you to pass out of here with the lives of other men in your hands. I hope that is clear, gentlemen?'

There was a chorus of 'Yes, Captain', and 'Yes, Sir'.

'One more thing before we go in for dinner. This is a new Officer Cadet Training Unit and all the staff have been assembled from other units. As you will probably have noticed, the camp has been built in a hurry. For most of the indoor classes we shall use the Towers and, eventually, you will all be accommodated up there. In the meantime, you'll have to do the best you can down here in these huts. This may not be what some of you are used to; but I ask you to remember that we're as new here as you are – we'll just have to try to get on together as best we can.'

He referred to his list. 'When we go in to dinner, I'd like Cameron and d'Arcy to sit either side of me. Don't worry – it's an ordeal you'll all have to suffer, two by two!'

'This really is too much,' Willoughby said. 'My brother went to Sandhurst. They had one batman between two! And here *we* are in a damned pigsty!'

Arthur Godson looked round the dormitory, saw the

twelve beds, each with its side cabinet for odds and ends, its wooden locker giving privacy from the bed next in line. The stove was burning well in the centre of the room and the place was decidedly warm. The lavatories were at one end of the room; the twelve of them shared three. The two bathrooms were at the other end and so far the water had run too hot to use without adding some cold. It was a damned sight posher than the tin tub in front of the fire at home.

'It seems all right to me,' he said impetuously. 'After all, we are in the army. And this is a lot better than the naval barracks we were in!'

'Dear boy,' Willoughby said, 'it's entirely a question of what you've been used to! Some of us were not brought up in pigsties.'

Wilfred looked up from his seat at the table, where he'd been shining his shoes, buffing the toe-caps to get a polish on them.

'Afore you get started,' he said, deliberately thickening his northern accent, 'you'd do well to remember we're all in this together. If we start by getting toffee-nosed with each other, there's going to be trouble among us, and we shall be so busy fighting among ourselves we'll never notice when they put us back on the train to return us to our units. So, I'd take it kindly if you didn't call my brother, *dear boy*. That's if you don't want me to thump you!'

Willoughby stared at him. '*You* thump *me*?' he said incredulously. 'The captain of boxing at Harrow . . . ?'

'It makes no difference to me if you were captain of rounders. Next time you call our lad, *dear boy*, I'll shut your mouth for you.'

Neither of them had seen Captain Nesbitt enter the hut. 'Everything all right in here?' he asked. 'Settling down, are you?'

They all sprang to attention when he spoke; he walked

across to the stove and stood beside it, warming his hands. 'Stand easy,' he said, 'and go about your business.' He looked across the room at Wilfred Godson, sitting at the table with his shoe covering one hand like a glove, the polishing rag in the other hand. 'What's *your* name?' he asked quietly.

'Godson, Captain. Wilfred Godson.'

'Ah, yes. One of the two brothers.'

'Yes, Sir. That's my brother over there, sitting on his bed.'

Captain Nesbitt took a pipe from the pocket of his jacket, checked that it contained a fill of tobacco, and lit it slowly with a wooden match he took from a box. Though he had told them all to be at ease, and most of the cadets had carried on with what they'd been doing before the Captain arrived, Wilfred couldn't start his polishing again, feeling conspicuous seated beside the Captain at the table. He could smell the strong odour of pipe tobacco and of polished leather which doubtless came from the gleaming belt and strap the Captain wore, that Wilfred already knew was called a Sam Browne. If ever he qualified as an officer, he knew he'd be entitled to wear one. And one of those neat uniforms with the large baggy pockets. My, they'd think he looked grand when he walked down to the Snug at the Raven wearing a uniform like that. Carrying a stick, and with a flat cap on his head! That'd set Old Quaytown buzzing, and no mistake – Reuben's lads a couple of officers!

He'd approached the War Office Selection Board with no actual hope of being chosen for officer training and, though he'd done all the tests conscientiously as well as he could, he hadn't been surprised when the Board had called him in to tell him he hadn't passed for the Navy. He'd been astounded when they'd told him, however, that they could pass him for the Army.

'There's no demerit in this,' the Chairman of the Board

had insisted. 'The Navy requires one set of abilities and potentialities, the Army another. We don't want you to accept our suggestion that you try for a commission in the Army with any thought in your mind that you're settling for second best.'

His surprise had been complete when they'd offered Arthur exactly the same alternative.

Captain Nesbitt was looking idly, it seemed, round the room, glancing at each bed, seeing the pyjamas men were laying out, the leather cases in which some carried their washing equipment. Wilfred and Arthur had thought themselves very grand with the small toilet cases their Aunt Eleanor had given them as a going-away present but some of the cases of their fellow cadets surpassed anything Wilfred had ever seen, with their silver mounted bottles and jars, the silver cases for toothbrush, toothpaste, styptic pencil which Wilfred had watched d'Arcy use that morning when he'd nicked himself shaving. Wilfred at nineteen had no need to shave; surprisingly Arthur, a year younger, already possessed a black bristly stubble if he didn't shave every second day.

'Your father's a fisherman?' Captain Nesbitt said quietly.

'Aye, Captain,' Wilfred said, unconsciously lapsing into northern accents at the thought of his father, Reuben. 'The Godsons have always been fishermen sailing out of Ravenswyke.'

'That's up near Whitby, if memory serves me right.'

'Aye. I mean, yes, Captain. But now my Dad's in the Army in France.'

'I'd have thought they'd have needed him for the Navy ...'

'My grandad was in the Army. Killed in the last war, in France.'

'We lost a lot of men in that war. We shall lose a lot more in this. And a disproportinate number of them will be officers. And junior officers, at that. I hope you know what you've let yourself in for by volunteering to come here.'

Wilfred laughed nervously. 'Us Godsons have always been ones for having a go,' he said. 'We couldn't let them down at home.'

'No, I guess you couldn't!' When the Captain spoke again, his voice was little more than a whisper. 'You'll find that a lot of people are not used to seeing a man polishing his shoes at table,' he said. 'You might do better to sit by the side of your bed for that.'

Wilfred coloured, realising he was committing a social error, but recognising that the Captain had taken the trouble to inform him so quietly the others wouldn't hear. 'I'm afraid I've a lot to learn, Captain,' he said, trying to lower his shoe out of sight between his knees. 'I hope that won't count against me. Or my brother.'

The Captain reached across and grasped the other shoe, which was lying on the bench. He took the rag from Wilfred's hand. 'You'll find you get a better shine,' he said, laying his pipe on the table, 'if you spit on the polish. That's why they call it spit-and-polish!' Without hesitation, he spat loudly on the toe-cap of the shoe. Wilfred saw Willoughby and d'Arcy look across the barrack room, each with an expression of distaste, but the Captain ignored them as he rubbed vigorously. As he rubbed, he said, again quietly, 'Of course it won't tell against you. The days of that kind of snobbery are past. People are saying this war will soon be over, but I personally don't believe it. We shall need as many good junior officers as we can find, and they won't all be found in the public schools. Don't misunderstand me; I have nothing against a private education, in fact I had the benefit of one myself. You all arrive here unknown, untried, untaught and untested. What we can make of you will be the measure of *our* abilities as much as yours. For a start, I suggest it's worthwhile to keep your eyes open and watch how the others behave. Then you won't cause them any unnecessary offence, and you won't have to spend your life threatening to thump them whenever they offend you!'

Wilfred coloured again. So, the Captain *had* heard his remark!

'I hope we shall all get on very well,' Nesbitt said as he put the shoe on the bench and got up from the table. 'Believe me, I realise what an ordeal the social side of being an officer must be for young lads who haven't been taught the intricacies of social etiquette. Let's face it – good manners are no more than a set of rules to make it easy for us all to get on together in a wider society. And I'm afraid you'll soon learn that good manners are not conspicuous among the rich, the privileged, or the well-educated! There, you see what a good shine that bit of spit brought to your toe-cap? There's a moral somewhere there, if only we could take time to work it out.'

'Won't it be funny, Mam, when Wilfred and Arthur pass as officers. I'd love to see them come walking up the street in their uniforms. I bet that'll make people stand up and stare!'

'Get on with that sewing,' Emily Godson said. 'And you, John, get on with your homework instead of gawping in that *Picture Post*.'

Emily sat by the fire, heavy again with disappointment. Winnie Clewson had had a letter that day from her son, and he was in the same lot as Reuben in France. Winnie had brought the letter round because, nosey devil, she'd asked the postman if he'd brought one for Emily Godson and he'd said, no, before he'd thought to say it was none of her business. 'It's funny to see Reuben walking about with his sergeant's stripes,' Frank Clewson had written. 'There's talk he's going to be made sgt-major.' Just that.

Not a word to say how her Reuben was keeping. How he was looking. How he was faring over there in France.

She turned when the door opened, admitting a cold draught, and Anne came in with her cloth coat wrapped tight about her. 'I think it's going to to snow,' she said as she took off her coat and threw it over the back of the chair.

'Hang it up, there's a good girl,' Emily said absently, staring into the flickering flames of the fire that gave her no comfort.

Anne came to sit in Reuben's chair, her hands extended towards the blaze. 'God, it's cold out there,' she said. Automatically, Emily swung the back of her hand across the girl's face. 'Don't blaspheme,' she said, but her voice lacked sternness.

'You're in my chair, our Annie,' John cried from the table. 'I shall be finished here in a minute.'

'When you've finished, you can have your chair,' Emily said, 'and not before.'

Strictly speaking, the chair was Reuben's, but family tradition had it that to sit in it was the prerogative of the oldest male Godson left at home. With Wilfred and Arthur, and their father Reuben, away in the Army, the chair rightly belonged to John.

Emily sighed; so many of the old customs seemed to be disappearing all too quickly. When she was a lass, no-one would ever have thought of sitting in the chair of the head of the household. She could count on one hand the number of times she'd sat there during her entire married life.

'Bring that buffet up to t'hearth, if tha's cold,' she said to Anne. 'I don't know what's getting into t'pair of you. You taking your dad's chair, and Eliza walking around with a bit of a lad from Newquay Town. If I ever see the pair of you together . . . ' she said to Eliza.

'I've asked you times to call me Liz, Mam,' Eliza said,

plaintively. 'Surely I've got a right to be called what I want . . . ?'

'A *right*, you young missy? You've got a right to be proud of the name you were given at your baptism, the name me and your dad chose for you. And that's as far as it goes.'

John closed his book with a snap. Damn evenings got longer and longer with his mam and the girls snapping at each other. He wished his dad was home, or Wilfred and Arthur . . . 'I'm going to have a walk down to t'slip,' he said, 'see how the *Hope* is doing.'

'It'll not run away,' Emily said. 'At least, it hasn't during all my years.'

'Aye, well, like, I'll just go and make sure everything's tied down. If it's going to blow up . . . '

Emily let him go; she knew he was feeling the same restlessness that lay like a clammy hand on all of them this November, the first winter of the war. She glanced up at the mantelpiece where she kept the ration books in their buff-coloured covers. Hardly enough in them to keep body and soul together, she told herself. Still, it did mean that everybody was in the same boat. There'd been a lot of complaints already that Fewster was unfair when it came to handing out the meat, and several times already she'd found a slice of liver under the small scrag-end joint she'd ordered. Of course, liver, being offal, wasn't on the official rationing, but Fewster gave it out sparingly to his old customers. So far the war had brought no real hardship to any of them, but she was more ready to let John take out the boat these days, now that the fish came in handy as a meal. Silas Redfern had been on to her again, and she'd pushed John into doing his homework. The lad had no interest in studies, in any kind of school-work. She'd told him that he'd need to learn arithmetic if ever he wanted to get into the Navy, but not even that had spurred him on.

'I'll leave t'school just as soon as I might,' he said. 'Be happy that our Wilfred and Arthur have all the brains in the family. We shall need somebody to help my dad wi' t' boat after the war is over, and I can't see a couple of officers settling down to shoot fifty fathoms of line! Or to bait a couple of hundred hooks!'

Emily knew he was right, of course. In her heart she didn't want either Wilfred or Arthur to go back to fishing after the war. She knew nothing would ever deter Reuben, or John for that matter. They were both from the same cast, both men of the sea, neither one of them happy on dry land. But Wilfred and Arthur, both of whom had had a good education, thanks to their natural ability to learn, were cut out for better things. Wilfred was going to be a marine biologist, whatever that might mean, and Arthur had set his mind to being a naval architect. And good luck to both of them.

'Mind you wrap up warm,' she said to John as he put on his overcoat and wound his scarf round his throat. 'And see you're back in here by nine o'clock!'

Liz glanced at John as he went out, and Emily failed to see the wink of understanding that passed between them, since she was looking in the fire once again, and thinking about Reuben. Liz watched him go, her fingers deftly folding back the hem of the petticoat into which she was sewing a lock of her own hair. The petticoat would be worn by Elsie Milner the following week, when she wed Mark Adam Tockett, and an old Yorkshire custom decreed that the lock of hair would ensure an early wedding for Liz. She smiled at Anne who was sitting back in the chair now that John had gone, enjoying the unaccustomed warmth and comfort close by the hearth and the blazing fire.

John didn't hesitate, but turned right as he left the house, down the narrow, steep, cobbled street that had borne his family name for more generations than anyone could remember. As always when he was heading towards the dock, his blood quickened. A few late gulls wheeled overhead, cawking in the keen November air which smelled of kelp, fresh as a cold bath after the warm, domestic smokiness of indoors. The twilight lingered over the slate roofs of the houses lower down the hill, and fire-smoke lifted lazily above them, weaving patterns. He paused, as he always did, by the gap between Clewson's and Bredford's, catching his first wide angle of Ravenswyke Bay below and Tockett House on the cliff at the far side, a single light glinting for a moment and then disappearing as, no doubt, Netta adjusted the black-out curtains.

There'd be a moon later, he knew with the weather-wisdom of a sailor, and tomorrow the catch would be good. Some said the moon sent the fish deeper in the water, others said it brought them nearer the surface. John knew that fish behave differently and what would set a cod down would happen bring a flounder or a sole up. He knew with the quiet certainty of a craft handed down from father to son through the generations, that tomorrow would be a good day for sole. And sole fetched a price these days.

How could he avoid school, and yet go out on the boat? He could pretend a sore throat, but that would keep him in the house, with the stink of vinegar and brown paper in his nose all day. At the first sign of a sore throat, his mam would rub his neck with stinking goose fat, soak a piece of brown paper in vinegar, and bind it round his neck with an old woollen sock.

How about a sprained ankle? Then he couldn't walk half way *up* the bank to school, but he could hobble down and *sit* in the boat. *That* might work! The problem of evading school still occupied his mind as he arrived at the bottom of the street, coming out past the new Post Office and the Raven pub, past the shed Old Millie Harrison let them use for storing their tackle, now that so many tourists had brought thievery to Ravenswyke. In his dad's time, a fisherman could leave his tackle in the boat all night, high and dry on the slip, and nobody would think of touching it. A man could bait his hooks, spread a bit of tarpaulin over them, and go into the Snug for a couple of glasses of beer before setting out. But only the previous week the Bredfords had lost a coil of a hundred feet of good line. They needed Millie Harrison's shed, with a stout lock on the door to which they all had a key, to protect their stuff these days.

He went to the gunwales of the *Hope* on its cradle by the top of the slip and, without thinking, rubbed his hands along the worn varnish. Come the spring, he'd need to get glass-paper and a brush to that, if his dad, Reuben, wasn't to skelp him when he came home on leave and saw the state of the boat. He checked that the tiller was stowed, lashed under the thwarts. He wanted to look at the pintles – when he'd lifted off the rudder, the last time he'd been out, it had felt as if there was quite a bit of play in the rudder bearing. That'd be the case if the brass bushing was becoming worn. He stuck his little finger into the bushed hole of the pintle; the inside of the lining felt smooth and round. Sometimes a bit of sand, a chip of rock, even a bit of shell, could get in there, riding under the collar, and abrade the brass during the countless times the rudder swung backwards and forwards in the course of a trip. This felt smooth and circular to his finger tip. Happen it had been his imagination but he made a resolve to check it in daylight before he took the *Hope* out again. Once that bush became worn into an oval, the heavy seas, constantly pounding the rudder from the stern, would increase the size of the oval, until the rudder would smash from side to side with a force sufficient to snap the pintle rod, even though it was made of forged steel.

He climbed into the *Hope* and felt the pintle rod,

three-quarters of an inch in diameter. It felt smooth all along its length, though a bit of a shoulder had been worn on it where it seated into the collar. He'd need to look at that, too, when the light was better.

He'd been so preoccupied with the rudder and the pintle rod that he hadn't heard Tommy Thompson approach. 'I wondered if you'd be coming out tonight,' Tommy said.

'I couldn't stand it at home; the three of them get on my wick!'

Tommy had three sisters, all younger than him. 'I know what you mean,' he said. 'Here, I've pinched a couple of my dad's cigs. You can have one, if you've a mind.'

He handed over the cigarette and John looked curiously at its oval shape. 'What's this then?' he asked. 'It's a funny shape for a cig.'

'Passing Clouds. My dad keeps 'em in a pink packet in t'cupboard for smoking on a Sunday. He says they make a change from Gold Flake.'

'My dad doesn't smoke,' John said, crouching in the lee of the boat to light up, puffing generously to start the tip of the cigarette glowing, and coughing with effort.

'Take it easy,' Tommy Thompson said. 'They say as cigs is going to be hard to come by during the war. All the tobacco is imported, and they need the space in the ships to fetch food.'

'They're trying to stop us going out because of the mines and the submarines,' John said, leaning his back against the side of the boat, looking out over the ocean. 'It's funny to think of submarines out there, isn't it, below t'surface, with a bit of a telescope sticking up. It must be bloody horrible locked up in one of them things, deep down in t'water. I wonder if they can see fish through t'telescope.'

'It's called a periscope . . . '

'Aye. Well, what I can't understand is, when they send off these torpedoes, how is it that the torpedo doesn't get all wet, eh? How is it that, when it hits a boat, it explodes. Like that mine I found – how come the water didn't get into it to spoil it, eh? These are smashing cigs . . . '

'My dad keeps them for a Sunday . . . '

'My dad had his bath on a Saturday night – we all did – and kept his clean shirt for a Sunday. We all did. Now it's only the four of us, we have a bath on a Monday after mam's done t'washing.'

'We don't have a bath. We have to wash all over, standing up in t'kitchen.'

'Tockett has six baths, all in separate rooms. Wi' big taps that give hot water and cold, and a little spray thing you hold in your hand to wash the soap off. They say the house has a boiler big as a factory boiler with, like, hooks that drop the coke in and fetch out the ashes. Must be a marvellous thing to watch it working.'

'It must be nice to have a bath when you want one. When I had scabies I had to go to the Municipal Baths in Leeds – honest they had a tub there so big you could have got four in it – but it was full of some sulphur stuff that stank horrible. And I had to wash my hair in it. I thought I'd die. But it cured my scabies.'

'What on earth is *scabies*?'

'It's like a rash you get and can't get rid of without this sulphur stuff.'

'That must have been awful!'

'It was. I've had so many diseases,' Tommy Thompson said proudly. 'I've had mumps, and measles, and whooping cough, and even diphtheria. When I had diphtheria, I had to go into Isolation Hospital. They thought I was going to die, and mam brought a clean nightshirt for me to be laid out in. But I didn't know owt about that – I was in a *coma*. Have you ever been in a coma?'

'I can't say I have,' John said.

'Aye, but then you're young yet. You haven't started working, yet.'

'Neither have you, if what I hear tell about Dobbin's place is true!'

Tommy Thompson had left school at fifteen, and was now working at Dobbin's, one of the new shops in Newquay Town.

'You can hardly call weighing taters and bagging up sugar *work*!' John said. 'I've been *working* ever since I were old enough and strong enough to grab the tiller of this boat. If you'd been out in a gale, struggling to get your lines back up to avoid losing them, hauling them while you balance in t' scuppers with every wave coming inboard and swirling round your ankles, trying to drag you back overboard with it, you'd know what work means. I've been tied to that mast in more storms than you've had hot dinners! And that's *work*, believe me.'

Tommy's face glistened with enthusiasm. 'All right, John,' he said eagerly, 'take us out wi' you! I won't be a burden to you, I can promise. Take us out and then, happen, your mam'd have a bit of respect!'

'Godsons never take nobody out with 'em,' John said with pride, albeit somewhat pompously.

'Your dad used to take Batty out wi' him, so I've heard.'

'That was different,' John said. 'Batty was out of work wi' nowt coming in, and so my dad took him out to help him. Batty was the first, and I reckon he'll be the last. Any road, you didn't come down here to talk about fishing or comas or owt like that. You came to see if I had a message for you from our lass. Well, she says to tell you she can't manage for a day or two because mam's keeping an eye on her and she's doing this sewing for Elsie Milner's wedding. Oh, aye, and I'm supposed to say to you that nowt's changed, whatever that may mean. It all seems a bit daft to me!'

'Aye, happen it is a bit daft, to you!' Tommy Thompson said, though he seemed to have been pleased enough with what John had told him, especially that last bit. 'I'm going in t' Snug. It's a pity you're not older, else I'd take you with me and buy you a drink.'

'Take me with you . . . ?' John said with scorn. 'I can take myself, if I've a mind . . . ' That was a big secret John had been hugging to himself for days. He knew that, local tongues being what they were, eventually his mam would find it out but for the moment he was pleased to keep it to himself. Ever since he'd rushed into the Raven to tell Ephraim Hardcastle about the mine, and to speak to the police on the telephone, Ephraim had allowed him to go into the Snug and drink a glass of cider. Of course he had to sit in the dark corner by the window well away from the fire, and he knew he'd have to keep his own counsel and not draw attention to himself. The discovery of the mine seemed to have drawn him into the ranks of the fishermen – after an adventure like that, he was accepted as one of them, an adult, one of the elite of an exclusive club centred on the Snug of the Raven Hotel. The first time he'd been in there after the mine incident, he'd been standing in the middle of a crowd of the fishermen, the Bredfords, the Clewsons, George-Willie Mountjoy, as they'd moved across the Slip. He'd been telling them yet again how he'd manoeuvred his line round the anchor chain of the mine when suddenly he'd found himself inside the Snug with George-Willie asking him what he'd have. 'I know what he'll have,' Ephraim had said, smiling at him. 'He'll have a cider for a while or two.'

The second time he'd gone in, he'd had no money in his pocket. 'No,' he'd said, 'I'll not have owt,' but Ephraim had stood a glass of cider in front of him and had said – 'You can bring us a bit of fish when you've a mind!'

Now it was an understood thing that every time John returned from fishing, he'd sort out a chubby plaice, or a sole, or a cod, wrap it in newspaper, and give it inconspicuously to Ephraim behind the bar. And he could go into the Snug any time he liked, and drink a glass of cider. It was a heady experience for a lad going on fifteen who'd be leaving school when they broke up for Christmas in a couple of weeks' time.

The day after school ended he resolved that whatever the weather might be, John Godson would be out for his first day's work as a professional fisherman. With the *Hope of Ravenswyke's* tiller clasped firmly in his already experienced hands. 'Come on, Tommy,' he said magnanimously, 'I've got my spending money in my pocket. I'll buy you half a pint of beer! Happen then you can stop mooning over our lass for half-an-hour while we have a game of dominoes.' Unfortunately, his tongue let him down. He'd meant to say, dominoes, but instead pronounced the word the way he had ever since he was a baby, calling the game *donimoes*. Tommy Thompson was still hooting with laughter as they pushed open the door of the Snug and passed through into the smoke-filled beery atmosphere, and walked with pretended confidence up to the bar.

'Bloody hell!' Old Bill Clewson said as he watched them come in. 'I never thought to see the day as a Godson would bring a Newquay Towner in here! Silas Godson, aye, and John's dad, Reuben, would have a fit if they could see this day!'

'Hold thy noise, Dad,' Tom Clewson said. 'That bloody mine could have got us on the *Marguerite*. I reckon John Godson has a right to bring anybody he wants into here! Any road, I want to talk to him.'

He got up and walked to the bar. 'What you both having?' he asked, before either had chance to give his order.

'Cider?' John asked, looking at Ephraim, who winked at him.

'Half of mild,' Tommy Thompson said, overwhelmed by being invited by one of the fishing community. Though he'd been in here many times to drink, he'd been aware that he was tolerated by the men from Old Quaytown, nothing more. They always separated. The fishermen sat round the fire, looking into its flames and not saying much; the Newquay Towners congregated round the bar and seemed to chatter a lot.

'I'd like a word, John, if you've a minute,' Tom Clewson said.

'Well,' John said, looking at Tommy to imply that he'd come in with him and didn't feel he could desert him now they were inside, 'aye, if it's summat important?'

'You've seen the Naval Directive? About not going on fishing on account of the mines and the submarines . . .?'

'Aye, I've seen it. I read it when that fellow nailed it to t' board.'

'Well, some of us thinks it's not right. We want to have a meeting here, tomorrow, before t' tide. Will you come?'

John felt the burst of relief in him. 'Come?' he asked, 'of course I'll come. When has there been a meeting without a Godson there . . . ?' He repeated the same thought to his mam when he got home, just before nine o'clock. 'They're having a meeting. When has there been a meeting without a Godson present? My father'd skelp me if I wa'nt there . . . '

'But you've got school . . . ' she pleaded hopelessly.

'School, Mam? Nay, where's your sense of what's right? Do you think I should be up there, adding two and two and doing history, at a time they're holding a meeting down in t'Snug that concerns our very lives . . . ' Of course, he was playing the drama of the situation for all it was worth. He walked across the room and stood beneath the beam on which the name of every Godson, since the building of the cottage, had been carved – every male heir to the Godson name. Of course, his name would never be there – Wilfred would get that distinction after

Reuben had passed away. He lifted his hand and was just able to touch the old carved beam.

'I'd be failing in my duty as a Godson, Mam, if I wasn't there tomorrow!' he said. Anne tittered but he quelled her with a look. In truth, he felt himself growing into the stature of the leader of the Godsons in the absence of his father and brothers. He had totally persuaded himself that his presence the following day was vital, irrespective of the demands of school.

'And I'll be the one'll have to face Mr Redfern when he comes down complaining,' his mam said.

'You tell him, Mam, that some things are more important in life than poring over books. Tell him that! He'll understand.'

'My, isn't it marvellous what a glass of cider can do!' Anne said, complete in her disloyalty.

'Our Annie, I'll bray thee!' John said, his pomposity pricked like a hot-air balloon.

'It didn't need you to tell tales, Anne,' Emily Godson said. 'I've known about the Snug ever since the first night. Just like I know who it was broke the china dog that used to be on your Aunt Eleanor's mantelpiece. All right, John, you needn't go to school in the morning. But the minute that meeting's over, off you go up t'bank, you hear me?'

'That'll depend what the meeting decides, won't it?' he said, cheeky now that he had made his point.

High tide was at twelve o'clock the following day; by unspoken consensus the fishermen assembled in the Snug at ten o'clock for their meeting. John Godson, one of the first to arrive with his baskets of line and his pail of bait, found himself a seat near the door. As his fingers worked deftly preparing the mussels and fixing them firmly on the hooks, his eyes were busy looking round the room as the dozen fishermen assembled. In his father's time, he reflected, a meeting like this would have brought twenty or more. Now they were a bare dozen and that included old Bill Clewson who hadn't been out on a boat in years. And Walter Craggs, the agent who sold their catch in Whitby market. Arthur Fearon, who once had been the fishermen's agent, had made it a full-time job but Walter Craggs did it part-time only, making up his money by running a haulage service with his Foden lorry. 'My God,' John thought, 'there will soon be so few of us left we shan't be able to get enough together to hold a meeting!'

It had been a cold morning when John left the house at seven, eager to be ready before the meeting took place to launch the *Hope* first down the Slip at high tide. He didn't intend to go up the bank to school and knew in his heart that his mam wouldn't press him. An understanding had grown between them since his dad, Reuben, went away. Although she might talk firmly with him about schooling and Silas Redfern's complaints, provided he didn't bring the truant officer down to the house, she wouldn't interfere with his occasional fishing. She knew very well that the moment he left school he would take complete command of the *Hope* as his way of life. He might as well get used to it, and keep his hand in practice. Well, that was the way she rationalised it to herself. She knew she could do nothing to stop it, and was a practical enough person not to take on a fight she couldn't hope to win.

Walter Bredford, from the *Nelson*, opened the meeting. 'The Navy is saying we shouldn't go out – they're trying to put a ban on us. Since so many boats have been hit wi' mines, and since the submarines have surfaced off Scarborough and destroyed a couple of boats, the Navy says we should only go out of Whitby, and in convoy, wi' a Navy boat to look after us like a flock of bloody sheep!'

There was a growl when he mentioned Whitby. The fishermen of Ravenswyke, with their difficult conditions of launching and berthing, regarded the men from Whitby, with their much easier handling in the deep open-mouthed port, as a bunch of softies. Whitby boats were bigger, and took a bigger catch, often coming into Ravenswyke Bay to do it. And the new trawlers that dredged their otter-boards along the sea bed killing next season's spawn, all worked out of Whitby – no wonder the rivalry between the two places was intense.

'It's all part of the plan,' George-Willie Mountjoy said, 'to close Ravenswyke down for fishing and get us all working out of Whitby. I shouldn't wonder if that bugger Mark Adam Tockett wasn't behind it, an' all. Once he's closed us down, there'll be no stopping his plans to sell this place right out from under us, the way he tried to do before, until Reuben stopped his caper!'

At the mention of Reuben Godson, several of them looked across the room at John Godson, sitting quietly, baiting his hooks. 'Aye, what does John think of it, since he's a right . . . ?' Tom Clewson said.

'And the only one so far who's got near a mine . . . ?' George-Willie added.

John was nervous with all eyes upon him. But he was a fisherman, sort-of. At least, he would be once he'd left school in a few weeks. And he *had* fished the *Hope* alongside the rest of them. And, he *was* a Godson!

'I think we should fight any move to close us down and move us to Whitby,' he said slowly, his voice faltering at first but gathering strength as he went on, 'since there's always been fishing out of Ravenswyke as long as there's been a beam in our sitting room!'

There was a murmur of approval. All knew about the beam on which the name of the head of the Godson family had been carved, generation after generation, going all the way back to the fifteenth century. That beam belonged as much to Ravenswyke as to the Godsons.

'A man's got a right, it seems to me,' he said, his voice

growing in conviction, 'to earn his money in any honest way he can. I wish there was more of us, more boats, just like in my dad and grandad's time. I wish they'd let some of the lads who are wasting their time in the Army, come back home and get some of the boats out of the sheds and into t' water.'

'Tha's not afraid of a submarine, then, young John?' Alf Corley asked. Alf's coble, the *Princess*, had made the journey back from Whitby, to work out of Ravenswyke. It had a brand new diesel engine and Alf had made a success of it with his sons, Peter and Maurice. Both of them were now in the war, and Alf would have been with them if he hadn't lost half a lung in the last war.

'Well, let's put it this way, Alf,' John said, with a smile on his lips. 'I don't know if I'm afraid of them because I've never seen one, but I don't lie abed nights thinking about them!'

Ephraim Hardcastle had come into the Snug. As owner of the pub, he was virtually a member of the fishermen's meeting though he knew better than to express an opinion. The conversation became general and voices began to get heated, raised in anger as the fishermen argued about the 'plot' to drive them all out of Ravenswyke.

'You'll never get any sense out of them, John,' Ephraim said quietly. 'Somebody's got to take a lead and tell 'em what to do, else they'll still be arguing in here when the tide comes!'

'Happen you're right,' John said, looking round at the heated faces. The Clewsons were in favour of taking a deputation to the Navy Headquarters in Whitby. Others were saying they should take shotguns out with them and blast any Navy boats out of the water who tried to interfere with them.

Finally, in a grumbling silence, John piped up, his thin voice not yet grown to maturity but his determination evident for all to see.

'We've been fishing out of Ravenswyke for upwards of five hundred years,' he said, 'and I suggest that we carry on doing it the way we've always done. No need for deputations – why should we offer them the chance to make it more official than it already is? So far, it seems to me, all they've said is that they *recommend* we don't go fishing out of Ravenswyke, that we take our boats to Whitby and fish in convoy under the protection of the Navy boat. Well, frankly, it seems to me a Navy boat is just as capable of being hit by a mine as a fishing boat and as for the submarines, well, if they come to the surface and see a Navy boat they're going to start shooting. My Dad told me a tale about a submarine, during the last war, that came to the surface and when he saw the fisherman, he bought his catch. There was no Navy about, then!'

'So, what's it to be then, young John?' George-Willie Mountjoy asked. 'Tell us, what's to be done . . . ?'

'Aye, John,' Walter Bredford said, 'tha's the Godson now. So tell us, what's to be done?'

John looked about him again and gulped, suddenly aware of the awesome responsibility, suddenly realising for the first time that these mature men were waiting for the word of a schoolboy. Easy enough to spout out the first thing that came to his mind, but was that the right thing? Would he regret it afterwards? He tried to think the way he guessed his dad, Reuben, might have thought, but it was hard even to bring the image of his father's face to his mind, let alone to solve the problem the way his father would have done. He longed to say 'you must make up your own minds,' but he knew that wouldn't do. They wanted a decision out of him, and they wanted to follow him when he set out to put that decision into operation. All he could do was cling to the past, to tradition. He knew that once they started out from Whitby the fishing industry, such as it was, in Ravenswyke would be dead for ever. The men, and the sons of the men, would never come back to fish the more difficult landing once they'd become accustomed to the deeper water, where the boats could be moored alongside the harbour and taken in and out irrespective of the tides.

But, if that was the way of things, what right did he have to influence men to change it? Wasn't it time to give up Ravenswyke, to move the boats, to go with the times? They could still live here in Old Quaytown and travel to and from Whitby by one means or another. They would be able to step straight on to the decks of the boats, moored alongside the quay, start the engines, and be away in minutes instead of their present method of having to launch the boats cumbersomely into the heavy waves of a high tide, or wait until the lowest tide, and drag the boats with all their weight across the difficult slate ledges of the scaurs that lay immediately off-shore. He could remember the boats that had had their bottoms ripped out, coming home when the tide was less than full.

But, if they went to Whitby ...

If the men started to drift away ...

If they tired of the five mile journey to and from Whitby and rented cottages down by the harbour ...

If Ravenswyke had started its death throes by the time his dad, Reuben, came back from the war ...

'This war won't last for ever,' he said, 'and when the men come back, they'll want summat to come home to, rather than an abandoned village. It seems to me that it's up to us to keep things going. The Navy can make a lot of noise, but what do they know about it? If we go out, we go! Happen they can fetch us back in once, twice, but they'll get fed up of it before we do. And, meanwhile, we're keeping the place going, keeping it alive for the men who'll be coming home. My dad would bray me if he returned and found the *Hope* lolling against a safe berth in Whitby Harbour. He'd think I'd gone soft in t' head!'

There was a roar of approval. No delegation. No

representations. They'd carry on as they'd always carried on. They'd go out fishing, and neither the mines, the submarines, nor the combined might of the German and the British navies would stop them.

'You'll be the first off, I reckon?' Alf Corley asked John, smiling.

'I reckon there's no need to change the habits of a lifetime,' John said, 'not even for the Royal bloody Navy!' He hefted his baskets of baited line, and went out through the door. Instinctively, he glanced up at Tockett Top and saw only the thin white November clouds. The sea was running large, and he'd need all his skill to get off the Slip without being skewed sideways on to the rock on which the Raven had been built. They heaved and dragged the *Hope* until it was lying at the top of the wooden rails of the Slip. He put the sweeps into the rowlocks, sat facing the stern, his boots against the blocks, his backside firm on the centre thwart.

'On the next one,' he shouted.

They waited until the wave rode in, hissing and curling up the slope of the Slip to scurry round their ankles, then in one concerted heave, they pushed the *Hope* into its back-tow. The boat went sliding down the wooden rails, the keel riding on to the drag of the wave; John pulled with both oars as soon as he felt the hull lift so that the boat was water-borne. The *Hope* went straight as an arrow between the rocks of the Raven on one side, the edge of the Slip on the other. He took his sight-line, keeping the pitch of Clewson's down-bank cottage roof in line with the bell on top of the chapel, knowing that if he could maintain that straight line, he'd launch safely. He had to give a touch more with his left hand, since his left arm had always been the weaker one. Up sweeps, quickly feathered on the forward push, then dig in, not too deep, and a slow even pull back, with all the strength of his muscles in it, holding the *Hope* straight through the next wave that came curling up and under him, angling to try to smash his stern to starboard, to dash the *Hope* against the Raven rocks. He checked with his right hand, increased the pull with his left, and felt the nose of the *Hope* swing over, putting him back on his sight-line.

Alf Corley was paying out the stern line, standing at the head of the Slip watching every movement of John's progress, shaking his head at the stubborn young bugger who always insisted on the Godson right to be first off.

Corley's cousin, Robin Peck, was standing by the *Princess* which would be next off; it would have been infinitely easier for the two of them to lead the way down the Slip but they knew none of the fishermen would permit that.

If the *Hope* went out, it led. It went first, cleared the rocks, and then assisted the others out. Reuben himself had designed the ritual when the scaurs had been churned up in a pre-war storm to make the landing even more difficult than it had always been. The *Hope* went out, using oars. Once clear of the landing, they'd either hoist sail, depending on the lie of the wind, or they'd start the engine. A line would be paid out from the stern and then, when the *Hope* was clear, they'd use that line to drag out the second boat. The second would drag the third, the third the fourth. It was hazardous, but there was no safer way of doing it.

John shipped the oars in the gunwales, and started his engine since the wind was thin and mean. He stood next to the engine casing, watching them on shore as they lifted and shoved the *Princess* to the top of the Slip. He saw Alf and his cousin, Robin Peck, get into the boat. 'The next wave ought to do it,' he thought. Sure enough, when the next wave came, Alf held up his arm and John opened his throttle. The tow-rope came up out of the water, taking some of the strain, starting the *Princess* sliding. As soon as John saw the movement, he opened the throttle wide and the *Princess* rushed down the Slip straight as an arrow. As soon as John saw it was safely launched, he untied the tow-line from the stern-post and cast it overboard.

He could smell the sole in the water, and was eager to be away. He waved his hand and saw an answering flash from the end of the alley that came out behind the Raven. He knew his mam always stood there, and watched him go, whether she'd sanctioned his departure or not.

CHAPTER FOUR

Ravenswyke Church was full to capacity for the wedding of Mark Adam Tockett and Elsie Milner, with the County families occupying the right hand pews, and the folks of Old Quaytown the left hand. There'd been talk, mostly inspired by the wicked tongue of Connie Cathcart, of boycotting Elsie's wedding. After all, though she lived in a cottage in Old Quaytown, she didn't come of a fishing family and wasn't rightly one of them, or so Connie had maliciously said on every possible occasion since the wedding was announced.

But on the day of the wedding, tradition won. Elsie was an Old Quaytowner; they'd not let her be wed alone.

Elsie wore a plain two-piece suit in bottle green over a lime green blouse, with a hat whose veil hung down over her face though it did nothing to hide the intense sparkle in her eyes. Both Eliza and Anne waited on her at the altar, though their role was midway between bridesmaids and matrons-of-honour.

Mark Adam was wearing his uniform of captain of the Yorkshire Regiment; his best man was Ezra Thrummell, who now ran the family business of Thrummell and Slade, the largest solicitor's practice in the district. The service was conducted by the Reverend Michael Roberts; it was the first wedding he'd solemnized in his new living, and he was more nervous even than the bridegroom.

Eliza adored the church and always had for as long as she could remember. It had been a favourite place of hers ever since she'd been taken there one Sunday afternoon to Sunday School, now that Captain Walham was too old to look after the young ones in the Methodist Chapel down the bank. She'd enjoyed climbing to the top of the bank to look over the roof of the cottages of Old Quaytown nestling below; it had always seemed entirely appropriate to her that the Church should occupy this commanding position as if, in its benevolence, it stood guard on all of them. When she prayed by her bedside at night and lifted her head, it was to the tangible building above rather than a nebulous God in the Heavens.

Often she would walk up the bank and go into the Church, for no other reason than to sit quietly in one of the pews, looking about her in awe at the high vaulted ceiling, the beautifully carved oak of the lectern and the altar, the decorations on the edge of the pulpit that had been carved by Simon Marriott of Goathland, signed with his symbol of an ear of wheat. Though she wasn't very good about the house, as her mam always complained, she soon was drawn into the ritual of cleaning the Church and would sit for hours happily polishing the brass-work, keeping a shine on it into which she would gaze and dream. It seemed to her that she had been born with a forbidden dream inside her; as she grew through her teens, the dream became more and more a secret wish she sometimes felt would burst inside her. Eliza adored Elsie Milner because of one thing; Elsie had successfully escaped from Old Quaytown twice now. Once she had left Ravenswyke to go to live and work in Leeds with her friend, Emma Baxter. She'd met a man who'd taken her all over Europe, to Paris and Rome, Venice and Baden-Baden. Eliza almost choked with pleasure when Elsie told her of those trips, those days she'd spent travelling. Her man had killed himself when he got into financial trouble – 'Did you love him?' Eliza had asked every time Elsie Milner talked briefly of his death – and she'd returned to Old Quaytown.

'I would never have come back!' the younger girl always declared passionately, but Elsie Milner always smiled and said, 'We never know how long our roots can be until we try to pull them up!'

It was Eliza's guilty secret that she suspected she had no roots, no knot of loyalty binding her to Old Quaytown. Only this passionate desire to see more of the world she knew was over the top of the bank. She and her sister, Anne, had many arguments about it. 'I want to get away,' she'd say, in the dark privacy of their bedroom when they'd be lying awake at night, waiting for sleep; Anne would grumble when Eliza wanted to talk and say, 'Old Quaytown's all right. Better than living over there, in Newquay Town!'

Newquay Town was the furthest foreign place Anne could imagine but then she was a year younger than her sister and her longings had not yet found expression within her.

Eliza was the first to hug Elsie when they came out of the vestry, though Mark had clasped Elsie's hand in his and his eyes gleamed with the pride of a mature man forty-five years of age. Nothing he'd ever achieved, either here in Yorkshire or in the City of London, gave him such a reason for happiness as his marriage to Elsie. He saw Eliza Godson reach round and squeeze his bride; it was a pleasure shared and multiplied.

'You're wearing the petticoat?' Eliza asked, even though she'd watched Elsie put it on.

'Of course I am . . . '

Eliza squeezed her again. 'Thanks,' she said, 'thanks a lot!'

The reception was held in the Royal Dock Hotel in Whitby with the buffet set all along one side of the Grand Ballroom. No-one from Old Quaytown had ever seen such a spread and wouldn't again, now that rationing was in force.

'We shan't be able to serve any meals in the Hotel for a week,' the manager said when Mark complimented him – 'I've used up our entire allocation!'

Beer barrels, and spirits bottles on tables, had been set up in the alcove that abutted the ballroom and, despite the lateness of the year, there were massed banks of flowers everywhere.

Mark had agreed with his bride that they should depart from the tradition of a sit-down meal, with all the speeches and toasts. When the wedding cake was wheeled in on its trolley, the five tiers glistening with icing sugar and silver ball decorations, the manager of the hotel, who was acting as Master of Ceremonies, tapped a gong for silence, and Mark Adam said, very simply, his hand in Elsie's, 'Thank you all for coming to see me married to the most wonderful woman in the world!'

There was a roar of applause as Elsie plunged the knife into the cake, and then the hotel waiters busied themselves demolishing it, and handing round the pieces on small plates.

Nat Gonella, the trumpeter, had brought his band from Leeds; as soon as the cake had been cut the musicians came on to the bandstand, and started to play for dancing. Mark Adam led Elsie out on the floor and they performed a ceremonial round while the people clapped them, their faces already flushed with the beer and the spirits that were flowing so copiously.

Among the faces Mark Adam noticed was that of Emily Godson, who was standing at the edge of the floor with her two daughters, and her son John, for once wearing a collar and tie and a tweed suit with a crease down the trousers.

Mark stopped impulsively in front of her. 'I'm sure we're all sorry about one thing, today,' he said gently. 'That Reuben couldn't be here among us, nor Arthur and Wilfred!'

There were tears lurking at the corners of her eyes as she nodded. 'I'm sure he's with us in spirit, Mr Tockett, wherever he might be! And the two lads, as well!'

'I'm sure they are.'

Emily looked at Elsie, Tockett as she now was. All the memories flashed through her mind – the time she'd tried to kill herself, because she thought that her Reuben favoured Elsie above her, the way Elsie had come back, like a whipped dog, from her adventures abroad and, at first, Emily had felt threatened yet again.

'Elsie,' she said, 'I wish you both a long and happy life together.'

Elsie laughed. 'I reckon, between us, we've caught the two best men in the whole of Ravenswyke!' she said.

Emily smiled at that. 'I reckon we have that!' she said.

Both of them knew, without a further word being said, that it was the ending of a long time of inescapable antagonism between them.

'When Mrs Tockett comes back from her honeymoon,' Anne burst in excitedly, 'she's going to teach our Liz to talk French!'

'Our Liz, as you call her, had better learn to talk English first,' Emily said, laughing. Today, she couldn't be angry. Today, she couldn't object to the whims of a young girl. Today, in some curious way, she didn't really mind that Reuben was not by her side.

Today, she was telling herself, today the woman she'd always feared as being more attractive, more worldly, more intelligent, more desirable than she herself could ever be, had married another man. At last, Emily Godson was free!

She stepped forward and hugged Elsie Tockett. 'I really hope as you'll both be very happy,' she said, 'though my heart quails when I think of all them windows you'll have to clean in that big barn of a house you've taken over!'

'Don't be daft, Mam,' Liz said. 'Mrs Tockett will have servants to do all that, won't she, Mr Tockett?'

'I think that might be arranged,' Mark Adam said, smiling tenderly.

Tommy Thompson had been hovering diffidently on the edge of the group. 'Best of luck, Mr and Mrs Tockett,' he said as he stepped forward. 'Can I ask your daughter to dance, Mrs Godson?'

'Aye, lad, tha'd better, else she'll die of waiting,' Emily said.

'I'm going to learn to talk French,' Liz said, as she stepped forward with her hands raised to clasp his for the slow foxtrot that Anne and she had practised for so long in the bedroom. 'And it's all right to call me Liz!'

Connie Cathcart had established herself in a corner of the ballroom, with her cronies about her. Netta, the Tockett housekeeper, was sitting on the sofa by her side, a glass of sweet sherry held like a mayor's mace in her hand. Margery Mountjoy, Old Millie Harrison, and Mrs Probert from the Post Office sat side by side on stuffed chairs, solemn as a jury with a guilty verdict.

Mark had been cornered by a group of his business acquaintances and raucous laughter indicated the traditional ribaldry of the aftermath of a wedding; Elsie had left them to it and was walking slowly around the ballroom's perimeter accepting the kindly compliments of the guests. She dreaded the moment she'd arrive in the corner where Connie Cathcart had established herself; the County folk, friends of the Tockett family, had all accepted her completely and sincerely and she had no fears on their account. Her eyes locked into Connie's as she approached; she saw the smile of triumph on the other woman's lips and knew that today, if only today, she was vulnerable. She saw Connie turn away and mutter something to Netta, whose eyes hardened to a basilisk stare as she saw her new employer approach. Netta presented a problem to Elsie. Mark had said he didn't particularly want to keep Netta, since she was such a curmudgeon, and had given Elsie the right to replace any of the staff who didn't suit her. Netta came of an Old Quaytown family – her grandfather had fished alongside Silas Godson and her father for several years had been the fishermen's agent. He'd had no sons, and the boat had been sold on his death. Netta had been in service in Whitby and had been brought back to Ravenswyke for the job of housekeeper at the Tocketts. She had a bit of money put by, and Elsie suspected that, if she lost her job, she'd stay in the village, living in the family cottage in Old Quaytown, a constant thorn in Elsie's side. It would be hard to say who had the worse tongue, Netta or Connie.

Elsie spoke first. 'Don't get up, Netta,' she said, though Netta had shown no sign of rising from her seat at the approach of her new employer. 'Just for today, I think we might leave formality behind us!'

Connie hadn't lost her smile. 'Well, Mrs Tockett,' she said, 'we always knew you'd do it. We always knew you'd catch yourself a good husband in the end.'

'Aye, better a man on the rebound than no man at all,' Mrs Probert added.

Elsie felt humiliated, and defeated. She cursed herself inwardly for caring what these vicious women thought or said but she couldn't escape the fact that she *did* care. Today, of all days, couldn't they forget their animosity? Couldn't they give her a crumb of friendship?

'If your mother could have seen you now, she'd have wanted to get married herself,' Old Millie Harrison cackled, her toothless gums working with glee.

Elsie couldn't think of a single thing to say; today of all days, she didn't want to descend to their level, to indulge in a verbal brawl with them. She felt the tears begin to form behind her eyes but knew she mustn't give them the satisfaction of seeing her cry. Nor must she let them drive her away. Netta was looking sharply at her, her eyes probing for any weakness she could exploit. She hardly noticed the touch on her elbow but heard the voice in her ear.

'Excuse me, Mrs Tockett,' John Godson said, 'I've been wanting a word with you. I got this card from my dad today. He asked me to read it to you, like a wedding telegram. It says . . . ' He coughed as he held the postcard high, squinting at it. 'When Mark Tockett chose you above all others, he took a good friend of the Godsons, and of all the folk of Old Quaytown. Best wishes for a happy life.'

She turned to him, her eyes gleaming with tears of joy that didn't shame her. 'He said that?' she asked. 'Your dad, Reuben Godson, said that?'

'Aye,' he said, 'it's here in black and white . . . Now, Mrs Tockett, will you give us a dance, though I'll ask your pardon in advance for stepping on your feet. I'm not much on this dancing lark . . . ' He took her in his arms, and they set off across the floor.

'You dear, sweet, lovable liar,' she said when they were away from Connie's corner and all the gossips. 'There were nowt written on the back of that card!'

He laughed. 'You know that, and I do,' he said, 'but it's given that lot summat to talk about, hasn't it?'

They danced a few steps, Elsie floating in sheer joy.

'Any road,' he said, 'if my dad *was* here, he'd 'a said summat like that!'

Tommy Thompson sat on the back seat of the charabanc Mark Tockett had hired to take the villagers to the wedding, and to bring them home afterwards.

'You looked smashing today,' he whispered to Liz, sitting beside him.

'Only today, then . . . ?'

'Nay, I didn't mean that! You look smashing every day.'

'I don't . . . '

'Yes, you do . . . '

Liz curled up in the corner. Today, she thought, was the best day she'd ever had. All the people she'd talked to, all the new young men she'd danced with! Even Robert Thrummell had asked her for a dance! Thank God she and Anne had spent all that time practising on the bedroom floor with the wind-up gramophone going, playing the records they'd borrowed from Ephraim Hardcastle. Robert Thrummell must be at least twenty, and going to Oxford University to study law. One day, he'd take over his father's business. 'Have you ever been abroad?' she'd asked him, and had almost fainted with pleasure when he'd said, yes, actually, he'd just come back from Paris when war was declared. Apparently, he'd tried to join the Army, but they'd insisted he stay at the University until he'd finished his course. Then he'd be going into the Army, to be an officer.

She glanced sideways at Tommy Thompson. What *would* he say if she told him Robert Thrummell had asked to drive her home after the wedding celebrations, in his dad's car? What *would* he say if he knew she'd said, no, not today, and that Robert Thrummell had pressed her to see him again and she'd agreed to meet him outside the Church the following day, and go for a ride in his car across the moor as far as Pickering to take tea in the hotel there . . . ?

And, what would her mam say, if ever she found out . . . ?

'Shall us go for a walk along t'cliff top tomorrow,' Tommy Thompson, unsuspecting, asked.

'I'm afraid I've got a previous engagement for tomorrow, Tommy,' Liz said.

'Oh, bloody hell!'

CHAPTER FIVE

Major Sharp smiled when he saw Sgt Reuben Godson walk across the plank floor towards his improvised desk. Though Sgt Godson had attended the NCOs' Course at Sandhurst, with its training in military 'bull', he still rolled when he walked, as if adjusting to the pitch and toss of the deck of a boat.

Sgt Godson halted, his hands firmly pressed down the seams of his trousers according to regulations, but somehow lacking the military precision of an automaton such as, for example, Sgt-Major Griffiths, who was standing beside the desk ramrod straight.

'At ease, Sergeant,' Major Sharp said. 'You asked to see me?'

He heard the sgt-major suck in his breath in disapproval of his unmilitariness; dammit, this wasn't the Frontiers of India, the Khyber Pass, the Indian Mutiny. Major Sharp was a business man, not a soldier, with a large engineering company which he'd left in the capable hands of his crippled brother for the duration. Sgt Godson was a fisherman, not a soldier.

'Yes, Major, I did.'

'What about, Sergeant? Look, draw up that chair and sit down, if it makes you feel more comfortable . . . '

Again that hiss of disapproval. Even standing at ease, the sgt-major was drawn tight as a muscle, quivering to snap to a position of attention.

Sgt Godson took the chair, spun it round, and seated himself comfortably on it, totally relaxed. 'Yes, Major, well, you see, I want to put in an application but I thought I'd mention it first . . . '

'Applications should be given to me, Sergeant, in writing,' the sgt-major said instantly. 'You ought to know the procedures, with three stripes on your arm . . . !'

The Major held up a limp hand. 'Let Sgt Godson have his say, Sgt-Major,' he said gently. 'Right, Sergeant, what is this application? For compassionate leave . . . ?'

'No, Major, for transfer.'

'And you wanted to have a word . . . ?'

'Yes, Major. I wanted you to understand that I didn't want to leave the unit because of any dissatisfaction!'

'I see. Well, that's very thoughtful of you. What is the reason, in that case?'

'I was a volunteer, Major. I volunteered for the Navy, being a fisherman and more at home with boats. Now I find myself in the Army. It's just that I think I'd be more useful if I were doing something with boats. I feel so useless here, in France, waiting for something that seems as if it's never going to happen. At least, if I was in the Navy, I could be teaching the lads something about boats.'

Major Sharp sighed. 'Your application for a transfer will be the nineteenth I've had this week, Sgt Godson,' he said. 'Like you, everyone is growing bored of waiting for something that seems as if it's never going to happen. You know, because you went to fetch them, that we already have had two absentees. Now we have a third one, Private Cosgrove; he speaks perfect French since his father married a Frenchwoman at the end of the last war. He volunteered for Intelligence, and wound up here, in the Infantry. My guess is that he's gone down to his mother's village, and we shan't see him again in a hurry.'

Sgt Godson knew about Cosgrove, who had been in his platoon. Cosgrove had itched to be doing something more active than the constant drill and weapons training.

'Ours not to reason why, Sergeant,' the sgt-major said. 'Ours to do or die!'

'It's early days, Sgt Godson,' Major Sharp said. 'We're here because of our alliance with the French, because of Mr Chamberlain's promises. We don't know how we're going to fight this war when it comes. We will certainly need a lot of different talents. Don't ask me how I can foresee our needing a fisherman such as yourself in a land-based war. All I can ask you to do is to reconsider your application. Obviously, if you want to submit it through channels, you have that right, just as you had the right which you exercised to turn down the promotion to sgt-major that was offered to you before Christmas last year. But don't forget what I have said – there may come a time we shall need men of many dissimilar talents, especially among the NCOs, and I'd like to feel that when and if that time comes, I would have your services and support to rely on.'

Reuben Godson knew the interview was over. He stood up, replaced the chair, stood briefly to attention in front of the desk before executing an about-turn and marching from the room.

Back in the farmhouse in the billet he shared with three other sergeants, he sat on his bed. It'd be time to go for supper in five minutes. The platoon had finished its day's training; the lads would be getting washed and brushed, ready for an evening in the nearby town of Pincheville. He could go on the transport with them, spend his time in a bar which would be full of other soldiers. Or he could go to the quayside, look at the fishing boats many of which still went out seining. How he'd love a night out with the nets – he bet the fish would be running these clear cloudless February nights. His mind was soon made up; he went to the sergeants' mess and quickly ate the evening stew.

He was on his way out of the dining-room as Sgt-Major

Griffiths was coming in. 'You made me look a proper Charlie this afternoon, Godson,' Griffiths barked. 'You know damn well as all applications has to be put in through me, and countersigned by the platoon commander before they're submitted to the 2 i/c. That's the Army Regulation, *and* the CO's ruling. Major Sharp doesn't run this Company, thank God. Next time, let's have it done the pukka way, according to Regs, right?'

'Right, Sgt-Major.'

The sgt-major's features softened and he put his hand on Reuben Godson's arm. 'Your trouble, lad, is that you worry too much,' he said. 'You ought to have let them jump you up to CSM when they wanted to, then you wouldn't have been so damned bored as you are now. I don't blame you. Believe me, after all the fighting I've seen, I'm itching to get back into it. But you'll have to learn the soldier's way of thinking. When you have the good fortune to land on your feet in a cushy billet like this one, then enjoy it while it lasts. Because it won't last for long, I can tell you. How old are you, Godson?'

'Coming on forty . . . '

'Then that's what's wrong. You've got the forty year itch. Take the advice of an old soldier. Get yourself down into Pincheville to the place in the Rue des Soissons, and dip your wick. That'll make you feel like a man again!' He laughed coarsely as he pushed open the door of the dining-room and went in. Reuben smiled ruefully as he went back into his own billet, combed his hair, adjusted his army cap, and walked down the street to where the transport would be waiting outside the Company Office.

Anyone below the rank of sergeant wishing to ride on the transport had to be carrying a chitty signed by the sgt-major; he stood watching the guard check them one by one as the other ranks climbed aboard for their night out on the town. He noticed that one or two of the lads were not wearing strictly regimental gear – some of them kept a best suit, even stitched and soaped an extra special crease down the trousers and took in the waist of the battledress jacket to try to make themselves look a little smarter. This evening he didn't care and didn't interfere. When the lorry was full, he climbed in the passenger seat and the lorry set off to travel the eight kilometres into the glamour of 'the big city'.

Pincheville was a small fishing community before the war, with half a dozen small hotels, a couple of pensions that accommodated families from the Normandy hinterland. It had fifty bars, all tiny, a Mairie, and two cinemas. The house in the Rue des Soissons had been equipped quickly when the troops arrived – a dozen girls, most of them the overflow of Dieppe and Cherbourg, worked there under the supervision of a Parisian *Madame*, and the weekly inspection of a local doctor. It was a well-run establishment, and the British Army cast a blind eye on it. The *Madame* had carefully set her prices to be the equivalent of a day's pay and had already sent out on the street a girl she'd discovered robbing her client.

The transport stopped a hundred metres from the door, in the Place des Soissons, next to a bar that had quickly been converted into a *café-chantant* by knocking a hole through into what had been a storage barn at the back.

Each evening, a trio of piano, violin and accordion played sentimental French tunes, and a male dancer and his partner alternated in singing huskily into the microphone. The *Chat Noir*, as it had been called, could accommodate a couple of hundred soldiers, plus the twenty or more girls who'd travelled from inland to ply their wares as free-lances. Apart from the girls, one or two Parisian opportunists, and taxi-drivers, the *Chat Noir* was usually devoid of Frenchmen or their womenfolk, who preferred to eat and drink in the cafés around the quay to which Reuben hurried.

The quay was not dissimilar to that of Whitby, he

thought. Two sides, one for the importation of timber and other goods, the other for the fishermen. A railway line that ran down one side only. A fish landing dock, with its market where, each day, the boxes of fish would be spread out and sorted for selling to the wholesalers. At least twenty fishing boats were still moored at the quay, stern on, he noticed, each with its own mooring no doubt fixed on a block in the water; it'd make sense along that crowded quay to come in backwards, catch your mooring, and then back gently up to the quayside for off-loading. He noticed that each boat had its winch gear for purse-seining, and its drums of wire rope, most of which was rusty. Although contemptuous of the condition of most of the boats, he walked along the line looking at each one of them, drinking in the familiar smell, hearing the gulls overhead. Of course the land here was flat, unlike Ravenswyke which rose steeply from the quayside, and the street to his left was dotted with cafés and small restaurants. The atmosphere, too, contained a mixture of seaweed and kelp, fish, and the spicy odours of cooking and wine he'd come to associate with the French way of life. One or two fishermen on the boats smiled up at him, no doubt recognising a kindred spirit from his gait and the quick movements of his eyes.

About half the boats had left port, to judge from the gaps; as he walked along, he heard one or two more take off, noting the way their stern lines were jury-rigged to the mooring pontoons so that all the mate had to do was release the bow line and throw it in the water to the starboard side. The boats seemed to carry a larger crew than he was accustomed to with as many as five or six men to work them; but then, he told himself, they'd need that many to handle the winches and the heavy wire rope. He noticed that each of them used his riding lights, and a forward facing beam, to clear the dock but, as they moved down towards the lighthouse at the end of the mole that came in from the starboard side, the lights were hooded and the tiny deck lights were quickly lost in the blackness of the night. There'd been much talk of German submarines working down this coast, surfacing in the middle of a fishing fleet and opening fire with a deck cannon to sink the boats one by one. He'd heard that they'd taken ten boats out of Cherbourg like that, in December.

The door of a café in the centre of the quay opened and closed again and he went towards its welcoming light. The room inside was warm, with a wood stove in the centre of the room providing the blast of heat that greeted him as he made his way to the bar. Three tables were surrounded by families who seemed to be eating supper – there was a dish of mussels in the centre of one table with steam coming out of the pot. Two men were standing at the bar and both had glasses of white wine in front of them. He looked along the bar at the dish of hard-boiled eggs, the salt and pepper pot, the bottles behind the bar with their necks sticking out of what looked like a zinc tray. The bottles on the shelf behind the bar all had unfamiliar labels but he'd grown used to that in the four months he'd been in France.

'White wine?' he asked, pronouncing the words carefully, not yet bold enough to try his rudimentary French.

'*Vin blanc*?'

'Yes. *Oui*!'

The bartender, a man of at least seventy, placed a glass in front of him, swung a bottle with no label out of the zinc tray, and poured the glass full. He was short, with a white stubble on his chin, wearing a collarless shirt without a tie, and braces. Hung over his shoulder was a wiping cloth stained with gouts of red wine. 'English?' he asked, his voice a croaking rasp.

'Aye – I mean, yes.'

The man spoke English with an accent Reuben didn't

think was French. 'When I used to go out, in the old days, we used to put in to Falmouth. When I broke my back, falling across the winch, I was in hospital in Falmouth. Two years it took to get me right.'

'It must have been a bad one . . . ?'

'Yes. I was pinned under the wire. They had to saw through it to release me. They all thought I was dead. I should have been. Still, good comes out of bad, they say. I met my wife while I was in the hospital. *Oui*, and I learned to talk in English.'

Reuben had finished his glass of wine and, without being asked, the old man filled it for him. 'On me,' he said. 'We don't get many soldiers down here. Mostly they go to the Black Cat. Mademoiselle from Armentiers and all that. Paul, up there, is making a fortune. But then, he always does. It's not the fishermen who make money . . .'

Reuben laughed. 'You're right there,' he said.

The old man looked at him. 'Something familiar about you,' he said. 'I haven't seen you before, have I?'

Reuben chuckled. 'You can smell me,' he said. 'I have a boat. The *Hope of Ravenswyke*. A twenty-five-foot coble. I've been fishing every day of my life, until I got into this lot!'

There was a rapid exchange between the old man behind the bar and a man sitting at the nearby table with his family, but Reuben, who'd learned only a few familiar phrases, couldn't catch it.

The man seated with his family, a stocky man who looked Reuben's age, got up and came to the bar. 'You, fish man?' he asked.

Reuben nodded. The man looked at his glass then picked it up and threw its contents into the zinc sink. The old man, cackling, produced another bottle, again without a label, and poured the glass full again.

'This wine good,' the short man said. 'Me, Louis. This,'

he said with a wide sweep of his arm, 'my bar. This, my papa. This, my wife. I speaking English good, from my mama!'

'He would never listen, and never learn,' the old man said. 'Always wanting to run out with the girls when his mama wanted to teach him. Now he's speaking it like what you call, the proverbial Spanish Cow!'

'Come to please, sit down!' Louis said.

Reuben willingly joined them at the table. Three women, three men, and four children aged about five or six. A pot of mussels took pride of place in the centre of the table, with a dish of what looked like eel, fried in oil. As if by magic, a plate appeared in front of him, a fork and a knife, and a cut of the long French bread. Louis had brought his glass from the counter and set that beside him. 'Attention,' he said, 'this wine, extra strong!'

Reuben felt himself relaxing in the warm, friendly, family atmosphere. He couldn't understand a word of what was being said by the others but their total acceptance of him as a fellow fisherman was obvious. Louis maintained a constant barrage of English and French, appealing to his papa when there was a particular word he didn't know, or one of Reuben's north country phrases he couldn't understand. By the end of the meal, everyone at the table knew about Ravenswyke and the Yorkshire coast, about the fishing, lining, fetching lobsters and crabs with lobster-pots, netting – not the purse-seining they were used to – the difficulties of getting into and out of the Slip. The latter drew expressions of astonishment from them – *'Il n'y a pas de quai?'* they kept asking incredulously – and Reuben had to explain how they launched the boats one by one and then brought them back in again all on the high tide.

It was one o'clock by the time he looked at the watch Emily had bought him as a going-away present.

The transport back to the camp had left at twelve-thirty!

Despite their protestations that he could stay the night, that they'd find him a bed, that they could get out the *camionette* to take him back, he insisted on walking. 'It'll clear my head,' he said. 'You were right; that wine is strong!'

Eight, nine kilometres. The road to the camp was straight. He'd do it in a couple of hours if he got a move on, he told himself. The night was cold but the previous week's snow had all melted in the few days of unseasonable sunshine they'd all been enjoying in the camp. He soon settled into the rhythm of walking, trudging up the slight rise from the port along the edge of the wide road. Any man used to plodding the hills and cliffs of North Yorkshire can take the miles in his stride; despite being a fisherman, Reuben had enjoyed walking up the Bank and out on to the moors, happy once in a while to turn his back on the sea. He was carried along by the euphoria of the pleasant evening he'd just spent, the simple unassuming friendship of the people of the port, the fishermen and their wives. Aye, it'd been grand to sit next to a woman again and not some painted floosie after your money; it'd been grand to get the female smell in his nostrils after the reek of men's sweat in the camp. It'd been painfully nostalgic, too, to soak in the atmosphere of a quayside, the odour of fish that lingers forever in a fisherman's woollens, and to talk about boats, and lines, nets, anchors, waves and tides. By gum, he told himself, that'd been a grand evening. No wonder he hadn't noticed the hours slipping by.

He'd gone about four kilometres when the moon came out so that he could see a long way ahead. The road stretched before him like a winding ribbon with trees on each side that had lost their leaves. He saw the well-tended fields, the orchards, the neat farmhouses, the hay stacks. No denying, he told himself, it's a lush landscape all right. Very different from the bleak moors on which he'd spent his youth. It was a short step from that observation to wondering if the people themselves – not the hardened fishermen he'd spent his evening with, but the men who worked these inland farms – would be tough if it came to fighting a war. Major Sharp had said that at the moment the British were showing a presence because of political treaties, but that it wouldn't be long before the Germans turned their attentions away from the East, from Czechoslovakia and Poland, to the West.

Every week, either Major Sharp, or the Commanding Officer, Lt-Colonel Britten, would gather the Battalion together and give them a talk, trying to interest them in the larger picture of what was happening in Europe, no doubt to divert their minds from the total inactivity within the Battalion and Company lines, other than spit-and-polish and weapons training. After the Colonel's talk, the Company Commander, Captain Brooks, and the Platoon Commander, Lieutenant Smythe, would take over, producing the large maps of Europe, showing what the Germans were doing. The Colonel was a fanatic about all his men knowing what he called 'the larger picture'. Often when he passed a man in the tiny village where they were billeted, he'd stop him and bark questions at him. 'Do you think the Russians will succeed in Finland? Why do the Germans need Silesia? How did the Germans take Poland so easily?' and woe betide even the humblest soldier who didn't have some sort of answer to give.

One of his favourite questions, and one he'd asked Reuben when he'd turned down his promotion to sgt-major, was – What about the French? Will they fight? Will they put up a good show, eh? Or will they run? The Colonel, it was rumoured, had no time for the French!

Would they fight? – Reuben asked himself.

Would they see these lush farms destroyed, the way the

Colonel had told them the farmlands of Poland had been destroyed, with the farmhouses burned down, the local population slaughtered?

The fishermen had been very determined – when the Germans came, they'd put their families into the boats with their few prized possessions, and they'd sail away to England, to the south-coast ports. 'The English will look after us,' they'd said with a naive, almost childish, simplicity and faith.

There'd been no suggestion that they'd stand and fight. Several complete families, Reuben had learned, had already gone. To Falmouth or Brixham. One family had travelled as far as Canada, but they owned a thirty-five footer, rigged for sail.

As he marched along the road in the cold moonlit night thinking of these things, Reuben became slowly conscious that the inside of his left boot, by the knuckle of his big toe, was beginning to chafe. He stopped beside the road, unfastened his boot, and saw that the walking had rubbed a hole in his sock. He cursed his stupidity; he had meant to change those socks in the quartermaster's store when he'd seen they were thin; socks went to the laundry and you never knew which pair you'd get back. The edges of the hole had doubled back and had pressed against his skin to make a small blister which had burst; he took the sock off and replaced the boot without a sock in it, placing the sock in the inner pocket of his battledress blouse before setting off again. He'd turned his belt round while he'd been bending over his boot; he pulled the holster of his Webley back to his front, where it wouldn't bang as he walked along.

They were supposed to carry rifles everywhere they went in France but the NCOs had talked with the RSM, who'd talked with the CO. Now, anyone of the rank of sergeant and above was permitted to carry a pistol when he left the camp, rather than a cumbersome rifle. And men below the rank of sergeant were permitted to go into the town without any weapons.

After all, they weren't at war with France – they were only there as a political presence, a gesture of Chamberlain's good faith!

The road was totally deserted at that time of night; each farmhouse he passed, set back in its fields, was totally dark. Once a dog barked in the distance but soon stopped. The trees beside the road cast dark shadows in the harsh moonlight, and he walked along the side of the macadam to still the ring of his boots. Now he could hear no sound other than the rasp of the serge of his trousers. The sergeant who'd taught them field-craft, an ex-poacher turned gamekeeper, had taught them to keep their feet apart when they crossed ground at night to prevent even that small sound escaping from them to betray their movement; Reuben Godson tried it, feeling slightly ridiculous, waddling along with his feet apart, but noticing how even the tiniest rasp disappeared, leaving only the sound of his breathing and the slap of his pistol holster against his leg.

The camp was about a mile away – he couldn't get used to thinking in kilometres – when he came to the crest of a small hill and paused with his back to one of the trees. He glanced at his watch – half past three. Below him he could see the plain and the village around which the battalion was camped. He could see the artillery lines away to the left, with the guns camouflaged beneath netting which did nothing to hide their outline from the ground but presumably masked them from the air. Over on the right, about a mile from the village, was a unit of the cavalry – but they rode in tanks rather than on horses. Several of the officers had brought horses with them and a pack of hounds and hunted regularly across the fields. Rumour had it they'd brought new tanks with them, of a modern design, that were being developed before the war but now had been rushed into production. It was said the artillery also had a new gun, as yet untested. There had been many complaints that Britain ought to have foreseen the rise of Germany, ought to have prepared for this war much more thoroughly. The Colonel said many people had understood the dangers and spoken in Parliament about them, but their voices had not been heard. He had even warned them that perhaps there'd be a change of government, with Lord Halifax taking over from Neville Chamberlain, a politician whom the commanding officer appeared to despise as much as he despised the French.

It was all very much of a muchness to Reuben – he wasn't a political man and the machinations of governments meant little to him. The Germans had started a war and, when there was a war, you had to go to fight, to stop it. And then you returned home and picked up the pieces of your real life. Of course, his own dad, Silas Godson, hadn't returned home from the last war and his brother Lewis had come back with only one lung working but that was the chance you took. Just as every time you took out a boat, you took a chance on no storm blowing up before you got back in.

When the sound first came to him he ignored it, but then its insistent *cheep* forced itself into his consciousness.

It sounded like an Army radio, sending morse code. They'd all been taught morse code, and communicated between the platoons and the company headquarters on the exercises they did by morse. When the high-pitched *cheep cheep* stopped, he heard the harder clack he now instantly recognised as a morse key.

He was puzzled as to what the sound could mean.

Somebody using a radio, sending morse, at this time of night?

His first thought was that perhaps a section of the artillery, or the cavalry, were having a night exercise – he knew no exercise was scheduled for the infantry battalion.

If they *were* having an exercise, perhaps they'd have transport somewhere nearby, and he could get a lift the last mile into camp – his foot had continued to pain him as his boot had rubbed more and more skin from his blistered big toe.

He looked around. Patch of scrub to the right of the road and a track leading into it. Nothing to the left of the road except the line of trees spaced widely apart. Whoever was sending the morse would have to be in the scrub, with a truck parked out of sight. He walked slowly down the track, still making no noise. If it was the artillery, he didn't want them leaping out at him thinking he was one of the exercise umpires, or tossing a thunderflash at his feet and shouting, bang you're dead, thinking he was the opposition.

A man, a Frenchman by the look of him and the way he was dressed, was squatting beneath a tree in the centre of the scrub. He was wearing headphones, with one of the cups not clamped over his ear. The radio was in a hole beneath the tree and a wire ran from it, up into the tree branches. A bicycle was propped against the tree and the man was drawing power from an accumulator strapped to its pannier.

The Frenchman was so intent on sending his message that he didn't hear Reuben come into the clearing, stop, duck back behind the tree again.

Reuben unbuttoned the cover of his holster and took out his Webley. He pushed the safety catch forward with his thumb, then stepped out from behind the tree.

The Frenchman had finished his transmission, apparently, and was busy pulling the aerial wire down out of the tree. He'd already unclipped the leads from the accumulator.

Reuben felt a bit ridiculous with a gun in his hand, pointed at the Frenchman. 'That's it,' he said, 'what are you doing?' It sounded daft, even to him. It was perfectly obvious what the Frenchman was doing – he was sending a message by radio at three-thirty in the morning from the depths of a copse overlooking the British Army encampment. He was spying, that's what he was doing! 'You've been spying, haven't you?' Reuben said, again feeling ridiculous.

The Frenchman was quick, no doubt trained for such an emergency, and the knife he'd probably held up his sleeve flashed across the clearing, struck the gun, knocking it sideways, and then stuck in Reuben's arm. The Frenchman followed it across the clearing, his right arm bent and held across his throat. As he came near he slashed with his arm and hit Reuben across the throat, causing him to gag. This *was* something he knew about; he'd been in too many rough-house fights in Whitby not to be able to defend himself. Despite the pain in his arm where the knife was stuck, and the gagging in his throat, he banged his forehead forwards, the hard nut of his skull hitting square between the Frenchman's eyes. There was a loud crack and the man staggered backwards. Reuben reached across, grabbed the handle of the knife and pulled it out. The gun had dropped from his hand and he took a quick pace forward to put his foot on it, grinding it into the leaf-mould of the clearing. He'd no idea how to fight with a knife but he held it close to his body as he went after the Frenchman, letting it sway from side to side. The Frenchman, afraid of the blade, looked up at Reuben in terror and put out his hand, saying, '*Non, non.*'

Reuben grabbed the Frenchman's wrist and yanked him forward, using his right foot to kick the Frenchman's feet from under him. As the Frenchman fell, his arm twisted in Reuben's grasp and made a crack. The Frenchman screamed as he fell to the ground, his arm at an impossible angle to his body. Reuben bent over him, not knowing what to do next. Blood was running down his own arm into his hand but he could still flex his fingers though the movement sent stabs of pain up his forearm.

The Frenchman wasn't going anywhere; he crouched on his knees, holding his hand to prevent his dislocated elbow from moving, and his face worked in pain. Reuben stepped back from him and retrieved the Webley. He put the knife in the pistol holster, took out his handkerchief and poked it inside the gash in his uniform from which the blood was pouring.

First aid. Tourniquet to stem the flow of blood. Don't leave the tourniquet on too long or you'll lose the use of the limb. Mile to go, could he walk a mile? What about the Frenchman? His mind free-wheeled along these thoughts in no disciplined way. He knew one thing; come what may, he had to hang on to the Frenchman somehow.

Farmhouse? But what if the French were all in collusion? How would they react, seeing an Englishman bring in one of their own kind?

No. If they were in collusion, the radio would have been hidden in or near a farmhouse.

He took the lanyard from his battledress – the lanyard that ought to have been attached to his pistol by Army Regulations, but hadn't been, and looked round for a piece of twig, a stick, anything. He couldn't find anything on the ground and tried, one-handed, to break a piece from one of the shrubs. He couldn't do it, couldn't exert the force single-handed to break it. He tore it off the trunk of the shrub but now it was too cumbersome.

'Come on,' he said, 'get up!'

The Frenchman looked at him without comprehension. Reuben opened his lanyard and slipped it round the Frenchman's neck in a loop. He pulled the lanyard, not caring if he choked the Frenchman or not. Already he was beginning to feel light-headed, and knew he had to get the Frenchman out of that copse before he passed out. The Frenchman whimpered, but he came to his feet and started to stagger after Reuben, holding his arm to his side as they stumbled, locked together by that lanyard, along the track that led to the road.

When they arrived by the roadside, Reuben looked right and left, seeing no farmhouse, realising he couldn't last very much longer. He drew the Frenchman under the nearest tree, reached up, and could touch the lowest branch, which had been sawn off about six inches from the trunk. He looped the lanyard over it and drew the knot tight. The Frenchman started to choke, thinking Reuben meant to hang him and not realising that Reuben was incapable of much more effort.

Reuben had just remembered. Louis had said to him the previous evening that if Reuben wanted to stay, the *camionette* left Pincheville early when the first fishing boats returned, taking a load of fish to Corderie. If only he could hold out long enough . . . ! Louis would know what to do with the Frenchman. Louis couldn't be one of the spies . . . !

'Who are you, you bastard,' he said, shaking the Frenchman's arm so violently the Frenchman started to scream with pain, 'what do you mean by it, eh? You, a Frenchman, spying on the British, your friends, your bloody friends, do you hear me, who've come over here to help you . . . '

He hardly knew what he was saying, only that he was possessed by such a rage that this man should betray the very people who'd come to help him and his country.

'Oh bloody hell!' he said, and reached down and tore at the small pocket in the front of his trousers. He'd completely forgotten he carried a field dressing; dammit, the pocket was designed for a field dressing and he had one in it, not like the silly buggers who took their field dressings out and either used the pocket to carry their fags, or pressed them flat to improve the look of the trousers . . . He tore the paper wrapping from the dressing and the bandage unfolded itself and dangled from his hand. He unbuttoned the cuff of his jacket and his shirt and pulled them back.

'You move, you bastard, and I'll break the other arm!' The discovery of the field dressing had sent adrenalin coursing through his veins – he bared the wound, saw the clean cut from which the blood was welling, and slapped the dressing over it. Then he wound the bandage round it, as tight as he could manage one-handed. The blood still seeped through the lint and the bandage but it didn't seem to be coming as quickly.

The Frenchman had gone quiet.

Reuben whirled around quickly.

The Frenchman had passed out, had fallen forward, and was being strangled by the lanyard. Reuben cursed, reached up, and slipped the loop off the tree. He slid back the slip knot that held the noose tight round the Frenchman's throat, and put his ear close to the Frenchman's face. Thank God he was still breathing, though the air was rattling in and out as if he was in the last stages of bronchitis. Reuben hunkered down beside him, knowing there was nothing he could do but wait.

And try to stay conscious.

He stayed as he was, hunkered down and still, moving only the fingers of his injured arm from time to time to keep the circulation flowing in them. The blood appeared to have congealed on his wound, which had gone numb. As he waited he thought, not of the Frenchman or his spying, but of the fishermen in Pincheville, the shape and rigging of their boats, the method of working their nets. Then he began thinking of distant Ravenswyke, and the *Hope*, and wondering how his lass, Emily, as he always thought of her, was getting on. Several times in the last week he had thought to send her a line, but he wasn't such a dab hand at letter writing. He thought about his two lads, Wilfred and Arthur, gone to train to be officers, and of the two lasses, Eliza and Anne, left at home. Eleanor, his sister, away in York driving an ambulance. The other fishermen in Old Quaytown, the Snug at the Raven. And that took his thoughts away to Leeds, of all places, and to Emma Thoroughgood, as she'd been called before she married Stanley Baxter, the first woman he'd ever taken to bed, in the big front room of the Raven Hotel! From Emma Thoroughgood, his thoughts skipped to Elsie Milner, who had married Mark Adam Tockett. Elsie had been one of his first *friends*, aye, he could call her that, his first real friend. And the source of Emily's jealousy all those years ago.

His waking thoughts must have become dreams without him realising it, because he awoke to see the soldier bending over him, wearing the crash helmet of a despatch rider, and heard a voice saying, 'Sergeant? You all right, Sergeant?'

He shook his head. 'Aye, lad, I'm all right,' he said. 'Look to yon bugger.'

The despatch rider looked at the Frenchman then turned to Reuben. 'He's dead, Sergeant,' he said, 'he's dead! What happened?'

'You'd better get down to t' camp, and fetch t' orderly officer quickly as you can.'

The despatch-rider looked uncertain. 'I've just come from there, Sergeant. I'm on my way to Brigade HQ.'

'Don't argue, lad,' Reuben said. 'Get back to the camp and turn out the guard. Ask the Guard Commander to get the Orderly Officer, as quick as you can, and bring him up here. And that's an order. I'll carry the can if anybody says owt to you.'

'Will you be all right, then?'

'Look, I've been sitting here for four hours waiting for somebody to come along this road. Another half an hour won't kill me.'

The despatch-rider got back on his motor cycle, kicked

it into life, did an about-turn and set off. Reuben knew that by the time he arrived, the Orderly Officer would most probably be inspecting the guard before they changed at eight o'clock. With luck, they'd be back in ten minutes.

The despatch-rider must have been persuasive; the Orderly Officer and Sgt Williams, the Guard Commander, arrived in eight minutes. The Orderly Officer was Reuben's own platoon commander, Lieutenant Smythe.

'What the devil is happening, Sgt Godson?' he said, as he sprang out of the pick-up truck. 'In view of what the DR told me, I've asked them to roust out an ambulance. I can see we'll need one.'

Reuben had stood up but made no attempt to salute. Lt Smythe saw the blood on his arm. 'What happened to you?' he asked. 'And what happened to him?' pointing to the dead man.

'I found him in the woods, Lieutenant. He was sending morse on a radio he's got hidden back there. When I held my gun on him, he went for me with a knife . . . '

'A radio? In the wood? Where? Are you fit enough to show me?'

Reuben set off down the path with Lt Smythe and Sgt Williams following. Smythe whistled when he saw the radio in the hole dug beneath the tree trunk, and the wooden lid on which twigs had been stapled to camouflage it. He saw the bicycle and the accumulator wrapped in sacking.

'Are you all right, Sgt Godson?' he asked. 'Can you last a while longer?'

'Yes, Sir.'

'In that case, Sgt Williams, get back to the camp as fast as you can. Go to the Officers' Mess where you should find Major Sharp at breakfast. Give him my compliments, and ask him to come out here immediately. Tell him this word: Carbuncle. Understand?'

'Carbuncle,' the sergeant repeated. It had to be a code word.

'You sit down on that stump,' Lt Smythe said when Williams had gone. 'I'll be back in a minute.' He went rapidly up the path and Reuben heard him grunting then saw him walk down the pathway, carrying the Frenchman in his arms.

'The fewer people who see him, the better,' he said. 'Now, take it easy while I have at look at that arm of yours.'

He peeled back the sleeve of Reuben's battledress and his shirt, and slowly unwound the bandage part of the field dressing. The final layers were stuck with congealed blood. 'Look,' he said, 'I think the best thing is to leave that alone for the MO when he gets here, assuming he comes with the ambulance.' Almost as if on cue, they heard the squeal of brakes, then the sound of voices.

'They should be around here somewhere,' someone said.

The lieutenant went back up the track and came back a minute later with the Unit Medical Officer, who took one look at the bandage on Reuben's arm, then removed it layer by layer. He examined the wound.

'Move your fingers, Sergeant,' he said.

Reuben flexed them, feeling the pain up his arm.

The Medical Officer gripped his hand. 'Right, squeeze my hand tightly,' he said, 'tight as you can.'

Reuben gripped, noting how the MO was bending his wrist.

'You're a lucky lad, Sergeant,' he said. 'He didn't get a ligament.'

The medical orderly had come down the track, carrying a green tin box.

'Just dust it, and bandage it again,' the MO said to him. 'I'll put a couple of stitches in it when we get back to camp.' He moved to the Frenchman, felt his pulse, lifted his eyelids, let his head fall back. 'Dead,' he said, 'shovel him into the ambulance and we'll look at him later.'

'Do you mind if we keep him here until Major Sharp arrives? I think it's a *carbuncle!*'

'Like that, is it? Well, a few minutes here or there isn't going to hurt him now, is it? And my eggs and bacon will be cold by now, anyway. I'll send the ambulance back. You, Sergeant, come straight to sick bay when you get back to camp, and I'll put a couple of stitches in your arm.'

'Yes, Captain.'

It took Major Sharp only five minutes to arrive, after the ambulance had left. He had obviously been briefed, and walked down the track into the copse. Lt Smythe saluted, and Major Sharp saluted back, preoccupied by what he could see. He looked first at the radio, the accumulator, the wire stretching up.

'You haven't touched anything, Sergeant, have you?' he asked quickly.

'No, Sir.'

'You, Lieutenant?'

'No, Sir.'

'Good, then unless he spun the dial when he finished transmitting, we'll have the wavelength. Anybody searched him?'

'No, Sir.'

'Right, let's all clear out of here. Sgt Harrison?'

Sgt Harrison, who worked in Headquarters and occasionally gave the platoons lectures on security, came out of the thickness of the copse. Reuben hadn't even known he was there.

'It's all yours, Sergeant,' Major Sharp said. He turned to Lt Smythe and Sgt Godson. 'I suggest we get the hell out of here.'

Reuben rode in the back of the Humber Estate car the Commanding Officer used but fell asleep during the short ride back to camp. When he woke up, they were outside the CO's office.

'Do you think you can manage, Sergeant, just for a little while longer?' the Major asked.

'I can try, Sir, but you may have to waken me up again! Like, I'm sorry, but I can't seem to keep my eyes open.'

They went without ceremony into the Commanding Officer's office, which had a sofa across one wall, and several chairs around a table. Reuben stood briefly to attention, but Lt-Col Britten waved him to a chair. His keen eyes beneath beetling eyebrows stared into Reuben's face.

'I know you're beat, Sergeant,' he said. 'Loss of blood does that faster than anything else. But try to hang on long enough to tell us exactly what happened. Time may be an important factor in this.' Reuben described everything from the moment he'd heard the sound of morse coming from the copse, and the clack of a morse key. Neither the Colonel nor Major Sharp interrupted him. He told exactly how he'd tied the lanyard to the tree, how he must have passed out without realising it, and come round again thinking the Frenchman was still alive because he could hear the rattle in his throat.

When he'd finished, the Colonel looked at Major Sharp. 'That seems all very clear to me,' he said, 'do *you* have any questions?'

'Only one,' Major Sharp said. 'I'd like you to tell me again, Sergeant, exactly what happened at the end of the transmission. You said, he finished sending morse; there was an answer; he reached forward and switched up a button; then he started to pull the wire out of the tree.'

'That's right, Major.'

'He didn't touch the tuning dial; you're certain of that?'

'Yes, Major, I'm certain.'

The major sat back in his chair, a huge smile on his face. 'Well done, Sergeant,' he said, 'we've got the frequency!'

Reuben didn't hear the last part of the sentence. He'd fallen asleep again.

CHAPTER SIX

As luck would have it, Anne had just finished dusting Eleanor's room when her aunt arrived from York, wearing trousers and her Ambulance Driver's uniform, with its green peaked cap firmly held down on her curling blond hair. Anne could have finished the job hours ago, but she'd been entranced, as usual, by the lovely things her aunt had collected over the years, the cups and saucers, figurines in real china, little inlaid boxes in lacquer and mother of pearl containing her jewellery. Perhaps Anne's favourite was the clock on the mantelpiece, its round brass case supported from beneath by a gilded Atlas figure, standing firmly on a base of green onyx, that Aunt Eleanor had told her came from Italy.

'My, you keep it all looking nice and tidy for me,' Eleanor said, adjusting the position of one of the figurines on the top of the dresser a couple of inches to the left. 'It's a pleasure to come back home.'

She took off her cap, looked quickly in the mirror as she patted her curls, then put her arms round Anne's shoulders and pecked her on the cheek.

Anne, as always, was excited by the smell of her aunt, that faint delicate odour of bath oil and perfume that lingered on her skin. Last time she and Liz had been into Whitby on a Saturday, they'd spent half an hour in the chemist's shop, sniffing at the bottles of samples he had on the perfume counter, finally selecting the bottle of Rose Water that was all they could afford from their pocket money savings. 'It must be good,' Liz had told her, 'since it's threepence a bottle.'

But it didn't smell anything like the stuff her Aunt Eleanor wore and she swopped it with Susan Featherly for two handkerchieves.

'Now, tell me, what have you been doing?' Eleanor asked, as she sat in her chair, sighing as she relaxed. Frankly, she would rather have arrived at her home without her niece being there; she'd like to take off her work clothes and have a wash but she knew Anne was very fond of her, and looked after her rooms while she was away. Years ago, Reuben had built this extension to the Godson house for Eleanor and she had two whole rooms to herself, into which the rest of the family never penetrated without knocking. She'd bought her own furniture and even had a sink in the corner with a gas boiler over it to provide hot water. She'd made a curtain and Reuben had hung it for her so that the sink corner was hidden from view. He'd laughed.

'What's so bad about washing your hands that you don't want nobody to see you doing it,' he said, remembering the number of times both he and Eleanor, as kids, had been dropped into the same tub of water in front of the fire for the weekly bath, often in the water in which the clothes had been washed.

'You don't understand, Reuben,' Eleanor had said. 'I don't want to spend my time sitting here, looking at a sink and a gas boiler, do I?'

Reuben hadn't been able to understand. The Godson home had been one of the first to have gas laid on to it when they'd opened the gasworks behind Grinklegate; they'd been the first to have gaslight instead of lamps and candles, the first to have one of the new-fangled copper boilers that delivered hot water through a heating coil. Now the whole of Godson Street was lit by electric lamps and, before he went away, Reuben had been talking about replacing the gas boilers with what they called electric immersion heaters, since the gas coils banged and clanked, and sometimes seemed on the point of exploding. One or two had exploded, but mostly up at the top of the Bank where the gas supply was always doubtful.

'Many folks, still drawing water from the tap and warming it on the fire, would be happy to look at an inside sink,' Reuben had said gruffly, 'with a gas boiler beside it on t' wall!'

'Close the sink curtain, Anne, there's a good girl, and tell me what you've been doing.'

Emily had lit the fire when she knew Eleanor was coming home for a few days, and the room was warm as toast. Eleanor took off her shoes and wriggled her toes in the warmth.

'There isn't owt to tell,' Anne said, crimsoning with embarrassment. She never cared to be the focus of attention, to be asked to speak out. School had been an agony for her when she'd been asked to stand up and answer questions or recite the poetry lesson. She'd been pleased when, like Liz, she'd been allowed to leave at fifteen though the family had held council, and Aunt Eleanor in particular had tried to insist that Anne be made to stay on for the extra two years.

'Isn't *anything* to tell, you mean, Anne,' Eleanor said automatically.

'Well, you know what I mean . . . Nowt, I mean, nothing much happens around here. Nothing's happened since you've been away.'

'I can see that,' Eleanor said, smiling. 'Elsie Milner married Mr Tockett; Millie Harrison was taken off to the County Hospital after she had a stroke; they had to launch the lifeboat when Alf Corley nearly ran aground on High Tor when his engine broke down; lightning hit the bakery and blew out the ovens; the Bridge café fell down into the brook; that dreadful man Sampson was taken away by the police because he half-killed his wife when he came home drunk and his children have been taken into care; the Germans have invaded Norway and it looks as if the British troops are going to be pushed out, or taken prisoner, and your dad's been given a medal!'

'Crikey, Aunt Eleanor, you know it all already.'

'I ought to! Liz guessed what train I'd be on, and came to meet me. Like a newspaper, she is!'

'Aye, well, she always did have the gift of the gab, our Liz did,' Anne said grumpily. 'She'd talk the hind leg off a donkey! The number of times she's kept me awake half the night, chattering away like a monkey . . . ! No wonder I like going in to sleep with mi' mam!

Eleanor reached out her hand, took Anne's, and drew her to the side of the chair. Anne sat on the velvet arm, and Eleanor put her hand on Anne's waist.

'You mustn't be jealous of your sister, Anne,' she said. 'She's a year older than you are. In a year or two's time, there'll be nothing to choose between the two of you, believe me. You'll be just as pretty as she is; you'll have just as good a figure; your hair, if you go on brushing it the way I've always told you, will be just as shiny . . . '

'You think my figure will grow, Aunt Eleanor . . . ?' Anne asked anxiously .

Eleanor glanced at Anne's almost flat chest. 'Give it time, Anne,' she said. 'Many young girls start late.' She remembered the way she had felt at that age, when all the girls in her class at the local school had started their periods, and she hadn't. How they all had breasts, and she hadn't. It had given her a year of absolute misery!

Anne was staring into the fire, her expression woebegone. 'Liz has got a boy-friend,' she said enviously.

'So I heard. Tommy Thompson . . . ?'

'Oh no, he's old hat! No, she keeps company with a right toff – no less than Robert Thrummell . . . '

'Young master Robert. I used to work for his grandfather.'

'I know, Aunt Eleanor. He takes her all over, in his car. He's waiting for his papers to go into the Army. He's going to be an officer!'

Eleanor whistled. She remembered young Robert coming into the office, always very correct, very well-composed. It had been natural to assume he'd take over the business one day. Eleanor had always thought him a colourless lad who would never have made anything if he'd had to fend for himself. The Thrummell name had opened all doors to him, of course, especially since they were saying his dad, Ezra, was buying his way into a knighthood by taking on all the charity work and free committees he could. Now Ezra was sitting on the Civil Defence Commission, representing the civilian population, it could only be a matter of time before he received the award on which he'd set his heart. Eleanor knew him as a pompous opportunist and had always been pleased she'd worked for his father, and not him. If his father had stayed active in the business she might have remained with them rather than volunteering for the Female Auxiliary Nursing Yeomanry, the FANY. She wouldn't have been accepted for that snobbish and exclusive Service if Thrummell hadn't spoken for her!

Anne looked shyly round at her aunt's face, seeing her gazing into the fire no doubt recapturing her memories of the Thrummell family. Eleanor had a long thin face with even features, lovely soft blond brown hair which she kept in immaculate condition – Anne had never seen her in disarray, never seen her without a dab of powder on her cheeks, even a touch of lipstick on her lips. From looking at her aunt's cosmetics, carefully arranged on her dressing table in front of the mirror, Anne knew she used a little rouge, though Anne herself, making up furtively when she was supposed to be cleaning her Aunt's room, had never been able to smear the rouge on without it showing as two ugly red blotches on her cheeks.

Of course, everybody knew Aunt Eleanor's tragic story, how she'd been married to Terry Pitt who'd been killed in the last war, how she'd been pregnant but the baby had been born dead, how she'd gone a bit potty and, it was said, been responsible for the death of Anne's younger brother, Amos, so that Reuben had had to have her put away. Eleanor was forty-one, a year older than Reuben, Anne's dad but, somehow, Anne didn't think of her as an old person. She'd kept herself young by being always attractive, always neat and tidy, always totally correct.

'Why have you never got married again, Aunt Eleanor?' Anne asked. The minute she'd said the words, she regretted them. Her aunt had always been such a *private* person who resented any intrusion.

Eleanor nearly spoke the usual answer when people asked her that question – don't be nosey, it's none of your business! But then she looked up at Anne's young, serious, troubled face and recognised the question as part of the symptom of Anne's uneasiness, a manifestation of her puberty.

'I'll tell you, Anne, and then you must go because I want to get out of these clothes – I was working half of last night and I can still smell the oil from that ambulance. I've never married again, not for any romantic reason, but because I've always wanted to do things with my life I couldn't do if I'd promised to look after a husband. You remember how I used to organise the musical events for the Philosophical Society – I couldn't have done that if I'd had a husband to look after. I want to read a lot of books, to improve my mind; I want to go and look at a lot of pictures for the same interest. And I couldn't do that if I was married, with a husband and babies to look after, now could I? Being a wife and a mother is a big responsibility, but I don't want to take it on. Perhaps you'll think I'm selfish – a lot of people do!'

'No, Aunt Eleanor, I don't,' Anne said vehemently. 'Anyway, *I'm* never going to get married, either!'

Eleanor smiled at her, knowing what forces were at work in her. 'It's early days yet,' she said. 'There's no reason to make up your mind too quickly. Or too soon. Now, get off with you! I want to get changed!'

When Anne had gone, Eleanor took off her clothes and put on the velvet dressing gown she'd bought herself the previous year. She was lazy, loth to get washed and go down into the house below where she knew Emily would have prepared a meal for her, as she always did when Eleanor returned. Practical, sensible, maternal Emily, Eleanor thought, though somewhat ruefully, would never know the anguish she had been spared by her marriage to Reuben!

She turned on the portable wireless that had been a going-away present from the staff of Thrummell and Slade, when she had left to join the FANY.

The midday news came on. Third of May. The British troops had been withdrawn from Andalsnes, north of Bergen, Norway. Neville Chamberlain had been to see the King.

The window of her room looked out over the roofs of the houses built lower down the cliff of Old Quaytown, directly east across the North Sea. Over there, and to the north, British soldiers were being killed by the Germans, driven from the soil of Norway into the sea.

Perhaps, if only, if only she'd been born a male, she'd be over there with them, all her dilemmas resolved . . .

'You have your wish, Sgt-Major Godson,' Major Sharp said. 'The order has just come through and I thought you'd want to know right away. They've accepted your application for Special Services. You're to report back to Blighty immediately, to Portsmouth.'

Reuben smiled happily. They'd given him no option to refuse the promotion to sergeant-major after the spy incident and Major Sharp had asked if he wanted to reconsider his application for transfer. He'd thought about it for a few days but, during that time, the Unit had been visited by a team of two officers and a regimental sergeant-major. All three had been impressive men and when the Unit had assembled, they had given a talk in which each of the three gave a smooth but unprofessional performance. They'd said the future war would need to be fought, sometimes, in unconventional ways. They were looking for men of the highest personal courage and initiative to join a unit called the Special Services. It would be no good asking them in detail what the Special Services would do, because no-one knew, as yet. But they'd be organised in small squads, most probably called Commandos, and each Commando would learn to work independently. Some would specialise in operations that started by air, others by sea, and others overland. The Commandos would be volunteers, and they were going to be in the district for two days to give potential candidates a preliminary examination.

Reuben had withdrawn his previous application, and had asked instead to be considered for this Special Services. But first, he had to submit himself to a barrage of questions from Lt-Colonel Britten.

'Lot of damned glamour boys,' the Colonel had said. 'This war, like all other wars, will be won by good men on the ground, by the Infantry! Not the Cavalry, the Gunners, the Sappers, or the Special Services, but the foot-sloggers, the Infantry. And we shall need good men, just as they will. If you put forward this application,

Sgt-Major, you do so against my express wishes and desires!'

It appeared that the Commando recruiting team had arrived with a brief direct from the War Office, cutting across all normal lines of command, and the Colonel didn't like it.

Reuben persisted. The idea of amphibious warfare appealed to him; if he could combine his duty to fight the war with his love of boats, he knew he'd be a happier man for the years he knew the war would last.

'I'd like to give it a try, Colonel,' he'd said and the Colonel had grumpily dismissed him.

'The CO wants to see you before you go, Sgt-Major,' Major Sharp said. 'I'll wheel you in there at nine o'clock, then you'll still be in time for the boat to Blighty from Dieppe.'

'Disappointed in you, Sgt-Major Godson,' the CO said. 'You know, your medal was a personal recommendation from me. I was even thinking of putting you forward for Officer Selection, if I could have your word that, after commissioning, you'd come back to the Infantry in the Regiment. You'll be on attachment in your new lot; don't forget your first loyalty is to the Yorkshire Regiment, and not to this bunch of cowboys! Sorry to see you go! Best wishes to you and all that rubbish, but you know what I mean, eh?'

'I know what you mean, Colonel,' Reuben said quietly. 'But I wish you would understand my point of view. I know that going away from the Unit could be thought of as disloyalty – especially since, as you've reminded me, you've given me promotion and have personally recommended me for the Military Medal. But boats are in my blood, and have been in the blood of my family since the fifteenth century. The mistake was mine; I thought as I'd be happy helping to fight the war on dry land, but I've found that half of me isn't being used, half of my experience and knowledge is crying out to be used. If part of this Special Services unit is to be amphibious, they'll be able to use me to the full, and that's where I'd like to be.'

The Colonel coughed and shuffled his papers from embarrassment. 'Yes, Sgt-Major, I can understand that,' he said. 'I expect one becomes too paternal about the men in one's battalion since we spend so much time trying to foster a family feeling. But I don't like to lose good men and, for a peacetime soldier, you've come along very well. So, go with my good wishes; I hope you'll succeed in finding what you're looking for in these Special Services. I can only regret that we weren't able to give it to you here.'

Reuben saluted, and marched out, a burden of guilt removed from him by the Colonel's kindly remarks.

Elsie Tockett was only half awake when Mark Adam came into the bedroom. He was carrying, on a tray, a cup of tea, a slice of toast, and a boiled egg with a neat silver cover on it.

'Elsie,' he said, his voice low, 'it's me, Mark! Sorry to waken you at such an ungodly hour!'

She struggled awake, and sat up in the large double bed, arranging the pillows behind her back so that he could set the tray down on her lap.

'Whatever time did you get here?' she asked, puzzled. 'I thought you weren't coming back from London until Friday?'

'I drove up during the night,' he said. 'The roads were bad or I'd have been here sooner.'

'Roads bad, first week in May?'

'Jammed with traffic, all going south. Elsie, I've got my recall. I've to join the regiment as soon as possible. There's some sort of an emergency. I've heard a rumour that the Germans are preparing for some sort of advance, but nobody knows where. I've also heard that they're trying to get rid of Neville Chamberlain, to replace him with somebody else, probably Lord Halifax.'

'He'll make just as much a mess of it as Chamberlain,' she said. 'He's just another appeaser, just like the rest! They need a man who can go in there and tell the Germans it's all got to stop. They need a strong man!'

She drank her tea but ignored the egg. He reached across the bed to kiss her forehead but, uninhibitedly, she lifted her face to kiss him on the lips. 'A kiss on the forehead isn't much good after you've been away three days,' she said. 'If you've been driving all night you'll be tired. Better get your clothes off, and slip in here beside me, where it's warm.'

'Then I'd be more tired still!' he protested. After the rather formal marriage he'd enjoyed with his wife, Hester, who never did anything sexual spontaneously during the latter years of their marriage after the children were born, he found Elsie's direct approach pleasing, and flattering. She made no secret of the fact that often she desired him physically, she wanted him sexually. It had been a new experience for him, rejuvenating in its forthrightness.

Elsie herself had been astounded by the extent of her own sexuality. She'd thought that as she reached forty, the well of her desires would most probably run dry but it seemed as if the reverse was the case, and she overflowed with desire for Mark. It had been many years since she had known orgasm; when it happened to her the first time Mark made love to her, gently, and kindly, on their wedding night, and then fiercely and passionately as the night went into day, she had believed it was because it had been a long time since she'd been with a man sexually. The residents of Old Quaytown who'd dismissed her all her life as promiscuous had never realised she was, in her own way, totally selective, and totally faithful to each man she chose. The minute her interest in Mark

Adam Tockett had been kindled, she had looked at no other man. She had gone into marriage expecting a quiet dignified life, with security and authority, and had been amazed when they had begun to revel in each other's bodies, to behave in private like a pair of juvenile newly-weds who've just discovered the delights of sexuality for the first time.

She'd been reluctant to talk about him rejoining his regiment; she'd known it was going to happen one day soon. Surely, she consoled herself, at forty-five they'd give him some kind of office job, possibly somewhere near at hand. The war needed younger men!

'I thought that perhaps you'd heard some more about going into the Ministry of Supply?' she said quietly. He'd been given an offer to work for the Ministry, possibly running a manufacturing company somewhere here in the North, but he'd surprised her by saying he had no interest in doing that. 'I didn't get to do any fighting in the last lot,' he'd said defensively.

She knew the story; he'd insisted on giving her the details before they were married of how he'd been 'suspended' from his regiment because of a homosexual offence. How he'd come back home in disgrace, had been thrashed by his father, and practically forced into his marriage with Hester Gramond. Of course, a much embroidered version of the story had run wild through the district, but he hadn't spared himself in making certain Elsie knew every detail of it. She knew damned well that a lot of young men experiment with homosexuality, just as a lot of girls form attachments which can progress as far as touching, and playing with each other. 'Just because you once had homosexual relationships doesn't mean you're a homosexual,' she'd said at the time. 'From what I've heard about these boys' schools, ninety per cent of the lads have a go at it, one time or another!'

'All right,' she'd said, 'I know you didn't do any fighting

last time, and we don't need to go into the reasons for that all over again, but I don't see why you need to sacrifice yourself in this lot. Not if you're usable elsewhere.'

He couldn't see it with her logic. He'd gone to the Colonel of his regiment and had offered his services as an infantry officer. 'We'll call you, the moment we need you,' the Colonel had said. 'At the moment, we're pushing through as many young officers as we can. I've had an application to join from a couple of youngsters from your part of the world. Godson, I think the name is. Two brothers. Anything in the cupboard locally I ought to know about?'

'They're two good lads from a first class family who've been fishermen since the fifteenth century,' Mark Adam had said enthusiastically. 'I'd accept them like a shot if it were up to me.'

Now the time had come for the forty-fives. Mark Adam would go in as a captain and take over immediate command of a company. All his officers would be raw, straight from OCTU. His men would mostly be recruits who'd done the basic six weeks' army indoctrination training, and then had completed the nine weeks' infantry course. 'With luck,' his commanding officer had said, 'we'll find you a few experienced senior NCOs but they're as short as gold dust and just as valuable.'

'I shall be in camp quite near here,' he said to Elsie as she sipped the tea he'd brought her. 'It's supposed to be a military secret, but it'll be outside Pickering somewhere. They're putting up some kind of ready-made hut for the battalion offices, and the rest of us will go under canvas. That's if they can find enough tents for us all. I will be able to come home more or less every second night.'

'And how long will *that* last?' Elsie said, feeling unaccountably shrewish, wishing she could be easy and relaxed. Already she had a hollow in her stomach from the knowledge he'd be gone. The camp outside Pickering could only be for a short time before he went to the real fighting Army somewhere. She wished so much she could smile, and say something brave and unselfish, but she felt ugly, ugly from sleep, from desire for him, from a reluctance to accept his male feeling that he had to run away to do what he called his duty, squandering the life they wanted to spend together.

'I don't know, love,' he said, surprised by her tone of voice. 'It won't be up to *me* to decide, will it? But they'll have to give us all time to knit together into one unit, so that we learn how to work together . . . '

Now she realised why she felt ugly; she felt excluded from this particular world of men, who could go anywhere, and do anything, who could live in tented camps and 'learn how to work together,' as he had put it.

'Do they have women in infantry companies?' she asked, forcing herself to speak lightly. 'I could come and be your orderly, make your bed, cook your meals, even learn to drive your car. And, when you went into battle, I could be your bearer, carry your rifle for you, and your spare ammunition . . . '

He seated himself beside her on the bed. 'There's nothing I'd like better, or worse,' he said. 'I want you back here at home, warm and safe for me to come back to!'

She buried her head in his shoulder, and couldn't prevent herself from crying. 'Only this once,' she said when she could draw breath. 'Just let me have a little cry and then it'll be all over, I promise you.'

Wilfred and Arthur returned to Ravenswyke on the same day that Winston Churchill, and not Lord Halifax as everyone had expected, was made Prime Minister. Emily Godson had received an invitation from the War Office, with a first class rail warrant, to attend the Passing-Out Parade at Selcombe Towers, the Stately Home in which her two sons had been changed from cadets into fully-fledged Second-Lieutenants, each with a pip on his shoulder, and under his arm a stick of cane, wrapped in leather. A representative of Gieves, the Savile Row tailors and military outfitters, had set up a branch in Selcombe village and all the young men without family tailors had gone there to be outfitted. It was the first time either Wilfred, or Arthur, had owned a suit specially tailored for them; they gave their equipment to John, Anne, and Liz, who had come to the station for the arrival of the train, and marched side by side down the long slope that led to Old Quaytown below. While their kit was carried through the Backs, they marched down and alongside the the Cut, as far as the Raven Hotel; their orderly progress became something of a rout as women rushed out of their cottages to greet them, to clutch at the barathea of their uniforms, to hug them and plant kisses on their cheeks as if they were the returning heroes of some valiant campaign.

'By gow, the Jerries had better watch out when you pair get there,' Winnie Clewson said. It was typical of most of the remarks they'd heard, most of the suggestions that once the two Godson boys went across to Europe and took over the conduct of the war, it would soon be all over!

Ephraim Hardcastle was standing outside the Snug when they arrived in triumph, surrounded by a crowd of every young lad and lass in Old Quaytown. He held a glass of whisky in each hand.

'Get them down, the pair of you!' he said. They stood to attention, clinked the glasses together, then drained them in one gulp that brought tears to Arthur's eyes.

'I reckon as we're right proud of you,' Ephraim said, 'you being officers an' all. If only your dad could be here to see this day!' The doorway of the Snug was filled with the fishermen who'd not gone to war, each with a drink in his hand.

'Come in and have a drink,' Old Bill Clewson said. 'We moan wet the baby's head!'

'It's not a christening, silly old bugger,' George-Willie Mountjoy said. 'Anyroad, they'll want to get up t'hill, to their mam.'

'To get changed,' Walter Bredford said. 'They'll be bringing t'*Hope* out, on t'tide, I reckon. John's got t'hooks baited, ready!'

Wilfred looked at Arthur. It'd be a lark, sure enough, to take out the *Hope*. But Arthur shook his head. 'Mam'll want us by her side for an hour or two,' he said. 'We can't let her down. Not today!'

Emily was waiting inside the house when they arrived. 'Wipe your feet,' she said. 'Our Liz has cleaned the place through for you!'

Their equipment had been stacked on the sofa that ran along the back of the room; they threw their caps and sticks on top of the pile and rushed across, both trying to grab her round the waist as if in a rugby tackle. 'Give over!' she kept saying, 'give over!' but she couldn't have stopped them even if she'd wanted to from hugging her and squeezing her until she *had* to tell them to stop.

'You're taking all t' breath out of me,' she said. 'Stand back, stand back, and let's have a look at the pair of you!'

They stood back from her, side by side in military precision, while her eyes greedily took in the details of their uniforms, their Sam Browne belts, the gold gleaming star on each shoulder. They'd chosen to wear their service dress uniforms rather than the plainer battledress; she'd never seen them looking so well, so grown up, so proud and dignified.

'So,' she said after she'd devoured them with her eyes, 'you're a pair of officers, eh? I never thought I'd see the day that grown men would be calling my sons Lieutenant . . . '

'They don't, Mam,' Arthur said happily. 'They call us

Mister! Everybody with only one pip on his shoulder, is called Mister.'

Liz and Anne were standing beside them both looking enraptured by the uniforms.

'A right pair of toffs, eh, Liz ... Anne ... ?' Emily said.

Wilfred turned. 'What's all this Liz business, then?'

'It's my name! Anyway, mam said I could! Though Robert calls me Eliza!'

'Who's Robert, when he's at home ... ?' Wilfred asked.

'It's her fella.' Anne said, 'Robert Thrummell.'

'Thrummell, indeed.'

'He's gone to Sandhurst,' Liz said. 'He's going into the Guards!'

Wilfred looked at Arthur and winked. 'The Guards, my dear chap, eh what?' he said, giving an imitation of so many of the upper class cadets they'd had to suffer during their officer training.

John pushed his way past Liz. 'Eh, our Wilfred, eh, Arthur; I've baited three baskets of line. Bags of sole about. You coming out, then?'

'Sole, eh?'

'And I got thirty pounds of haddock, yesterday, and ten six-pounder cods. Navy says we're not allowed out, but we go, all the same. I've been doing a bit of netting. You should've seen t' mackerel – I could've leaned over t' side and scooped 'em out in my mam's pinny! Alf Corley got on t' rocks again – that engine of his, and brand new. Bredford pulled out a funny bugger ... '

'Stop swearing, our John,' Anne said quickly, looking at mam, who hadn't taken her eyes off the two older lads.

'It went six feet,' John said, excited, 'and had a head on it the size of t' copper, I'm not kidding. You coming out, then?'

Wilfred held up his hand to stop the flow. 'Not today, John,' he said. 'Happen tomorrow. We want to talk to mam a bit, you know.'

'Nay, lad,' Emily said, 'you can go out if you've a mind. T'talking will still be here, when you get back.'

Arthur shook his head and Wilfred saw it. 'No,' Wilfred said. 'Us'll not go out today.'

'Bloody hell!' John said, 'and I've prepared *three* baskets!'

This time Emily's hand swung out and caught his ear, though with no strength behind it. 'Stop swearing, John,' she said. 'Just because you go into t' Snug, it doesn't mean you can bring their language back up here!'

'Go into t' Snug!' Wilfred said. 'How long has this been happening, then?'

'Ever since I caught yon mine ... ' John said complacently.

Arthur had drawn his mam aside while the other two talked. 'You ought to have used that warrant and come to the Passing Out Parade, Mam,' he said. 'All the other mams were there, and sisters. It was a right grand occasion!'

She put her arm round him. 'I'm not one much for grand occasions, Arthur,' she said. 'I'd rather see you the way I have done, all here together, in your new uniforms. Anyway, you know how I always cry when I'm happy and the mothers of all your grand friends would have wondered what I was crying about!'

He hugged her. 'Aye, well it was a bit toffee-nosed,' he said, 'though I'd have liked you to see it.'

'What's to happen to you now?' she asked anxiously. 'You'll not be going to France right away?'

He shook his head. 'No,' he said, 'we shall have to join our regiment first of all.'

'Why did you both choose the – what's it called – Royal

West Kents? Why didn't you go into t' Yorkshire Regiment, like your dad?'

'We thought about it, honest, we did. And we talked about it. And finally we reckoned we could never keep straight faces if we were posted to the same unit as our dad! Imagine us having to call him sgt-major, and him having to call us sir!'

'Yes, I can see what you mean. It could be a bit embarrassing, both sides. When do you have to go to this – Royal West Kents? And where is it?'

'We go down to the depot in Maidstone in three weeks' time.'

'And that's it, then . . . ?'

'Aye, Mam, that's it!'

A tear had formed in the corner of her eye, but she brushed it away. 'Well, make the most of it while you're here. Bed's made up, wi' clean sheets and a bottle in. You'll be wanting to take a walk round, see all your mates, I expect. I'll have your tea on t'table at six – Fewster's given me a nice bit of liver since I told him you were coming home today. And a rice pudding – I thought you'd like that.'

They didn't speak of the gulf that both knew had opened between them, now that they were officers and, by any account, had risen in the simple scale of Emily's values. They'd gone away boys, both of them, and had come back gentlemen and, try as she might, looking at them in their newly tailored uniforms, hearing the changes they hadn't realised had taken place in their voices, seeing the confident manner in which they held themselves like men of self-assurance the world over, she couldn't see them as her boys. She'd never been a possessive mother, had never sought to hold any member of her family to her apron strings. Even when they'd been tiny tots, she'd let them wander out of the cottage, up and down the backs, down to the Slip, out on the *Hope*. When their brother,

Amos, had died, well, it'd been the will of God to take him and, though she'd mourned him grievously, she'd let his image go. In the same way that now she knew she'd let the images of Wilfred and Arthur as boys slip away. They were men now, and gentlemen at that, and she'd never be at ease or comfortable with them again.

'That's if you still like rice pudding?' she asked.

He squeezed her again. 'Mam, anything you make, we like. You know that. And I couldn't think of anything I'd rather have for my tea than a bit of home-cooked liver, and a rice pudding!'

'Right,' she said. 'Now, would you like to take all your stuff upstairs and unpack it, while I get John's bit of snap ready, since he's going out. I'll come up and look at all your things, a bit later, when I've got myself sorted out a bit!'

In some curious, undefinable, way, they all knew a change had taken place between Arthur and Wilfred. Wilfred was the older one, by a year, and had always looked after Arthur but now he seemed to defer to his younger brother.

'You ought to have seen Arthur, Mam, swaggering along at the head of the platoon, then marching out in front of the whole parade . . . '

'What was that for . . . ?' Emily asked. 'Hadn't done nothing wrong, had he? You hadn't let him get into trouble . . . ?'

'Trouble, Mam? Hasn't he told you? Haven't you told our mam, Arthur?'

'I didn't get round to mentioning it,' Arthur said quietly. 'Any road, what does it matter . . . '

'Arthur got the Stick of Honour,' Wilfred said, 'for being the best cadet!'

Emily looked at Arthur. 'You never!' she said. 'Why didn't you tell us?'

'Aye, well, it wasn't anything,' Arthur said. 'I reckon

I was just lucky, that's all, and made all my mistakes when nobody was looking!'

Emily looked from Arthur to Wilfred. Now she could understand what had happened between them and how the balance of seniority between them had altered. Without thinking, she looked up at the beam above the boys' heads, on which the name of every heir to the Godson name had been carved down through the ages. The last name on it was that of her husband, Reuben. The next name, by right, would be Wilfred, her first born. Wilfred saw her look up at the beam and understood why.

'Come on, young John,' he said, 'let's you and me take out the *Hope* and see what kind of a mess you make of it!'

He hefted his bag and took it upstairs. When he came down, he was wearing his old serge trousers, his heavy boots with their soles made from an old car tyre, his thick jumper with his round-necked fisherman's smock in faded thick blue cotton over it. Both Emily and Arthur watched him, mute, praying he would invite Arthur to come with him, but he avoided his brother's eye.

'Back on t' tide, Mam!' he said, as the countless generations had said before him.

'Aye, lad, back on t'tide. I'll have t' kettle on t' hob!'

It had started to rain as he and John walked down Godson Street over the slippery cobblestones, past the stone built houses and down the steps. Featherly's dog rushed to the gate across the pinafore sized garden and barked at them; Wilfred settled the basket under his arm and held out his hand for the dog to nuzzle. 'Daft ha'porth,' he said, 'it's nobbut me!'

'He remembers you,' John said, 'he smells you!'

Wilfred could *smell* Old Quaytown and was at home and familiar with it. Alpha Zelta they'd given him at the OCTU. Alpha for his ability to learn the new things quickly, to know them completely, and Zelta, the lowest category, for his leadership ability. He hadn't told anybody, not even Arthur, about his interview with Captain Nesbitt, his Assessment Prelim, as they called it.

'I don't see that I can send you forward, Godson W.,' Captain Nesbitt had said regretfully. 'I could recommend you if it was solely a matter of knowledge; you have an ability to assimilate knowledge as well as any other cadet on the course. But there seems to be a streak of what I can only call deference in you. You always try to persuade other people, and then defer to them if your arguments fail. Leading a platoon, Godson W, is not a matter of deference; you must learn to be positive, to give orders and then stick by them. You have to learn to be something of a dictator! Not the Chairman of the Committee!'

'I'll try, Captain Nesbitt, I'll try,' Wilfred had promised. He *had* tried, but it had not come easy, with the result that he'd only just scraped through with the Zelta category, the lowest on which he could pass.

Now he had three weeks in which to put it all behind him; three weeks to wipe out the bad memory of his OCTU failures, to get back his confidence in himself.

'We'll fish the south run, off Tockett Top, today,' he said when they'd launched, and were drawing out the *Princess*.

'I thought we might go north, try to find a cold stream . . . ?' John said.

'South!'

John was tending the baskets under the mast, and looked up at Wilfred sitting in the stern with the tiller in his hands. 'Aye aye, skipper!' he said, a smile playing across his face.

They sailed across the ocean in companionable silence. The day was cold, and they'd have a cold evening to look forward to, and no hope of coming back in before morning light. Wilfred's hand was cold, not yet hardened again to the sea temperature. He huddled down more comfortably, putting the tiller under his arm and sticking his hand in the pocket of his smock where he could feel the hank of whipping twine he'd put there the last time he'd been out. The sea had that cold heavy oily feel to it, and the sky was overcast, though the wind was driving inland, keeping Tockett Top clear. They'd need to stay well away from the lee shore of the rocky coast; days like this, and nights, many an incautious boat had foundered, especially before they'd all acquired engines to help them out in an emergency. They were proceeding under sail; they'd used the engine to get them off the Slip, but then had hoisted sail and switched the engine off.

'You've got the forestay too tight, young 'un,' Wilfred said, feeling it in the tiller. 'And your port stay is too slack. The *Hope* wallows like a sea-cow on this tack!'

John smiled again, knowing the handling of a boat is an individual thing; any helmsman who knows what's going on will complain of another's rigging of the boat. 'If you're coming out wi' me, we'll have to change 'em,' he said. 'Personally, I like a bit of helm. It means you can get around quicker!'

'Look who's talking,' Wilfred said. 'I was the one taught thee to sail!'

John didn't feel like arguing though, in some inner way, he knew his brother was spoiling for a quarrel. While he had no objection to a good barney, and was prepared to defend his point of view about anything to anybody, he sensed this wouldn't be a fair fight. He sensed that Wilfred was like a boil, waiting to burst, full of heat and pus.

'We'll re-rig her tomorrow,' he said, 'if you've a mind to.'

The evening had started to draw in as the last line went down on its pig-lead.

John chucked out the sheet anchor, and opened the snap

box his mam had filled; he was seething with resentment but trying not to show it. Everything he'd done had been wrong, and Wilfred had found constant fault with him. When he'd been rash enough to sniff the water and suggest they were over a good place, Wilfred had snapped at him, 'I were picking fishing grounds when you were picking your nose!'

Worst of all, Wilfred had broken the unbreakable rule, of shouting while the crew was shooting the lines. As a result, John had looked up and the next hook, plucked off the side of the basket by the pull of the line already down, had stuck in the ball of his thumb and ripped out a chunk of his flesh as big as a pea. And then, to cap it all, Wilfred had said, 'If you'd been paying attention to what you were doing, that wouldn't have happened!'

It was the unfairness more than anything else that riled him. He had been paying attention, until Wilfred had shouted, 'What's that, what's that out there?' The *that* had been an abandoned jerry-can that doubtless had fallen over the side of some boat or other, plying the coastal trade under Navy escort.

He opened the snap tin in silence and passed Wilfred a thick sandwich and a cup of the piping hot tea from the thermos flask. He didn't wait for his own tea, but took his sandwich up into the bows, squatting before the mast, watching the sun go down. Nothing soothed him more than watching the sunset over the water; somehow, it almost seemed a kindly event, as if the sun were saying – that's it for the day, I'll see you tomorrow. The clouds had turned yellow with the refraction, and the sky behind them, briefly seen through holes, was that insipid blue he associated with the change of season.

'Bloody hell,' he thought. It wasn't going to be much fun fishing with Wilfred if this was the way he was going to carry on, finding fault with everything, moody and sullen. John had so looked forward to this day when his brothers would be home and the three of them could go out together for a bit of a lark. More than anything else, he wanted them to see how he'd learned while they'd been away, and how he'd looked after the *Hope* in their absence, stoning the deck, varnishing the woodwork, scraping the metal. Every bit of rope on board was correctly spliced and fitted, with all the ends lashed and whipped, seized with tallow the way he'd learned. He'd greased all the blocks, replaced any worn pins, even painted the anchor with silver metal paint. The baskets had been cleaned with all the broken ends of withy cut neat so that they couldn't snag the line, and the lines themselves had been laid with the precision of a mill bobbin. Not one word, not one single word of recognition or praise.

'Tea up, young 'un!' Wilfred called but he paid him no heed, not trusting himself to speak. He rode the bow of the *Hope* up and down, its sheet anchor holding it before the wind, the mainsail skegged tight, the foresail down. Now the sun had started to dip behind the clouds of the horizon; the temperature dropped. He could see the *Princess*, working the cold streams of the north run with the *Nelson* and the *Marguerite* and wished he was over there with them. This part of the ocean felt flaccid and empty, devoid of marine life. Hell, Wilfred knew better than he did! It was true what Wilfred had said, that he'd been picking fishing grounds when John had been picking his nose! Not that he remembered ever being a nose-picker; it was just an expression folks used though he'd never thought to hear it from his own brother.

Bugger it! He'd saved his pocket money, and a share of the catch was his by right. He could ask mam, who held the purse-strings in his dad's absence, to advance him thirty pounds out of the catch money, which was less than his entitlement, and take that pram off young Brawnham. Once, the Brawnhams had been a fishing family, but one by one they'd left the sea. Now, their fifteen-footer never came out of the shed and Millie Harrison had said a year back that anybody could have it for twenty-five guineas. He'd need to spend a lot on refurbishing it, possibly as much as five pounds, but then he could have his *own* boat, and not have to go out with *anybody*, not even Wilfred. When his dad came home, the two of them could fish side by side, two boats, and double the catch. That's what he'd do. He'd take the *Sybil* tomorrow, lodge the twenty-five guineas with Mrs Harrison, get it out onto t'Slip, and start work on it. With luck, he'd have it in t' water by the end of the week and then he could tell Wilfred to take a running jump!

He smelled the tea without turning his head round, and felt the touch of Wilfred's hand on his shoulder. 'Here's your tea, young 'un,' Wilfred said.

He took the thermos cup but didn't turn round. He knew that if *he'd* been skippering the boat, the snap time would have been over ten minutes ago. Now they'd have to haul like hell to get the lines up in the last of the light. And tradition had it that the youngest on board the *Hope* always started the haul, and handed over when he pulled up the first fish. It'd be a bloody long haul tonight, since he hadn't smelled a fish all the time they'd been there!

John was right; there wasn't a single fish on the first line, though most of the bait had been eaten. John knew the answer but said nothing, not wanting to risk another reprimand. The place Wilfred had chosen was teeming with May spry, and they'd pick a hook clean without getting caught by it.

Two codling on the second line; they weighed four pounds between the pair of them!

'Nay, I moan as well go on pulling,' John said when Wilfred who, at least, had remembered *that* tradition, offered to pull the rest of the line inboard. John's thumb was hurting like hell where the salt water got in and the line chafed, but he was good for another few fathoms. They did a bit better with the third basket, since spry feed mostly near the surface. Six fat soles, a really good cod that'd touch ten pounds, and a bloody great hake.

'They're selling hake in t' fish-and-chip shop,' John said, breaking the hostile silence that had fallen over the boat. 'Us'll get a price for that! Though us'll have to skin it, first.'

'I'll take care of that,' Wilfred said quickly. Skinning a hake was not a pleasant job since it was abrasive, with hundreds of tiny spines that could rasp your knuckles to the bone if the skin was hard to pull, and your fingers slipped off the pincers with which you gripped it.

'Aye, that's a job for an expert. A novice like me could make a right mess of it,' John said grumpily.

The last three fish on the line were big horse-mackerel. 'How did them buggers get down there?' John wondered. Still, with the spines drawn, they'd make a meal at home, split and fried in Quaker Oats.

He said nothing as he eyed the box of fish – the worst catch he'd had since the last November storm. The evening light had almost gone; he reached beside the engine box and drew out the cone of sail he kept there, getting warm, and drew it over his shoulders like a cape, with his hands poking through the two improvised arm holes. He opened the bait bucket with its mussels and sprats then stood with his back to the mast, drawing the line towards the spare basket, setting it with a flick of his wrist until he came to the first leader and the first hook. Over across the water he could see the lamps lighted on the *Princess* and the other boats.

'Damn fools,' he said out loud. 'No wonder the Navy's chasing us if they're lighting lamps.' It'd be a certain draw for any submarines that happened to be lurking in the ocean, a sure indication, too, that a fishing village was nearby, since the boats never went very far from home these days. Damned lamps kill a man's night vision, anyway. The stars would be out soon, and John would be able to see clear as day once he got his night eyes. In the meanwhile, he could bait the lines by touch if necessary.

'Shall I do a basket?' Wilfred asked, but John shook his head.

'There isn't room for the two of us in t'dark,' he said. It wasn't strictly true but two men with their backs to the mast needed to be in some sort of harmony and rhythm. 'You have t'first kip, if you've a mind.'

Wilfred seemed to have lost all his fight when he'd seen what little fish had been on the lines; he knew the reason as well as John – dammit, he was planning to be a marine biologist, wasn't he, so he ought to know! But smelling the fish beneath the surface of the ocean is very much a matter of habit.

If he'd consulted John, if he'd deferred to his more up-to-date knowledge of how the fish had been running . . . But that was the deference thing again – the Zelta for leadership. And it was a well respected tradition that the skipper of a boat made the decisions . . . He knew he'd been wrong, badly wrong, and that irked him. He knew he'd behaved badly towards his brother, and that irked him even more.

'Eh, young 'un,' he said, 'tha' keeps t' boat looking nice.' He reverted to the accent of his boyhood, before the Grammar School, the University, the OCTU, had all worked on his speech.

'Aye, well, it's in t' family, isn't it?' John said, not to be appeased, not to be so easily mollified, now that his mind was set on the *Sybil* and his independence. Bugger t' *Hope*! he thought. Let it rot in t' bloody shed until they came home, then they could rig it any way they bloody well wanted!

He went to sleep squatting on his heels with his back

jammed against the mast, the canvas cape wrapped round him for warmth. He'd rather sleep at the bottom of a mast than tucked up in bed, nights like this when the air was nippy but not too cold, when the early rains had come and gone, when the night wind was gentle about your ears. He'd pulled the cap forward so that the peak covered his forehead, and had tucked his hands inside the cape and wrapped them round his balls for warmth. He fell easily into a dreamless sleep though he knew Wilfred had come awake as he'd finished baiting the lines and would doubtless have liked a bit of a chat. Well, bugger him! Let him sit there at the tiller, and work out for himself whatever was bothering him! That was the last thought John remembered before the thunderous crash brought him awake.

They'd drifted slowly southwards as he'd known they would and he could see nothing amiss forward.

'There,' he heard Wilfred shouting, 'look north!'

He swung round and couldn't believe his eyes; dawn had not yet come but the surface of the water was bright with that pre-dawn sheen of blue mist. Appearing out of it, about three miles away, was a bulk he instantly recognised as that of a German submarine!

'Bloody hell,' he shouted, 'it's a sub. Start t' motor!'

As he spoke he heard another thunderous crash and now he could see the submarine was firing a gun on its deck, but away from them. As he watched, suddenly there was a gout of bright light, and another explosion that rent the thin pre-dawn mist aside to reveal a collier, one of the many that still plied along this coast with coals from the Durham mines. The shot the submarine had fired must have got the engine room; the collier had blown apart and, as they watched, it split in two and started to slip into the water. They could see the crew leaping off the sides, but there'd be no hope for them in the maelstrom that would follow the boat down, the dreadful suction that would pull anything it caught down into the depths.

There was nothing they could do but watch; the submarine klaxon sounded and the men on its foredeck scampered back into the conning tower amidships; within seconds they heard the clang of the lid, and the sub began to sink in the water.

'Us can't let it get away!' John howled, but Wilfred shrugged his shoulders, knowing there was nothing they could do.

'We'd better get over there,' he said, 'just in case any of 'em has survived.' He started the engine and they motored across the surface of the water, which was now as still as a mill-pond. As they raced forward, they saw the *Princess* coming south, obviously with the same intention.

Both of them circled the place, but beyond floating wood from boxes, a pullover, cork floats and mooring ropes, they found nothing in the oil slick.

The *Princess* pulled alongside; automatically John looked at the catch boxes and his face went grim when he saw how full they were – Alf Corley must have pulled in over fifty stones of best cod, with a couple of boxes of soles, and even a few haddocks to put the jam on it.

'We were straight in the line of fire,' Alf Corley said. He'd eyed their meagre catch but hadn't said anything about it.

'Bugger woke me up!' John said. 'Makes you feel eerie, doesn't it, to think that bugger's lurking down there somewhere.'

'Nay, he'll be off. They can move like hell under water,' Alf said. 'He'll be miles away already.'

'Well, the Navy will be here, soon. They'll have sent a message from t' coastguards.' With the outbreak of war, a coastguard station had been founded on the cliff-edge to the north of Ravenswyke, with direct telephone communication to Whitby. Manned day and night by volunteers, it was their observer who spotted the *Princess* going on to the rocks by High Tor, and had called out the lifeboat.

'You going to shoot your lines again?' John asked casually, but Alf Corley shook his head.

'No,' he said, 'yon bugger's shaken us a bit. I reckon me and the lads will settle for what we've got.'

He opened the engine and the *Princess* drew away. They'd have to wait a couple of hours before it would be high tide again and they could get up on the Slip, but there was always plenty to keep them occupied on a boat.

'What about it, *skipper*? Are we going to shoot the lines again?' John made no comment that could be construed as criticism or approval.

Wilfred shook his head. 'We've got off to a bad start, young 'un,' he said, 'and mostly it's my fault. I came out for the wrong reason. I don't expect you to understand, but it was to spite our Arthur, to show him who was the oldest! And in the process, I made a mess of it for you as well! Like, I'm sorry! Though I realise anybody can say they're sorry, afterwards!'

John was not a lad to hold grudges. Suddenly he realised how foolish, how disloyal to the family his thoughts about buying the *Sybil* had been. The Godsons sailed the *Hope*; that's all there was to it. The oldest Godson at home sailed the *Hope*. Right now, that was his brother, Wilfred.

'You don't have to say you're sorry to me,' he said. 'The *Hope's* yours while you're home. Where we fish, and how, is your choice. And if we come back in wi' empty boxes, who gives a bugger? There's always another tide, that's for sure, and plenty more fish in t' sea!'

Wilfred heard the words of conciliation, but sensed the undercurrent of disappointment, of wounded pride that the *Hope* would return to the Slip with less fish than the others. He looked up at the coming dawn, estimating the time available to them before the tide was high.

'Tell you what, young 'un,' he said, 'grab hold of this tiller. You find the fish for us, and I'll fetch 'em up.'

John scrambled to the stern of the boat, his face creased with delight. 'Bugger it, tha's on!' he said joyfully. He kicked the throttle of the engine to full, opened the mainsail to take advantage of the following pre-dawn wind. The *Hope* surged over the water, heading north. 'Take t' pig off,' he said. 'We'll try them all shallow!'

When the sky begins to lighten, some fish come closer to the surface where they can more easily see the food, shoaling sometimes as little as three fathoms down or so. It took them five minutes to reach a place on the ocean which John, by sense alone, felt would be full of fish.

'I'm going in a big circle,' he said, 'so you'll have plenty of room to chuck it.' He throttled back so that the boat was moving comfortably across the water, with the mainsail tied tightly down amidships. He knew he'd drift when the wind came hard abeam, making their circle more like an oval, but at least if Wilfred stumbled he'd have the boom near at hand to grab. And there'd be no risk of a Chinaman, when the boom swings violently from one side to the other, knocking him overboard.

Wilfred was clumsy at first and nicked his fingers a couple of times as he fumbled the hooks over the basket edge, but soon he took back the rhythm, and the line went overboard easily and smoothly, especially since the drag was out at an angle, rather than straight astern. He knew John was favouring him, making it easier for him, but since his apology he had felt a catharsis; the two of them were as one again, brothers, Godsons of Ravenswyke. He concentrated all his efforts on getting out the three baskets of line as fast and as neat as he could, noting how well John had baited them so that none of the morsels dropped from the hooks to foul the lines in the basket. The lines themselves had been laid with a neat precision he knew he couldn't achieve. When the last line end, with its float, went out and they were steaming away and clear, he came back to the stern, wiping his hands on a bit of rag.

'By gow, John,' he said, 'You laid them lines a fair treat an' all. I reckon as our dad couldn't have lain 'em any better!'

John grinned with happiness. He stood up, holding the tiller with the side of his knee pressing against the push of the waves. The pain in his thumb end was forgotten, and with it his thoughts about buying the *Sybil*, striking out for independence. He looked up into Wilfred's face, flushed after the work of throwing out the line. He knew how his back and shoulders would be aching from the awkward movement in a cramped stance.

'Turn round,' he said, 'and let's have a go at you.'

Wilfred turned round and squatted in front of John, who remembered the countless times their dad had done this to them. He dug his two thumbs into the wool of Wilfred's sweater, where his shoulder blades met, and pushed down hard. Wilfred groaned, but he pushed again, working the tense muscles, pressing into them to relieve the tension and cramp.

'By gow, young'un, that hurts!' Wilfred complained good-humouredly. 'You been weight-lifting or summat?'

'Hold still and don't fight me!'

Slowly he kneaded with the balls of his thumbs while Wilfred squirmed. It was hurting John a sight more than Wilfred, each pressure sending a stab of pain through the wound the hook had made, but he gritted his teeth and carried on. The message had a practical purpose if Wilfred was going to be able to get the lines up quickly again, after John had lifted as far as the first fish. He'd seen too many fishermen who'd taken a sudden cramp, and wrapped the lines and barbed hooks round themselves during the pull!

'Aye, you should be all right now!' he said. 'Your neck's as soft as a babby's.'

Wilfred stood up and flexed his muscles. 'I could have done with that a time or two when we were on the course!' he said.

He sat on the gunwale by the stern seat, and took his cigarette tin out of his pocket. 'You started smoking yet, young 'un?'

John laughed. 'What do you think?' he said.

'And drinking, eh? In the Snug. I hope you're not courting yet? Haven't got any lasses into trouble!'

John coloured. 'Plenty of time for that,' he said. 'After the war is over. You got a girl?'

'Not exactly,' Wilfred said. 'I've got my eye on a couple!'

'Safety in numbers, isn't that what they always say?' John said wisely, as he lit the cigarette Wilfred had given him.

When they'd finished smoking and had eaten their morning snap and drunk the remains of the tea from the thermos, John turned the boat around and headed back towards the fishing ground.

'Do you reckon it's too soon to lift 'em, Wilfred?' he asked, deferring to his older brother.

'You're the skipper, young 'un!'

'Right. Grab hold of t' tiller, and I'll make a start on it.'

'You were right, young 'un!' Wilfred said as he eyed the filled fish boxes when they approached the Slip. 'If we'd have gone where you said last evening, we wouldn't have had a wasted night!'

The *Princess*, the *Rose* and the *Nelson* were already drawn up the Slip when they came in with the *Marguerite* behind them. A crowd had assembled in the cold post-dawn light, and Wilfred could see Arthur among them, and their mother. John was on the tiller, coaxing the engine slowly along so that they moved forward towards the sloping runway up which the boat would be dragged on its cradle. The cradle was already down in the water. Wilfred was standing in the bow, ready to catch the line when Alf Corley threw it.

He turned to the stern, looking past the mast and the boom round which the sail had been lashed tight. 'All right, young 'un?' he shouted but his words were blown away in the fresh wind that had come up with the first light.

John saw his lips move and knew what the words would be; he held up his hand and Wilfred turned round and waved to Alf, who threw the sand-filled purse at the end of the line, tossing it in a neat arc that put in safely in Wilfred's arms. He brought the line rapidly in, hand over hand, and John felt the nose of the boat dragging round. This was the dangerous moment; the boat was slewing under the bow weight of the line, neutralising the positive drag of the motor and the rudder. If a wave came up and under the stern, it could swing them violently to one side or the other, smashing them against the rocks of the Raven, or the wall of the port side of the Slip. He teased the throttle forward a touch to take the weight off the bows since Wilfred, no doubt fatigued after his first night's fishing, was fumbling the line in a bit. Now the steel rope came inboard, with its snap hook on the end, and Wilfred fastened it over the cleat in the bow. Peter Corley was on the winch.

'Back everybody,' he yelled and opened up the throttle. The drum started to turn and the steel-wire rope tightened, pulling the *Hope* bows on to the Slip. John used the rudder to gentle the stern over, until they were inside the rods sticking up from the cradle. Wilfred had run amidships. He picked up the first rod, plucking it out of the cradle, hooking the eye of the rope to which it was attached at the bottom on to the amidships cleat of the *Hope*. He dashed round in front of the mast in time to get the other rod, pick up that rope, and slip it on to the cleat so that the cradle and the boat were effectively tied together. The cradle started to rumble along the slip beneath them, and the *Hope* rode up and out of the water, high and dry on the top of the Slip, where the fishermen could manhandle it to the flat apron of concrete next to the Raven, right in front of the door of the Snug.

The crowd parted as Arthur and Emily Godson came forward; John had jumped over the stern and was standing at the top of the Slip, watching the *Marguerite* come in, a fisherman to the last. Wilfred lifted the boxes to the stern one at a time, and Walter Craggs was stacking them on the flat bed of his lorry, next to the boxes from the other boats.

'By gow, you've done well!' he said, as he took the cod, the two boxes of sole, the whole box of haddock. John had wrapped a haddock and a fat sole in a paper to take home, another sole for Ephraim. As he had wrapped it, Wilfred had asked what it was. 'That's my beer money!' John had said, and Wilfred had laughed, remembering the way he'd paid for the things he wanted with fresh fish!

Emily Godson was standing with her purse clasped in her hand, a woollen shawl drawn round her shoulders on top of her tweed coat. 'We heard the explosion,' she said, 'but we couldn't see nowt!'

Wilfred knew what that must have meant, how every family with a fisherman out that night would have dressed and come down to the Slip, waiting for news.

'Didn't the coastguard come down?' he asked.

'Ephraim telephoned from the Raven. They said as they couldn't make out what it was on account of the mist!'

Wilfred cursed, realising the anxious hours the people had spent before the first boat hove into view when the morning mist disappeared. 'I thought the coastguard would have seen it all . . . '

'Alf Corley said it was a collier. Split in two by a submarine . . . ?'

'Aye, that's right!' The crowd had solidified round them now that the fish had been taken off.

'Did you see it, Wilfred, did you see them fire the gun?' Johnny Eagle asked. At nine, he was more interested in the submarine's guns than colliers.

'Aye, we saw it. We heard the first one, and then saw them fire the second one. I reckon it must have hit the boiler – the collier just kind-of blew in two at the middle. It were gone within a minute. They can't have felt nowt!'

Jenny Bideford crossed herself. 'We all thought it might be the *Hope*, Wilfred,' she said. He looked from her to Georgina Coombs; John saw him, and read his glance perfectly.

'Safety in numbers, eh, Wilfred,' he whispered. 'What's for breakfast, Mam?' he asked. 'I could eat a horse!'

She put her arm round his waist and, for a moment, he was surprised and pleased. She felt warm and smelled of home; it had been a longer and colder night than he realised and his bones were chilled. 'I told our Liz to get some porridge ready for you. It'll warm you up . . . '

'Wi' honey?'

'Honey, indeed? On a Thursday? You'd eat us into t' poorhouse, given a chance!'

Arthur walked up the hill alongside Wilfred. 'You did well!' he said. 'Still haven't lost your touch, I see!'

'Thanks to our John! Where I set us, we'd have been lucky to catch a cold. The young 'un's got our dad's nose, which is more than I can say for myself.'

'Aye, but you've been away with your mind on other things.'

'Happen I have!'

They clattered up the cobbles side by side in silence, but it had none of the warm companionable feeling Wilfred had just experienced out on the boat with John. Arthur knew it and was wise enough to know the reason for it. At this moment the leadership abilities, which had won him a Sword of Honour at the OCTU, failed him entirely.

'I haven't told Mam or any of the others,' he said when, as always, they paused to look out over the ocean at the gap between the houses, with their own house the first round the next bend, 'but I met Walter Brackley coming up the street when we were coming down. He was bringing us a telegram apiece.'

'Dad?' Wilfred asked instantly.

'No. We've got to join the West Kents fast as we can. We're to pick up a warrant from the RTO and get back, today if possible!'

CHAPTER SEVEN

Churchill declared his personal war on Germany by dropping a bomb; it was a symbolic gesture, for no-one had ever dropped a bomb on Germany before. But it revealed to the world quite clearly that Churchill didn't intend to follow the appeasement line of his predecessors; he was going to fight.

Mark Adam Tockett's newly formed battalion was given two weeks in camp near Pickering, barely time to assemble their troops, supplies, and equipment and to get to know each others' names, and then sent south, by troop train, heading for France.

Wilfred and Arthur Godson, by coincidence they thought, but because he had asked for them, were in Capt Tockett's company. Wilfred Godson had A platoon, Arthur had B platoon, and C platoon went to a newly commissioned officer who'd formerly been a clerk in Mark's London office.

Sgt-Major Reuben Godson, MM, was posted to Portsmouth, then sent to Falmouth. He was placed in charge of a group of men, all formerly connected in one way or the other with the sea, and told to train them in the craft of handling small boats. They wore a hotch-potch of clothing over denim battledress with no badges of rank. Sgt Godson was issued with a Colt .45 automatic, and a knife which fitted down the tabs that had been sewn into the seams of the trousers of his battledress. He examined it carefully, then went into Falmouth Town and found a ship's chandler, from whom he bought a Sheffield steel, wooden-handled gutting knife of the same make he'd always used in Ravenswyke.

On 15 May, Holland surrendered to the advancing German forces who used a type of warfare no-one had ever seen before, a *Blitzkrieg* in which the might of the German armoured war machine rolled unstoppably across the landscape, destroying all before it.

On 16 May, Captain Tockett's company landed at Boulogne amidst scenes of great confusion. The battalion's orders were to move towards Arras, already known to be in German hands. They were twenty miles down the road, when they were ordered to change direction, and turn left for Ypres.

The Germans had taken a line from Arras to the south of the coast below Boulogne; now they began to push north. With the Germans to the south, and to the north-east, the British Army was effectively trapped.

The Commanding Officer of Mark Tockett's battalion called his three Company Commanders into the headquarters he had improvised at the road-side.

'I've just received a signal from Brigade HQ,' he said sombrely. 'The battalion will make its way, independently, to Dunkirk, where transport is being assembled to take us back to England.'

'What a cock-up, Sir,' Captain Mills-Webb, in charge of B Company, said.

'Cock-up is the only suitable description,' the Colonel said. 'Obviously, we shall try to get to Dunkirk as a single unit, but if that fails, and I anticipate that if similar orders have gone to all units, then the roads will be choked with people, we may have to split up. It will be the responsibility of each of you to get his entire company, his entire company, you hear me, on to those docks ready for embarkation. We may be beaten this time, gentlemen, we may be running with our tails between our legs, but I want to see this battalion reassembled in its entirety, back in

England, ready to train and train, thirsting for the time we shall return to do battle with the Germans, here on European soil!'

'And there endeth the Lesson,' Mills-Webb whispered to Mark Tockett. 'Rally round the flag, boys, and three cheers for St George! As for me, sod the roads. I'm going to take a compass in my hand, and head along the straight compass bearing for Dunkirk. And any bloody Kraut who gets in my way will get the foresight of my Webley up his nostrils!'

On 24 May 1940 Hitler arrived at the headquarters of Field Marshal von Runstedt and confirmed that, despite Brauschitsch's urgings, the German advance would halt, 'for regrouping'. Herman Goering, Marshal of the Luftwaffe, recently recovered from one of his frequent bouts of drug-taking, launched the available might of his air strike capability against the beaches of the tiny fishing town of Dunkirk, from which the Allies hoped to evacuate, by every possible means, the beaten armies.

Every available small boat, many manned by civilian volunteers, set sail from the south coast ports of England for France, and the troops were cheered by the sight of the massive flotilla that arrived off France's shores on the 27 and 28 May; despite the bombardment of the Luftwaffe planes, many tens of thousand soldiers were embarked, to start their perilous run to safety. Many never made it as the Stukas flew overhead, discharging their cannons at any target they could find.

Sgt-Major Godson arrived on the beach south of Dunkirk, piloting a thirty-foot dory not dissimilar to the *Hope of Ravenswyke*. He dropped his anchor fifty feet beyond the surging wave-front of the beach, and paid the line out slowly as the boat was carried forward by the rush of the tide. Many men didn't wait for him to reach the shore line; they scrambled up to their armpits in water to be dragged over the gunwales and flop across the thwarts of the boat. There were hundreds of men on the beach of this tiny cove and his was one of only three boats taking them off. As he watched, a twenty-foot dory was swamped by the sheer weight of men trying to clamber aboard and he knew he faced a similar fate. He pulled the engine into reverse and ran backwards against the oncoming waves, every one of which threatened to smash over his stern and swamp him. The boat was rocking fore and aft, and he saw one man's face disappear in a bloody mess as the boat's gunwales lifted violently up under his chin.

'Sharkey,' he yelled, 'you'll have to beat 'em off – there's no other way!' Sgt Sharkey looked back at him, his face green with fear. Now the weight of men clasping the port side of the boat had tipped it at an impossible angle. One wave under the starboard side, one lift, and the boat would turn turtle.

'Grab that tiller,' Reuben yelled to Bill Williams, 'and keep us moving slowly backwards. Keep your stern on to the waves, for God's sake, or you'll swamp us.'

He raced forward along the port side of the boat, reaching down to prise fingers loose.

'We'll come back for you,' he said, looking into the water-logged faces appealing to him. He had to fight his way through the press of bodies, calling, 'We'll come back for you, we'll come back for you,' but still the hands clutched, still the weight dragged them down.

He picked men up by handfuls of their clothing and threw them over to the starboard side, hoping to balance the weight, but still the clutching hands dragged them down.

Then, reluctantly, and hating the necessity of it, he started to chop with the hard blade of his hands at the wrists of the men holding the gunwales. Bodies were piled one on top of the other across the decks, and the water line was within six inches of the gunwales. As he chopped, so the men fell back, their wrists numbed by the blow. He threw more men across the boat, and went forward again, chopping hands, sickened by what he was doing but seaman enough to recognise the need for it. As men's hands were caught by the blows, they let go and drifted away from the boat, looks of reproach, of hate, of horror distorting their features.

'I'm sorry,' he said, 'I'm sorry. We'll come back, I promise we will,' but still he needed to chop.

One man reached in with his other hand and grabbed Reuben's ankle, screaming through the foam of sea-water in his mouth. Reuben felt himself pulled sideways and knew he'd go overboard if he didn't do something. He couldn't bring himself to look, but kicked upwards with the foot the man was holding. He felt the sickening crunch as his boot went forward into the man's face, the blow breaking his grip. As he moved forward again, he saw the man floating on his back, his face a bloodied mess, and Reuben wanted to be sick but knew that any weakening, any softening on his part, and the boat and all in her would be lost.

Now the boat was back in the deeps, and had righted itself since only four men were hanging on. One man had another man hanging to his back, clinging like a limpet with his hands round the first man's throat. Reuben saw that the man nearest the boat couldn't breathe and was slowly being choked by the man on his back. He sprang forward to try to catch the man's arms to liberate him, but before he could get through the mêlée of bodies, legs, and arms of those who had successfully climbed aboard, the first man lost his grip, gasping as his burden choked him, and sank beneath the next breaking wave.

There had been no time to think of anything save the retreat from the beach; the yells of the men ashore, the crash of gunfire, the whee and zip of the bullets from the

Stukas which roared overhead, the crump and spray of their bombs exploding in the water among the floating bodies, tinging the wavetops red with blood, had deadened Reuben's mind. He dashed back to the stern and took the tiller of the dory, handing Williams the anchor warp.

'Keep bringing it in,' he shouted. As they drew level with the anchor, he went wide. Williams waited until they overrode the anchor itself, liberating it from its hold in the sandy bottom, and then yanked it inboard.

'Now get amidships and arrange the weight,' Reuben yelled. 'I want all the ballast amidships, and away from the gunwales!'

Williams and Sgt Sharkey worked together, moving the men by force if necessary so that they were all huddled as tight as possible amidships, with only their feet spread out into the gunwales. They were still carrying too much weight, and the boat wallowed like a sea cow, each successive wave dashing in over the stern and running foaming along the decks. Reuben looked over his shoulder, rapidly estimating. He knew he had no alternative but to turn the boat bows on to the waves, but feared what would happen when he was half way through the turn and the next one smacked them on the beam. In one way, the excessive weight would help since the gunwales were low in the water, but that could bring the wave up and over them, to swamp them in the scurrying flood of tons of water. It would all be a matter of timing, but couldn't be delayed.

He waited out two waves, trying for the aftermath of the seventh, which in Northern waters was usually the big one. As he saw the big one coming, he rammed the gear lever from reverse into forward and then, as the swell began and the boat started to lift, he rammed the tiller hard over, hoping to ride his beam up on the crest of the wave, ready to drop down the other side, bows first. His plan worked at first. The boat managed to get beam about for the top of the wave and flipped neatly over it. He saw the chasm of the back of the wave opened before him and held the rudder over, hoping the aftermath of the wavetop would kick under his stern and bring his bows round. But the ballast weight was too much; the boat was too sluggish and didn't come round in time so that it lay wallowing at the bottom of the trough with the crest of the next wave towering twelve feet above them.

'Hang on!' Reuben yelled and grabbed the transom as the wave bore down, its sheer weight of water cascading on the deck of the boat driving it down and under, lifting the gunwales with its next surging force. The boat rose rapidly in the surge but the weight was on the port side and they came up the wave, beam on, canted over to what Reuben feared was an impossible angle. The men who hadn't found anything to cling to saw themselves looking over the canted deck of the boat into a menacing dark green abyss of water; the meagre hold their feet had on the gunwale was broken, and several of them went topsy-turvy off the deck, as if diving into the deep. The wave came down in a thunderous foam and Reuben heard the yells of fear and the cries, but he was holding on to the transom with one hand, the tiller with the other, fighting to keep them apart, to hold the tiller over to slew the boat, if they rode the wave at this impossible angle, back into the flow of the tide.

For one brief moment, he seemed to be standing on the hand holding the tiller. He could see nothing of the sky, only dark green water and white-lashed, foam tops, and spray that sent rainbows into his eyes and then, with a sickening judder, the tub slowly came back up on to the wave, bows on, breasting the next wavetop, sending tracers of spume past their heads, but level, horizontal, and bows on, heading for England.

There was no respite for the men on board who were

stunned by the violence of the waves. As they tried to sit upright, a Stuka came in from the north, hugging the sea, its guns chattering death and fire at them. Reuben saw the dance of the bullets on the water as they approached the boat and knew there was nothing he could do. The bullets swept across the water tops at them, chattering from the guns of the plane above. Fascinated, he saw them approach, then sweep the boat and the water at each side. He heard a man scream amidships, saw a spray of blood, but his attention was caught by a string of bombs that seemed to be floating down from the belly of the plane in a slow arc that would surely coincide with the boat's path. He knew if he veered the boat to right or left he would swamp her in the next wave, but it took all his seaman's resolution not to push the tiller hard aport, but to watch the waves and stay dead square on to them, despite the three bombs. They hit the water a hundred yards in front of him and almost immediately exploded throwing up a curtain of water through which the boat sailed. The bow lifted but here the weight aboard helped rather than hindered, since the boat lifted with no indication of turning turtle. The shock of the explosion in the sea was a giant thump that slammed the wooden hull; it must have been a well-built vessel since the hull shuddered, swelled, and then settled back into its caulked shape, before ploughing on against the waves.

All around them Reuben could see the debris floating in the water, and bodies with their uniforms ballooned with air keeping them afloat. He saw the red tabs of a Staff Officer, the pips of a Captain, the stripes of a Corporal. Another boat was drifting across his bows; it was a dinghy about fifteen feet long with its foresail in tatters, its mainsail holding firm abeam the wind. Normally used by its skipper and a crew of one for week-end amusement, the dinghy had crossed the Channel at the stern of a motorised vessel and was now attempting to make its way back under sail. The skipper was wearing a dark, navy-blue blazer and a yellow sou' wester hat, with bright yellow waterproof trousers. Nine people were huddled in the dinghy, two on the foredeck, and it was bobbing up and down like a cork. The skipper, Reuben noticed, had a pipe clenched between his teeth, the bowl upside down.

As Reuben watched, the wind blew more strongly on the mainsail and the boat slowly tipped over, its passengers sliding into the sea but still hanging on. As the boat had gone slowly over the skipper, no doubt used to the manoeuvre, slid over the windward side of the dinghy, and stood on the keel. The boat slowly righted itself and the skipper jumped inboard again, with his passengers scrambling back over the gunwales. The whole operation had taken less than a minute, while Reuben sailed past, the diesel engine of the dory thumping smoothly and evenly, dragging them over the water at about five knots, straight and even despite the wallow across the beam.

The soldiers on board were all shivering with the cold. 'Get them to huddle closer together,' Reuben instructed Sgt Sharkey, 'else they'll freeze to death.'

The soldiers moved as close as they could, wrapping their arms around each other, snuggling close. Williams pulled a piece of tarpaulin they used as a sheet anchor from the locker and draped it across and in front of the men in the bows; that way they were protected from the worst of the waves' impact.

Planes whined in the sky overhead and the crump of explosions was a constant shock to their ears as they made their way from the beach. An old collier had been hit and was slowly sinking in their path, its superstructure burning fiercely. Reuben set a course to pass it on the windward side but could still smell the stink of burning oil and the even more horrible odour of burning flesh. Now that they were out of the line of the headlands, the boat pitched as well as wallowed and several men, jammed among the bodies on the deck, were sickened by the odour from the collier and vomited; there was nowhere to throw up except over the backs of the men jammed all together. Soon even the hardiest among them had been affected, and the decks were awash with spew. Reuben deliberately turned the boat ten degrees to the next big wave which curled along the starboard side and washed the men and the decks in a deluge of clean water.

There was no need to check the compass as he motored along the lanes of the flotilla heading back across the Channel; one or two lone Stukas machine-gunned and bombed them, but the main effort was concentrated on the beaches behind them.

He looked at the soldiers huddled on his decks. What a monumental disaster it had all been, he thought. If he hadn't volunteered for Special Services and been sent back to Britain for training, he would have been among them, or among the thousands who must have died by the roadside on their way to the beaches. More than anything else he was angered by the uselessness of his life since he'd joined the forces, the way he'd been pushed into the Army despite his volunteering for the Navy, the way he'd been sent to France where the only action he'd seen had been the purely fortuitous capture of a French spy.

He'd wanted to refuse the Military Medal, as he'd first refused the promotion to sergeant-major, since he didn't feel he'd done anything to merit either award. All useless, useless! At least, if he'd been in the Navy he could have been training lads to handle the many types of boat they'd need if they were to land small forces on the mainland of Europe. He'd have been able to pass on his knowledge of wind, weather, tide, and primitive navigation. Better still, he now realised, he should have stayed home in Old Quaytown, gone fishing every day, done his bit by providing food for the beleaguered island. Him and John, working side by side. They'd have dragged home some boxes, and no mistake! Emily always told him about John's catches when she wrote her weekly letter; the lad seemed to know what he was about. It was a pity about the schooling; happen, after the war, John could make it up by going to a night school.

The soldiers sat on the deck like so many landed cod with no energy left for anything except holding on to the canting deck of the boat. Now they were in the middle of the Channel and each successive roll meant a change of weight, a new grip. One of the men in the middle seemed to be slumped down, his body pushing against the others.

'Get in there, Sgt Sharkey,' Reuben said, 'and see if you can do ought for that lad.'

Sharkey, like Reuben, was a peacetime fisherman though he worked the trawlers out of Fleetwood; he edged his way forward into the press of bodies, skilfully balancing himself as he made his progress towards the man amidships. When he arrived, he bent over the man, then looked back at Reuben and drew his hand across his throat in a gesture no one could misunderstand. The soldier was dead. Reuben could hear nothing but the pantomime was self-explanatory. The two soldiers next to the body, doubtless apathetic, were signalling for Sgt Sharkey to throw the corpse overboard. Sharkey didn't want to do that. He pushed his way through the press of bodies to the case of the fish-hold and tied the body to the rope that secured the hatch cover. One or two of the men near the hatch cover protested at having a corpse beside them, but Sgt Sharkey told them to shut up, indicating by gesture that it wasn't too late to throw them overboard.

He came back to the stern and sat on the thwart beside Reuben. 'Would you credit it,' he said, his voice disgusted.

'Aye, there's many a man behaves in strange ways

when he's lost hope!' Reuben said. 'I'd be inclined to agree with 'em myself. There's going to be so many dead and dying when we get there, that another will only be a burden to them.'

'He's got a family somewhere,' Sgt Sharkey said. 'I'd like to think that my family would know I'd been brought home, if anything happened to me.'

Reuben thought back over his life; how many men he'd known go down in the sea, how many men with their pockets weighted with stones so they wouldn't float and suffer a lingering death. Maybe it was only the small boat men, in intimate contact with the water over the gunwales, who felt that way. The men in the trawlers had little actual contact with the sea from the decks of their vessels; they could sleep some nights in the warmth of a cabin under blankets, instead of squatting at the stern or the mast-foot. They rode the trawlers just like a man might ride an omnibus or a charabanc.

'There's nowt wrong with the sea for a grave, Sergeant,' he said. 'Next one dies, we'll heave 'em both overboard, and that's an order. Get that lad's paybook and identity discs, ready for if he has to go. Then, at least, his widow's pension, if he's married, won't be delayed.'

Reuben made three crossings, but Sgt Sharkey didn't come with him again. Reuben didn't want him; he chose a corporal who'd fished off Filey sands, Bodey, a thin spare Yorkshireman with arms like whipcord. Williams came with them; Sgt Sharkey and Williams had almost come to blows when they'd had to throw four men overboard during the first crossing, since the dead bodies were crashing about and interfering with the holds of the living soldiers as they rode the storm that came up when they were entering Dover's outer harbour.

On the third crossing, Williams was hit by a Stuka bullet that took away half his shoulder. Reuben brought him to the stern and lashed his wound as best he could, knitting the edges of the torn flesh together after he'd poked as much engine room waste as he could into it, to try to stem the flow of blood. Bodey had taken one look at it and had shaken his head. On that trip they had twelve casualties from Stuka raids and the deck of the boat was peppered with splinters.

Once again Reuben had been sickened by the sheer weight of numbers trying to get aboard, and the total collapse of any sort of organisation on the beaches. The men should have been held back, clear of the beaches, and a beach marshal should have watched the boats arrive, assessing how many each could take and sending the men down in units. Each time, Reuben had had to clear the gunwales of the boat by force, looking into the men's pleading eyes, saying, next time, next time, we'll be back, I promise! Each time, he'd taken a dangerous weight of men on board; he knew it was only his personal experience with small craft that enabled them to cross the Channel safely with such a press of men on board. The second and the third time he'd even started out overloaded, but had guessed he'd be certain to lose some of the men before he got into the dangerous high waves of the Channel's open sea.

More and more men cursed the total absence of the RAF and the way the German Luftwaffe seemed able to roam the beaches with impunity, firing their cannons and dropping bombs among the massed men. Some of the British anti-aircraft guns were firing from the hinterland behind the beaches, but they were largely ineffectual, and many of them were knocked out by the planes' bombardment.

When Reuben tied up the third time, a harassed major came running along the wharf, a clip-board in his hands.

'You're to stand down,' he said. 'No more trips for the time being!' Though Reuben was exhausted, he reckoned he'd be good for one more round voyage before he'd have to pack in.

'I can manage another one, Major,' he said, but the major shook his head.

'It's suicide over there,' he said. 'We're losing the majority of the boats. No point in sacrificing men uselessly. The Met men say the weather is coming down, and then the planes won't be able to fly, and then we can try again.'

Bodey and Reuben helped Williams off the boat; he was already as near death as it was possible to be without actually dying. A stretcher bearer ran along the wharf-side carrying a stretcher.

'Give us hold,' Reuben said, 'and you go to see to somebody else. Where do we take him?'

'There's a Casualty Reception Centre straight ahead,' the orderly said. 'They're flooded out, so you'll just have to dump him anywhere you can. But don't leave the stretcher – we're short of *them*.'

Reuben and Bodey carried Williams up the wharf through the streams of men coming from the other vessels that had got through. Evening was coming, and the few flares that had been lit on the top of poles cast an eerie, blue-white light over everything, staining the blood that was everywhere black, making already drawn faces into death's head skulls from which black eye sockets barely revealed the life within. Men were carrying men on their backs, in their arms, on their shoulders. Men dragged themselves along without an arm, some without a leg. Several blinded men were being guided by others, their arms outstretched, their new loss of sight terrifying them into crying out, whimpering as they stumbled on obstructions they'd never see again.

When they arrived at the end of the wharf, Reuben saw the CRC away to the right. 'Come on,' he said to Bodey, and they carried the stretcher out of the queue of men shuffling forward, and round the back of a large brown canvas marquee.

They entered the marquee whose walls were lined with beds; Reuben could see the doctors working their way down the sides, going from bed to bed without looking beyond the man they were attending. Reuben saw one young doctor who was coming to the end of the row.

'Quick,' he said to Bodey, 'drop him in here.' They put the stretcher in the space between the last bed but one, and the last. Only two men lay between Williams and the doctor.

'He'll be all right now,' Reuben said, as they made their way out of the front of the tent, past the queue of men waiting to walk, or be carried, in.

Bodey was chuckling as they walked along. 'Nowt stops thee, does it, Sgt-Major,' he said, 'Tha stops at nowt! Now let's see thee find summat to sup and summat to eat – I'm absolutely bloody famished!'

It was raining when the order came to start the flotilla again; the Stukas were grounded by the bad weather the Met men had predicted.

'I reckon the two of us can manage,' Reuben said, looking at Bodey for confirmation.

'Aye, Sgt-Major, I reckon we can! And it'll leave room to bring another God-forsaken bugger back with us.'

While Bodey had eaten and drunk his fill, Reuben had been on the scrounge and had gathered together a number of field ration packs, and blankets, with which he'd loaded the boat. He'd also fixed a number of ropes to the boat which was festooned like a Christmas tree. Now the survivors would have something to hang on to on the journey home. He'd been into the repair yard at the back of the docks and had found a large quantity of cork floats which he'd loaded on to a hand-cart, wheeling them to the boat and tipping them into the fish hold to increase the buoyancy.

Bodey brought him a packet of sandwiches and a couple of bottles of beer from the Salvation Army van; he wolfed them down as Bodey took them out of the harbour, realising for the first time how long it'd been since he'd eaten anything. The journey out was peaceful through the rain; they'd found waterproof suits; Bodey's was several sizes too large, but at least it kept off the driving rain and let his body heat develop.

Though they couldn't see more than a hundred yards ahead of them, Reuben knew where to head by instinct and didn't need to refer to the compass; the engine was working a treat, pulling them along across the wavetops, since the tide was running north-east in the Channel. Bodey was sitting at the stern with Reuben when suddenly he sniffed, and looked over the side.

Reuben smiled at him. 'I've been smelling 'em for the last five minutes,' he said. 'By gow, I'd like to drop a line or two among that lot!'

Both fishermen at heart and by instinct, they knew when they were motoring through the shoals; down there, both knew, the cod were streaming with the tide, and soles, plaice, haddock! And they were riding above them!

'Breaks your heart, doesn't it, Sgt-Major?' Bodey said.

They went back to the cove they'd used before and Reuben's heart sank when he saw the men lining the beach like lice. From somewhere, Bodey had acquired a policeman's truncheon which he produced from beneath his waterproofs and hung on its thong from his wrist.

'Last time, one of 'em nearly pulled me overboard,' he said grimly. 'I'm not having that again!'

They went in stern first, paying the anchor warp over the bows, the engine idling them backwards towards the throng. Within seconds, the water round them was churning with bodies thrashing their way out to the boat. The soldiers had thrown away their rifles and equipment; some had taken off their boots to enable them to swim more easily. Four of them had improvised a raft and were paddling it like mad through the deeper water.

'Tha'll never get to England on that,' Bodey yelled good-humouredly. 'Tha'd better get aboard!' He was standing in the gunwales, reaching down and yanking them over the side, one at a time; Reuben saw that he'd lashed himself to the mast; nobody was going to pull Bodey overboard this time!

'Pack together, pack close together,' Reuben shouted. He pushed the men forward when they tried to squat on the deck immediately in front of the tiller, giving him no room to manoeuvre the boat. 'Sit on the box,' he yelled, 'and open your legs so's next man can sit between!' He saw the deterioration that had taken place in the men's morale. These men were like zombies, with all the fight knocked out of them. Suddenly he saw a familiar flash, a face he thought he knew but couldn't immediately put a name to, and then another, and then another.

'Th'art welcome, little bonnie bird!' one of the men, a burly sergeant, said, and Reuben placed him instantly.

'Tha comes from Staithes . . . '

'An' tha's Reuben Godson, *Hope of Ravenswyke*. I might have known tha'd be around here, somewhere!' The sergeant seemed to come to life. 'Come on then,' he bellowed, reverting to his rank of authority. 'There's room for ten more in there. Hodge up a bit, come on!'

He worked like a demon, packing the men closer together, pushing them with his brawny arms when they were slow to move, sliding them along the deck.

'That's right, lift thy knee so's he can slide under. There, i'n't that more comfortable. Come on then, hodge up!'

Within minutes, it seemed to Reuben, the moment he feared came to being. The boat was full; there were a thousand more bodies thrashing around them in the water, and at least fifty pairs of hands clutching at the gunwales, which were now within six inches of the water. Once again the boat was wallowing and he couldn't, he truly couldn't, take on another body.

The sergeant was standing in the gunwales shouting helplessly, 'That's enough for the *Skylark*, that's enough!' So far, he'd retained his good humour but now, Reuben knew, the mood would rapidly change.

He looked at Bodey who shrugged his shoulders, then hefted his truncheon.

'Get up into t' bows, Sergeant,' he said. 'Start to pull in that anchor rope as we draw forward. Whatever you do, don't let it go, since I have to leave the tiller. It'll take a bloody good pull!'

Best to get the sergeant out of the way, with what they had to do. As soon as the sergeant started pulling, he slammed the gear into neutral and left the tiller. Once again, his dreadful ordeal began as he bent over the gunwales, staring into the wide-open panic-stricken eyes of the soldiers, mostly young lads, and began his litany.

'We can't take any more. We'll come back. I promise! We'll come back, I promise.'

The eyes stared uncomprehending at him, and mouths worked. 'You'll not leave us, you'll not leave us!' The soldiers began to scream in panic at the thought of being so close and yet being refused. Arms came over the gunwhales as they tried desperately to get a hold inboard. Reuben was too experienced by now to offer them an ankle to grab; his hand rose and mercilessly chopped at wrists, breaking the soldiers' grasps.

He heard screams as Bodey wielded the truncheon and the sergeant bellowed from the bows. 'What are you *doing*?'

'Pull that bloody anchor rope, Sergeant,' Reuben yelled above the plaintive noise of the screams, 'else we'll all founder!'

And then, throught a mist of spray and tears of regret, he saw a face that stopped his heart for a beat. 'Arthur,' he yelled. 'Arthur!'

Wilfred was treading water by Arthur's side, and behind them, Mark Adam Tockett. Arthur went to plunge forward through the water, pulling the men aside like waterlogged rats. 'Dad,' he yelled, 'hang on, we're coming!'

Wilfred stayed where he was, still treading water, and grabbed at Arthur's epaulette, holding him back. Reuben saw Wilfred's gesture, watched him shake his head from side to side, knowing his dad had no room for them aboard the boat.

Reuben saw his two sons through a haze of turmoil; what could he do? There were many men between them and the boat, men who had an equal right to consideration. But he knew that this would probably be his last trip; when he'd left, the Major had told him that the Germans were drawing ever nearer the beach and soon the lift must stop.

'If it hadn't been for the tanks and the German infantry stopping,' the Major had said in wonderment, 'they'd have been in Dunkirk already and our casualties and prisoners of war would have reached the hundreds of thousands!' He'd told Reuben that, at best, the British had expected to be able to lift off fifty thousand or so, leaving the rest to their fate. They hadn't anticipated the size of the fleet of small boats that would risk the Channel in late May, the bombs and guns of the Stukas, the vagaries of wind and weather, to bring home as many men as possible. It had been estimated, the Major had told Reuben, that a quarter of a million men had been saved. But this trip, on the 2nd of June, would most probably be the last.

Arthur was still struggling with Wilfred, trying to force his way through the press of men, but Mark Tockett was treading water quietly behind them, waiting to see what would happen.

What *could* happen? What *could* Reuben do? The boat already had its full complement. To take any more would surely risk the lives of everyone aboard by taxing Reuben's skill to the uttermost. The weather was bad, the waves were high, and they'd need all the freeboard they had to get through.

But, to leave his own sons on the shores of France, facing certain imprisonment, or death . . . !

If only they'd been closer . . . !

If only they'd been up to the gunwales and he could have pulled them aboard . . . !

Then Wilfred made the gesture Reuben had seen so many times when they'd been out in the boat together, when one of them had been in the bows controlling a line and the other had been in the stern, with the tiller and the engine. It was an upwards shake of his head, a clear unmistakeable signal they'd used to each other a thousand times.

It meant, 'Go!'

It meant, 'Go now, and fast!'

Whether it meant, chuck the lines, drop the anchor, get under the wave, throw the mooring, it still spelled, 'Go, go now, go fast!'

Reuben kicked the lever into drive, heard Bodey shout, 'Anchor free' and bent down to open the throttle. Tears coursed down the sea-water on his cheeks in an uncontrollable flood. His own two lads . . . Emily's lads . . . Godsons, of Ravenswyke . . . !

When he saw the sand-filled purse of the mooring rope he moved instinctively, picked it up, saw its line coiled in the stern locker, then turned and, in one long swift easy movement, tossed it out over the water, as so many times he'd cast the mooring rope of the *Hope* up on to the slip. The sand-filled purse described its slow arc and he saw the look in Wilfred's eyes. The purse dropped in the water not inches from his face and he wound it round his waist in a flash, tying the rope instinctively into a bowline. He reached out his hands and grabbed Arthur and Mark Tockett to him, twisting so that his back was towards the boat. Reuben pressed the throttle open and the boat surged through the water, tightening the rope, drawing Wilfred, Arthur, and Mark Tockett through the throng of soldiers all shrieking and screaming to be taken. The movement was too fast for any other to grasp the rope. Wilfred was being dragged backwards, his head clear of the waves, clutching the other two in his arms. Reuben knew the drag would be terrible unless the other two could get an independent grip of the rope, and Wilfred wouldn't be able to survive it for long. As soon as they were clear of the crowds, he eased back on the throttle but grabbed at the rope and pulled, keeping it tight so that they wouldn't sink. He abandoned the tiller and, hand over hand, dragged them rapidly towards the stern of the boat.

'That's it, Wilfred,' he shouted, and his son let go of the others, turning and leaping up out of the water to hold the transom. 'Get our Arthur,' he said, 'I think he's drowning with all the water he's swallowed!'

Bodey had come to the stern and he reached down and grabbed Arthur's epaulettes, pulling him slowly over the gunwales. Arthur was gasping and coughing, with water streaming out of his nostrils, but Bodey turned him over on his face and left him, reaching down again for Mark Tockett.

'Come on, Captain,' he said, 'come aboard!'

Mark Tockett flopped on to the deck. 'Thanks,' he said, and then the sea-water came rushing out of his mouth in a thin watery spew.

Reuben pulled Wilfred over the transom. 'Tha'll have to work thy passage,' he said. 'Grab some of them blankets from t' stern locker and start handing 'em around!' He looked at Wilfred's epaulettes on which the cotton star was showing. 'That's if you're not too grand, Sir!'

Wilfred tried to laugh but, like the others, he had a lungful of sea-water and barely had time to turn his head towards the side before the thin stream spewed from him.

Reuben had opened the throttle and the boat moved sluggishly forward again. He knew he'd loaded beyond the safety point but, what the hell. It all depended on him now, didn't it, on his seamanship. And he knew he'd get them across the Channel, come what may!

'Get up, Arthur,' he said, 'and break out them field ration packs. I reckon you must all be starved by now!'

Mark Tockett had seated himself on the edge of the throng of men, tucking himself into them instinctively, knowing how much depended on them keeping an even ballast. He looked up at Reuben, and winked, and Reuben winked back.

'Tha' always wanted to come out on a boat wi t' Godsons,' Reuben said. 'Happen now you've got your wish!'

'Happen I have,' Mark Tockett said, 'and thanks!'

Six men were washed overboard when they reached the sea outside the headland, despite the ropes that Reuben had fixed across the deck. The men, Reuben reckoned, had been too exhausted, too apathetic, even to hold on. All the survivors were in a state of shock; they'd waited on the beach for days under the constant strafing and bombardment of the planes which only the bad weather had halted.

'This is the third boat we tried to get on,' Wilfred said,

'but they were fighting like animals. We were lucky to get all of our lads, all who managed to get as far as the beach, on to some kind of transport.'

'And you three stayed behind, eh?' Reuben asked.

'We couldn't leave Captain Tockett, and he wanted to see the Company safe.'

'Bloody heroes, that's what you are!'

'If we hadn't got on this, we were going to leave the beach and strike out south, to see if we could find a boat of our own somewhere. Anything would have done!'

'Aye, I reckon it would,' Reuben said. Among the many craft he'd seen on the water had been a hastily improvised raft, with a pole for a mast, and a bed-sheet for a sail, with a rowing oar for a rudder. The man on it would have got safely across, he believed, if a Stuka hadn't chosen the raft deliberately as its target and blown it out of the water.

'Wrap yourself up warm, lad,' he said, 'and get some of that food down you! You'll be starved after waiting in t' water all that time. We'll have to get you back home, let your mam get some decent grub into you!'

'Is that what they're doing?' Wilfred asked.

'Aye, they're sending 'em all home. Them as has got a home to go to. Some of the lads we've brought out are French; it'll be a long time before they get home again, by their own firesides!'

CHAPTER EIGHT

Wilfred Godson and Georgina Coombs were married in September of 1940; Arthur Godson was the best man, and Liz and Anne Godson were bridesmaids. Jenny Bideford didn't attend the wedding; she joined the ATS in York when she heard about the engagement. Due to the war-time restrictions there was no village celebration; Emily and Eleanor represented the Godsons; Georgina's uncle, who'd been crippled in the potash mines, leaned on his stick and gave the bride away, and the wedding breakfast, a present from Captain Tockett and his wife, Elsie, was held at the Royal Hotel, Whitby. Elsie Tockett also dug into the extensive stocks of Tockett House, and gave them two pairs of Irish linen sheets and pillowcases, for a double bed.

Though there was to be no official 'do', the entire village turned out to watch the ceremony in the church at which, once again, the Reverend Michael Roberts officiated. There'd been a rush of weddings in 1940; he'd lost all his former nervousness as he performed the rites.

'What *are* you getting married for, our Wilfred?' John Godson had asked the night before the wedding when the men gave him a stag party in the Snug of the Raven.

'Tha'll learn, soon enough,' old Bill Clewson had cackled, 'if tha' hasn't learned already!'

'I wouldn't have thought you'd get married, Wilfred, with all the uncertainty about the future,' Arthur had said. Though neither of them had referred to the boat incident in the weeks they'd been at home, waiting for recall, both knew that Wilfred had recovered his confidence in himself. Okay, he'd told himself, so I wasn't any good at OCTU, so I did get the lowest category for leadership, but when that boat was about to leave without me, I didn't break down as Arthur did and blubber like a babby, trying to take precedence over men who had every bit as much right as I did.

He'd recognised it was a pure coincidence that the boat was skippered by their own dad, but that didn't give them any special privileges over the other waiting, desperate, men. Of course, what their dad had done by throwing Wilfred the line was a special family thing – the point was, they hadn't cheated, they hadn't knocked down other men to get aboard, and Reuben had made sure they both worked their passage. If it hadn't been for Wilfred lending his weight to the tiller when the boat was wallowing in the high seas, knowing just how to help his dad keep the boat on the waves, well, they might not have got through. Wilfred had no conscience about being on the boat, but he couldn't have downed another man, any other man, to get there. In this way, he knew he'd bested Arthur, who might be better when it came to the exercises in an OCTU but who, so far as Wilfred was concerned, had failed the practical test.

Though he never uttered a word of reproach, Captain Tockett had known it, too; needing an officer to help him reform the Company and gather its men together, he'd asked Wilfred to volunteer. When the Company had reassembled in the same camp near Pickering from which they'd started for France, Captain Tockett named Wilfred as his second-in-command, and gave him his second pip before the normal probationary period for 2nd Lieutenants had expired.

As a result of his new duties, Wilfred could only get a week-end pass for his honeymoon; they spent it in the

Royal Hotel where they'd held the wedding breakfast, since there didn't seem any point in going elsewhere.

When Emily returned from the wedding, she sat in the living room, her face flushed with the wine she'd drunk. Eleanor had had to leave on the first train back to York, since she was on duty that night. The two girls, Anne and Liz, were attending the social being held in the old Library, and John was out at sea, fishing. She sat in her own chair, gazing across at Reuben's chair, wondering where he might be. They'd given him seven days leave after Dunkirk and he'd come home to spend the time with her, bringing Bodey with him. Bodey had no living relatives, and they put him up for the seven days. Reuben had formed a real attachment to the little wiry man, and Emily liked him, too, since he was always cheery, easy to please, mucking in with whatever domestic arrangements, not fussy about food, even helping her with the washing up and drying, which Reuben himself rarely did!

She had felt a bit sorry, at first, that Reuben hadn't come home alone, so they could sit by the fireside of an evening and talk to each other, but she could see it was good for Reuben to have found a pal, a man he could talk with, drink with, swap fishing yarns. She had felt a tinge of jealousy when she had discovered how close they were, but she realised as, bit by bit, they told her the story of their voyages across the Channel, the horrible stories of the men trying to scramble on the boat, that men sharing such a terrible experience would necessarily be drawn close to each other, closer than any woman could ever hope to come. And, she told herself, there was always their big, warm, double bed and they could lie there holding each other close after they'd made love, and talk all night if they wanted!

Now they'd both gone, hoping to rejoin the same unit, and she hadn't the faintest idea where they were. The last letter she'd had from Reuben, two weeks ago, had said he was leaving the place where he'd been and going to another place where he wouldn't be able to write for a while. Meanwhile, he was keeping well, and missing her, and his stomach pains had disappeared, and Bodey sent his regards and best wishes and had been made up to sergeant.

She'd been so proud of Reuben with his Military Medal ribbon on his chest; but had been discomfited when he refused to talk about it, as if it were a subject he'd prefer to avoid. He'd told her the bald outlines of how he'd found a spy in a wood and had arrested him; she'd seen the awful wound in his arm which had left a scar that would stay with him for the rest of his life. She'd laughed when he'd shown her the wound stripe he was permitted to sew on his arm, but more than anything, she was proud of the crown he wore below it. Company Sergeant-Major Godson, MM. My, how grand it all was!

That sounded so much better than Warrant Officer, Second Class!

At heart, though, she knew he was still her Reuben.

One thing had puzzled her. While he'd been home, and despite Bodey's suggestion, he hadn't once taken out the *Hope*. He'd helped them bait the lines, mended the lobster pots, waited on the Slip to see them back in, but he hadn't taken the tiller of the *Hope* in his hand. Not once. When she saw him come home, without giving her notice, she'd resigned herself to him taking out the *Hope* on the next tide. But he'd sent the lads out with it, and hadn't once gone himself.

She knew she'd have to stir herself if she was to sort out the bedrooms. Wilfred and his wife would move into the room that recently had been John's. John would go with Arthur into the back bedroom, next to the girls' bedroom. Eleanor had even offered Wilfred and Georgina the use of her place but Wilfred had refused, Emily had been pleased to note. Eleanor was all right in small doses but she'd become that old-maidy and finicky – why, she'd even taken to using a napkin when she ate her meals – she'd said it was since she was clumsy and didn't want to stain her uniform. No, Emily could put up with Eleanor very well at mealtimes, and occasionally for a bit of a chat, but she was always pleased when Eleanor retired to her own quarters, and sat there playing the wireless or the wind-up gramophone to herself.

Of course, Eleanor's place, built specially on the back for her by Reuben, had its own door that gave on to Baker's Walk above – though the Old Bakery hadn't been used as a bakehouse for over two hundred years, being replaced by the one across from the Bridge, the Walk still retained its old name. Emily knew that sometimes Eleanor slipped out of an evening. It hadn't taken Emily long to learn where she went; the new – that's to say, fifty years old – hotel at the top of the Bank, the George Hotel, permitted ladies to sit in the cocktail bar of an evening, all very grand, and many of the posher ladies whose husbands were retired ship's captains, or army officers, had taken to congregating there after supper. They said that all the parish councillors were elected in the cocktail lounge of the George before their names ever appeared on the paper for the vote.

Emily was amused at the thought of the tittle-tattle that must pass up there – she'd never had any desire to go out of an evening to seek the company of other women. She was always happy to attend the village's own events, the weddings and baptisms, the birthday parties and Chapel socials, the dances and bring-and-buy sales in the Parish Rooms of the Chapel, so energetically organised by Captain Walham, retired from the sea. She liked nothing better than sitting beside the dance floor, watching the young folk doing the waltzes and veletas, even the exotic rumbas and dashing tangos that seemed to be creeping in now that most people had the wireless. The biggest part she ever wanted to play in these events was, occasionally, to draw the raffle tickets out of the hat to see who'd won the box of chocolates, the cake or the bottle of whisky.

Several large houses had been built on the top of the Bank on land the Tocketts had once owned. It had become fashionable for wealthy merchants and tradespeople from Leeds to build a place 'by the sea'. The houses all had imposing names, like The Laurels, The Willows, Ocean-View; some were odd combinations like 'Dunromin,' or – and this one had given Emily and the villagers of Old Quaytown a laugh – 'Hersanmine'. Most people didn't get it when the carved oak nameplate went up – 'you have to say the words out loud, *Hers, and, mine*,' Emily had explained to Millie Harrison, who still hadn't understood. The ladies of the Bank Top could always be recognised; they walked about in tweed suits, wore hats and thick lisle stockings and well polished brown brogues shoes. And they all had voices like sea-gulls; cawking away.

Yes, the old place was beginning to see changes, Emily realised. It was being separated, like fresh milk will separate, into different levels. Once the folks of Old Quaytown had been the aristocracy of Ravenswyke, with the people in Newquay Town being regarded as second best. Now the segregation was Bank Top, Grinklegate, Old Quaytown, with Newquay Town still last and despised. Of course, Tockett House still ruled the roost, but not in the same way it had in James Henry Tockett's time; the sight of James Henry Tockett being driven through the village, first in his carriage, then in his motor-car – and he was the first in the district to have one of them – drove fear into the hearts of his tenants of Newquay Town, and brought derision to the lips of the fishing community, who'd traditionally prided themselves on tugging the forelock to no man! Mark Tockett seemed to spend most of his time in London and anyway, was not a man to be feared. He went into the Raven to take a drink, would help launch a boat if he happened to be standing by, and now was one of the officers of the Royal West Kent Regiment, just like her own two boys. Of course, he'd crowned it all by marrying Elsie Milner-as-was, a local girl.

She wished she knew where her Reuben was, that night.

She heard the footsteps on the doorstep shortly before ten, and the whispering voices. Some lad, she imagined, who'd seen the two lasses nicely to the door when the social ended.

The door opened and Liz poked her head in, a curious cheeky look on her face. 'Mam,' she said tentatively.

'What is it, Liz?'

'Mam! A couple of lads have seen us home. Can we give 'em a cup of cocoa?'

'Cocoa? Haven't they got cocoa at home, then?'

'They've come a long way!'

'Aye? Well, fetch 'em into t' light where we can see 'em.' It'd be Grimthorpe's lads from Overbank, the village a couple of miles into the moors. She'd seen them several times coming down into Old Quaytown's social events, since there wasn't much doing in Overbank with only one pub to go to of an evening. 'Who is it, the Grimthorpe lads?'

The man who came in first had shoulders on him like a barn door and seemed to fill the room. He was wearing a suit of a kind she'd never seen before, with pleats in the back of his jacket, and a tie so multicoloured as to dazzle your eyes.

'Who on earth might you be?' she asked.

'Dodds, Ma'am. My friends call me Pete.'

He spoke in a way she'd heard occasionally on the wireless. 'You're American, aren't you?' she asked him.

'Reckon as I am, Ma'am!'

He was followed into the room by another man just as large, though less colourfully dressed. 'Good evening,

Mrs Godson,' the other man said, and his accent was much less thick. 'Hugh Dubiel's my name, Mrs Godson.'

'Dubiel – that's a funny name.'

'Canadian, Mrs Godson. My ancestors were French stock.'

'Ah, I see, that explains it. Well, you'd both better come in and sit yourselves down while I make the cocoa.'

She could see her two girls were as pleased as punch, and as proud as peacocks with their two 'friends'. Emily quickly saw that Liz devoted herself to this Pete, while Anne had linked herself to Hugh Dubiel.

Both men were looking around the room with eyes like chapel hat-pegs, saying, wow, wow, under their breath. Emily went to the stove in the corner of the kitchen, which abutted the living room, and mixed half milk, half water in the pan. She added a little from their precious store of sugar, and the cocoa powder, and started to stir it on the heat.

'What's that!' Pete had asked incredulously, and Liz was showing him the carved beam. His head was almost on a level with it and he reached out his hand and stroked it reverently as if it were a church relic or an aged work of art. 'See this, Hugh,' he said. '1479. Wow!'

Hugh was examining the table that Emily knew had been in the family four hundred years. To her it was a nice old table, polished and maintained throughout the years. The Godson meals had been eaten at it, the Godson children had got out their books to study at it, the Godson men had wrestled with their fish accounts on its darkened surface.

'Holy Cow!' Hugh said. 'Sorry, Mrs Godson, but I've never seen furniture as old as that before.'

'Nowt to be sorry about, lad. It's nobbut an old table!'

She spent the next hour bringing out the things that to

her were ordinary, but which seemed to fill the two lads with astonishment. Lace shawls great-grandmother Godson had made, the meerschaum pipe grandfather Godson had brought back from a voyage to Europe, in its velvet lined cardboard case, the Cross, with its mussel-shell mother-of-pearl inlay that had been carved and dated by Ebenezer Godson in 1595, the scrim that Josiah Godson had carved when he went to sea on whaling expeditions. They exclaimed with delight when she'd made her own cup of tea, and poured the milk into it from a milk-jug in the shape of a cow. It had belonged to her maternal grandmother and Emily had used it all her life without it being damaged in any way.

'Back home,' Pete said in awe, 'a piece like that would be kept in the cupboard behind glass!'

'It's nobbut an old milk jug,' Emily said, 'though we have kept it for best!'

Both Pete and Hugh, it transpired, had grown tired of waiting for America to come into the war. Hugh had been living in New York – the very name brought a glaze to Liz's eyes – and had thought to go back to Canada to enlist. Pete had met a seaman travelling a cargo ship across the Atlantic with vital food supplies, and impetuously had begged a lift for both of them. Now they were in what they called the UK, they were hoping to enlist in the British Army, though Pete wasn't sure what it would do to his American citizenship if he joined 'a foreign Army'.

'Nay, this isn't a *foreign* Army,' Emily said good-humouredly, 'this is t' *British* Army!'

'It's *foreign* to them, Mam,' Anne whispered.

Meanwhile, they'd got a job on a site in the middle of the moors, building a small aerodrome. 'It's all helping you guys fight the war,' Pete said.

Emily had questioned them carefully, not being obvious, gathering the facts one at a time without the boys being aware of what she was doing. Pete was twenty-four and his father had his own hardware store in the Village.

'That's Greenwich Village, Ma'am,' he explained, 'and that's not to be confused with Greenwich, Connecticut!' Pete had been to what he called 'college' to study economics, before the war, and what he regarded as the injustice of American Isolationism had forced him to come overseas to see what he, individually, could do. Hugh had been to the same college; his father was a High School teacher in Montreal, Canada, but Hugh had been restless to see America and New York in particular.

'Canada, Mrs Godson, is a provincial country, full of inhibitions.'

'We had some Canadian soldiers here, once,' Anne said. 'You could have joined the Canadian Army if you'd wanted.'

He shook his head. 'No way I'd want to join up with a bunch of Canadians,' he said firmly.

Emily reproached him. 'You shouldn't speak badly of your own country and your own kind, lad,' she said. 'You've got to accept your own, with all their faults and failings!'

When the two strangers and the two girls were talking together, and Emily went back to the kitchen to wash out the teapot, to stand it ready on the hob for John when he came back in on the tide, she looked back at the group in the sitting room. Aye, the two lasses were growing up. They'd want to meet the lads, to go out with them. She'd felt a bit strange when the Thrummell lad had come calling for Liz, but that hadn't lasted too long. Liz had dismissed him as 'toffee-nosed', her term of condemnation for anyone who put on airs.

'Right, you two,' she said to the girls, 'it's time you were getting up them stairs!'

The two lads took their cue immediately. 'It's time we

were getting back,' they said. 'It's a long walk over the moors!'

'Couple of strong healthy lads like you,' Emily said, 'you'll be in bed inside the hour!'

Pete paused at the door. 'You've made us welcome, Ma'am,' he said. 'I'd like to ask your permission to call again, if we may!'

'You're both welcome,' Emily said, 'so long as you behave yourselves wi' my lasses!'

Liz was scandalised by her mother's forthright speech. 'Mam,' she said reproachfully, but Emily paid her no heed.

'You'll have to take us as you find us,' she said. 'And you mustn't take offence if we speak our minds. We're not much for beating around the bush in Old Quaytown!'

'It's been a pleasure, Mrs Godson,' Hugh Dubiel said, as he drew the door shut behind them.

'Right, the pair of you, washed and straight into bed!' Emily said. 'And I'll not have you talking all night!'

She lay in her own bed, hearing the girls whispering to each other in the next room, but too drowsy to reprimand them, to prick the bubble of their young pleasures.

As the German Fleet became more active in the North Sea, especially the submarines, the Navy insisted, and the fishermen accepted, that they should keep closer inshore, setting an informal two mile limit. The fishermen didn't really mind; now that the trawlers were mostly engaged on mine-sweeping and the spawn was left undisturbed on the bed of the ocean, the quantity of fish they could catch greatly increased. In the mackerel season, when the weather was usually fine, the shoals were so thick it was as much as a fisherman could do to land them. It seemed as if the fish were on a suicide mission, scrambling together in the water off the end of the Beck so thick that on one occasion Alf Corley put his hand in and started to pick them out alive, catching them by the tail and flinging them into the boat. If John hadn't seen him doing it, he'd have believed it was just another fisherman's tale in the Snug of the Raven. Many times he'd netted so many himself that he'd been unable to drag the net in single-handed and had had to let a few of them spill out. He'd worked on the problem and now had a hand-winch aboard the *Hope* amidships, since he still refused to take a crew member with him. Whenever Wilfred came home on leave, he went out with John. Arthur could never be persuaded to accompany them; it seemed as if he'd lost all interest in the *Hope*.

Those early days of the war had been a proving time for John; he'd grown bigger, stronger, and more confident of himself. Wilfred had prospered, too, and there was talk of him being made a Captain. Arthur had got his second pip but that, he said deprecatingly, was a matter of routine. It almost seemed as if, Wilfred thought, Arthur had shot his bolt at OCTU, had put all his endeavours into winning that honour, and had nothing left for the actual business of *being* an officer, of leading his men by inspiring them. Mark Tockett had been promoted to Major though he was still in charge of the Company which hadn't been sent back abroad, either to North Africa or the Far East, the only zones where fighting was taking place apart from sporadic outbursts. They had all been put on alert several times; once there was a rumour they were to go out to Greece to join the Australians and New Zealanders and they were all put on forty-eight-hour stand-by, but that came to nothing.

Meanwhile, they trained and trained, going on schemes in the mountains of Scotland and Wales, always returning to the camp near Pickering which was now a sizeable establishment, with wooden and corrugated-iron huts, mess-halls, and offices. The officers were housed in Benton Hall, about half a mile from the camp, each with his own room, each with a batman to look after him. Dinner was taken in the former dining-room of the Hall; the officer commanding the Battalion, Lieutenant-Colonel Simmonds, MC, was a stickler for mess discipline and insisted on all the officers attending the Dining-In nights. Benton Hall also accommodated a detachment of the Honourable Artillery Company, a unit of the Royal Army Medical Corps, and several officers of the Pioneer Corps, but the latter made their own messing arrangements, and used the Hall only for sleeping.

Arthur would have found it difficult to explain in Old Quaytown, but he could no longer support the differences in his two lives. He couldn't spend the greater part of his time living in an aristocrat's mansion, eating carefully prepared meals in the Mess, being served by the Mess waiters with all the ritual of the peacetime Army, having everything he wore cleaned, brushed, and pressed for him by a batman, being addressed as Sir most of the time, and then return to Old Quaytown where he shared a poky bedroom, ate his meals off the table in the one living-room where all the family would be chattering, take out the fishing boat and work like a dog pulling in lines and nets, squatting beneath the mast for an hour's sleep, performing his natural functions over the side of the boat within full view of his brothers. He kept these feelings to himself as much as possible, especially when he returned to Old Quaytown; he'd asked himself many times – was there something unnatural about him that he should think these things about his own family?

In a sense it was worse having Wilfred with him all the time. If his two lives had been two quite separate packets, he could have picked one up, and left the other down, at will. But Wilfred, who seemed not to have this dreadful dichotomy, was always there as a silent reproach. Wilfred had mastered the art of switching one life on and the other off. In the Mess he behaved impeccably, subduing his

Yorkshire accent, discussing the affairs of the day, the conduct of the war, the vintage of wines, with great composure. It seemed as if, when he crossed the Cut leading to Old Quaytown, everything about him changed; his voice thickened, even his gait took on its seaman's roll, his manner coarsened so that he was completely at home with people like Alf Corley, Bill Fellows, George-Willie Mountjoy, in the Snug. Arthur's trouble, he told himself, was that he couldn't make this quick switch. He needed time to adjust.

'Tha's not happy, is tha', lad?' his mother had said the last time he'd been home on leave. 'There's summat bothering thee!' How could he tell her that one of the things that bothered him was the fear that, in the Mess, he'd slip back into the use of those very words, thee, tha', thy, summat, and then he'd lose, or he'd feel he'd lost, all his well-preserved dignity.

'It's not my way to pry,' his mother had continued. 'Tha' knows I'm here, in t' absence of your dad, if tha' wants to get ought off your chest!'

How could he tell her, without causing her irreparable damage, that her very homeliness, the simplicity of their lives, was like an anchor holding him moored to Old Quaytown and their house in the street that even bore their family name. He'd listened to Wilfred talking in the Snug one evening, when he'd gone in desperation to see if he couldn't absorb himself once again in its homely atmosphere, saying 'Old Quaytown gives us all summat to hang on to in a changing world, it's like a token of everything that's permanent in a transient life.' The rest of them had nodded when Wilfred had said that, even though they might not know the meaning of the word *transient*. If Arthur had used such a word, there'd have been hoots of laughter and – look who's being toffee-nosed now wi' his long words!

It was probably for one reason more than any other,

Arthur realised, that he'd begun to resent his older brother – Wilfred possessed the gift of simplification. He could explain recondite ideas to fishermen, or simple values to high-ranking officers without ever seeming out of place. He could teach his men the multitude of details they needed to know to safeguard themselves when they returned to the fighting, he could be lenient and benevolent, yet, with one whiplash of his tongue, he could reduce a fool or a miscreant to a quivering sorry mess. He could look at what seemed an insolubly complicated problem and say 'Ah, that's simple!' and reduce it to its elements. Or he could devise sophisticated techniques that, since they depended on a chain of simple matters, were invariably successful.

'Tha' moan't be jealous of Wilfred because he's a bit older,' Emily had said, thinking in her simplistic way that she'd solved the problem of what was wrong with Arthur.

'It's not that, Mother!' he said with exasperation.

'Tha' used to call me *Mam*! Our Wilfred still calls me *Mam*!'

Damn our Wilfred, he felt like shouting at her, but he couldn't. He put his arms round her shoulders, kissed her forehead, and said, 'And you'll always be *Mam* to me, too, even if I prefer to call you *Mother*!'

'You mun have it your own way!' she said. 'Just one thing, lad. When you go chasing your rainbows, don't leave your family too far behind. Happen a time might come as you'll need 'em!'

John had come into the house from the yard with his baited baskets and heard what his mam said. She turned on him. 'How many times have I to tell you not to bring t' baskets in here. Your dad allus took them out the yard door!'

'I forgot my cigs,' he said. 'Ephraim let us have five each in t' Snug at dinner-time. Art coming out then,

Arthur,' he said, teasingly. 'Mackerel's jumping into your hand again!'

'No, I've a bit of reading to do,' Arthur said. It was his standard excuse. 'War won't go on for ever, and I don't want to be left behind.'

John grinned at him. 'Tha'll make thyself poorly with all that reading,' he said, 'else tha'll lose thy eyesight! Any road, our Wilfred's coming wi' me, and the pair of you must get sick of the sight of each other, in t' Army together, an' all!'

John picked up his packet of five Woodbines, and went back out of the door into the yard, still carrying the baited baskets, leaving behind an odour of unfresh fish.

'Times I've told him not to bring the baskets in here,' Emily said, flustered by the smell, looking at Arthur's wrinkled nose.

John paused by the gate door, and pulled his cap firmly down on his head. He heard Wilfred come clattering across the yard, with Georgina's lighter steps behind him.

'Come on, then,' he said, 'if we're going. Us'll miss t' tide'. He glanced at Georgina and smiled. 'You'll have to let him get away a bit faster, missis,' he said. She winked at him; since she'd come to live with the Godsons, she and John had formed a firm friendship. She'd slipped on her coat and walked down the cobbled street with them, proud of her husband, Wilfred, happy to be a Godson, happy to be walking down the street with them to the *Hope*. Her father had been a fisherman – Reuben had maintained that Fred Coombs was one of the best. He'd been one of the first to put an engine on board his boat and the engine had killed him. He'd been twirling the starting handle, the engine had backfired, smashed his arm, and thrown him over the side. A storm was blowing at the time and he'd gone straight under, never to be seen again. Georgina's brother, called Fred like his father, had tried his hand at fishing without success; he'd worked in the potash mines alongside his uncle but hadn't made a go of that. Finally, he'd gone off into the West Riding of Yorkshire, and had been picked out of the River Aire one morning. The police established that the last time he'd been seen alive, he was staggering along Bridge Street, dead drunk.

It was a matter of great pride to Georgina that she'd come back into the world of fishermen with the Godson family. Anyway, she knew she loved Wilfred, and would have married him no matter what his job in life might be. And, for him to go off and get himself made an officer! Who would have thought it all the years they'd been seeing each other in and around Old Quaytown, that one day she, and not any of the other girls who fancied him, would have been his wife, the wife of a Godson and an *officer*!

The fishermen were all standing round the top of the Slip when they arrived.

'We thought as how you weren't coming,' Alf said, 'We were just about to launch t' *Princess*!'

'Not coming, a day like this?' John looked up at the sky, at the clear cloudless heavens, the brilliant glow of the blue air above them lifting spray off the wavetops to a phosphorescent sparkle that spoke of a perfect fishing day.

'What you brought t' baskets for?' Alf asked, mystified. 'You'll fill yourself netting today!'

'Happen we might,' John said, wearing his cheeky look.

He'd been to Whitby that morning and had seen the mackerel lying in the fishsheds by the ton. The price would be rock-bottom, hardly worth sending the stuff to market. So, he'd had a bit of an idea . . .

'You're a mug to go lining, a day like this,' Walter Bredford said. He, too, couldn't understand what John was doing, and the lack of knowledge bothered him. A wise fisherman kept one eye on the weather, and the other on the Godsons. 'You can see t' mackerel from t' cliff top,' he said, 'churning away in t' water like sprats!'

'Aye, happen you can,' John said. 'But has any of you taken t' trouble to find out what t' market's like? You won't earn dinner money wi' mackerel today, I can tell you. They were shovelling 'em in Whitby, shovelling 'em!'

'Nay, bloody hell!' Walter Bredford said. 'I wish I'd set a couple of baskets if that's the way it is!'

'Now you see why I've set mine,' John said. 'I'm going lining. I can always come back for mackerel if there's nowt doing!'

He could see Bredford looking up at his house, back at the state of the tide, knowing there wouldn't be much time.

'Run up to t' house,' he said to his wife Millie, 'and fetch us a couple of baskets. Be sharp, like! What us'll do,' he said to his lads, 'is fetch in a net of mackerel and use 'em as bait to go lining.'

It was the only thing they could do, and make the tide.

The *Hope* was first off with Wilfred at the helm, John standing by the bows to keep her off the rocks if the bows swung over in the waves. The *Princess* followed; Alf Corley had given John a wink, happy because he never travelled without a couple of baited baskets, whatever fish may be running. Clewson brought the *Marguerite* off a treat, but then had to wait in the water for Millie Bredford to come running back, three baskets in her arms. Poor woman had been almost up to the top of the bank on which Old Quaytown was built. The Bredford cottage was one of the uppermost since the Bredford family had only lived in Old Quaytown for a hundred and fifty years. By the time the *Nelson* got off, the Godsons had already started to shoot the first line off Tockett Top.

When the lines were down, John Godson came and sat

at the stern with Wilfred, to eat their snap. It was three o'clock in the afternoon, sunny but cold out on the water. A few white clouds had appeared, drifting slowly though low down; when one of them obscured the sun John felt a shiver of cold run through him.

'You know, I think I've caught a bit of summat,' he said. 'The cold's running through my bones.'

Wilfred felt his brother's forehead. 'Aye, you're a bit warm,' he said, 'happen you're running a temperature!'

'I've had a bit of a headache all day today.'

'Silly lad, young 'un. You ought to have said summat, and I'd have fetched t' boat out on my own!'

'Nay, you'll not be here for long. I wouldn't want to miss coming out with you, while you're about!'

Wilfred put his hand on John's shoulder. 'Tha' mun take care of thysen!' he said, relapsing into the broad speech that was like a secret language between them, used only when they were alone together. Now that Wilfred was so much away and in the company of men from other parts of the country, he consciously tried to change his speech to a middle-class accentless sound, modelling himself – though he told no-one this – on the sound of the voice of Frank Phillips, the BBC radio announcer who read the nine o'clock news. It seemed to Wilfred that Frank Phillips' voice was the clearest, and most understandable, he'd ever heard.

'Wilfred,' John said, when they'd eaten their sandwiches. 'Tell us; what's it like being married?'

'What's it like . . . ? How do you mean?'

'You know, like, what's it like!' His already flushed face coloured even more. 'I don't mean, you know, in t' bed! I mean, what's it like having somebody there all the time. Somebody, like, who depends on you . . . '

'Oh, that!' Wilfred said. 'It's champion! You know, young 'un, it's like having another self. There's always things we can't say to anybody, when we're single, in case they'll laugh or take it amiss, but when you're married, it's having somebody to share everything with. Georgina always wants to know everything about what happens when we're out fishing; I have to tell her everything. Where we went, what the weather was like, if the sea was rough, how many lines we shot, who shot 'em, how much we picked up, who brought it in, who took the tiller coming home, if we hoisted sail or relied on the engine, how you behaved yourself . . . !'

'Well, the bloody nerve . . . '

'No, I don't mean that in any wrong way. No, Georgina's interested, you know, really interested . . . And its champion having somebody to tell about it all. Especially when we do well, or when we get a big 'un, or when we hooked that big haddock through the gills, and that time we got the devil fish and we had to cut off the hook and drop it back else it'd have poisoned us if we touched it with our bare hands.' He watched John while he was talking to him, saw how interested he was in Georgina's reactions.

'Sometimes,' John said, 'when you get back in, you want to talk to somebody fit to choke. I find it. I can't talk to Mam because she's seen it all, and every time I start to speak she goes into one of her tales about what happened to Dad in 1935 . . . '

'That's because she misses him so, John. You mustn't begrudge her that!'

'I don't, believe me, I don't. I just sit there and let her talk. But it must be nice to get somebody off on your own, to be able to talk to them. Else, just to sit quiet with 'em, while they're darning your socks . . . '

'It is, an' all! Young 'un, tha'll have to get thyself a lass of thy own!'

John looked away, muttering 'never, never!', but Wilfred turned his face back. 'You've got yourself a lass, haven't you, young 'un?' he said.

John looked miserable. 'What put that idea into your mind?' he said sulkily.

Now Wilfred understood. 'You've got your eye on somebody, but she hasn't said she'll have you yet, is that it?'

'It's nowt to do wi' you!' John said. 'How long are we going to leave them lines down. Until t' fish is all rotten?'

Wilfred smiled to himself, careful not to let it show on his face. Fancy that! The young 'un was smitten with some lass! And she, like lasses all the world over, was probably playing hard to get!

'Don't worry, young 'un,' he said, 'it'll all come right in the end.'

'Plenty more fish in t' sea!' John said, and immediately felt happier now that Wilfred knew of his dilemma.

John got up at twelve the following day, ate his dinner, then went down to the *Hope* and worked on the rigging for an hour, replacing one of the shrouds which seemed to be worn. He was sitting on the boat when the girls who worked in the offices of the Gas Company started to come back after their dinner-hour.

The fourth was Grace Marsh.

She paused by the boat. 'What are you doing?' she asked innocently.

'I'm making a gallows, to hang myself!' he said cheerfully.

'You got problems, then?'

Grace Marsh had been a class below him in the Ravenswyke school, not that he'd ever paid her, or any of the other girls, much attention. She had bright ginger hair and a freckled complexion – that was what had first attracted his eye when she'd started coming past the Slip each day on her way to her first job in the Gas Company's office after she'd left school in June. It had taken him some time to start to talk to her; it wasn't until she'd actually stood by the boat for five minutes, watching him work, that he'd summoned up the courage to say anything. Even now, he blushed to remember what his first words had been. 'What do *you* want, then?'

She should have gone away, offended, but she hadn't. 'I was only *looking*!' she'd said politely.

He'd blundered on. 'It doesn't cost nowt to look!'

'My!' she'd said, 'aren't we grand, now that we're sailing the boat instead of coming at the bottom of the class all the time!' With that, she'd tossed her ginger curls and had left, walking with great dignity around the head of the Slip, and over the paved steps that led to the Gas Works and the Company office.

He'd watched her furtively whenever he was on the Slip during any of the four times a day she came by. Lately, he'd taken to carrying the baskets down, empty, if he knew it was one of Grace's times, and sitting on the stern to bait them. He'd done it yesterday in the rain, which was probably where he'd caught his cold! She hadn't stopped by the boat, nor looked at him once, after that time, until the evening he'd gone to the social in the Parish Rooms, hoping to see her. She'd come in among a crowd that included Phil Mountjoy and Maurice Corley, and the six of them had been laughing at some joke Maurice, who was going on twenty at the time, had obviously been making. Maurice was what was known as a wag and certainly a smooth talker. Apparently, he'd appeared before a Tribunal and had got a deferment of military service. Nobody knew on what grounds, and nobody asked in Old Quaytown, since the gossips all were silent on the matter of military service. If a man didn't care to go then that was his affair. Somehow, four or five of the lads who should have been called up had wangled a deferment and none of them was despised for it.

Ephraim said it came from olden times, when every one

of the inhabitants of Old Quaytown, one way or another, had been involved in smuggling. Those years, Ephraim said, had planted the seed of disrespect into every one of the inhabitants, disrespect for authority that would never completely disappear. It had nothing to do with the law; there was no crime in Old Quaytown and, before new people started to appear across the Cut, no-one had ever bothered to lock his door. The law was the law, but some of the more tiresome requirements of those in authority were frequently ignored. Fewster, for example, administered the meat ration with scant respect for coupons. If he had the meat, he gave it to the people who'd always been his customers irrespective of the number of coupons they might have in some arbitrary book. If the young Mrs Fellows needed a cut of lamb when her relatives came, she got it. When Connie Cathcart lay ill of pneumonia, her daughter got beef to make her a beef tea.

'It's money that rations meat in Old Quaytown,' he'd said. 'Nobody's going to go mad having joints on a Tuesday because nobody can afford it, not even us, who own the damned shop!'

Nobody believed the latter part of his sentence; Fewster was reckoned to have a penny or two socked away under his bed for a rainy day. But the principle was right. For hundreds of years, what the folk of Old Quaytown ate had been rationed anyway, by their purses and their natural sense of thrift.

And to hell with authority!

John wondered how the hell Maurice Corley had got round them on the Tribunal, so that he could appear at this social, cracking his jokes, having all the girls in stitches laughing at him. Suddenly, John had a longing, a feeling of something he'd missed being out on the boat so much. He knew he wouldn't have been at ease in such a social party, couldn't have thought of a single joke to tell that would have made them laugh. He knew plenty of jokes, but they were all the kind the fishermen told in the Snug, most of them mucky and far too rude for mixed company. He could talk endlessly about the waves, the weather, the habits of fish, the way and places fish feed in. But how could that interest anybody like Grace Marsh? Her family came from the top of the Bank. Her father had been a whaler who'd retired to build himself a house overlooking the water. Their house had a whalebone arch at the front gate and featured on the postcards that had been made from photographs. Bank Top, it was called. Her room was the top left-hand one at the front. John had walked past it several times since she'd first stopped by the boat for that bit of a chat, hoping he might fall in with her, naturally, as she made her way back from the top fish-and-chip shop of an evening, or coming out to post a letter, owt like that. But he'd never once clapped eyes on her.

Oddly enough, that social was the first time he'd ever talked to her. She'd seen him sitting in the corner, a half-pint of lemonade shandy in his hand, and had detached herself from the party and come over to sit next to him.

'What a noise they make,' she said, 'going on and on, telling their silly stories. I kept wishing I might be out on that boat of yours, away from them all. I bet you wish you were out right now, where there's peace and quiet?'

'I'd rather be sitting here, next to you!' John had said shyly.

Her eyes gleamed at him. 'That's better,' she'd said. 'I knew you could say something nice, if you tried!'

Well, he had tried, hadn't he? For more than four weeks, since that first evening, he'd been thinking of something nice to say when she wasn't around, and saying it when he got the chance when he saw her. She'd started coming back early from her dinner so that she could spend five minutes talking to him before she had to go back to work; she'd even come down a couple of mornings early, and they'd chatted while the tide rose to full. And always, he'd tried to think of nice things to say.

'I like the colour of your hair.'

'It's awful. I wish it was blond.'

'I like the way you do your hair.'

'Mam wants me to have it permed.'

'That's a nice coat.'

'This old thing? It belonged to my auntie.'

'It must be nice working for t' Gas Company.'

'It's horrible, and smelly.'

The nicest thing he'd been able to think of to say had come three nights ago. 'There's another social on Saturday!'

And then had come the disaster of her reply. 'Don't I know! Maurice and Phil have *both* asked me to go with them. I don't know which one to choose.'

An instant pall of gloom had settled over him. Both Maurice *and* Phil. Bloody hell! What hope did anybody have, competing with them? 'Well, you'll just have to make up your mind, won't you,' he said and turned back to his work ignoring her.

Since then he'd been in the doldrums, culminating in his question to Wilfred. He *was* smitten with Grace, no two ways about it, and he couldn't put her out of his mind, no matter how hard he tried. When they'd come back in at three o'clock in the morning, they'd sat on the rail at the end of the Slip, below the dark, silent Raven, reluctant to climb the hill to go home to bed. The early gulls had begun wheeling about; the air had that saline iodine tang that was like wine to them both.

'I shall miss this, young 'un, when I'm sent overseas,' Wilfred had said, but John had been too immersed in his disappointment to reply.

Then Wilfred had turned to him. 'Young 'un,' he'd said, 'you remember all that time ago when we came in and

Georgina *and* Jenny Bideford were waiting for us, and you said there's safety in numbers. You were right, then. I'll bet you one thing; if Georgina hadn't seen that Jenny Bideford was keen on me, she'd have kept *me* dangling on a bit of string a bit longer, just as your lass is dangling you. You've got to get yourself another lass and make a fuss of her. Then this lass of yours will come round!'

It had sounded marvellous at three o'clock in the morning, with Wilfred, an Army Officer, speaking confidently, but now, ten hours later, John had to find the courage from somewhere to put the plan into action. He'd worked out a plan during his dinner. Grace Marsh was there, standing beside the boat. Now, did he have the courage to put the plan into action?

'You're making a *what* . . . ?' she asked.

'I told you, I'm making a gallows to hang myself!'

'Whatever for . . . ?'

He came and squatted on the side of the boat, his face near to hers, so near he could see the marvellous green colour of her eyes, the freckles, the lovely red hair, and waves of love rolled over him.

'Well,' he said, 'you can keep a secret, can you?'

'Of course. Don't you trust me . . . ?'

'It's because I trust you that I'm asking your advice. I can't give you any names, but two girls have asked me to take them to the social, and I don't want to take either. But they keep asking me. They simply won't let me alone. There's only one way out of it – I've got to hang myself!'

'You're joking,' she said. 'You're pulling my leg!'

'Aye, happen I *was* joking. About hanging myself. But not about these two separate girls. What am I to do?'

'Who are they?' she asked, puzzling her way through the names of the girls of the village. 'Molly Cathcart? Winifred Probert? Nancy, from the bakery?'

'No, I can't tell you their names,' John said, 'that wouldn't be right. What am I to do?'

'Tell them you're going with somebody else . . . ' she said.

'But I can't lie to them! And there's nobody else I'd like to go with. Except you!' There, he'd said it. He hadn't been shy or blundering, and he'd said it.

'Then tell them you're going with me . . . ' she said, 'and there's an end to your problem!'

'Would you? I mean, will you, go to the social with me?'

'Of course I will. I don't want you hanging yourself all over t' dock!'

He smiled. When he got home, the first thing he'd tell Anne and Liz when he saw them would be that he couldn't take them to the social because he was booked. To go with Grace Marsh!

CHAPTER NINE

Reuben Godson and Bodey sat on the stern thwart of the black rubber dinghy looking at the sporadic outbursts of firing on the cliffs of Dieppe above.

What a damned fiasco it had been! What a waste of men's lives, of youth, and eager enthusiasm!

How appalling that men could be launched into such a foolhardy, ill-conceived, badly prepared and executed enterprise!

The raid on Dieppe had been designed to test the ability of the Allied forces to land on the continent of Europe; there had been rumours that it had been pushed through against the objections of sensible people in order to give the Canadians, who had been its principal victims, a role to play in the war. As a political gesture, it had turned into an unprecedented disaster.

Reuben and Bodey, members of the Special Boat Service of Combined Operations, had been given command of one of the twenty-foot rubber dinghies in which many of the Canadian troops had been landed, along with a detachment of British Commandos. Reuben had been too busy ferrying soldiers between the warships moored out in the roads and the beaches, to watch the progress of the inland battle. The first he knew of the disaster was when the troops started to come back down the cliffs to the beach, raked by fire from strategically placed German machine-gun nests.

It was like Dunkirk, all over again, the same young faces in the water pleading to be taken aboard the boat, the same overcrowding, the same 'Trust us, we'll come back for you, we'll come back', the same hands clutching the ropes lashed to the side of the dinghy, the same chopping motion of the hard blade of *his* hand, the same shell-shocked faces looking up at him with an insupportable hatred in their eyes.

The seas off Dieppe were turbulent and the insubstantial dinghy bucketed up and down, almost impossible to manoeuvre. Reuben and Bodey had trained with the rubber dinghies off the west coast of Scotland, learning as best they could how to handle the wayward craft, longing for the firm manoeuvrability of a wooden hull below their feet instead of these damned elongated sausages in which a man could neither stand nor sit. They were powered by a small petrol engine bolted to a board across the stern; Reuben had quickly learned that to do anything with the damned things, you had to ballast the bows to stop them slipping sideways across the wavetops. He hated the craft with a passion, but accepted that they could get closer with them than with a wooden keel-boat which would smash itself on the rocks and run aground on the beaches.

They'd made six trips, taking men in under cover of darkness; only after the sixth did they learn they had been directed by the Embarkation Officer to the wrong beach! They'd refuelled, lain off the beach in the Channel waiting for the radio, bolted amidships, to come alive with orders and instructions for them. And when, finally, the orders had come, they'd been shocked by what they'd learned. 'Go in again and try to get as many off as you can!'

The whole enterprise had been a disaster.

Now they were floating across the water. They had twenty men on board, most of whom were wounded. They'd thrown four dead men back into the sea! The petrol engine had failed; when Bodey, who could strip an outboard motor blindfold and put it together again in a force four gale, had examined it, he'd shaken his head.

'Rings have cracked,' he said. 'It's a goner!'

The coast was a mile away but the tide was setting south-west, carrying them further out into the Channel and the Atlantic Ocean. If they survived that long! The waves were running anywhere between twelve and twenty feet high – unheard of for mid-August when the Channel usually hides its malevolence beneath a calm surface – and already the two sides had punctured with the constant flexing motion and were losing air. The dinghy wallowed in the waves broken-backed and ungainly, skimming the wavetops or dropping into the troughs as the whim took it, and there was nothing that Reuben could do. Even Bodey had been seasick; Reuben knew his stomach wouldn't hold out very long.

He looked at his compass to verify what he already knew from the stars; ahead of them were the open three thousand miles of the Atlantic Ocean, as far as Bermuda and South America. And there was little he could do to stop them floating into it, or running into the shores of Occupied France.

The Canadian soldiers on board were huddled down below the rounded edges with the water lashing over them as every wave came in; there was an incessant yarking and heaving as the impossible motion made men sick and sick again, even when there was nothing left inside them to come out and relieve the pain. They were rolling about insensible to their predicament, most of them with blood being washed out of their open wounds by the immersion in salt water that effectively prevented any clotting.

'We've got to devise some kind of rudder,' Reuben said, 'a mast, and a sail.'

'I'm that bad, Reuben,' Bodey said miserably. 'I've never known owt like it!'

Reuben put his arm round Bodey's shoulder. 'Come on,

Bodey,' he said, 'you've got to hang on. We've got to get control of this boat again, else there's no way we can survive!'

Reuben went forward and prised one of the floorboards up. Since the side-panels had punctured, the thwart had worked loose and washed overboard before they'd had chance to stop it; the floorboard was ineffective at that point. He brought it back to the stern, humping it over the bodies of the men who were lying there. As he came back he noticed that one man was lying on his back with his open mouth full of sea-water; as the boat flexed, the next wave rolled under him, lifted him, and hung him over the side. Reuben grabbed the dead man's ankles and heaved, knowing there was nothing else he could do, hardened to death by those he had witnessed in the past hours.

'What can we do with this, Bodey?' he asked, bending over the stern to examine the engine mount.

'I don't know, Reuben,' Bodey said apathetically, hugging his knees, flexing them to ease the pain in his belly.

'If we could lash it to the engine, sticking down into the water, and then tie something to it for a tiller, we could steer the damn boat!' Reuben said. 'Unlash some of the rope from the sides, where it's threaded through the eyelets! Come on, Bodey, stir yourself. Tha's not giving in now!'

Bodey managed to struggle to his knees and crawl along the side of the boat through the mêlée of wounded men. Another one had died, but he left him where he was, rolling in the bottom of the dinghy, while he pulled the loop of rope through the eyelets. When he'd finished, he'd managed to free about five yards; he brought it back to the stern and offered the end of it to Reuben. The boat swung round and up, round and down, and once again the pain pierced his belly.

'I've got nowt left to chuck up,' he said, his voice creased with anguish.

'Then stop thinking about it,' Reuben said. 'Give us a hand here.'

The engine was swinging from side to side on its mount! Bodey grabbed the throttle handle and held it steady while Reuben tried to lower the floorboard into the water, pushing it down against its buoyancy, pulling it to the side of the engine cover so that he could get a loop round it. It took all the strength of his right arm to hold the wood down, and then he found it was impossible to keep it from lashing from side to side in the movement of the waves, especially since it jutted out at least nine inches behind the engine cover.

It was made of three-quarter-inch plywood; they wouldn't be able to split it along its length to make it the same width as the engine cover.

'Sit on my feet,' Reuben said. He bent over the stern while Bodey held his legs down; that way he could work a loop on to the rope, and draw it down and round the plywood floor board, catching it round the engine cover and yanking it tight. It took ten such loops before he was satisfied that it would hold; when he came back inboard, he tried the throttle handle of the engine, and was able to move the plywood like a rudder, though the short throttle handle took all his strength.

'We need more leverage,' he said.

One of the soldiers had slung his rifle over his shoulder; they lashed that to the throttle handle with the rifle sling, giving them the leverage they needed. Now Reuben could do something about the direction in which the boat was moving.

'We'll try to go north,' he said. 'If the tide is pushing us west-south-west we should be able to move across it with that rudder. Meanwhile, I'll try to work out what we can do about a sail.'

First he had to consider how to erect a mast! He scouted among the men lying in the boat – no other had brought his rifle on board.

'You taking us back to England?' one of them groaned as he lay indifferently across another man's body.

'That's what I'm trying to do,' Reuben said.

There was nothing on board he could use for a mast. He cursed the loss of the oars; he'd instructed two of the soldiers to row when the engine had failed, and had passed the oars to them. One of them had lost his oar overboard before he could put it into the rowlock; the other had been doing his best to help the boat into some sort of stability when the damned plastic rowlock had broken and the oar had slipped out of the rower's hands into the sea. If he'd had the oars he could have rigged a mast, even gaff rigged a sail. If . . . If . . .

He took up another floorboard; it was about two feet wide and seven feet long. The wind was coming from behind them, running them south-east. What they needed was a vane that would drive them north. He freed another length of rope from the eyelets on the port side and lashed a loop of it round the end of the board, with the ends in the eyelets. Now the floorboard was standing upright in the centre of the boat and only the bottom of it needed holding. He got another piece of rope from the forward eyelets, but it was too short. He needed something to jam the bottom of the upright board amidships, some weight, something solid.

He went round the men in the boat. Five of them had died, and he dragged their bodies amidships, jamming them beneath the thwarts so that their bodies held the bottom of his improvised vane at an angle of forty-five degrees to the line of the boat. As soon as he'd jammed them there, he noticed the difference in the motion of the boat. Now it was being impelled by the weight of air trapped by the vane.

'Sail the bloody thing, Bodey,' he yelled triumphantly and saw to his relief that a smile had come to Bodey's face now that they had the craft under some sort of control. It wasn't much, but they were making a knot or so against the run of the tide, moving west by north-west instead of being carried helplessly to the west.

The euphoria of the controlled motion communicated itself to the soldiers nearest the stern, who were affected by Reuben and Bodey's upsurge of spirits.

'Tha's done it again, Reuben,' Bodey was shouting, slapping Reuben on the back. 'Haven't I allus said, nothing beats thee!' The pain in his gut was forgotten now that they were actually *sailing* again. He rested the rifle/tiller against his arm, cheating it over a little, striking a balance between the angle of the improvised rudder and the run of the water, gaining a northerly point before centralising the tiller again. It was an old sailor's trick to gain a degree or two on the wind, sawing the dinghy across the wavetops. One soldier crawled up to the stern; blood running freely from a cut at the base of his scalp mingled with salt water on his face.

'Congratulations, Sgt-Major,' he said. 'And thanks for saving us – we wouldn't have lasted long back there.'

'British, aren't you, Lieutenant?' Reuben asked, seeing the cloth pip on the epaulette of his jumping jacket.

'Canadian, actually. I emigrated there, three years ago, with my family. I joined the Army when war broke out.'

'Are these your men?' Reuben asked quietly.

'No. I was separated from my unit. I think they all died, anyway, poor devils. We were pinned down and they mortared the hell out of us. The explosion of one of the mortar bombs picked me up and dropped me over a cliff edge. I fell fifteen feet or so and that saved my life. Then I crawled down the cliff and out on to the beach.'

'May I know your name, Sir?' Reuben asked.

'Bill Loder. I don't think we need the *sir* bit any more. I think you'd better call me plain Bill!'

'Right, Bill. Let's have a look at that wound on your head.'

The dinghy was still sawing about in the waves, and Reuben had to hold Bill's shoulders with his hands while he examined the wound. It was deep and ragged and it seemed to have broken bone in the bottom of the cut.

'I can't see out of this eye,' Bill said, 'and I have no feeling down my other side.'

'You'd better try to jam yourself somewhere,' Reuben said. 'I used my field dressing on that other lad, and the boat's first aid supply has washed overboard.' He'd noticed the Lieutenant's field dressing pocket was empty, but wasn't certain that it would be a good idea to cover the wound anyway, if bits of broken bone were floating about in it. Better that the sea-water washed them out and kept the wound clean.

Another man had crawled to the stern. 'Peter Lockney,' he said, 'another Englishman turned Canadian. Where have you been living, Lieutenant?'

'Toronto.'

'I was Montreal myself.'

Reuben looked at him and couldn't see an obvious wound. 'You all right?' he asked. 'Are you wounded?'

'Only in my mind, Sgt-Major,' Lockney said. 'I'm just so bloody angry, so pissed off with the entire fucking cock-up! I might have a bit of a shell-shock; three lads in front of me were blown up in a minefield and I woke up a couple of hours later with my head against a stone wall.'

One by one the survivors came towards the back of the boat. Lockney, Bill Loder, Hiram Saul, Klaus Cevicec, Andreas Volotim, Kurt Rosenberg – they formed a small League of Nations with the countries of their origin. None had lived long in Canada – they'd gone there from Europe in the years around 1935 from either economic, political, or religious pressures. They'd never expected to return to Europe. But then, they hadn't anticipated a world war.

They sat in a group around the stern, huddled together for warmth, as the night gradually wore out and the first streaks of a cold grey dawn showed themselves reluctantly behind them. Reuben counted them; when dawn came, eight of the men left in the dinghy were still alive, though most were now suffering from exposure. They stacked the dead bodies around the bottom of the improvised wind-vane, holding it firm against the pressure of the pre-dawn wind which drove aboard like knives, chilling them to the marrow. Only Reuben and Bodey were wearing waterproofs and for a moment Reuben thought of offering his round, but he knew they needed him to survive, and he wouldn't live long if he removed that final protection.

Hiram Saul died around eight o'clock, and Bill Loder soon after.

Occasionally they saw boat activity on the horizon, but Reuben knew they were so low down in the water and waves that they wouldn't be spotted unless somebody came close. Even then, if the look-out weren't sharp, they'd be missed.

He was incredibly thirsty, knowing he'd swallowed some of the sea-water during the previous night, while he'd been fixing the rudder. Again he cursed the lack of preparedness; all the dinghies should have been equipped with survival kit for just such an emergency, but they'd been stripped bare so that they could carry more men more quickly into the shoreline.

Klaus Cevicec died at midday; when Reuben picked him up to place his body with the others amidships, to distribute the ballast and to hold down the vane, he discovered that Cevicec's right leg flopped uselessly; his knee had been broken but he'd said nothing about it.

Endlessly he asked himself what he could do to increase the chances of survival for those who remained; he knew the cold and the wind could strip life from a man within hours, if he didn't have food to give him some internal warmth.

'How are you feeling, Bodey?' he asked after Cevicec had died.

'All right, I guess. Thirsty, hungry, cold, wet, miserable, with a pain the size of a football in my guts. But apart from that, all right!'

'There's a rotten job to be done,' Reuben said. 'Do you feel up to it?'

Bodey looked at him. 'Aye,' he said, 'if you think it needs doing.'

'We need protection from the wind and the water. The dead men won't miss their jackets, but these lads could use 'em. Do you think you could dig among that lot, and strip off their jackets to hand round?'

Bodey looked green. 'I'll be honest with you,' Reuben said. 'I don't think I could bring myself to do it. That's why I'm asking you! I honestly don't think I could do it.'

'Well, I'll be buggered!' Bodey said. 'That's first time I've ever heard thee admit there was summat tha' couldn't do! I'm not so sure as I can do it myself. But, I'll have a go!'

He gave Reuben the rifle/tiller and crawled forward. Reuben saw him pause by the stack of dead men then tentatively hold out his hands and pull the first pair of legs apart so that he could unbutton the camouflage smock where it fastened in the man's crotch between his legs. His body bent and heaved, but his stomach was empty and only a few drops of bile escaped from his throat. He flipped the man over and pulled the smock up the man's back, then over his head. The body flopped obscenely away from him, then came back and landed in his lap.

Reuben heard him groan but he carried on removing the smock. He crawled back to the stern, and handed the smock to Kurt Rosenberg, who pulled it over his head, already more dead than alive but recognising the need for added protection.

They saw a plane fly overhead, but were too apathetic to wave to it.

A destroyer steamed down the Channel, about three miles distant from them, but they had no hope of being seen in the leaden grey day with its lowering skies that seemed ready to drop rain. It was the coldest August day Reuben could remember since the lousy summer of 1933 when Marty Gainer had gone fishing off Ravenswyke without his jacket, had caught pneumonia, and was dead within a week.

'Let's sing a song,' he said to Rosenberg.

'What do you suggest?'

Bodey came back with another smock which he gave to Andreas Volotim.

Reuben could only think of one song.

> Pussy can sit by the fire and sing,
> Pussy can climb a tree
> Or play wi' a silly old ball o' string
> To amuse hersen, not me!
> So I like Bingo my dog because,
> Bingo knows how to behave,
> An' Bingo's the best dog as ever there was,
> An' I am the man in the cave!

'The last line, it do not make sense,' Volotim said in the thick accent of his Russian motherland. 'Vot it means?'

'I don't know,' Reuben admitted. 'I've never known! My mam used to sing that song to us when we were little. I had four brothers and a sister. My dad, Silas was his name, and all my brothers – well, not Lewis, he was later – were killed in t' war. Not this war, last war.'

'What's tha' talking about, Reuben,' Bodey asked, his voice indistinct since, as he discovered by speaking, his tongue had swollen so that it seemed to fill his mouth.

'I don't rightly know!'

Volotim died about nine o'clock. He was sitting near the stern, riding the motion of the boat as he rocked himself from side to side chanting a Russian dirge. Finally, he fell silent as he slowly ran out of voice, then shuddered with all his being as if shaken by a violent palsy. When it ended, he slowly toppled over backwards.

Kurt Rosenberg, Bodey, and Reuben Godson hunched at the stern of the boat in the darkness of their second night and headed slowly west by north-west.

'Sing us that song again, Reuben,' Bodey said, speaking with difficulty. 'Go on, sing it for us!'

'I don't know . . . as I can!' Reuben said.

'Go on. Try . . . !'

The sound rose slowly, and followed them across the wallowing ocean.

> Pussy can sit by the fire, an' sing,
> Pussy can climb a tree
> Or play wi' a silly old ball of string
> To amuse hersen, not me . . .

The aeroplane came down the coastline and they heard the Whitby sirens sounding across the flat moors at the top of the Bank; those who had Anderson shelters in their gardens wondered if they should go into them but in many cases it would have meant taking out the gardening tools, the wheelbarrow, the potted plants. Anderson shelters, provided free on application by the Council, made useful garden sheds, though the Wardens became very upset if they saw them being used for that purpose.

Those who had no Anderson shelter came out into the streets and stared upwards; the plane was trailing a cloud of grey-black smoke behind it, and its engine sounded clattery.

'It's a Dornier,' they said. 'It's a Messerschmidt, it's a Fokker.'

Whatever it was, the aeroplane was clearly in trouble and, over Ravenswyke, the engine started cutting out then starting again with that fearful clatter, as if there were loose nuts and bolts caught in it. Once over Ravenswyke, the plane headed in a circle that took it first out to sea and then back inland again.

John Godson and the other fishermen were gathered on the concrete apron by the Raven, drinks in their hands. It was twelve o'clock; high-tide would be around one o'clock and already they had baited their hooks ready to sail out.

'It's a Dornier,' Old Bill Fellows said, but the other fishermen laughed; it was well-known that Old Bill couldn't see more than a hundred yards any more.

Alf Corley had heard the crash of the guns earlier, and the explosion of the bombs. 'They're giving it to Middlesbrough again,' he'd said.

The daylight raids had increased in number; a flotilla would come in out of the sun during the late morning, running up the coast so low the folks in Ravenswyke could read every marking; the ack-ack guns on the moor would open up but the planes were too low, usually, for the fire to be effective, or for the radar to get an accurate track of them. Sometimes, the planes came down to sea level; they seemed to make a point of High Tor, then dip as they turned, and roar past Ravenswyke below the level of the cliffs, heading north for the industrial towns; when John had been walking along the clifftop with Grace one day he'd seen the planes and was actually looking down on them, able to distinguish the men in the cockpits quite distinctly. It had given him a strange feeling, seeming to personalise the bombing. Those were actual men attacking, not some anonymous black shape seen indistinctly through clouds. Grace had been terrified out of her wits, of course, but John didn't mind. It'd given him an excuse to put his arm round her shoulders when they sat down on the springy turf at the cliff's edge, and she'd clung to him fervently while he'd kissed her.

'Yon bugger's been hit,' Alf Corley said, as the plane circled overhead, trailing its smoke.

As if to confirm what he said, a black dot separated from the plane, and began to drop through the sky; a second or two later, a grey cloud appeared above the dot, whose fall was arrested. The grey cloud opened out and settled in the sky.

'It's a bloody parachute,' John yelled excitedly. 'A bloody parachute.'

Now they were all looking upwards and the men who'd been in the Snug came streaming out when they heard the shouts. John watched the figure coming down then shouted, 'Come on, let's launch t' *Hope*! He's coming down in t' sea!'

Mad with excitement, he rushed to the *Hope* on its cradle and the rest rushed with him.

'Us'll come with you?' Alf said, asking. It would never do to get into another man's boat without an invitation.

'Aye,' John said. 'You Alf, Peter and Maurice . . . '

'I'll get my shotgun,' Ephraim Hardcastle said, determined not to be left out.

'Make it quick.'

They were ready to launch down the Slip when Ephraim came out with the gun and clambered over the side. Walter Bredford and George-Willie Mountjoy had also been invited on board, and they set off in a fever of excitement. The *Hope* and the parachutist both hit the water at the same time; the parachutist was about a half mile off, due east of the Slip and the mouth of the Cut. The fishermen all crowded into the bows as John raced forward on his maximum revs but then Ephraim shouted, 'You'd better all stand back – he might have a gun!'

They went back to the mast, but John was heading in a circle round the man they could see floating in the water, using the dog-paddle to keep himself afloat, the grey canopy of his parachute lying on the water beside him.

Ephraim poised himself on the bows, the shotgun raised to his shoulder dramatically. 'Don't move!' he shouted, and John chuckled. What did Ephraim think the poor half-drowned bugger was going to do – chuck a bomb at him?

He worked the tiller, cut the engine, and slewed the back of the boat over, placing himself neatly by the side of the floating figure. The fishermen had all rushed for the stern and were extending hands overboard to help the flier into the boat; John saw he was a young lad, couldn't be more than Wilfred's age, with a shock of blond hair and a leather flying jacket; as he came over the side they saw the flash of the lambswool lining of his boots; water ran from inside his leather helmet down his face as they put him on the fish-box amidships. Ephraim stood over him, the shotgun barrels only twelve inches from the flier's neck.

'Put that bloody thing down,' Alf Corley said. 'If tha' pulls t' trigger tha'll blow a hole in t' bottom of t' *Hope*.'

It was John's boat and he was skipper. He gave the tiller to Maurice Corley and said, 'Head us back in, eh?' while he went forward through the throng.

'German?' he asked.

'Yes.'

'Ah, you talk English?'

'A little!'

'Well, you bugger, what're we going to do with you, eh? You been dropping bombs on Middlesbrough, eh? Killing people. English people!'

'It's the war!'

Bredford was seething with anger; a cousin had been killed working in a factory in Birmingham. 'Bloody murderer,' he said, then reached in, grabbed the German's hair and clouted the side of his neck.

'Here, hang on,' John said. It didn't seem right to set on the defenceless man. Not so many of them.

'Chuck him overboard, and let him swim back to bloody Germany!' Bredford said. 'Nay, hang on!' John said with a skipper's authority the other fishermen would recognise. 'This is a Godson boat! We'll have nobody beaten about on this boat!' He couldn't have explained why, but it didn't seem right.

'What are we going to do with him, then, John?' Ephraim asked.

John chuckled. 'First thing I'm going to do,' he said, 'is a bit of salvage.' He went to the side and grabbed the line lying in the water. As he pulled it inboard, the parachute came slowly with it, scooping up the water. He drew it slowly inboard, fold by fold.

'That'll save Mam a few coupons,' he said. 'I don't reckon as it'd be any good to Jerry there, where he's going!'

'What's going to happen to him?' Peter Corley asked, but John pointed towards the Slip where he'd already seen the village constable on his bicycle, wearing his tin helmet, and carrying his gasmask case over his shoulder.

'Francis will take care of him,' he said, 'though he'll probably shit hisself before he gets him into t' lock-up!'

The prisoner looked from one to the other, obviously not too sure of their rapid-fire Yorkshire dialect. 'I am prisoner-of-war!' he said two or three times.

'Aye, lad,' John said, 'tha's a prisoner-of-war, and tha' can count thy lucky stars it's us as took thee, for many a lad round here would have pushed your head under t' water and held it there!'

They ran the boat up the Slip but left it on its cradle; as usual when anything happened, the folks of Old Quaytown had gathered round the Slip top; John saw his mam and his sisters before the crowd rushed forward to surround them as one by one they climbed off the boat.

'Here, you are, Mr Francis!' John said. 'He's all yours.'

He'd bundled up the parachute and had wrapped the cords tight round it.

'Is that his parachute?' the constable asked ponderously.

'Well, it's not his nightie, is it . . . ?'

'I shall need that for evidence . . . '

'Evidence of what . . . '

'Of his method of entry into the country . . . '

The fishermen laughed at him, and John slapped the bows of the *Hope*. 'That's his method of entry into the country, Mr Francis,' he said. 'Tha' can take that wi' thee, if tha's a mind!'

'There's no need to be cheeky, young Godson,' Francis said, his dignity hurt.

'Aren't you interested in the German, then?' Mrs Bredford said. 'With you lot chinwagging about evidence, he could have been half-way up t' Bank by now!'

Ephraim was still holding the shotgun pointing at the German's legs.

'Since you're armed,' the constable said, 'you'd better get back into the pub. We can't have you discharging firearms in a public place, can we.' He approached the German. 'Right, lad,' he said, 'do you understand me?'

'Yes.'

'You're a German aeroplane flier, right?'

'Yes. But now I am prisoner-of-war by Geneva Convention.'

The last words were lost in a shriek from the edge of the crowd. When she'd heard they'd caught a German,

Connie Cathcart, who'd been in the Post Office at the top of the Bank at the time, had come running down the hill. When she saw the German standing in the middle of the crowd, she launched herself through it and before anybody could stop her, she'd raked her fingernails down his face, gouging for his eyes, leaving trails of blood down his cheeks.

'You murdering swine!' she shouted. 'You murdering swine!'

The crowd polarised instantly, several of the women beginning to echo Connie Cathcart's shouts, and others battling with them to keep them off the German. Within a flash he was engulfed in a punching, kicking, scratching crowd, his arms held across his face to try to protect himself from their savage vulture-like attacks. Suddenly each of them could name a relative killed either at Dunkirk, or in the bombardments of the English cities, a wounded man, a prisoner-of-war, a cripple. Suddenly, here was a live enemy on whom they could vent all their frustrations, all their problems and difficulties during this time of war.

The men leaped in among the women, pushing, pulling, dragging them off the German, and among them was Bredford, the man who'd wanted to kill him out there on the *Hope*. Kill him, yes, a clean chop and then back into the ocean, but not to see the man torn to pieces alive. Slowly they dragged the women off him, seeing what a sorry mess he now looked with his uniform ripped, chunks torn out of his hair, leaving his bloody scalp exposed, his face raked by fingernails and gleaming crimson with blood.

He was shouting and shrieking, sobbing with fear, when the men made a ring round him, the constable looped one link of the pair of handcuffs over his wrist, and he was led in the centre of the solid phalanx off the Slip and up the hill towards the police house half-way up the Bank.

The coastguard station had rung Whitby; the Army would soon arrive to pick him up and take him into military custody. Meanwhile the women moved away from the Slip in small groups, arguing loudly with each other, the very loudness of their voices an expression of the guilt they now felt for the sudden blood-lust that had overtaken them all.

'When I looked at him,' Emily said to John Godson when he returned from fishing on the next tide to find her sitting up waiting for him, 'I saw your dad, and all the lads left behind at Dunkirk. I saw all the planes running over the beaches the way your dad told us, shooting down at the innocent lads below, and our Wilfred and Arthur standing there in the water with nothing they could do except wait for the next plane to come. Like the rest of the women, I wanted to get in there and tear him to pieces with my own hands. I had that lust to do it, I could hardly keep my hands to myself!'

Tired though he was, he put his arm round her shoulder. 'I think I know how you felt, Mam,' he said. 'But it's all over now!'

'It isn't, you know, John!' she said. 'A lot of us learned something about ourselves this day that we didn't know before. We learned what animals we all are, inside us, and how little it takes to bring it out of us again! A lot of us won't find it easy to live with that, you know!'

'Nay, Mam, you're not an animal!' John said. 'You moan't go thinking like that about yourself!' But he knew, because he'd seen the women's faces as they tore at that German lad, that what his mam said was true.

'Take that parachute thing and burn it,' Emily said. 'I know you meant well, but I couldn't bear to have it in the house!'

John Godson crawled along the side of the hedge. Maurice Corley and Peter were behind him. He stopped and waited until Maurice drew level. 'Your Peter's making a bloody awful noise,' he said, 'can't you keep him a bit more quiet?'

'I'll try,' Maurice said. 'How much further do you reckon it is?'

'Not very far. Carter said it were just over the rise by Mammon's Shoulders, and they're over there!'

He pointed right; the solid bulk of the clump of stones that, since time immemorial, had been called Mammon's Shoulders without anybody knowing why, was outlined against the moonglow, which cast a deep shadow on the side of the row along which they were crawling. It wasn't a cultivated hedge – more a row of clumps of gorse and heather, and once or twice John's knee had landed on a spine. The brow of the small hill rose in front of them, and they crawled steadily forward; sheep skittered to their right with their hoofs clinking on stones so John wasn't really afraid they'd be heard, even with the noise Peter Corley was making, and the snuffling. He wasn't very happy with their enterprise, and would have preferred to stay at home, but Maurice had coerced him into making up the three they'd need.

Slowly they crawled up the rise then hunkered down in the lee of a wall; it was there before them, its shape clearly outlined in the moon.

Carter, the man who drove the post-office van, had told them that the German's plane had come down near Mammon's Shoulders, and hadn't caught fire. Apparently the Army was keeping a guard on it until the Air Force could send an expert to look at it, to see if it contained any new inventions they didn't know about. Carter was always a mine of information; while he'd been out fishing, John had brooded about what he'd said, and then talked with Maurice when they came back in.

'You know, Maurice, I'd love to have a bit of that plane,' he'd said. 'Summat to shove on t' mantelpiece in my room. Somehow, I feel that plane is mine, since it was the *Hope* that fetched the lad in. I'd just love summat out of it, as a keepsake.'

'I wouldn't mind, either,' Maurice said, and then the idea had been born to creep up during the night hours, to try to filch something from it. Anything would do, John told himself, though he'd prefer something with a bit of German writing on it, so that he could say – that's a bit of Germany. Germany seemed so far away, so un-understandable. When he'd taken Grace to the pictures in Whitby and they'd seen the Gaumont British newsreels there'd been many shots of Germans, many aerial photographs of bombing raids on German cities, and the very ordinariness of the people and the land they lived in had seemed bizarre to him. If they were as monstrous as everybody said, why did they look such ordinary people, living in such ordinary places? A little bit of that plane would focus everything for him.

There were two soldiers, wearing greatcoats, and tin helmets, with rifles slung over their shoulders. They were sitting on the wall about twenty yards from the plane with their backs to it, and smoking cigarettes which they made no attempt to hide. They were talking normally to each other and one was describing his work in Sheffield. Apparently, John learned as he listened, the man had been a machinist in a factory. The other man had been a sheep farmer in Wales and their lives, prior to joining the same Army unit, couldn't have been more dissimilar.

'We'll go round the back,' John hissed to Maurice. 'They don't think anybody's about else they wouldn't be sitting there smoking.'

They worked their way slowly until the plane was between them and the two guards, then crawled cautiously forward until they were within touching distance of the plane, which had ploughed a furrow in the ground before smacking its nose into the stone wall. The fabric was dark green, with black and white markings on it and a swastika.

'I'd love to find summat wi' a swastika on it,' John said.

They were all surprised to see how small the plane was; they had thought of it as being enormous but they could see there would barely be enough room for a man to stand up inside the fuselage. The front was all crumpled and one of the two engines had smashed back into the wing, snapping it almost free of the body. The plane had two seats beneath plastic domes, the forward one of which had been slid forward on a rail. John carefully prised himself up the side until he could look over the edge of the cockpit, seeing all the clocks, as he thought they were, on the panel. He had no idea how a plane worked – he'd never taken any interest in them – but he guessed this would be the driving seat, and the seat behind would be for a gunner or the man who dropped the bombs.

'If I hodge up, I can get over the edge,' John said, 'and then I can crawl back inside, see what I can find.'

'Oh, John, do you think you ought! Let's get off home,' Peter Corley said.

'You keep an eye out,' John said. 'I'm going over.'

There were two footrests in the side of the plane, obviously to help the pilot climb up into the cockpit. John used them, keeping his body pressed tight against the plane's skin, to lift himself up. He could see the backs of the sentries, and the glow of their cigarettes, but they were paying the plane no attention as he slithered over the lip of the cockpit, behind the seat.

Once there, he found himself in a tunnel, and immediately his hand touched a pair of headphones. 'Bloody hell,' he said silently. That would make a marvellous souvenir. Maybe Phillips, in the wireless shop, could show him how to connect them into the wireless he had in his room, when he'd had it mended.

He crawled slowly along. The path here was about five feet long, and there were rails along the floor which seemed to have buckled. Ahead of him were two scoops coming down from above, bolted into the floor, each about six inches wide and semi-circular.

He eased his head round one and looked upwards. His face was three inches from the smashed face of a dead man!

He stifled a scream that came to his lips as a great gulp – surely, he told himself quickly, they wouldn't have left a dead man in here . . . It couldn't be a dead man, it was some kind of a ghost or something. With his mind whirling he started to back away and then he heard the sound outside the plane of the squeal of a car's brakes, and a loud crisp voice said:

'Nobody's touched anything?' Another voice said, 'No, Sir, them was the instructions.'

Another voice said, 'We might as well as get started, Wing-Commander.'

Yet another voice said, 'Right, MacBane, it's in your hands,' and suddenly the plane was flooded with light which seeped into the interior through all the cracks in the fuselage.

John tried to turn round, but couldn't.

He tried to go backwards, but his trousers stuck on a shard of metal.

'Help,' he cried weakly, and heard someone outside say:

'Wing-Commander, I think there's a survivor trapped in there. I heard a voice!'

'A voice, a survivor, how's that possible.'

Another voice said, 'They usually fly with a bomb-aimer, Sir.'

The rear canopy was pulled back with a screeching sound and John said, 'Help, help me,' again.

'Damn it, you're right, Flight-Lieutenant,' the first

voice said. The dead body was lifted carefully, the straps unbuckled, and John saw the legs in flying boots disappearing upwards.

There was a silence. 'You heard a *voice*, Sergeant? This man's been dead since the crash!'

'I heard a voice, Wing-Commander! Definitely heard a voice!'

'Help!' John said. 'I'm stuck inside here!'

They all heard that and the beam of a torch played over John's face. 'There's a young fellow inside here, Wing-Commander,' the voice said. 'It must have been him I heard!'

'Then get him out, Sergeant,' the Wing-Commander said testily. 'We haven't got all night and there's a Heinkel we have to look at over by Danby!'

It took ten minutes to extricate John from the fuselage; he looked about for Maurice or Peter Corley but they must have fled at the approach of the Air Force staff car, which was now parked with its headlights illuminating the plane. Beside it was a truck the back of which, John could see, was filled with equipment. The Wing-Commander, if that was the man with all the rings round his epaulettes, was standing in front of John, literally quivering with rage.

'Who the devil are you,' he was saying, 'and how the devil did you get in there!' Without waiting for the reply he turned to the two sentries who were standing rigidly to attention behind him.

'What do you mean by it, eh? You're supposed to be guarding the plane and you let any Tom, Dick, and Harry scramble about inside it . . . ?'

John looked around at the group, mortally afraid. Would they shoot him for a spy, a saboteur, an *enemy*?

'I was only looking to find a bit of summat wi' a swastika on it,' he said in his own defence. 'It was my boat as fetched the pilot out of t' water!'

'What's your name, lad, and where do you come from?'

the Air Force sergeant asked, his voice paternal and kindly.

'John Godson. I come from Ravenswyke.'

'And you were looking for something with a swastika on it, as a souvenir?'

'Aye. I weren't *pinching*! It were just for a souvenir.'

'And you haven't taken anything . . . ? You haven't got anything in your pocket?'

'No, I haven't.'

The Wing-Commander was fuming with impatience. 'Get rid of him, Sergeant. We have too much work here to bother with souvenir hunters. But let me give you this warning, young lad. If I ever catch you near one of my planes again . . . '

John didn't hear him; he was already twenty yards away, legging it for all he was worth across the moor.

The sun came out on the fourth morning, and Reuben got up from the thwart at the stern and walked forward to the bows of the rubber dinghy, which had now collapsed in the centre. Both halves of the boat were wallowing in the water in the shape of a V, and he had to splash through waves to get from one to the other. He knew that the weight of the corpses clustered at the bottom of the vane was dragging the boat down into the water amidships, and the bodies themselves were beginning to bloat and swish backwards and forwards. The vane itself was shaking at its top. He knew it wouldn't stay upright for much longer, but lacked the energy to consider the problem in any practical way. When he was standing in the bows, he tried to urinate, feeling as if his bladder was about to burst but only a few drops, that ate acidly at his flesh, escaped from him. He stood in the bows looking across the ocean; the sun was rising rapidly over the stern, which meant they were heading more west than they should be and he could see no land to the north, where it should have been if their direction had been maintained. During the nights, when he had drifted in a sleep-like coma, the boat must have veered, something that would never have happened if he'd been steering the *Hope*. He could sleep perfectly at the *Hope*'s tiller and any change of direction, any alteration in the wind, would immediately awaken him better than any alarm clock. But this wallowing tub ... He'd conceived a tremendous hate for the craft, as if its own insufficiencies were responsible for his predicament. 'If only I'd had a *boat* under me ... ,' he'd muttered often during the night. But this black, slimy, wallowing thing ...!

He noticed that the air was escaping from the bows which were no longer firm and resilient. He knew he ought to get the air pump from the stern and use it to pump some more pressure into the bows but, lacking faith, he couldn't be bothered. If the damned floppy thing was going to sink then, damn it, let it!

He sloshed his way back through the centre section to the stern and saw that Bodey had let go of the tiller.

'Bodey,' he said, chiding, 'steer the bloody thing, can't you?' At least, he meant to say that, but only a mumble came out of his mouth, his tongue was so swollen. He must have chewed on it during the night; when he wiped his mouth with the back of his hand he saw his wrist was flecked with blood. Bodey's eyes were closed and Reuben leaned forward to shake him. As he grasped Bodey's shoulder, Bodey fell forward into the water which was swishing around the stern.

'Nay, Bodey,' Reuben said, 'sit upright. Tha'll get thy face all wet!'

He reached down and tried to lift Bodey's shoulders up, but realised he lacked the strength. He knelt on the floorboard in the water and heaved Bodey upright.

'Nay, come on, lad,' he said, 'we've been through too much together for thee to quit now!' He thought he was talking to Bodey, but no sound but an indistinct mumble was coming from his mouth. 'Remember, when I fell out of the boat off Falmouth and would have got myself chewed up by t' propeller if tha' hadn't fetched me back in? Remember when we went down to get that mine off t' pilings, and I made a mess of it, and tha' dragged me out through t' water? Damned near drowned me, but at least, the mine didn't get me. Come on, Bodey, set yourself up again. Remember, I told thee, tha' could come out wi' t' *Hope* next time we go back home for leave. Remember, I'm going to buy thee t' *Sybil* after t' war, and tha' can pay me back from t' catch, just like my dad set up a few in his time. We mayn't have much, but tha's welcome to what we have, if tha'll sit up straight.'

Bodey's eyes opened but he could see nothing through them since they were focused on the distant, empty, horizons.

Neither of them had spoken when Rosenberg had died. While he was still alive, he'd taken something out of his pocket and had sat there stroking it. Reuben had wanted to ask him what it was, but was already having difficulty speaking. Rosenberg's mouth was working, and Reuben noticed he'd lost his bottom teeth, which must have been a false set. When he'd finished, after hours of stroking whatever it was he was holding in his hands, he put it back in his pocket and curled up sideways on the rubber side. The next wave had rolled inboard, then rolled out again, taking Rosenberg with it.

'Come on, Bodey!' Reuben said, trying to get through to him. 'It's thee and me again, thee and me!'

But Bodey didn't speak.

Reuben struggled to get Bodey upright, and then tucked Bodey's ice-cold hands into the pockets of his waterproof. He jammed Bodey's feet under the thwart so that he wouldn't be washed overboard, looked up scanning the sky, and used the tiller to point them north. The wind had changed and was coming from the south-east. If only, if only, they hadn't already floated past Land's End. He jammed himself on the back thwart, locking his legs around Bodey's and the tiller under his arm. 'North,' he told himself, 'north.' He said it over and over again in his mind, north, north, as he drifted into a state of blissful memory-filled unconsciousness.

'You're looking a bit poorly, Georgina,' Emily said. They were sitting together by the fireside and Georgina had just lit the lamp so that she could see to do a bit of sewing. John was out with Grace – Emily had only given permission for Pete and Hugh to take Anne and Liz to the dance in Whitby if John and Grace went too, believing there was safety in numbers. Eleanor was down in the south of England somewhere on some kind of special training, which left only Georgina to keep her company. She was pleased to have Wilfred's wife with her; a quiet, unassuming girl; Georgina and Emily were alike in so many ways. Both were home-bodies, preferring to sit by the fireside over any gallivanting. There was a bring-and-buy sale this evening, in aid of the Soldiers, Sailors, and Air Force Families' Fund, and many of the wartime grass-widows would be there, chatting and drinking a port-and-lemon before returning to lonely firesides. Emily was glad to be here with Georgina, her knitting in her hands. 'Yes, you *are* looking poorly!'

She'd guessed, of course, but was waiting for Georgina to speak. It didn't do to push these things – the lass would tell Emily when she wanted her to know. Happen she was waiting until she'd seen Wilfred again, to tell him first.

'It's nothing, Mam,' Georgina said, 'I'm just a bit off colour!'

'Aye, well, you'd better take good care of yourself. I don't want our Wilfred thinking I've let you neglect yourself when he comes home again.'

'You think he'll come home again, Mam?' Georgina asked wistfully, staring into the fire, reaching out for the poker and disturbing the few lumps Emily had put on there when they'd sat down.

'Nay, love, of course he'll come home again. Whatever can you be thinking of . . . ? It's touch and go whether he'll come home first, or Reuben. Reuben will have a shock when he walks in and sees you there, won't he, Wilfred's bride! And stop poking the fire, love. That coal's got to last us, you know!'

'Sorry, Mam,' Georgina said. 'I'm that restless, somehow . . . '

'If you've ought on your mind . . . women's got to stand together, you know, while the men's away . . . !'

Knit one, purl one, knit one, purl one, she kept the even rhythm going, not needing to look down at the needles to know where she was with this roll-neck seaman's sweater she was making for when Reuben came back home and went to sea again. It was an act of faith. Susan Corley had said – 'I don't know how you can go on knitting like that, not knowing what's going to happen!' Alf Corley had got his call-up papers, but it was reckoned to be a mistake, and they'd finally sent for Maurice *and* Peter.

'I was half way through making a pair of socks for our Peter, but I can't bear to look at them now, can't seem to thoil the time!'

'Life goes on, Georgina,' Emily said, 'renewing itself like the rise and fall of the tide. You learn that, as a fisherman's wife. Nothing is ever as important as the next tide. You learn to gauge your life by it, even though the next tide might be the one that takes your man. You learn to get everything settled before the tide, since you never know. You'll never catch a fisherman's wife sending her man out on the ocean hungry, or angry, or with new problems. You'd be surprised how many fishermen say their goodbyes in t' bed! And a woman never refuses, else she'll send him away unhappy, and spend all the time between tides in fretting herself!'

'And when he doesn't come back, Mam, as so many haven't over the years?'

'Aye, well, there's no short answer for that. It'd take a better woman wi' words than me to tell you about that. I've heard some of 'em say they're like a pot that's been emptied and nobody can fill it again. Very few fishermen's widows ever get married again, you know.'

'Damn boats. I wish they'd never been invented!' Georgina said. 'And the damn war the same!'

Emily smiled at her. 'Eh, why don't you make us both a nice cup of cocoa,' she said. 'Wi' real milk, not that powdered!'

'I couldn't face a cup of cocoa, Mam. It makes me feel sick just thinking of it! But I'll make one for you.'

'Sick, love? Whatever for . . . ?'

Georgina realised she'd given herself away. 'You know, don't you?' she asked. 'You've known all along!'

Emily smiled. 'Of course I know, love,' she said. 'Two women can't live in the same house without knowing about each other. Don't forget, you're like a daughter to me! I knew you'd missed, and then I knew when you started being sick. Our Wilfred were home eight weeks ago. I reckon it's then you started . . . '

The Godsons weren't a demonstrative lot, but Emily put out her hand and touched Georgina's arm. 'I'm right glad, love,' she said, 'and I reckon as our Wilfred will be chuffed! I shan't mention a word of it to him. That's a wife's privilege to tell her man she's having a baby!'

'I wanted to wait,' Georgina said, 'until after t' war!'

'Some things won't wait,' Emily said. 'That's human nature. We'll have to get you registered for the orange juice and the cod liver oil. And the extra milk. We shall have to start to take care of you! Have you worked out a date?'

Georgina smiled. 'Happen it might be your birthday present next year,' she said, 'to make you a grandma!'

'Oh Lord, I'd rather have a new pair of stockings,' Emily said. But she was joking. She couldn't have thought of anything she would rather have than a grandchild for her birthday. 'I bet Reuben will be as chuffed as Wilfred.'

It was a miracle, Janislas thought, that he'd seen them. He wouldn't have done, if he hadn't been up in the crows-nest looking for mines. He'd seen the floating black object, with something glittering on it. 'Mine ahead, Sir,' he'd reported down the handset that had been installed on the platform they'd built on the mast of the trawler.

'What type?' the cold, hard, metallic voice came back.

'Not yet identified, Sir,' Janislas reported.

He'd come to England from Poland via Dunkirk, walking across most of Germany and France on his way, discovering that he'd been advancing in front of the German *Blitzkrieg*. A teacher of English at the Warsaw Language Seminary, he had seen no future for himself or any other Pole in Warsaw. He'd hoped to be able to use his English, German, French, and Polish as an interpreter, or working in Intelligence; instead he'd been ordered to report to Looe, and had been attached to a minesweeper squadron, comprising mostly trawlers commandeered for the war, often with their own crews if they were willing to join the Royal Navy. Many of them weren't, preferring to let the trawlers go against the compensation they knew they'd get, and putting to sea in the small fishing boats on which most of them had started. Fishing was still a Reserved Occupation and most of them couldn't abide the Royal Navy types, with their spit-and-polish, their arrogance, and what the fishermen privately derided as their lack of practical seamanship.

Janislas, to his great surprise, enjoyed the life of the Minesweeper Squadron; he liked its simple directness and lack of complications. There are mines out there. Go out, find them, and destroy them!

'Description,' the young Sub-Lieutenant snapped.

'Black, two parts joined together, some kind of vane in the centre.'

'My God – self-propelled, do you think?'

'Could be, Sir.'

The officer on the bridge, twenty-four-year-old David Machin, RNVR, swallowed hard. There'd been talk of the Germans inventing self-propelled mines. After all, why not? Set a mine with some sort of vane on it, launch it from the shores of France. It would terrorize the sea-lanes by night, and create havoc on the shores of England if it got through. One chap from the Admiralty had said that if the Germans succeeded in working out the steering, they could launch millions of the damned things, as easily as throwing stones!

Commander Nicholson had dissented. 'Such a barbaric idea!' he'd snorted. 'And, anyway, it would close the Channel to German boats just as effectively as it would interfere with ours. The entire German Navy would have to go round the top of England . . . '

David Machin yelled for the radio operator. The procedure was unnecessary, since the radio had been installed in a small box aft of the steering wheel-house. 'Sparks,' he yelled, and the quiet voice came back through the panelling.

'Yes, David, you don't have to yell, you know. You're not on a destroyer now!'

'Unidentified mine ahead, may be one of those self-propelled jobs. We're going forward to investigate, but get a message back to Squadron Information Officer, just in case we catch a crab!'

The radio operator, a Chief Petty Officer who was also

second-in-command and had assimilated seamanship of a sort in his own one-hundred-foot steam-yacht before the war, sighed. Young David Machin definitely had the ability to dramatise himself and any situation into which the war put him.

'We're not going to catch a crab, David,' he said. 'We're just going to go a bit closer, then we'll get out our binoculars, and take a look at the damned thing!'

David turned to speak. It was a decided disadvantage having a millionaire who also happened to be chairman of the company you'd worked for in peacetime acting as second-in-command, definitely yet another of the inconveniences of this wretched business of the war!

'I still think that the Squadron Information Officer ought to be informed according to Naval Procedure,' he said stiffly.

'I'll get on to them right away, David. If you'd just waddle this tub a little bit closer, so that we can see the damned thing, I could even pass them a detailed description, couldn't I? Better than calling it two black things joined together with a vane in the middle.'

'Take the helm, Wilson,' David Machin said, 'and keep an eye on me, up in the bows. I'll make the usual hand-signals.'

'Aye aye, Skipper,' Wilson said.

David Machin hung his binoculars around his neck and climbed the steep deck leading to the bows of the converted trawler, past the fifty-millimetre cannon that had been mounted on what had been the hatch-cover of the forward hold.

He braced himself in the bows and raised the glasses to his eyes. He couldn't see a thing in the swelling waves. He glanced up at the crows-nest, and saw the direction of Janislas's pointing finger. He looked again, sweeping his glasses upwards across the waves in that direction. He saw the black object briefly but it was gone before he could focus on it. The boat was heading towards it; he waited a moment without his glasses to his eyes, hoping the better to find it through the expanded field of vision.

'There it is!' Janislas shouted, and gave the compass direction.

David Machin looked, then lifted his glasses.

'It's a damned rubber dinghy,' he said, 'a damned rubber dinghy!' His sense of disappointment was acute; he could have imagined how he'd be cheered in the wardroom if he'd been the first to spot a new type of floating mine, the first to either destroy it, or bring it safely in for examination. But a rubber dinghy! He could see the figure of a man at the stern, but surely he was dead, since he showed no sign of life. He turned his back and went back to the wheel-house. Dammit, if only he'd kept his mouth shut about passing a message to the Squadron I.O. He'd be a laughing stock now they'd reported a suspected new type of mine, and had found a blasted rubber dinghy with dead men on board! He'd half a mind to tell Janislas to pump a few bullets into the damned thing, and sink it. At least, he wouldn't have the embarrassment of towing the blasted thing back into the Looe dockside where they were berthed.

CPO Humberton was chuckling. 'Found a dinghy, have we, David?' he said. 'Not much danger of catching a crab with that, I'd think.'

'I intend to sink it,' he said, 'as a potential danger to shipping, and then we can get about our business of looking for mines.'

'They're all dead on board?'

'Of course they're dead. If not, they'd be standing up cheering, wouldn't they?'

'Maybe we should sound the klaxon . . . ?'

'Whatever for . . . ?'

Without waiting for instructions, Humberton pressed the button and the harsh tones of the klaxon horn sounded from the mast-head. Janislas had been looking through his binoculars, and now he shouted. 'The man in the stern is alive, Lieutenant! He's alive.'

'Now aren't you glad you didn't sink it?' Humberton said.

Without waiting for orders, he left the radio shack and went to the side of the boat; he waved his arm in a jerking motion and Wilson steered five degrees to starboard. He waved again, and they went starboard again, then he motioned with his hand for them to reduce speed. The boat, its engine cut, glided slowly forward against the thrust of the sea.

'Ahoy there,' he shouted. 'We've come to take you aboard.'

Reuben heard the voice, and turned his head. He'd heard the sound of the ship's engines; happen he ought to do something to avoid a collision. How often had he had his nets out at night, or his lines down, when some blundering fool had come down the coast along the fishing lanes, often with no look-out. Samson in the *Fancy Lady 111* had been cut in two by a collier and survived the night clinging to the hatch of the fish-hold. He ought to do something about the noise of that engine, coming closer, but he couldn't be bothered. And then he heard the noise change as the vessel, whatever it was, veered to his port, their starboard, off the collision course. And then he heard the voice . . .

Shouting 'Ahoy there . . . '

Was it just another of the many times he'd dreamed it, during the nights? Voices calling, ahoy there.

He could hardly be bothered to turn his head but he did. A boat. A trawler by the look of it, out of one of the Devon or Cornish ports, and a funny-looking bugger, certainly no fisherman, leaning over the side.

He tried to shout back, but couldn't, though he knew his face had cracked in a smile because the sores on the corners of his mouth hurt. He ought to do something, but he couldn't get his mind to work. Yes, he ought to lift his hand, to try to wave at them, the least he could do, to say hello. But he couldn't lift his hand. His arm had stiffened and locked around the tiller. All he could do was nod his head, but then lifting it up again took time and more energy than he felt he possessed. He heard another, younger voice firing questions.

'Who is it? What's his name? Where has he come from? What are all those bodies doing in the water?' and then he heard the other voice, the one that had said, 'Ahoy there', saying 'Why don't you shut up, David, and take over the helm!'

What happened afterwards was lost in delirium of hands, the rub of rough blankets on his skin, and smooth cottons, the hard questioning voices of men and the softer tones of women.

When finally he awoke, he came back to life slowly as a feather will bounce repeatedly on the ground and eventually lie, fragile. He heard voices asking questions, other voices furnishing answers, and both sets of voices were familiar and he didn't know for how long he had known them and when he had first heard them, but on one of his descents into a sort of reality that was ill-defined and out of focus, he recognised the face of his wife, Emily, and his son, John.

'It's me, Reuben, and our John, come to see how you are,' she said.

He drifted away again before he could try to fashion a reply, but before he went into his vague, dream-like trance, he felt her hand on his.

When he came back again, Emily was there again, but not his son, John.

'Where's our lad,' he asked slowly, 'out on t' tide?'

They were the first words he'd spoken since the death of Bodey.

'I told him to get back home,' she said. 'I can manage on my own now I know tha's all right. How are you feeling, Reuben?'

'I don't rightly know,' he said.

'That's to be expected. You've been out of it for three weeks now.'

'Like a long sleep . . . '

'Aye, a long sleep . . . '

'How long have you been here?'

'Going on a week now. I've been coming in every day and sitting with you.'

'You oughtn't to have bothered.'

'It's all right. I brought my knitting! I've nearly finished a new woolly for you . . . '

He smiled at her. 'So the time hasn't been wasted?'

'No, you couldn't hardly say it's been wasted! It's been a change for me to see thee, Reuben Godson, ligging a' bed! I mind the times you've sat by me, when I've been having t' little ones.'

'Where's Bodey?' he asked quietly.

'Aye, well, Reuben, Bodey's dead I'm afraid. And so was all the others in t' boat, so they tell me. You were the only one left. I told them, there's nowt on t' sea will take you, until you've a mind to go!'

'I thought I was a goner, Emily!' he said. 'I'd given up!'

'That I should live to see the day . . . ' she said. 'There's nowt beats thee!'

'That damned black rubber thing beat me. It wasn't like t' *Hope*.'

'They told me it was a miracle it was still floating. Seems like you'd rigged a sail on it, they told me. And a rudder! I told 'em, give my Reuben a bit of rope in his hands and he'd win the war for you! That made 'em laugh, right enough. Exposure, that's what got you. They say you've got to rest for a long time, build up your strength again.

They think I can take you home with me, in a few days' time. You'd like that, wouldn't you?'

'Aye,' he said, 'it's what I've been dreaming about. Walking up our lane, smelling a Yorkshire pudding in t' oven, a basket of fish in my arms, and thee, waiting to give us a kiss!'

'I'd have given you one earlier, but there's that many folks about! I reckon t' kisses can wait until tha's back home.'

'I reckon they can, lass!' he said, sinking back on his pillows. 'There'll be time for them, in abundance.'

BOOK TWO

May 1944

CHAPTER TEN

Elsie Tockett knocked on the door of the Godson house, then turned the handle and went in, calling her customary, 'It's only me, Elsie.'

Emily was baking, banging the bread dough up and down in the large glazed earthenware pot on the stool she'd put near the fire. There was an inviting odour of yeast and dough and the hot oven, and Emily's face was flushed with the heat and her exertions.

'Hello, love,' she said, wiping a wisp of hair from her forehead with her flour-coated forearm and leaving a smudge of white across her cheeks, 'you've brought Thomas, then?'

'He always wants to come with me,' Elsie said, 'and I know you don't mind!'

'Mind? Why, who could mind the sweet little bairn!' Emily said, looking at the three-year-old Tockett boy. 'You know, he's growing up to be a right Tockett, the spitting image of his grand-dad!'

'He's a handful, I can tell you,' Elsie said, taking off her simple brown fur toque hat and placing it on the peg behind the door.

'Nay, don't put that there!' Emily said disapprovingly. 'Put it on the dresser where no harm will befall it!' An expensive fur hat like that, hanging behind the door!

Elsie laughed. 'It's only a hat!' she said as she settled Thomas in his chair. 'Now sit quiet there, and behave yourself,' she said. 'You can see Auntie Emily is busy!'

'Nay, Elsie,' Emily said, embarrassed as always when

Elsie used that name. 'You moan't bring him up, you moan't bring a *Tockett* up to call me auntie! Whatever would his father think!'

'He can tell me what he thinks,' she said, 'when he gets back home. That's what I've come to tell you. He asked one of his friends who was posted back to England to ring me up. It's all very secret, but the battalion is coming back very soon. He thinks they'll get a bit of leave when they arrive! So, we'll be seeing Wilfred and Arthur back again.'

'Did he say ought else about the lads?' Emily asked anxiously. 'They're devils when it comes to writing!'

'No, except that they're well, and send you their love.' The latter was an invention of Elsie's. She'd been so busy asking Colonel Willoughby for news of Mark that she'd forgotten to ask if he had any news of the Godson boys.

'I wonder if that means that Eleanor will be coming back from Italy. It must be very strange for her to be driving an ambulance on them foreign roads, with all them soldiers and foreigners about!'

The two women conversed easily while Emily got on with her jobs. Elsie had taken to walking down into Old Quaytown when Thomas was old enough to be taken out in his pram, and then later in his push-chair. Ever since her marriage, she and Emily had been comfortable with each other. Without Mark, the Tockett House felt lonely all day long, especially since she had so little to do up there. When she'd got rid of Netta, she'd had the good fortune to find Jack Prendergast and his wife, whose cottage on the Bank had burned down when a spark fell in the thatch of the roof. Rendered homeless and without furniture overnight, they'd jumped at the chance to work at Tockett House. Jack Prendergast was a practical man who seemed able to turn his hand to anything and, with many builders and plumbers away at war, he'd needed all his skills to maintain the structure of the building, with such occasional professional help as he could find. Somehow, despite the demands of the fabric of the building, he'd managed to turn the gardens into a productive vegetable plot, and supplied many local shops in season. His wife, June, bustled about the house.

'Our place were that poky, Mrs Tockett,' she often said. 'Here, we have room to breathe. It's done Jack's asthma, as kept him out of the Army, a power of good!'

With June about, Elsie realised just how lazy Netta had been, standing on her dignity, delegating all the actual work to the army of servants she loved to command. June had two part-time helpers, and even managed to fit in the cooking when the cook left to work in a factory canteen.

'So, they're coming out of that Italy, and back home,' Emily said. 'Reuben will be happy to see them. Happen it'll do him a bit of good!'

'He's still the same?' Elsie asked. 'I saw him sitting outside the Raven when I passed by, but he was looking out to sea and didn't notice me!'

'Aye, lass,' Emily said, a frown crossing her face, 'he's still the same. He's going to York next week, to see a specialist.'

'Ah, well, that'll fix him up for certain,' Elsie said with an optimism she didn't feel.

Reuben had returned from the hospital after the Dieppe raid a totally changed man. No one noticed much difference in him, thinking he was still weakened by the exposure of floating for nights in the Channel, until someone remarked that Reuben seemed to have lost all interest in the *Hope*.

Four days after he'd come home, John had taken his mother on one side. 'There's summat wrong wi' Dad,' he'd said. 'Of course, when I asked him if he was coming out in t' boat when he got back and he said, not today, I thought it was just because he was tired of travelling. But

I've asked him every day now, and it's still t' same answer. And do you realise he's never walked down to see t' boat once?'

'Nay, that can't be right,' Emily protested. 'He went down there yesterday. I know, I smelled whisky on him, when he came back!'

'That's what I'm trying to tell you, Mam,' John said. 'He didn't even go down to t' Slip. He went to t' Laurel! Whenever have you heard of Dad drinking in Laurel? I can tell you Ephraim were grieved about it when they were talking in t' Snug today. Reuben Godson, a Godson, doing his drinking in t' Laurel? Whenever have you heard of ought like that!'

'Well, I never!' Emily had said. 'Well, I never!'

The fishermen of Old Quaytown regarded the Raven without question as their second home. They met in the Snug, they kept their boats outside its walls, they did their drinking inside. It was well known, even to the police, that Ephraim Hardcastle kept an open door for the fishermen regardless of licensing hours, and never refused one of them a drink. When the new constable turned up in 1943, a ruddy-faced former sergeant who'd retired and then joined the police again as a constable when the war broke out, he'd walked down to the Snug one night at midnight. The high tide was at one o'clock and they were all sitting in front of the fire, drinks in their hands.

He'd stood in the door, looked around, looked ostentatiously at his watch, and then had said, 'Reckon there's time for me to join you in one, before I go and check the Gas Works Office windows!'

The silence that had fallen over the room as he'd entered, became its original companionable murmur, and ever since that, they'd taken it in turns to leave a piece of fish behind the bar for him.

For Reuben to forsake that atmosphere to drink in the modern bar of the Laurel, where they served cocktails for tourists, black market whiskies, gins and rums for the people who'd come to live up-Bank and in Newquay Town, was regarded as an act of incomprehensible treachery by the Old Quaytowners.

After a month of asking Reuben when he was coming out on the *Hope*, John stopped mentioning it and simply went about his business, in which Reuben took not the slightest interest. John even baited the baskets down in Old Millie Harrison's shed, or on the side of the Slip when it was a fine day. Every time a cheque came from the fish agent, Walter Craggs, John would hand it silently to his mam, who'd take it and deposit it in the new branch of the Yorkshire Penny Savings Bank near the Post Office, that transacted business for two hours each Tuesday. As she deposited the cheque, she drew out a fifth of its amount in cash, kept a half of that for her housekeeping, and gave the balance to John in an envelope the bank supplied. She also had the allowance which Reuben had made to her when he'd joined the Army; that came through automatically but John was doing so well these days that she didn't need to draw on it very often.

Every second week, Reuben dressed in his battledress uniform and went into Whitby, where he paraded in front of the officer in charge of the Army Recruiting Centre and received a fortnight's Army pay, less the amount that had been sent to Emily by the Paymaster-General.

This had gone on since Reuben returned home in 1942; every three months or so he was instructed to appear before an Army Medical Board, or to see one of several consultants either in York, or in Whitby hospital. He'd seen the neurologist several times, and the psychologist, but each time he'd been graded unfit for duty and had been sent back home on 'indefinite medical leave'.

Anyone less concerned with accurate medical definitions would have diagnosed that Reuben had simply lost the will to fight.

And with it had gone his will, or so it seemed to Emily, to take an active part in anything.

Though they'd slept together in the double bed every night since he returned home, he'd never fulfilled his promise that there'd be abundant time for kisses! Or any other personal approaches, for that matter. He treated her constantly like a close friend, was good and kind to her, listened to her when she talked, did any small jobs she might ask of him with goodwill. But he never took her in his arms, not even when the bed was cold, and never made any sexual advances to her of any kind. If he complimented her on her appearance, or praised her for her cooking, it was totally dispassionately, totally as an outsider might compliment his hostess, or his landlady.

Emily was getting near breaking point, though no-one realised it except, perhaps, Elsie Tockett.

'You know, Emily,' Elsie said, when Emily had put the baking in the oven and had sat down at the table to drink the cup of tea Elsie had made, 'if ever, for any reason, you need a home to go to, a bed for the night, you can always come up to our place. We've beds galore! And no questions asked!'

Emily's eyes misted over as she looked at Elsie. 'Tha's good to me,' she said, 'and tha' knows more than tha' tells. I'm all right, yet! I've got our Martin to look after, you know, now that Georgina's gone into t' WRNS. That reminds me; it's about time I was getting him up from his sleep!'

'Why don't you let Thomas go up there,' Elsie said. 'You know where Martin's room is, don't you, Thomas?'

The lad had been busy with crayons on the end of the table, colouring the pages of a book. 'Yes, of *course* I know where it is!' he said.

'Well, don't get toffee-nosed about it!' she said, laughing. 'Go and waken him up and show him your drawing book.' The lad didn't need telling twice; he climbed down from the chair, clutching his book and his box of crayons, and marched self-importantly towards the door of the staircase. He turned with his hand on the knob. 'Shall I help him do a wee-wee?' he asked solemnly.

Emily nodded. 'Yes, help him do a wee-wee!' she said, then smiled as he opened the door and went into the downstairs back hall. 'He's like a brother to Martin,' she said. 'You're bringing him up very nicely. I imagine Mark will be very pleased when he gets home. After the war, he'll be going away to one of them boarding schools, I expect?'

Elsie could see that Emily was trying to change the subject, to take the focus of their conversation away from herself and her troubles. 'I meant what I said, you know. There's always a place for you in Tockett House, if you need it.'

Emily laughed nervously. 'Nay, what would I do in a grand place like that. I'd feel right out of it, up there!'

Elsie had invited her and the girls one afternoon for tea. Liz and Anne had been very excited to go and had dressed for the occasion. As if perversely, but from a deeper understanding of herself, Emily had worn her 'shopping' clothes, not what she thought of as her Sunday best, in which, she knew, she would have felt ill at ease. The entire occasion had been a great success as far as the girls were concerned, but a failure for Emily, since she had not felt comfortable for one second in such a grand place. It wasn't a question of wealth; the Godsons were by no means poor people and would finish the war with enough in the bank to buy Reuben any boat he wanted. The sheer size of the place, the unnecessary space of the place, had overawed her. She'd been taken round all the rooms by Elsie, with the two girls running ahead to look into everything, chattering like birds, asking questions about everything, but Emily, without meaning to, had constantly asked herself – 'why do they need such a big bedroom – why do they need such a big hallway – why do they need so many sheets and blankets – why, why?' The bedroom she shared with Reuben was big enough for their double bed, a bedside table, two wardrobes, and an old sea-chest and a chest of drawers. It was the largest room in the house and didn't measure more than four yards by five. The place where Elsie hung her clothes, what she called, to the girls' delight, her *dressing* room, was larger than Emily's bedroom, and even contained a sink with running hot and cold water!

'We could find you a small room, somewhere, if that was what you wanted,' Elsie said, persisting.

'Aye, well, I'm very grateful, but it hasn't come to that, yet!' Emily said.

Elsie could have shaken her with exasperation. She wanted so much to help if she could, but she'd known that, once Emily was safely married to Reuben, she'd become totally independent. All her emotions, all her feelings, were locked away inside herself where nobody could see them. Elsie knew that unless, somehow, she could break down that barrier, she'd never get Emily to admit that she needed help.

'You know, friends are friends in fair weather and foul,' she said. 'I hope I don't need to tell you that. When times were bad for me, the Godsons, first Lewis, and then Reuben, didn't turn their backs on me. If folks hadn't seen I had the support of the Godsons, and that even included Reuben's mother, Hannah, things would have gone hard for me in Old Quaytown. I'm not about to turn my back on a Godson now.'

'Nay, Elsie, love,' Emily protested, 'don't keep going on about it. I'm all right, I tell you. Any road, I'll make you a promise. If ever I need owt, I'll remember what you've said, and come to you first! Now, what about a piece of that jam pasty. It should be about ready now. And then, we'll fetch them lads down and I'll get Martin dressed. Our John will be in on t' tide and find me wi' nowt done!'

The tide came high at six o'clock, and John was first on it, with five boxes full. Walter Craggs was waiting and threw him the sand-filled purse at the end of the line, then went back to operate the winch. John went back to the stern and guided the *Hope* over the cradle; Craggs threw in the clutch to halt the boat while John connected the amidships lines, then opened up again to draw the boat and its cradle up the Slip.

Reuben was sitting outside the Snug; though he'd invented this manner of berthing the boat, he paid it no interest now, his eyes fixed out to sea. John glanced at him in exasperation, but didn't call out. If his dad wanted to sit there, well, let him! At least he'd stopped going to drink in the Laurel, and had come back to the Snug, though he rarely went inside until the evening drew in. He sat on the concrete apron, looking over the rail into the swirling waters beyond. When he'd first returned, the fishermen had greeted him, had even sat with him and chatted about things that used to interest them all, once upon a time. But it didn't take many hours of non-committal disinterested answers for them to remark that the evenings were getting chilly, and they'd be better doing their drinking sitting by the fire inside.

'Art coming inside then?' they'd ask. 'It's too cold to sit out here to sup when there's t' fire inside . . . '

Reuben would continue looking out to sea. 'You get on in,' he'd say. 'I'll be in presently!'

They'd had a number of meetings about fishing things such as what they should do now that boxes were becoming expensive and hard to find, about diesel supplies, about the rising price of rail transport, about whether they should increase the percentage they paid to Walter Craggs, the agent, when he asked for another five per cent to cover the rising costs of transport. When they called the first meeting, Reuben had been sitting on his chair outside the Snug and the rest of them inside, waiting for him to come in to get the meeting started. It had been assumed that, as ever, the senior Godson would start the meeting going.

Finally, Alf Corley had gone to the door and had called out – 'Reuben, we're waiting,' and had received the astonishing answer – 'You'd better go ahead without me!'

Since then, they'd always told Reuben when there was to be a meeting, but he'd never attended, and gradually the leadership had passed from the Godsons to Tom Clewson, who'd been rejected when he tried to join the Army on account of his flat feet.

John was thinking of this when he came into the Slip. By rights, if Clewson were leading the meetings, he ought to be first off on the tide. It was only proper! But, to be first off had always been the Godson way, and he told himself he'd be buggered afore he'd surrender it lightly. Though it'd been a heavy sea and a long and arduous pull, he shed his tiredness after he'd seen the *Hope* shipshape and had given his boxes to Walter Craggs; he went inside the Snug and got himself a half-pint of beer which he brought back out again. It was a quarter to seven, and he knew Mam would have his supper ready, and little Martin would be bathed and dressed and want to climb on his knee.

He'd forgo those pleasures for a while in favour of a talk; he seated himself at the table and lit a cigarette. Reuben didn't speak but looked at him with distant eyes.

'What do you see all the day, looking out there, Dad?' John asked quietly. 'Do you see t' *Hope* and me doing the work of two to keep us in business?'

Reuben didn't answer.

'I asked you a question, Dad. Do you see me hauling in t' lines with the tiller tied over because there's nobody to hold her steady, one foot in t' gunwales waiting for the next one to pitch me over? I don't carry t' stones in my pocket, as they say Uncle Lewis did when tha' knocked him overboard wi' t' boom . . . I tie mysen to t' mast!'

Still Reuben didn't respond.

'Do you see all t' fish that stays down there, as we could bring in to sell if only I had somebody to take half of t' work, and double t' catch! Dad, tha' knows I'll soon be old enough to please mysen in what I do, and where I go, but I'll be buggered if I'll stay here a day longer than this war lasts. I'll be gone, down to Hull, to t' trawlers, where I can get big money and no responsibility. Aye, and forget about being a Godson!'

When Reuben turned his face back to his son, John saw the tears in the corners of his dad's eyes, and heard his sibilant whisper. 'You must never say a thing like that to anybody, John,' he said. 'You must never say you'll forget about being a Godson. Don't you realise, it's being a Godson that keeps me going on with life. I'm sitting here because I'm a Godson, like my dad before me and my sons after me, because I've always prided myself on having that bit of strength in my backbone . . . '

John didn't know what to say. He held out his hand and placed it on his dad's sleeve. 'Don't take on, Dad,' he said. 'I only said that to make you talk to me! It kills me to know you're watching me come in, and never giving me a word, never a word, as if I were a stranger to you. And all the time you're looking out to sea. Come on, Dad, let's go home together. Mam'll have a bit of supper ready, and tha' can hold Martin on thy knee while I get myself washed. There's no need to take on . . . '

'When I look out to sea, John,' Reuben said quietly, 'there's faces looking at me. Everywhere I look, there's faces. Faces of young lads, some with blood running down them, some with half their heads shot away, but they all have eyes that look at me in hatred, in loathing, in pleading and longing. Take us on board, they're saying, and then I look along the decks and I see the bodies all piled up anyhow, and I know there's no room. Try as I might, John, I can't dismiss the faces from my mind. They're there, behind my eyelids when I lie in bed of a night and shut my eyes to try to get to sleep. If I wake up in t' night, they're still there, still looking at me. When I see a box of fish out of the corner of my eyes, the fish-eyes are the eyes of the lads I left behind on the beaches . . . '

Now the tears were coursing down his cheeks, and John looked around, embarrassed, to see if anybody was watching them. Connie Cathcart was climbing the steps that led over to the Gas Works; old Millie Harrison's nephew was standing outside the Post Office talking to Wendy Cartwright. But nobody was taking an interest in where they were sitting. Most folks, likely, would be at home, eating supper.

'Come on, Dad,' John pleaded. 'Let's get you up home. Take my word for it, one day the faces will fade away. One day, you'll wake up, and they'll be gone, and you can stop thinking about them. You know what they said in t' hospital. That you'd been a hero, that if you'd still been with your regiment, you'd have got a bar to that medal of yours; MM and Bar, that's what you'd have been. And they don't do that to people who've failed in what they had to do.'

'So many killed, John. Such a waste, and all staring at me . . . '

'Come home, Dad, come home,' John said. He stood up, went behind his father and raised him from the chair. His father didn't resist. John was astounded to see how flabby his father's skin and flesh had become. Of course, he hadn't touched him for the eighteen months he'd been home, but he could still remember as a lad before the war began that his father's flesh, whenever they'd come into contact, had been firm and solid. He best remembered his dad as a firm, solid man of enormous strength. The creature he half held in his own strong arms was flabby as an old man!

'Come on, I'm going to take thee home.'

'Never say tha'll forget tha's a Godson,' Reuben mumbled as John half led, half carried him, up the cobbled street to their house.

'Has summat happened?' Emily asked immediately, looking from Reuben's face to John's.

'No, nowt's happened,' John said, 'I don't think Dad's feeling too clever. I should put him to bed, and give him a couple of them pills he brought back from York last time.'

'They're that strong, John,' she said anxiously. 'He'll sleep till morn with a couple of them.'

'Happen that's what he needs,' John said. 'Happen that's what the poor bugger needs.'

For once Emily didn't chide him for swearing in the house. She bustled about making a cup of cocoa for Reuben. When Martin started chirping at John about sitting on his knee, she scooped him up and carried him upstairs.

John heard him wailing, 'But it's not my bed-time yet,' then he heard the bang of the bedroom door and the clatter of his mother's feet descending the stairs.

'I'll put him in Wilfred's bed,' he said. Reuben was sitting at the table as if in a coma, completely unaware of what was going on about him.

'You'll do no such thing!' she said. 'He'll sleep in his own bed, as always.' Emily was quite firm; she poured Reuben's cocoa drop by drop into his mouth, slipped in each of the two pills between sips, and then helped him start up the stairs. 'You get yourself washed,' she said to John, 'and I'll dish up your supper when I come down.

I've made a rabbit pie for you and the lasses, when they come in. They're on t' late shift for a couple of weeks starting today.'

Though they had a perfectly good bathroom out in the back yard John fetched a bowl of warm water and put it in front of the fire on his mam's baking stool.

He went upstairs and brought down Martin. 'Come on,' he said, 'I'm going to have my wash and you can sit quiet by t' fire.' He took his clean clothes downstairs – it was an act of faith, on this evening, to wash and change as thoroughly as Reuben had taught him all those years ago when they'd both come in from the sea.

'There's some, young John,' he'd said, 'as sits in their muck in t' house of an evening, but that's never been a Godson way. We allus wash ourselves, and change into clean clothes before we sit down for supper.' John would have had to admit that, once or twice, coming in dog-tired from a particularly heavy sea, he'd neglected to wash. Tonight, he wanted to do it his dad's way, or the way his dad, in his former family pride, had taught him. He stripped to the buff, wrapped a towel round his middle, and lathered himself thoroughly with the strong carbolic soap they'd always used. He dried the top half, then washed from his waist downwards in a cleansing ritual he did for his dad.

John had always worshipped Reuben more, he felt, than his brothers had. Of course, they'd had a good education and had become a bit la-di-da as a result, and maybe that explained why, although they both had good relationships with their father, they didn't idealise him, John felt, the way he did. They hadn't seen Reuben in his present condition; by the time he came back home, they'd left to go overseas, to prepare for the Italian Campaign.

Arthur had pulled John's leg, saying, 'Don't you envy us, going abroad to all these foreign places?'

'Don't you envy me,' John had said, 'sailing out each

tide on the *Hope*, wi' nobody like you to give me orders.'

He finished his wash, and was sitting in his clean shirt and trousers showing Martin how to draw a boat, the only thing he could draw, when the girls came home from work. For a long time they'd debated whether they were going to join the ATS or the WRNS, or go out to work locally. Liz had clinched it by saying that if they were moving about and Pete and Hugh were moving about, they'd never get to see each other. As it was, Pete and Hugh could always come to Ravenswyke whenever they were given leave from the American Army which they'd joined, eventually, in England. They'd been sent back to America for indoctrination, and then had been posted back to England. Now they were stationed in Lincolnshire, and managed to get week-end passes quite frequently, and to cadge a ride up to Ravenswyke. The last leave before they'd gone to America, they'd come to the house overladen with presents for everybody, including cigarettes for John. They'd spruced up in the boarding house where they always stayed when they came, up Bank, and had ridden the Jeep down to talk formally with Emily.

'Ma'am,' Pete had said, 'we understand it's the custom around these parts to ask for the hand of the girl you'd like to marry from her parents. Well, Ma'am, seeing your husband isn't around at the moment, and we're leaving tomorrow for the States, we'd like to ask you, Ma'am, could we, sort of . . . '

Here, his brash courage had failed him. John could remember the scene as if it had been yesterday. 'They want to get married, Mam,' he'd said, 'to Liz and Anne.'

Emily had been shaking her head, much to everyone's surprise. 'Oh no,' she'd said, 'I can't agree to that. You'll have to ask their dad about that.'

No matter how much Liz and Anne had pleaded, how

much they had cried and accused their mother of ruining their lives, breaking their hearts, spoiling their chances, standing in the way of their happiness – all phrases that were so effective in the magazines they read so avidly, but which failed utterly to move their own mother – she'd shake her head and say she was sorry, but they would have to ask their dad when he came home.

They'd waited; when Reuben returned to Ravenswyke they were so shocked to see his condition that it was weeks before they could bring themselves to ask him.

And all he'd said had been, 'You'll have to ask your Mam.'

That night, they'd looked at the engagement rings they both wore on strings round their necks, and had cried themselves to sleep. Perhaps, if they'd been permitted a normal engagement, they'd have been happier to join the forces to get away from home. But both of them recognised the time might come when their mother would need them here, in Ravenswyke, and they obtained work in the rubber factory outside Whitby.

Both of them felt that no more boring jobs had ever been invented. The rubber objects which, they were told, were used in motor vehicles, tanks, and aeroplanes, came past them on an endless belt. They picked one off the belt and, with the sharp knife provided, they trimmed the surplus rubber from the join of the moulding. Then they put the article on another belt and it was carried away, they neither knew, nor cared, where. The factory employed well over a hundred women, most of whom did that sort of job. Now the work had become automatic, and the girls could sit there and chat most of the day, their fingers busy trimming, trimming, while their minds, their eyes and their tongues were elsewhere. The factory worked twenty-four hours a day in three shifts, with the belts never stopping except for repairs, for tea and dinner breaks.

The highlight of the day was Music While You Work,

a continuous programme of music on the wireless that was fed throughout the factory louder even than the slap of the belts and the noise of the machines. Then, for a glorious thirty minutes, everyone would let go and sing at the tops of their voices, vying with each other to be the first to recognise the new tune when it came up in turn, belting out the words which they all learned from evening radio programmes, and from gramophone records they swapped among each other or, and this was Liz's favourite, from the pictures that showed each night in the Roxy, the Astor, or the Royal cinemas.

Liz went to see *all* the pictures and was a complete fan. She even used some of the good money she earned in the factory to buy the fan magazines, and the walls of her part of their joint bedroom were covered with photographs of Don Ameche, Alice Faye, Carmen Miranda, Clark Gable, Ronald Colman, Leslie Howard, Gary Cooper, Spencer Tracy, Myrna Loy, Betty Grable and the rest of the Hollywood stars. Pete had promised her that when he came to collect her when the war ended, to marry her and carry her away to America, abducting her if her parents hadn't yet agreed, carrying her away like the knights-of-old, they'd spend their honeymoon in Hollywood where, he'd insisted, she'd see all the big stars with her own eyes!

Anne had been hesitant. 'Hugh and me, well, we might just stay here. Hugh likes Ravenswyke and says he wouldn't mind settling here, maybe becoming a fisherman, buying his own boat. Him and John talk about nothing else . . . '

'A *fisherman*, when you could be living in New York, America? When you could be travelling all over America, the Grand Canyon, Arizona, Texas, *Chicago*! You must be crazy, Anne. Me and Pete, when he gets his demob, we're off, like a shot.'

'Happen you might change your mind,' Anne had said.

In Hugh's last letter, he'd told her about his conversation with Pete, and the informal suggestion that they might go part shares in a boat. Pete, so Hugh reported, had been very enthusiastic!

'You've not stopped in Whitby, then, to go to t' pictures tonight?' John said as they came in from work.

'Evidently not!' Liz said, pert with him as ever. 'Anyway, it's Starlight Ballroom on the wireless, from America. New York. Coast-to-Coast.'

'I don't know what tha's talking about half the time,' John said. 'It's rabbit pie for dinner. Mam's upstairs wi' Dad. He's not feeling too clever. There's a letter from Georgina on t' mantelpiece. We got five boxes today, and two of 'em were haddock.'

'Anything for us?' Anne asked anxiously.

'Nowt! I reckon as they've jilted you!'

Anne looked worried. 'Hugh said they might not be allowed to write from where they were going,' she said. 'I hope it's nowhere bad they're going, like Italy.'

They took off their outside coats and hung them on the peg behind the door. 'Elsie Tockett's been in here today,' Liz said. 'I can smell that smashing perfume she uses . . .'

'And I thought it were my fishing clothes!' John said, ducking as she aimed a blow at his head. The door to the bedroom steps opened and Emily came in.

'Don't make so much noise,' she said. 'Your dad's just gone off. He needs his sleep.'

The girls were silent. They couldn't understand what had happened to their father and in a sense resented him for staying at home when their men, and their brothers, were away fighting. They thought Reuben must, for some incomprehensible reason, be faking illness. They'd talked about it, in bed, but could come to no satisfactory conclusion.

'He *seems* to have got better,' Anne said, 'but there's something wrong there, in his mind.'

Liz was less sympathetic. 'I think he's just ducking out of it,' she said, 'and the reason he won't go fishing is because they'll know he's better. Pete was telling me . . .'

'*Pete* was telling me . . . !' Anne said. 'Don't you ever think anything out for yourself. Our dad was never a malingerer, and I don't believe for one minute he's starting to be one now! Hugh was telling *me*, when I wrote to him how Dad was, that a lot of the military hospitals have men from the fighting and they don't know what's wrong with them. Shell-shocked, some of them are, and some are half-crazy! This war is doing funny things to a lot of people, and it seems to me, and to Hugh, that that's what's happened to Dad. Like a kind of shell-shock.'

But Liz had not been convinced. Shell-shock was no part of her self-painted picture of war heroes. The films she saw in the cinema portrayed men as heroes or cowards, bad men or villains, cowboys and Indians, and nothing else. There were no half-measures in the world the picture screen portrayed. Noel Coward had made that quite clear in the navy film, *In Which We Serve!*

They gathered round the table, with John sitting at the head of it as had been his custom since all the other men went away.

Reuben always ate alone these days. 'Get on and have your supper,' he'd say, 'and your mam will dish me up a plate when I'm hungry.' It seemed as if he'd even abrogated being head of the family table.

Liz put Martin in his high chair, then sat on the bench with Anne. Emily brought the rabbit pie to the table, its golden crust smelling deliciously of meat and vegetables cooked in a rich stock.

'Save a leg for your dad,' she said, as Anne stood up to divide the pie into portions.

'I've got to hurry,' Liz said.

'Why, missie, what have *you* got that's so important . . . ?' Emily asked.

'Starlight Ballroom from New York. Coast-to-Coast.'

'Well, they'll wait until you've finished your dinner . . .'

'Oh, Mam . . . '

'And don't "oh, mam" me! I've got too much on my mind.'

They'd finished the rabbit pie all but the generous portion Emily had set aside for Reuben in case he should awaken and be hungry; Liz was in Aunt Eleanor's rooms listening on her wireless to Starlight Ballroom, and Anne was putting Martin to bed, when John heard the knock on the door.

'Grace Marsh said she might pop round this evening,' he'd said earlier. His mam couldn't resist a little smile; Grace Marsh was keen as mustard, but John was successfully holding her at arm's length. Emily thought her a pretty enough lass, but wasn't sure what sort of a wife she'd make for a fisherman with some of her fancy ways. But John knows his own mind best, she told herself.

'What's she coming round here for?' she asked. 'I'm not getting changed for her, you know.'

'Mam, I haven't asked you to get changed, have I?' John said patiently.

He had noticed, though, that when Emily had come downstairs again after he'd spoken, she was wearing a clean dress and had combed her hair.

He went to the door and opened it, but saw the bulk of Doctor Thwaite standing there instead of the expected Grace Marsh. 'Eh, Mam, it's t' doctor,' he said.

'Well, don't keep him standing there on t' doorstep! Come in, Doctor Thwaite.'

He came in, carrying his bag. 'I've just been to see Mrs

Cathcart,' he said, 'and I thought I'd call in to see how Reuben was keeping. I haven't seen him in the surgery for a week or two.'

'Sit yourself down, Doctor,' Emily said. 'John, pour the doctor a glass of whisky . . . '

'Well, since I've no more calls, so far as I know . . . '

'He's been very well lately,' Emily said. 'There's been no call for him to come up and waste your time, especially with Dr Suddaby in the Army.'

Dr Thwaite had been brought into the practice as a probationer in 1940 when he finished his internships. In 1941, when Dr Suddaby went to join the Army, he'd made Dr Thwaite a full partner. With the influx of industrial workers into the district, and the houses on the top of the Bank and in Newquay Town that seemed preferable to most people than the much bombed manufacturing towns of Yorkshire, he had his hands full of patients, and there was even talk of him bringing in another partner.

'I've had a letter,' Dr Thwaite said, 'from the Army authorities. They've asked me to give them a complete background to Reuben's life, a sort of case history, and to include my observations of his present condition.' The request had baffled him; the Army didn't usually ask civilian doctors for that sort of information, more's the pity, he privately thought. He could have told them, for instance, that the Dobbs family had a history of violence and then perhaps young Dobbs wouldn't have been called up – to face a charge, within three months, of murdering his sergeant.

John had poured the whisky and had set the bottle on its tray, with a jug of water the way he knew the doctor liked to take a drink when he'd finished his rounds. He seated himself at the table opposite the chair Dr Thwaite had taken. His mam sat at the table.

'I've been through the files,' Dr Thwaite said. 'I've a record of all the standard ailments your husband had. Dr

Gilchrist left a wonderful legacy to us with those files, I can tell you! But I was wondering, was there anything in your husband's life that might not have appeared in them, because he had no reason to consult a doctor?'

'What sort of thing do you mean, Doctor?' Emily asked.

'Well, the obvious one is – did he ever have a violent fall and bang his head? Did anything ever drop on his head and knock him unconscious for an hour or two?'

'I suppose he had the usual falls, and things banging his head. I remember he clouted hisself a time or two on the beam that used to run across the door of the baiting shed, out at the back, until he pulled the shed down to rebuild it with Eleanor's rooms. But, I can't remember owt bad enough to knock him unconscious for an hour or two . . . Can you recall owt, John? Owt in t' boat you might not have bothered to mention. You understand, Doctor, that my husband has never been much of a one for molly-coddling himself.'

'I know it, Emily. That's what makes his present condition seem so incomprehensible. Was there ever anything on the boat, John?'

'Not as I can remember. Nowt specific. I let the main gybe over one time and it cracked him across his shoulders and nearly knocked him out of the boat.' Both of them were thinking furiously, but could remember nothing specific. 'I dropped a box of fish on his head once and got myself a lathering!'

'Would you say that your father was a very strong, very active, very tough man, but never violent?' the doctor asked John.

'He weren't a coward, I can tell you. When we had that dispute with the fishermen from Scarborough who were coming up here and messing in our fishing grounds at mackerel time, he gave one or two of 'em a right clouting, I can tell you. One cheeky sod lost half his teeth!'

'John!' Emily said, 'such language, to the doctor.'

Dr Thwaite was smiling. 'I heard about that incident,' he said. 'I wasn't saying your dad was a coward, but that he would only offer violence if it was offered to him. He wasn't a man to throw his weight about . . . ?'

'One thing bothers me, Doctor,' John said quietly. 'We're sitting here talking about my dad as if he were already dead. Well, he isn't dead, yet.'

'I'm sorry,' Dr Thwaite said. 'I was only using the past tense to mean, before the present trouble. Before Dieppe. Before he was adrift on the ocean. I hope you understand that. Of course your dad isn't dead, and a lot of people are exercising their minds and their talents to see he gets back again, as soon as possible . . . ' The doctor's voice tailed away. Emily's eyes had filled with tears, and her body, turned quickly away from him, was being racked by deep gulping sobs.

John leaped to his feet and went to her, putting his arm round her shoulders. 'There, Mam, there,' he said. 'It's going to be all right.' He turned back to the doctor, his vehemence aroused by the sight of his mother's tears, his voice louder than usual. 'I'll tell you what's wrong with my dad!' he said. 'It's yon war and the daft things that are going on! It's him being pushed into t' Army when he ought to have been wi' t' boats! It's that bloody mess at Dunkirk when he had to pick my brothers, his own lads, out of t' water. It's Dieppe, that bloody mess! And most of all, it's his conscience that gives him no peace. He's a Godson, Dr Thwaite, and all his life that's meant that people have looked to him for help, for him to take the lead, to solve their problems. And when he couldn't do that, when he had to hit the wrists of the men who were trying to get in t' boat – if you can call that bloody apology of a rubber thing they put him in, a boat – he had to look into their eyes. Doctor, you've never looked over the side of a boat and seen a drowning man you can't help. Well,

I have! I was there when Farley were knocked over, when we were racing back in that storm, and I got the *Hope* within a hand stretch of him and leaned over the gunwale to get him in and couldn't, just couldn't reach, before the next wave come, and dashed him down into t' deeps.'

Now his voice had become a shout, but he was past caring. All his love for his dad boiled up in him and he could no more contain it than an overheated boiler can hold its steam.

'*It's the bloody eyes*, Doctor,' he said. 'You look in their eyes and they look in yours, and it's all you can bloody see, a pair of eyes burning their way into you because you can do bugger-all about it! That's what's wrong wi' my dad. That's why he can't sleep proper, why he can't sit down with other people to take his nourishment, when there's lads out there dead because he couldn't get them into his boat. It'd have been different if it had been a straight fight, but it wasn't. It was a mess, Doctor, just as Dunkirk was a mess, and my dad knows it! And that's what's wrong wi' him!'

Elsie Tockett stood beside Emily and squeezed her arm as Reuben walked along the row of fishermen who'd assembled on the Slip to see him off. The Army had sent transport for him, a Hillman pick-up truck with an ATS driver, an extremely large lady of around fifty. John was standing at the end of the line of fishermen, ready to sail out on the tide. 'Mind tha' keeps t' *Hope* in good nick,' Reuben said, smiling, 'else I'll skelp thee when I get home. And next time I get a bit of leave, us'll go out together! And I'll show thee where tha's going wrong!'

'Hey, Reuben, remember when we lined up like this for Fearon?' Old Bill Clewson cackled, his mouth opening in a toothless grin.

'There's lots of things I remember,' Reuben said, glancing up at the Raven Hotel, and the room that overlooked the ocean. Ephraim Hardcastle was standing in the doorway. He extended his fist above his head and shook it, pronouncing a silent 'Good Luck'.

Of the assembled crowd, only Emily could recognise the tension in Reuben's eyes, and knew he wasn't yet properly cured. After John's outburst – and how she'd been ashamed by his cursing and swearing at the *doctor* – she'd gone upstairs to find Reuben awake despite the sleeping pills she'd given him. He'd been lying still in bed and had obviously heard every word. Tears were pouring down his face, too, to match hers. She'd reached over and clasped him to her, falling half over the bed to hold and hug him, and they must have lain there, locked together, for half an hour.

The doctor, they learned later, had sent his report not to the Army authorities, but to Major Suddaby, RAMC, who worked in one of the hospitals and specialised in shell-shocked and other mentally injured patients. Suddaby had been to see Reuben for himself, had prescribed no medicine, but had talked to Reuben alone in the bedroom for an hour. Then he'd taken John on one side.

'I know what you think about the Army and the conduct of the war,' he'd said, 'and many of us agree with you on some points. We all do our best, but there are going to be the inevitable problems, wrong solutions, false starts, and just plain mistakes. I think it will help your dad,' he'd added, 'if he spends some time a little bit nearer the centre of things. I've therefore arranged for him to be given a posting to the part of the Army that deals with Planning. Now, this is what I want you to do. His posting will come through very quickly. I want you to be as supportive as you can be, during the period between now and his departure. Will you do that?'

'Yes, I'll try,' John had said. 'And, Doctor, or should I call you Major . . . ?'

'Either will do . . . '

'I'm, like, sorry I swore at Doctor Thwaite. I meant him no harm.'

'You put the fear of God into him, young John. Which, I suppose, is no bad thing, once in a while. But I'd make your apology to him, not me. If, as I hear, you're going to marry Grace Marsh, you'll maybe have need of his services someday.'

Since that day, John had spent more time with Reuben. He'd deliberately kept the boat on the Slip and had taken the opportunity to replace the propeller shaft housing, a messy lengthy job that needed two pairs of hands.

Reuben had watched him start the job, and then had wandered over. 'Tha'll score that bushing if tha's not careful,' he'd said. 'And bushings are hard to come by nowadays, I hear.'

'Cop hold of that prise bar, then,' John had said. 'If we both move it evenly, it should slip off easy enough.'

'I'll just put a bit more grease on the shaft,' Reuben said. 'That'll make it slide a bit easier.'

Greasing that shaft was the first actual job he'd done on the *Hope* since he'd been back.

For the next couple of days, they worked together. The boat was due for an overhaul, anyway, and the jobs went better when the two of them worked together.

Reuben's posting had arrived the third day. It gave him only two days in which to prepare himself.

The night before he left, John missed his dad after supper, when he went upstairs to fetch his cigs, and spent a quarter of an hour talking with Martin.

'Your dad's gone out,' Emily said, worried.

'He'll be down in t' Snug, I expect.'

'I wish you'd go down, and see . . . ' She was knitting and clacking her needles vigorously, showing her nervousness. Then she lay the knitting in her lap. 'I'm that worried about him going back,' she said. 'I don't think he's right yet, though he's been that much better since Dr

Suddaby came to see him! Go down to t' Snug, see if he's all right?'

'He'll be all right, Mam. Happen he feels like a bit of a natter and a game of dominoes. Anyway, it's been days since I've seen Grace . . . I thought I might go round there for half an hour.'

'Blood's thicker than water, young lad!'

'All right, Mam, if it'll please you, I'll go and see Grace for half-an-hour then I'll pop down to t' Snug, see if my dad's all right. But how can you expect me to get on wi' my courting . . . '

'I expect you'll manage, somehow,' she said. 'But don't bring him home late.'

It had been nearly closing time when John had walked into the Snug. Grace Marsh's mam had been out for the evening, and they'd spent their time alone on the front sofa. He was damned certain that Grace would have let him, tonight, if he'd insisted, but something had made him pull back at the last minute. Coming down the hill, he'd realised why. He knew now he wanted to marry Grace, not just mess about with her like so many people were doing now there was a war on. Peter Corley, on his last leave, had told John he could have a different woman every night if he wanted! They said that if you went into the cocktail bar of the Hotel at the top of the Bank . . .

He looked round the smoky room of the Snug, but couldn't see his dad.

'He hasn't been in all evening,' Ephraim said, when John asked what time his dad had left.

'Hasn't been in . . . ?'

'Not since the pair of you left at three o'clock to work on the *Hope*.'

'I wonder where he can be . . . ?'

Ephraim picked up the telephone, and wound the handle. 'Maisie, get me the Laurel, will you?' He waited a minute until they came on the line. 'Jack, this is Ephraim down at the Raven. Sorry to bother you when you're closing, but by any chance is Reuben with you? Reuben Godson?'

He waited while Jack spoke, then laughed. 'Well, you know how it is, with fishermen,' he said non-commitally, and hung up the telephone. 'Your dad hasn't been in the Laurel for a three-month,' he said, 'and he isn't in there tonight.'

John had left the Snug and had walked out on to the Slip, standing on the other side of the *Hope*, looking out over the water. It had been high tide at one o'clock, but the fish weren't running well this early June, and others had followed John's example to stay ashore and do odd repair jobs. He looked at the wrist-watch Grace had bought him the previous Christmas; eleven o'clock! Where should he start to look for his dad? It wasn't like him to wander far from the dock. Where could he be? Perhaps he'd walked up the Bank; the view from there on a moonlit night like this would be worth the walk – John and Grace often took their walks up there, to be alone for a bit of a cuddle, looking down on the silvered sea and the black slate of the scaurs that extended as far as the low water line. But why would his dad go up there?

His eyes had adjusted to the moonlight after the lamps of the Snug and he walked up the street to the place they all called the Cockpit, where his mam often stood to watch them after the launch. The bank sloped steeply down to the edges of the scaurs, slipping a bit every year, gradually eroding away. There'd been talk before the war of them building a breakwater here to hold back the cliffs – some had said the cost would run to hundreds of thousands of pounds and the Council had decided against it in favour of street lights. More and more the Council made its decisions by ignoring the needs of the fishing community in Old Quaytown and perhaps that was just, since Old Quaytown now represented only a quarter of the total population of Ravenswyke, and fishing, far from being the staple industry with twenty or more boats sailing out every day, was now in the hands of just a few of the longer-established families.

Ravenswyke, John thought scornfully, was becoming a residential and holiday village, with the preponderance of people old and retired. Once they'd had a large young population and the school had been bursting at the seams. Now Silas Redfern had classes of no more than fifteen of each age group, half of them townies from Leeds and Bradford, come with their parents to live in Newquay Town while their fathers, and often their mams, sought employment in Whitby's factories.

The sea was placid that night, and John stood on the edge of the Cockpit, his knees resting against the wall. Out there, he told himself, were mines and bloody submarines, the devils of the ocean. Out there were British boats, and planes flying overhead from Germany to bomb the manufacturing towns of England and Scotland. But the RAF went over there, as well, and bombed the industrial towns of the Ruhr, so perhaps there was some justice after all.

He saw the black speck on the ocean long before he realized what it was. He stared out, focusing his eyes against the dazzle of the liquid silver ocean. A boat. An eight footer. Bloody hell, it was Walter Craggs's boat, the one he used sometimes to set a few lobster pots of his own when the transport business fell a bit slack. He saw the man in the boat rowing with steady strokes, and knew instantly who it was. The tide was coming in; in half an hour he'd be able to run Craggs's boat right up the Slip.

'Well, I'll be buggered!' John said, as he walked slowly down the steep, cobbled street to the Raven at the bottom, past the stone houses, the little yards in which folks planted any flowers they could find. He felt a joy inside that he couldn't have explained, a sense of things coming right for a change, of the old order being re-established. Reuben, his dad, Reuben Godson, was back out on the water! And all was well in the world!

He stood at the top of the Slip as his dad rowed in, his strokes long and firm and steady, his direction true.

'Chuck us t' painter, Dad,' John said quietly, listening to the slap of the water against the boat sides, smelling the salt, seeing, against the mooned surface of the waters, the outline of his own dad, his true dad come back, it seemed, from the dead.

'It's a grand night,' Reuben said as he climbed out of the grounded boat, then helped John haul it scraping over the oiled concrete runway.

'Aye, it's a grand night for being out.'

'I reckon they'll be running tomorrow,' Reuben said when they'd lodged the boat firm in front of the new public lavatories the Council had built in 1939 on a grant from Captain Walham, who'd grown tired of visitors urinating against his sea-wall. 'You've nobbut an hour's work on the *Hope*. You'll be able to make t' tide after I'm gone.'

They walked back to the sea-wall. 'You're all right then, Dad? About going, I mean?'

'Aye, lad, I'm all right. You were right, you know. You said that one day the eyes would go away. Well, they've gone, let's hope forever!'

'Amen to that. I'll bet it were grand, to get back on t' water again.'

'I can't say as it were bad,' Reuben said, smiling. 'I'll be off, then, tomorrow, to see what's at the back of this war business. And then, when I return, I'll keep my promise and we shall take the *Hope* out together. Thee and me, the Godsons of Ravenswyke . . . '

'And Wilfred, and Arthur, Dad. Us'll have a fleet of boats. Don't forget, we've got to bring our Martin up to it!'

Reuben looked solemn. 'You'd better not count on

Wilfred or Arthur,' he said. 'Them two have tasted life away from t' nest. They'll not come back here, I can tell you. And Wilfred will want summat better for Martin, a better education, a softer way of life.' He smiled a cheeky smile. 'It'll be up to you, I reckon, to give us the next Godson of Ravenswyke. I see that Grace Marsh gives every appearance of being willing and eager!'

John felt himself colouring. 'Nay, Dad,' he said, 'I've not yet made up my mind. There's too many other fish in t' sea!'

'Take my advice, lad,' Reuben said. 'Grace Marsh is right for you! Never mind about the other fish in t' sea. Treat her right, and she'll be a grand wife for you. Believe me, I nearly made a mistake at your age, and it could have cost me your mam. Grace may seem a bit, well, flighty at the moment, but that's the way of young lasses. But you get that ring on her finger, as sharp as she'll have you, and you'll see she'll settle down.'

John felt such a glow of warmth at hearing his dad speak, taking on the role of adviser. John had always taken his problems to his dad, and had always respected the advice he'd received even though sometimes he hadn't followed it. More than anything else, he realized, he'd missed this role in his dad for the last eighteen months. Now his dad was prepared to speak out, to show an interest, and even to give advice. They walked together up the cobbled street.

'After t' war,' Reuben said with enthusiasm, 'we'll design a forty-footer together, thee and me, and we'll have Tockett build it for us. Broad in t' beam, two-stroke diesel engine . . . '

'*Two-stroke* . . . ? By gow, that'll be summat!'

'Wait, tha' hasn't heard all of it. Us'll have a generator working off t' engine . . . '

'A *generator* . . . ?'

'Aye . . . '

'Whatever for . . . ?'

Reuben stopped and turned to look at his son. 'Tha'll never guess!' he said. 'For an *electric winch*.'

'Nay, bloody hell!' The swear word leaped from John's mouth at the thought. Fancy the *Hope* with an electric winch! Bloody hell!

'And I'll tell you summat else,' Reuben said. 'Cotton line's finished! After the war, we'll be using nylon lines, and nylon nets, made from the same stuff they're using for parachutes, with ten times, a hundred times the breaking strain of best cotton!'

They set off walking again. 'It's going to be a new world, Dad,' John said as they turned into the door of their house, Godson Cottage, Godson Street, Ravenswyke.

John stood at the end of the line of fishermen, saluting his father's departure on the surface but, inside, celebrating his father's rebirth. The large ATS lady had climbed back into the Hillman pick-up, and there'd been laughter when they saw how the vehicle sank on its springs.

'Tha'll never get that back up t' Bank, missis,' Alf Corley had said, home on leave for a couple of weeks and aching to get back out on the water in the *Princess*.

Reuben was wearing his sergeant-major's battledress uniform, with the ribbon of his Military Medal sewn on. Emily had pressed his jacket and his trousers, had polished his boots and even rubbed that blanco stuff on his gaiters and his belt. They'd stowed his kitbag, his large and small pack, in the back of the pick-up, and he was ready to go. He took one last look around, obviously embarrassed and not knowing what to say.

'Well, goodbye, all!' was all he could think of.

The ATS woman had opened the passenger door, and he put his hand on the handle prior to getting into the vehicle.

'Hang on a minute,' John said, his voice loud and

penetrating. They all fell silent, and looked across at him. He cleared his throat and took a telegram out of his pocket.

Walter Brackley, who'd slipped it into his hand a bare hour ago, broke into a nervous laugh. 'It's a telegram, Reuben, come for your lad John.' Telegrams almost invariably contained bad news, but the look on John's face, and the cackle in Walter Brackley's voice dispelled any bad feelings the sight of the buff envelope would normally have caused.

'I got this telegram, from Major Suddaby. You know, the doctor. It says, "Before he leaves inform your father unofficially he is awarded bar to Military Medal due bravery Dieppe under adverse conditions and lives saved."' John's face was red as he came to the end of the one long sentence.

The whole dockside erupted in a salvo of cheers as the crowd pressed in, slapping Reuben's back and arms, shouting well done, Reuben, well done Reuben, over and over again. Emily had been swept along in front of the crowd and was lodged tight against Reuben.

'I allus told thee, tha' was a hero!' she said, looking into his eyes.

'Go on,' the crowd yelled, 'kiss him, kiss him, give him a kiss!' Mrs Probert of the Post Office was standing near to him and she reached up and gave him a quick peck on the cheek. The other women in the crowd, even Connie Cathcart who'd come down from her sick bed to see him off, crowded round him, each kissing him on the cheek.

'Nay missis,' he kept on saying, 'tha'll have thy husband after me!'

But finally, it was Emily's turn. He put his arms round her, hugged her to him, and kissed her full on the mouth.

'Nay, Reuben,' she protested when finally he let her go, 'whatever will t' folks think!'

But neither of them cared, at that moment, what anybody thought!

And, as Emily watched the car drive away up the Bank, she remembered the words she'd used to Georgina. A fisherman's wife sent her husband away happy. She hadn't gone on, as she might have done, to say a fisherman left his wife happy. They'd lain in each other's arms all night long after he'd come in with John. He'd told her about the faces, and how they'd now left him. He'd told her about the waste of lives, and how he could now find out what it was all for, what it was all about. And then, they'd made love together and, afterwards, they'd talked about themselves and laid their plans for after the war was over.

Just before she'd slipped into sleep, she'd heard him say, 'The first thing we'll do, when I come back from t' army, Emily. Do you know what it is, lass . . . ?'

'No,' she'd murmured sleepily.

'We'll strip this bedroom, and we'll repaper t' walls! Wi' roses, just like you've allus wanted . . . '

CHAPTER ELEVEN

Lt-Col Mark Tockett opened the door of the dining-room of the Palazio Urbano they used as Battalion Headquarters and went in. The battalion officers had been assembled by his second-in-command, Capt Godson; the room buzzed with conversation until Capt Godson saw his arrival. The officers got to their feet, and he could sense the strong undercurrent of excitement as he placed himself with his back to the fireplace.

'At ease, gentlemen,' he said.

For days, now, the battalion had run with rumours; they knew he would tell them the honest truth and not attempt to mask it with platitudes. They were past platitudes; for months they'd fought the rugged Italian Campaign, battling for every hill top, every mountain range in Southern Italy, every new bay along the coastline. It had been a hard fight with the Germans taking a terrible toll of their advancing forces. The battalion had been decimated; of all the officers present in the room, less than half had left England with the battalion on its initial posting. Lt-Col Tockett had only commanded them for three months, after the death of the previous Commanding Officer, but had already earned their respect. An older man than most of the other field officers, what he lacked in youthful drive and dash was adequately compensated by his organising ability. Many privately said that if he had been in command instead of the previous Lt-Col, they wouldn't have suffered half the casualties in badly planned operations.

‘I have no good news for you,’ he said quietly. ‘In fact, I have bad news. Our return to the UK has been delayed; we’re going back into the front for what I’m told is one more operation!’

He listened to the groans from around the room. The officers and men of his battalion were, he knew, tired and in need of leave but then so were most of the other battalions fighting in the Brigade.

‘As you all know, gentlemen, we pinned many hopes on the fall of Monte Cassino. We hoped – or rather, those God-like creatures in Army HQ who control all our destinies, hoped – that once the Monastery had fallen, we’d be able to push the Germans up into the plains of Northern Italy. Well, as you know, we have the Monastery, but the Germans are still firmly entrenched behind it and it looks as if it might take time to shift them. We are going to help the Brigade do that job! I don’t yet know the battle plan, but as soon as I do I shall hold an O-group meeting, and we’ll get on with it. Meanwhile I expect you to break it gently to your men that they’re not going home just yet, but our return to Blighty is postponed, not cancelled.’

When he finished speaking, a loud murmur of questions ran round the room. The disappointment on the face of each officer was plain to see. Wilfred looked at his brother, Arthur, still a lieutenant, and read the abject misery it portrayed. Arthur, he knew, had had a bellyful. On the last operation he’d been pinned down in a mountain gully which was swept by Spandau fire from two directions. As soon as the Germans had found the range, they’d started lobbing mortar bombs in there. The German use of mortars in the mountains was brilliant – it had become their most destructive weapon.

Of course, Wilfred told himself, Arthur ought not to have walked into the trap the Germans had deliberately set in that gully. He ought to have read the ground and known it was dangerous to go in there without support from the mountains above. If he'd taken his platoon round the edges of the gully he'd have spotted the Spandaus, and could have obliterated them by standard fire and movement methods. We all make mistakes, he thought, but that one was stupidly elementary!

As a result of his mistake, Arthur had been trapped in the gully for twenty-four hours under continuous mortar bombardment. When B-platoon had finally cleared the Spandaus and the mortars away, Arthur had two men left in his platoon, himself and Private Wickem. And both had the glazed expressions of shell-shock deeply etched on their faces.

When Lt-Colonel Tockett stopped speaking, Wilfred walked across the room to his brother.

'Well, young 'un,' he said, 'back in we go . . . !'

Arthur nodded in misery.

'Come into the bar and I'll buy you a drink,' Wilfred said.

Now that he'd been given his captaincy, he felt like the older brother again, despite Arthur's OCTU success. He'd shown that, in action, he was the more experienced, the wiser officer, and had spent much of his time doing what their mother had told him to do – looking after Arthur. Arthur's problem was that he couldn't plan very well; he couldn't think things out efficiently since he tended to be too preoccupied with details. He took finicky care in detail, often in situations which demanded a wider look at the overall prospects. Arthur couldn't stand back and say – this is the final objective, and the details can take care of themselves. Thus, he couldn't be flexible. He'd drawn a line on his map and had said to his platoon, this is the way we'll go. All very well, but the line went through the gully and he ought to have kept an open mind. When he saw the gully for the first time, he ought to have realised it was a likely situation for a trap, and been flexible enough to lead his men around it, along the gully's edges.

'Come on,' he said, 'the drinks are on me.'

'I wonder if that .303 ammunition has arrived,' Arthur said as they walked across the dining-room back to the bar, housed in what had been a corner of the Palazio's main foyer.

'Fancy us, a couple of Godson kids, living in a Palace,' Wilfred said, chuckling, trying to cheer up his brother.

'Do you know if that ammo has arrived?' Arthur asked, fretfully.

'Ammo, ammo, why are you going on about ammo? What'll you have to drink.'

'The last time I checked the platoon supplies,' Arthur explained pedantically, as if to a child, 'and found out how low we all were, I indented for some more to be brought back up to strength. We can't go back into the line if we don't have ammo, can we?'

Wilfred looked at him in amazement. 'Arthur,' he said, 'we've only just had word we're going back in there and already you're worrying your guts about details like ammo ... when the time comes to go back into the line, we'll have ammo coming out of our arse-holes, believe me...'

'I hope so,' Arthur said. 'A soldier can't fight without ammunition ... '

'Oh, bloody hell, Arthur. Stop nagging me about ammo. Just tell me what you want to drink ... '

'Have they any Gordons?'

'How the hell do I know if they have Gordons? You want a gin, right? It might be Booths, it might be Gordons, it might be London Dry. I don't know what they've sent up for us.' He turned to the barman. 'Wilkins,' he said, 'have we any Gordons Gin?'

'No, Captain,' Wilkins, the mess orderly behind the bar, said. 'I can do you a nice line in Tanqueray ... '

'It's Tanqueray,' Wilfred said to Arthur.

'What's that? I've never heard of it. What does it taste like?'

'It tastes like gin,' Wilkins said. Like all the other Mess servants, he'd had a bellyful of Lt Godson's finicky complaints.

Wilkins slowly and deliberately put a glass in front of Lt Godson, and another glass with the bottle of Tanqueray in front of his brother, the Captain. 'Perhaps *you'd* care to taste it, Captain,' he said, then walked down the bar to serve other officers.

Wilfred knew he ought to call Wilkins back, to reprimand him for dumb insolence, but frankly, he was tired of defending Arthur, of fighting petty battles for him. He poured two generous drinks, recorked the bottle, added tonic water, and carried the drinks to a corner of the foyer where there were two armchairs somewhat secluded from the rest.

'Come on, young 'un,' he said, 'bottoms up!'

Arthur was scanning his glass. 'They don't wash them very clean,' he said. 'Somebody ought to have a word with Harrington about it. If he's supposed to be Messing Officer, he's not doing much of a job of it.'

Wilfred seethed with anger but tried not to show it. Harrington, a pre-war hotel owner from Paignton, Devon, did a marvellous job of foraging for them. No matter where they'd been, he'd always found somewhere he could set up some sort of officers' mess, and give them something a little extra special in the way of drinks and food. Most probably he'd driven over to one of the American outfits specially to provide this gin for them. That very morning, they'd had tins of rolled bacon for breakfast – when Wilfred had complimented him and had asked where they came from, Harrington had smiled that slow Devonian smile of his.

'Ask no questions, Captain, you'll get no lies . . . ' he had said.

And here was Arthur knocking him because of a bit of a thumb-print on a glass!

'I remember you, Arthur, when you were picking your nose and stealing drinks out of t' glasses left on t' tables at t' Snug!'

Arthur's nose wrinkled in distaste. 'You always annoy me, Wilfred, when you put on this Old Quaytown accent of yours, and talk about our childhood there. We're ten thousand light years away from Old Quaytown now and I, for one, want to remain that way!'

'Why, you bloody little snob,' Wilfred said. 'If you ever say owt like that in our mam's hearing, I'll break your neck!' He took a big gulp of his drink, trying to settle his anger, remembering he'd brought Arthur into this corner for a purpose. But, by God, it was hard to do anything for the damned tyke! It took a great effort of will to calm himself, as on so many occasions during their service together in Italy. Arthur's great trouble seemed to be that he couldn't adapt to *any* situation. When other officers were delighted with the few luxuries that could be provided for them, Arthur criticised and carped.

That wasn't too important, but what worried Wilfred was that Arthur was exactly the same in his fighting. All war means taking chances, and sometimes you had to lead your men into situations that were far from ideal, relying on your own adaptability, and the skill you'd trained into your NCOs and men, to get you through. All the time, Arthur strove for a perfection of his own kind. Wilfred knew Arthur's men and NCOs hated him. Because, at the critical moment when a bit of dash and verve would see them through, he waited, looking for that extra bit of protection, that extra carpet of fire to be laid, before he would go forward. How many times had he heard Lt-Col Tockett bellowing down his radio, 'Move, man, move that

damned platoon of yours! What are you waiting for . . . '
and heard Arthur's reply, prim and dispassionate – 'I was waiting, Sir, for the covering fire to take full effect', or some such textbook classic OCTU answer that bore no relationship to the actual conditions of warfare. As a result, Arthur had lost more men than any other platoon commander, and more NCOs, and several times Wilfred had had to persuade Lt-Col Tockett not to replace him.

'Look, Arthur,' he said, 'I want to talk to thee . . . '

'Oh, God, not another Old Quaytown sermon!' Arthur said. 'As soon as you lapse into the archaic English forms of the second person singular I know . . . '

'Shut up, lad!' Wilfred said, his voice hardened into command. 'It's for your own good. Listen to what I have to say! There's a job going and I can get it for you. You'd be in charge of a Transit Camp, bringing new lads in, taking out the wounded. They need somebody to run it efficiently and I think it's just up your street. I've had a word with Colonel Tockett . . . ' He stopped when he saw Arthur's white face.

'You're trying to get rid of me,' Arthur said. 'Don't think I don't know what happened to Pringle, who was doing that job. His jeep ran over a mine – lucky devil was killed instantly . . . '

'That was a chance in ten thousand,' Wilfred said. 'That road was supposed to have been cleared by the Yanks . . .'

'But it hadn't, had it . . . ?'

'What happened to Pringle is a *detail*, Arthur. Look at the job from a wider point of view . . . '

'A *detail*. It killed Pringle, and I don't think he'd care to hear you calling it a *detail* . . . '

'Arthur, the job's yours. I'm advising you to take it,' Wilfred said, exhausted with his attempts to talk rationally with his brother. God, he'd like to see the back of him, to know he was somewhere safe. And, what was important, not leading innocent lads into battle. 'Will you do it?'

Arthur was shaking his head violently. 'Never!' he said. 'I'll never do a job like that. Anyway, it's you and me, isn't it. We promised we'd stay together . . . '

Wilfred felt the heavy load of his brother settle back on his shoulders. 'Aye, I reckon we did,' he said. He got up to leave. Now he'd have to persuade Lt-Col Tockett not to post Arthur out of the battalion.

'Nay, our Wilfred,' Arthur said, smiling and mimicking Wilfred's earlier Yorkshire accent, 'tha' can't go without letting me buy thee summat to sup!'

'Stick it up thy arse!' Wilfred said savagely, and strode from the foyer of the palace in search of Tockett.

The Panzer unit was hull down in trees at the bottom of the bluff, which ran sheer behind the position for a couple of hundred feet or more into impenetrable crags. Mark Tockett had assessed the position through the glasses which he passed to Wilfred.

'I don't like it, Captain,' he said. 'I just don't like it.'

Wilfred swept the ground ahead of them through his glasses. He and Lt-Col Tockett had moved forward ahead of Battalion Headquarters when they'd heard that A-Company was pinned down and already had heavy casualties. Now they could see why. The company had been trapped between three German units of Panzers. According to the message they'd received, one of the Panzer companies had hidden in trees and had held back, about half-a-mile to the right. They'd permitted the company to come half-way through them, and then the three prongs of the pincer had closed. They'd seeded the position in advance with well hidden snipers, and mines, and must already have sighted the mortars and zeroed them on to suitable locations into which they had rightly guessed the beleaguered Company would run.

A-Platoon of A-Company had run into a wood, advancing section by section over the rocks to the plateau on which the pine maquis grew. The Germans had waited, with infinite patience, until the Platoon had reformed in the wood, and had then mortared them to smithereens. The last message that Capt Mackenzie, the Company Commander, had received had been screamed over the radio by a wounded infantryman, who hadn't even finished the sentence.

'They're all dead, hey you, are you listening, they've all been . . .'

Anybody could have supplied the missing word.

B-Platoon had tried to scale the rocks to the right, and the Panzers had splashed them with the devastating fire of anti-personnel shells that exploded on contact with the rocks into a thousand killer fragments, whirring in all directions.

C-Platoon, led by Lt Arthur Godson, had been held back by Capt Mackenzie, in reserve. Now it was cut off from Company Headquarters by the tank units Tockett could see in the glasses. They couldn't go round; the tank units would have to be destroyed.

'What do you think, Wilfred?' Mark Tockett asked, dropping the rank. Wilfred knew he wasn't asking for a purely military appraisal; he was asking Wilfred if he thought Arthur was man enough, officer enough, leader enough, to succeed.

What could Wilfred say? They had to go forward; the battalion had to advance and was being held up by one position, that could be dealt with by one platoon, adequately led. If Arthur . . . He couldn't put his thoughts into exact words. He knew that, if they bypassed Arthur's platoon, that would destroy his brother in the battalion. On such occasions, word gets around, and men can be cruel. 'Did you see, when the going got tough, they pulled out that wanker Godson's platoon, and put us in!'

It would be a hard fought, but small action. Like the game of chess, in which both sides were preparing to exchange pawns, to clear the way for knights.

But one of the pawns was his own brother, Arthur! The man he'd promised to look after! He scanned the ground, looking at the entire situation, his mind racing to find a solution to the problem that wouldn't disgrace, or destroy, Arthur and his men.

All too clearly he saw it was a classic platoon action. One section to the right up those rocks, in amongst them. Covering fire with rifles and two-inch mortars while the other section crossed that small gully, and took up positions to the left of, and beside the tank position. From there they could lob everything they'd got on to the tanks, including incendiaries, H.E. and smoke. The smoke would destroy the tanks' field-of-view. The third section could then dash straight forward over the open ground; a few grenades lobbed into the tank slits and they'd clean the Germans out.

The platoon officer, on a job like that, would go in with the third section.

The Germans, in such a situation, anticipating a frontal assault, would sweep the ground with machine-gun fire at waist height.

There would inevitably be a few casualties. The misfortunes of war!

If the third section didn't move quickly, they'd be decimated. Since it would take the mortar crews only a short time to get the range of the two sections offering supporting fire, any delay would be fatal for the entire platoon, not just the third section.

If the tank position were not quickly neutralised, the pincer could reach further back, and squeeze the whole company, even threaten the entire battalion which, because of the nature of the ground, was extended along the line of advance.

It had all the hallmarks of a classic Kesselring rearguard action in which he risked the minimum force, i.e. the tanks, to gain the maximum advantage, i.e. a whole battalion and many hours if not days of delay.

And Arthur was the man at the centre of it all!

Wilfred swung the glasses around and up the rock-face. He grunted with satisfaction. It could work, it could just work, given the German mentality and their knowledge of the unpredictability of the British.

'Right of arc fifteen degrees, a track through rocks. A small force could find its way up there and "accidentally" disclose its position to the German tanks. They would assume that an attack was being planned from that direction and switch their guns from the forward facing fixed arcs, to fire up the mountain track. They would doubtless radio to the mortars, and switch the mortar target. That way, the frontal assault would have at least the time it would take them to traverse those machine-guns to get through.'

'And the feint, over the edge of those rocks . . . The men up there would be on a suicide mission . . . '

'No, Sir. As soon as they'd effectively revealed themselves and had seen the Germans start to traverse, they would advance northerly, over the rocks. They'd hole up and wait for the battalion to pass through the tanks.'

Lt-Col Tockett took the glasses and used them to scan the ground. 'It could work,' he admitted grudgingly. 'But it depends on how well the people up there can feint an assault without being hit by snipers. I don't suppose I need to ask which officer is going to lead the feint . . . ?'

'No, Sir. The other officers are all concerned with their companies.'

'Very well, you'd better get on with it!' He turned to his signaller. 'Message to all company commanders. O-group here, in ten minutes' time.'

Wilfred selected his team; five men from his previous company, four of whom had been in his platoon when he was a lieutenant. They pored over the large-scale map of the terrain and found the track clearly marked.

'Good, the Germans will know it's there,' Wilfred said.

'And have mined it, Capt?' Sgt Gosport asked. He'd been Wilfred Godson's first sergeant, when Wilfred joined the regiment after OCTU.

Corporal Evans had been a private in the platoon, and Wilfred had recommended him for his stripes. 'And booby-trapped, Capt?'

'Yes, mined and booby-trapped. That's how we're going to tip them off. We're going to explode one of the mines and a couple of the booby traps. How well can you scream, Saunders?'

'I'll manage something, Capt.' Saunders had also been in the platoon; Wilfred had recommended him for stripes but he'd lost them subsequently in a brawl with the MPs in Naples.

Stevenson and Viccars made up the party. Viccars was the mines and booby-traps expert who'd attended all the courses back in UK. Now he'd have a chance to prove how well he'd learned his lessons. Stevenson spoke fluent German; before the war he'd worked as a young lad in a Munich brewery.

'We're going to see if we can find a sniper with a radio,' Wilfred explained to Stevenson. 'If we can, you can send a message to say the British are coming over the side of the rocks, okay?'

'Okay, Captain. Jawohl, Herr Kapitän!'

'Beg pardon, Capt,' the quartermaster sergeant who was kitting them out said. 'You don't need to go looking for a radio. I've got one here we pinched a few miles back . . . '

The CQMS was a well-known scrounger; Wilfred

laughed and said, 'Why didn't I think to ask you, CQMS?' He took the khaki-green German handset with its extendable rod aerial. It would give them a range of a mile at least unless they went too far behind the rocks. Thank God it was a fixed frequency crystal; they'd pick up the tanks on one of the three pre-set frequencies.

Lt-Col Tockett came to see them start. When the men had filed out of the encampment, he held out his hand.

'Good luck, Wilfred,' he said.

'Thank you, Sir. We'll see you on the other side of the cliffs.'

'I hope you will.' Mark looked at Wilfred, wanting to say more but wondering how far he should go. Dammit, he'd known these lads all his life. He'd watched them grow up down there in Old Quaytown. He felt he had a duty, apart from anything else, to Reuben.

'I can't expect you to believe this, Wilfred,' he said, 'but one day you'll learn he's not worth it!'

Wilfred smiled, but the pain of the last few months showed through it. 'Blood is thicker than water, or commonsense, don't they say, Sir?'

'Yes, that's what they do say, damn them,' Mark Tockett said.

It was twelve o'clock and the blazing sun was high overhead. Wilfred could smell the dry arid herbs that managed somehow to grow in each crevice of this barren rocky maquis, where only goats and sheep could have survived throughout the ages. Viva Italia! Viva the sunny lemon groves, the orange trees of the travel books it had once amused him so much to read. Now the landscape had been devastated by mortar bombs, artillery shells, and the deliberate spoiled earth policy of the retreating German Army.

'Have you got them?' he asked Stevenson, who'd been

flicking the fixed frequency switch of the Siemens radio.

'Yes. Channel Two. An O-post has just given them an accurate picture of our battalion position. But so far, no mention of us.'

'Good. Keep listening.'

Wilfred had estimated it would take an hour and a half for them to get into position. The signal for the first part of Arthur's attack would be a round of red tracer fired from Wilfred's position. Arthur's two sections would move cautiously under cover of the rocks, with no attempt at fire and movement, no attempt to keep the Germans' heads down by rifle and mortar fire. Only when the two sections were in position, would Wilfred simulate his assault, and then Arthur spring the surprise.

'Move like hell when you go, young 'un,' Wilfred silently prayed.

'Sniper position ahead,' Sgt Gosport whispered. 'Do we take him?'

'No,' Wilfred said, 'we go round.'

There was no point in risking exposing themselves at this juncture, and the Germans always covered their snipers, one with another. Rocks ahead and an almost indistinguishable sheep-track.

'Keep off the track,' he heard Viccars whisper, but none of them needed to be told. They'd only gone a hundred yards, crawling their way from cover to cover, bending double and running where they could, then crawling again, when Wilfred saw Viccars jerking his thumb downwards. He looked over the edge of the rock and saw a thin tendril of what looked like vine, lying innocently across the path, where no vine could possibly grow.

Viccars went over the edge of the rock like an eel, grunted when he located the charge hidden beneath a flat stone. It took him only a few seconds to disconnect the spring-loaded firing clip and render the mine useless.

'Some Italian peasant is going to kick that with his foot, after the war is over!' he said when he rejoined them, 'but I'll be buggered if I was going to risk lifting it.' It was a favourite trick of the German minelayers to put a second charge beneath the first, as a booby-trap.

Now they had reached the beginning of the track that would eventually curve back and bring them to a position overlooking the tanks from the side. Wilfred looked at his watch; they were on schedule, moving tightly and easily, completely in tune as a unit. In his early days in Italy, he and Sgt Gosport had often taken out small patrols at night, probing the German positions. They'd developed a harmony of movement and understanding between them that Wilfred could still feel working. He beckoned left, and Sgt Gosport went up the side of the track to the left. Wilfred went to the right with Cpl Evans and Viccars, taking advantage of every fissure, every rock, to avoid sky-lining themselves. So far Wilfred was confident they hadn't been spotted by any of the O-posts or the snipers. Stevenson had listened constantly to the radio and had heard only reports of the movements Lt-Col Tockett had said he would continue to make among the companies, to keep the watchers orientated towards his direction.

He watched the fingers of his watch. At one-thirty exactly, he gave Saunders the red tracer round. Saunders took the magazine off his rifle, ejected the round he had in the breech, and inserted the tracer. He climbed the rock until he could find a fissure then he placed himself at the back of it, pointing his rifle at the rock above the German position.

Stevenson levelled the Mauser rifle the CQMS had given him; when Wilfred nodded he fired it and its distinctive sound echoed round the rocks. They heard Saunders scream; it was a blood-curdling yell of a man in his death throes and then he fired the red tracer. Stevenson was listening to his radio and all hell broke loose. He flicked round the channels and all of them were carrying voices.

Snipers are trained to hear the crack and thump of a rifle firing, and from the sound work out exactly where the shot comes from. Putting the rifle in the *back* of the fissure had deceived them all, it seemed. The mortars concealed in the rocks above the tank position all fired, but two hundred feet or more further down the mountainside.

Wilfred clamped the phones of his radio round his ears, and heard the distorted voice of Lt-Colonel Tockett himself.

'Bingo!' he said. 'Bingo!'

It was the signal they'd both agreed if the machine-guns on the tanks started to traverse.

Wilfred went to the edge of the rock and looked out between two rocks and down. Sure enough, the guns on the tanks, of which he could now see three, were traversing left moving through the complete arc of 125 degrees.

'Now,' he said out loud.

It had been arranged that the two-inch mortar groups of Arthur's platoon sections would start to fire when the guns reached a hundred degrees.

As if on cue, he heard the bangs of the mortars, saw the black objects lobbed into the air to fall round the tank positions. Many fell short, since the mortar teams misjudged the distance and the drop, and the crack of rifles came from round the position, as snipers saw targets among the mortar teams. First round, high explosive shells as arranged. Second round should be incendiaries, and were.

The third round should have been smoke. Somebody had made a cock-up. The mortar teams fired high explosive again.

'Run, Arthur, run!' Wilfred said, willing his brother to get off his belly and start the dash across the open ground in front of the tanks. If he didn't start now, he wouldn't make it before those machine-guns, already locked into the ends of their traverse, started back again. Once the machine-guns traversed back, they'd have no chance below. He turned and nodded to Stevenson, who opened up his microphone and screamed into it, in German.

'The frontal attack is a fake; I can see them coming over the back of the rocks.'

Immediately, the German mortar teams started a creeping barrage from the previous position up the rocks, laying a carpet of explosions that slowly crept up the rocks towards Wilfred's position.

The two-inch mortar teams fired incendiaries again.

Wilfred saw it in a blinding flash. Arthur had countermanded the battalion orders, and had ordered a double dose of HE and incendiaries. The stupid, bloody idiot. He'd doubled the dose, thinking it would give him greater security, instead of realising that, at this moment, he had no time for security or safety. He had to *move, move, move*.

The machine-guns started to traverse back.

The Germans were playing it safe, as Wilfred would have done in their position. They turned the mortars on to the heights, and swung the machine-guns of the tanks to cover the flat ground before them. With the nests of snipers midway between both, to fire at such targets as presented themselves. He replaced the earphones on his head.

Mark Tockett, speaking with a slow, clear, precise voice, spiky as ice crystals, was saying, 'I repeat, Lt Godson, I say again, start the assault with your section *now*!'

Wilfred heard a voice he recognised.

'Smoke going down in five seconds, *according to plan*!'

He heard the petulant note in his brother's voice, and knew his days as an officer in *this* battalion were finished.

'Not according to *my* plan!' Mark Tockett snapped back over the air. 'Move, for God's sake, man, move your damned self!'

In five seconds the guns would have completed their traverse. In ten seconds they would be locked back into the forward turret position, on fixed arcs, ready to fire.

'Get back over the mountain,' Wilfred called to Sgt Gosport. 'Saunders, give me that Lee Enfield. Stevenson, that satchel of grenades.'

They knew what he intended.

'We'd rather stay, Captain,' Sgt Gosport said, but Wilfred shook his head.

'No, Sergeant, this is family!' he said.

He waited until they had started down the side of the mountain, and then lobbed the first two grenades. They rolled and bounced fifty feet below the rock where he was crouched. As they exploded, Arthur started his smoke, but the canisters fell short, and the wind carried the smoke behind the tanks' positions. The range of the German mortars lifted, and now they started to cluster immediately below Wilfred's position. If only he could draw that machine-gun away from its forward pointing position! He could see the path to his right, and a gap in the rocks. He went swiftly behind the protection of the rocks to the gap and then sprinted across it. He had reached the far side of it when the sniper's bullet came, missing him by six inches. He crawled back, then ran again. This time, the bullet zipped within inches of his face and another one, from a different direction, snapped behind him. He crawled back, sweat pouring off him, and this time ran doubled over with his rifle poked above him, his hat dangling on the end of the gun.

When he arrived at the other side, there were three

holes through the centre of his cap. He looked over the edge; the second layer of smoke trailed wispily across the front of the tanks; it would be dissipated in a minute in the wind which blew up and across the tank position.

Then he saw Arthur's section rise, and start to run forward.

Wilfred flung himself down, aimed the Lee Enfield at the turret of the first tank, and started to fire, trying to put a round through the slits. It was a vain hope. Now the snipers' rounds were cracking round his position, and the tanks' machine-guns started to fire.

Arthur's section was running forward, their rifles held at waist height, firing blindly as they ran.

Wilfred took his eye from his back-sight and watched helplessly as the section was decimated. He saw the mortar bombs exploding round the tanks though they did little damage. Lt-Col Tockett had ordered the three-inch mortars to fire in support, and Brens from hastily arranged positions poured the high speed hell of their own creation into the tanks' positions. The crackle of explosions, the thunder of shells, the snap and whee of rifle bullets reached a crescendo, and then Wilfred saw his brother hit just as he was approaching that thin wisp of smoke, as tempting but as penetrable as a houri's veil.

The heavy machine-gun round stopped Arthur; he staggered and Wilfred could see his chest was covered with blood.

Sniper bullets hit him, and jerked him first this way and that, refusing to fall.

A mortar bomb exploded a yard in front of him and scattered what was left of him in an explosion of flesh and bone.

Wilfred hadn't realised it, but when the first bullet hit Arthur and stopped him, he had stood up yelling, 'Tha' waited too long, young 'un, tha' waited . . . too . . . bloody . . . long!'

The three sniper bullets that hit Wilfred killed him instantly.

CHAPTER TWELVE

Mark Tockett folded his napkin and replaced it in its silver ring.

'Your Mrs Prendergast is a wonderful find, Elsie,' he said.

Elsie had been worried that when he returned home he would find too many changes in the Tockett way of life but he had been so sombre, doubtless from his experiences in Italy, that he seemed to have little care for the details of domestic routine. She'd been aghast when she'd picked him up at the railway station and he had stepped off the train with his arm in a sling.

'You've been wounded,' she said, 'and you never mentioned a word of it in your letters or on the telephone!'

'It's nothing,' he said, 'not worth mentioning. I only wear the sling occasionally, when my arm is tired.'

The 'nothing' was a deep hole gouged in the flesh of his upper arm alongside his muscle by a mortar splinter. That night, when he'd taken his bath, she'd seen his naked body and had counted the lacerations six months of fighting had given him. She'd stroked every one in an orgy of tenderness, the tears bright in her eyes at the knowledge that men were being made to suffer so much, and yet could survive. Recently she'd started to work each second day in the hospital in Whitby, wheeling round a trolley of tea and biscuits, toffees, sometimes bars of chocolate and cigarettes from the ration they obtained. At least, that was the way it had started. Soon, she'd come to know their names, and had sat with them, to let them talk about their private lives, their hopes and fears. Many had been so badly wounded they'd never walk or work again, and were having immense problems adjusting to the loss of limbs, deafness and, in several terrible cases, blindness. At least, Mark had been able to walk when he'd come back, unlike so many of the poor devils she helped compose difficult letters home.

'You don't mind, then?' she asked.

'Mind what . . . ?'

'June doing the cooking, and Jack turning your flower beds and part of the lawn into the vegetable plot, and keeping sheep, and cows, and all the rabbits and chickens that seem to get everywhere. Oh, and eating in this one room instead of using the breakfast-room and the dining-room, and the black-out curtains instead of the velvet, and having forty-watt bulbs in some of the lights, and the heating turned off . . . '

'And sharing my bath with you . . . !' He reached over and took her hand. 'Elsie,' he said, 'I know how hard all this must have been for you and I'm bound to say I think you've managed marvellously. Anyway, this house is far too big for our requirements. I've been thinking for some time that I might even pull half of it down after the war – we don't need all these rooms so why shouldn't you shut down the ones we don't use? As to the Prendergasts, I think they were a wonderful find. It's so pleasant to see June bustling happily about, instead of sourpuss Netta!'

'And you don't mind not having a cook?'

'Elsie, I don't mind! If June is happy to cook *and* look after the house, so well and good. It's one less person about the place! Do you know that when I lived here as a boy, I could never ever find any privacy. There always seemed to be somebody about, either dusting, or sweeping, or cooking, or doing the garden, or washing the car that was already spotless! I think it's wonderful. For the first time, Tockett House is a home! And not like some damned cold Victorian museum! But you didn't need to lock all the silver away in the vault!' he added, smiling. The Tocketts had always had an eye for silverware and over the years had amassed a considerable collection. Now it was all in the iron-sided vault his grandfather had ordered to be built in a corner of the cellar.

'It was such a responsibility,' Elsie said. 'And, besides, think how much cleaning it took!'

'Well, at least you've left us our napkin rings . . . '

'And the salt and pepper. If you like, Mark, if you want to bring any people here for meals or anything, I'll get it all out and clean it for you . . . '

He squeezed her arm. 'No people for a while, Elsie. After the Godsons have been this evening, nobody but you, me, and Thomas. Dammit, a man has a right to get to know his own son!'

They went from the breakfast-room they now used for all their meals and Elsie called into the kitchen that they'd finished. When they went into the main drawing-room that Elsie had opened specially for Mark's return, the fire was blazing cheerfully with a couple of logs replacing the coal they'd normally be using. Jack Prendergast followed them in, wheeling a trolley on which June had set coffee and milk in the the Meissen jugs, with the Meissen coffee service. Elsie was amused to notice that, in honour of the Master's return, he'd donned the plain black alpaca jacket over a white shirt and a black tie. His black trousers held a knife-edged crease, and his patent leather shoes gleamed.

'Will you be taking cognac or liqueurs, Col Tockett?' he asked formally.

'I think a glass of brandy might fit the bill,' Mark Adam said. 'What about you, Elsie?'

She nodded. 'I'll have the same,' she said, brimming over with happiness that everything seemed to be going so well. She'd been so worried that when Mark Adam returned, after his high life in officers' messes, and being made a Lt-Col, though she still didn't understand why he was called simply, Colonel, he'd discover he'd made a ghastly mistake marrying a common girl from the village. She thought he might be vexed at the changes she'd felt obliged to make, that he might find Prendergast, so obviously untrained as a butler but doing his best, to be a ludicrous figure. But then, she realised, her husband had not been accustomed to seeing Jack Prendergast in any other role, as she had. She'd known June and Jack for many years as casual acquaintances; the sight of him in his alpaca had almost caused *her* to chuckle.

Prendergast withdrew, and she sat next to Mark Adam on the sofa that now faced the fire. With the two massive armchairs on each side of the marble fireplace, it formed an oasis of happiness and comfort. She'd put two small tables by the side of the sofa on which they could rest their coffee cups and glasses; Mark Adam stretched his arms upwards, sighing with contentment, then let out a groan as he felt the pain of his wound.

'You ought to wear your sling more often,' she chided him, but then he brought his arm down and rested it along the cushion behind her neck.

'If I wore that damned sling,' he said, 'I wouldn't be able to put my arm round you, now would I?'

She snuggled into him, happy to sit there quietly for a few minutes, before the Godsons arrived. She'd invited Reuben and Emily to come up for supper but Emily had demurred.

'I don't think Reuben would be very comfortable doing that,' she said. 'Maybe we could come up after supper is over, and just drink a cup of tea or summat, whatever you're having. But don't make anything special. You know how he's been since he got the telegram.'

Both Wilfred and Arthur had listed their father as next

of kin when they were commissioned. The War Office telegrams, announcing their death, had gone to him in the office in which he worked, one of the Planning Sections in Marylebone Road. He was permitted to live out of barracks, and had found a room with a Cypriot family in the Edgware Road. He usually arrived at his desk at eight o'clock – the telegrams were waiting for him, thoughtlessly put in his In-tray by the ATS clerk. He'd ripped them open without realising what they might be, since they constantly received cables from abroad, though usually via the Army Signals Office attached to their section.

'We regret to inform you of the death of your son, Wilfred, killed in action . . . ' The rest of the message was lost in a blur of incomprehension. Reuben picked up the other buff envelope and opened it. 'We regret to inform you of the death of your son, Arthur, killed in action . . . '

He'd sat at his desk, staring into space, unable to believe the evidence of his eyes. He was still sitting there when Sgt-Major Smitherson, the WO1 in charge of the section, arrived.

'Morning, Godson,' he said. 'Didn't get a bloody wink last night! I was down in the tube-station during the raid and a damned woman had hysterics half the . . . Godson, are you all right?'

He walked across the room to Reuben's desk, and reached out to touch his arm.

'Wake up, Godson,' he said. He'd seen it many times, after nights of no sleep, that a man would just simply nod off, with his eyes open sometimes. It didn't take him long to realise Godson hadn't nodded off.

'Maggie,' he bawled, 'fetch us a cup of coffee, jildi!' Not even his bellow, that once had caused men to leap to attention at five hundred yards, could penetrate Reuben's mind, which was in a tight closed circle, whirling constantly round the unacceptable fact – Wilfred, and Arthur, regret to inform you, killed in action . . . Wilfred and Arthur, both dead!

Smitherson looked at Godson's desk and luckily saw, and recognised, the telegrams. He'd had one himself, a couple of years ago. His lad, in North Africa, right after the campaign started. Kid of nineteen in the Tanks.

He drew up a chair and sat there looking at Godson until the coffee arrived. He put it into Godson's hand.

'Drink that, Godson,' he said, 'it'll do you good.' He turned to Maggie. 'How did them bloody telegrams get there?' he asked angrily.

'I put 'em in his In-tray, Sgt-Major, with the rest of the inbound mail.'

He flipped over the envelope. As he had guessed, it was addressed to Sgt-Major R. Godson, M.M., Operations Planning, Section 104.

'They had his bloody name on them, girl!' he said. 'Haven't you learned *nothing*! You only get them buggers if a next of kin is missing or killed. And you put the bloody things in his In-tray!'

Reuben felt the warm mug of coffee in his hand and automatically drank from it. Scalding hot, it shocked him into awareness, and he coughed and put the mug down. For the first time since he'd read the words, he saw his surroundings, the bare office adapted from a room in a hotel in the Marylebone Road, his Army desk and chair, the coconut matting on the floor, the green metal filing cabinets, the charts on the wall. He looked around him as if seeing it all for the first time, as if he had no place in it. He glanced at the lists which had suddenly become meaningless to him – lists of names of men to be moved about like pawns. Lists that came in to them from all the theatres of war, lists they compared with other lists, adding some names, subtracting some names, lists they gave to the pool of typists in the other offices along the floor of this hotel, who presumably typed them and then sent them out somewhere. The whole section, commanded by a Captain of the RASC who had been a bank manager before the war, contained fifty-five people, and was, itself, the subject of yet another list.

'Two of my lads,' he said to Smitherson. 'Dead. Killed in action.'

Smitherson turned to Maggie. 'Get out of here,' he said, 'and shut the bloody door behind you. Don't come back in until I shout for you, right!'

'Right, Sgt-Major,' she said huffily.

He walked across to his personal locker standing against the wall, and took a brown paper carrier bag out of it. From the bag he produced a bottle of Johnnie Walker whisky and a glass. He poured the glass brim-full of the whisky and put it on Godson's desk.

'Drink that, old lad,' he said. 'Then take a few days leave. I'll cover for you. Maggie!' he yelled, but this time he had to wait before she came in. 'I want a travel warrant, return to York, and a month's ration cards.'

'What name?'

'Sgt-Major Godson, R, MM,' he said, 'and get your arse moving!'

'You'd be lucky!' she said as she flounced out.

'And get a motor from the motor pool,' he said, 'and a driver. Front door, soon as you like.'

The whisky and the coffee took Reuben as far as his lodgings and then King's Cross Station. The ten o'clock train was late, and he managed to squeeze on it before it left, thirty minutes after time.

He hadn't telephoned ahead; he could have rung the Post Office to ask them to take a message up to Emily, or asked Ephraim Hardcastle to tell John if he was about, but he'd recovered himself sufficiently not to want to expose Emily to those hours of worrying, wondering why he was coming home unexpectedly. It had been six o'clock when he'd walked into the house. High tide had been at four o'clock, and John had already had his wash and was eating his supper. The two girls were on late shift, and were eating prior to going to Whitby to the factory. Martin had been sitting in his high chair and the sight of the little lad had driven a nail into his heart.

'Well, I never,' Emily had said. 'What's tha' doing home?' she asked. 'Have they given you a bit of extra leave, then?' She'd come across the room and had kissed him on the cheek, hugging him to her. John was clasping his arm, and the girls were crowding round.

'It's grandad,' Martin was shouting, banging his spoon on the tray of the high chair, 'Can I get down, grandad?'

Emily drew back from Reuben, sensing something in his rigidity. He pulled her back towards him and squeezed her tight, his cheek next to hers. Now her fears were confirmed.

'There's summat wrong, isn't there? Your old trouble, come back again? What is it, Reuben? Nay, come and sit by t' fire and have a cup of tea afore you get into it. Anne, take your dad's case up to our bedroom. Liz, finish giving our Martin his dinner. Come on, stir yourselves.'

She bustled them about briskly, and led Reuben across the room to his chair.

'Sit thysen down,' she said. 'John, pour a pot of tea for your dad.'

Though it was June, the fire had been lit but, with only a handful of coals in the bottom of the grate, it didn't give out much heat. He held out his hands and watched John mash the teapot again from the kettle that, blackened with age and use, stood always on the hob. His mind flicked back to the last war, when he was seventeen years old and, just like John, keeping the family going by running the *Hope*. His father, Silas, and his four brothers had all been away at war. His mother, Hannah, had been sitting by the fire when the telegrams came. Three of them together!

Three of his four brothers, Martyn, John, and Alan, all killed together. And now this. He drank the tea his son John had given him, then turned to Liz.

In some way it was easier to tell Liz rather than to face Emily and tell her, or face John.

'Liz, you'd better come and stand by your mam,' he said, 'I've brought bad news for her about our Wilfred and our Arthur.'

'Wilfred *and* Arthur,' Emily said at once.

He turned back to her. 'Aye, lass,' he said, 'both of 'em.'

'Gone . . . ?'

'I'm afraid so, lass. They've both gone!'

'Gone, *both* gone?' she said incredulously, her face wrinkling with disbelief.

'Tha'll have to face it, lass! Both of them. Killed in action . . . ' The sentence ended in a high pitched wail, and he buried his head in his hands, tears streaming from his eyes. John put his arm round him, and hugged him tight; Liz and Anne stood beside their mam, their hands round her waist. Both were crying and only Emily and John stood, stoically dry-eyed. Emily knew she'd cry later, in the privacy of her bedroom; right now her husband and her two girls needed all of her strength.

'Somebody will have to let Georgina know,' she said, 'in the Naval Mission in Washington. I wonder how we go about that . . . ?'

'We can send a telegram, Mam,' John said. 'She told me that if we heard we were to send her a telegram right away. Shall I go down to t' post office and knock on t' back door?'

'Nay, lad, you'd best stay wi' your dad. Anne can go with me. Liz, stir yourself and make a bit of supper for your dad. I don't know how long it'll take me down there.'

She put on her coat and, clutching her purse in her hand, set off with Anne down the cobbled street.

John put his arm round his dad's shoulders.

'Come on, Dad,' he said, 'let's take thee upstairs for a bit of a swill. It'll make you feel better.'

Suddenly, Liz was alone in the room. She sat on one of the chairs at the table looking vacantly towards the fire. This was something *she* understood. Family receives telegram announcing death of son. Grief. Tears. Survivors comforting each other, or being brave, holding back their tears. Cut to shot of inside of church, everybody in black, Vicar reading Bible and saying, The Lord Giveth, the Lord Taketh Away. She buried her head in her hands, wailing, 'Pete, oh Pete, don't get killed, don't get killed, will you?'

Elsie had been waiting for the sound of their voices in the hall, and immediately went out to greet them.

'Come in, Reuben, come in, Emily,' she said.

Emily was wearing her Sunday best, and Reuben his uniform, though with shoes instead of boots, and no gaiters. He had an open neck to his battle dress jacket, and was wearing a tie. The thin ribbon of his Military Medal and bar stood out against the dull khaki.

'Aye, come in, Reuben, come in, Emily,' Mark Tockett said. 'Come and sit by the fire. The evening's turned chilly for June.'

Now that they had come, Mark Tockett was ill-at-ease. He saw Reuben looking round the room and remembered the number of times he'd come up here to confront Mark's father, James Henry Tockett.

'You'll notice a number of changes since my father's time,' he said.

Reuben nodded. 'This always was a bit of a dark room,' he said. 'It seems to me you've lightened it a bit.'

Mark laughed. 'We took out a ton of massive dark

furniture,' he said. 'You could never walk round the room for all the old mahogany. And Mrs Tockett has changed all the curtains.'

It was a shock for Emily to hear him refer to Elsie as Mrs Tockett but she read it as a sign of the social distinction between them. Mark Adam Tockett would refer to her by her Christian name, but he'd expect *his* wife to be Mrs Tockett to all of them. She knew it wasn't snobbishness but the natural order of things. Even Eleanor these days called Elsie Mrs Tockett, and didn't use her Christian name, even though Elsie had asked her several times to do so.

'I seem to remember the pictures were different,' Reuben said.

'I didn't like all those gloomy ancestral portraits,' Elsie said cheerfully. 'They always seemed to be watching me everywhere I went!' Now the walls were hung with landscape paintings, mostly woodland scenes, but there were a couple of impressive dramatic sea-scapes by Ethel Walker. 'You've heard we've got a painter in Old Quaytown,' she said.

Reuben nodded. 'I've seen him down in the Snug a time or two. That Bartlett cottage has stood empty too long since we pulled Bartlett ashore off the beck in 1938.'

Emily's eyes misted over at the mention of Bartlett's death, reminding her of her own tragic loss. She'd cried enough that night Reuben had brought the news to last a lifetime and had fallen asleep long after dawn praising God that Reuben was no longer on active service and that fishermen, like her son John, were still on the list of reserved occupations.

'It's good of you to ask us up,' she said to Mark Tockett, hoping to get on with things. She hadn't come to hear a lot of chit-chat about painters, and furniture. She sipped her port, delicately, and put it down again, waiting for Mark Tockett to speak.

'Yes, well,' he said. 'It was good of you to come. You know I want to talk to you about your lads. It's a two-sided affair. I want you to know how it was at the end, and to tell you they both died quickly, and also to salve my own conscience. Since they were two of my own officers, I feel a sense of responsibility for them. I want to tell you that I didn't neglect them, that they didn't die through any carelessness of mine, through any error on my part that could have been avoided. I've written a lengthy report about Wilfred; it's my belief that the War Office might very well make him a posthumous award for his bravery.'

'Aye, he was a brave one, our Wilfred,' Reuben said quietly. For the first time in months, he saw eyes again, the eyes of the men pleading to let them on to the boat. He saw the eyes of his own son, Arthur, and those of Wilfred, telling him to go, forgiving him for going and leaving them behind on the beaches of Dunkirk.

'Our Arthur . . . ?' Emily asked quickly, 'what about him?'

'He died, Emily, in the line of duty. It was his duty to attack an enemy position and he did it. He was killed outright when a bullet hit him. He died at once . . . '

'And Wilfred . . . ?'

'He'd volunteered for a dangerous assignment, to try to take some of the pressure of the assault away from his brother. It was a brave thing to do, and he did it voluntarily.'

'To try to protect Arthur?'

Mark Tockett nodded. There was no point in blackening Arthur's name, in telling them it was their son's own fault he'd been killed, and that he'd taken a lot of good men to their deaths with him as a result. He knew, in fact, that a large measure of blame should rest on himself. He ought to have ignored Wilfred's pleadings and kicked Arthur out of the battalion, back to some administrative job where he wouldn't endanger men's lives by his over-caution, somewhere his total absorption in detail would have served him and the Army in good stead as an administrator. Arthur never was, and never could be, a fighter, a front-line man, an independent driving force capable, as his brother Wilfred was, of leading other men with dash and verve.

'Aye, I knew it'd be like that,' she said. 'He always looked after him.' She could remember so many times during their childhood when Wilfred had protected his brother, when he'd stuck up for him in family disputes, when he'd shielded him from Reuben's fatherly wrath. When Arthur had chucked the anchor overboard that one time, Wilfred said it was he who had untied it, and took Reuben's skelping. She wouldn't have known if she hadn't heard the two lads going on about it in the baiting shed, when they didn't know she could hear them, and Wilfred saying – if you do that again, I'll skelp you myself and not wait for dad! She remembered the number of times Wilfred had helped Arthur with his school homework and, when they went to the Grammar School together, how he'd coached the younger lad, night after night, even neglecting his own homework. Many a time, she'd come down the stairs and found Wilfred asleep over his books, trying to catch up on the time he'd given willingly to his brother.

Only one thing remained to puzzle her. Knowing what she had about the relationship between Wilfred and Arthur and the way Arthur many times, with that cheeky grin on his face, took advantage of it, how had it come about that she had been more fond of Arthur? She had to admit that he'd been her favourite among the boys! Especially since Amos had died when he was six years old. Could it be that she realised Arthur would *need* somebody to favour him? That Wilfred, a true Godson, needed nobody since he had the Godson family strength to see him through? And John seemed the same way inclined? Even facially, Arthur had more resembled the Ducketts than the Godsons. As he'd grown older he'd begun to look more and more like her dad rather than a Godson. Could it be that? A Duckett and not a true Godson? Anne was a Godson, certainly, and Liz a Duckett. How had it come about that she'd had two Ducketts in succession . . . ?

'I hope I needn't tell you,' Mark Adam Tockett was saying, 'how sorry I am about your two sons. If there had been anything I could have done, believe me, I would have done it.' He hated himself as the words came from his lips, but felt they were better said for the benefit of Reuben and his wife.

'You musn't grieve yourself over that side of it,' Reuben said. 'This whole damned war is a mess, and there's no greater tragedy than the loss, the useless loss, of so many lives. We all will have to learn to accept our losses and try to carry on as best we can.'

Mark Tockett held out his hand and Reuben shook it formally, before he and Emily started off from the house along Cliff Top to Old Quaytown awaiting them below. They didn't speak as they walked. Emily looked down and over the roof-tops of the old village clinging to the side of the steep cliffs; she looked out over the sea, her mind flooding with memories of the twenty-odd years of her marriage, her child-bearing, her motherhood. When they reached the top of Newquay Town, she put her hand in Reuben's. 'It used to be such a marvellous place,' she said, 'when you and I looked down on it as a young lad and lass. It always seemed to me to be the only place in the world I could ever imagine myself to be. But now, I don't know. Sometimes I get the fancy to go far away, anywhere, to leave it all behind somehow . . . '

'We're lucky, Emily,' he said, his hand clenching

around hers. 'We've still got three of 'em left. A bit of money in t' bank. And t' *Hope*.'

'Nay, Reuben, tha's forgetting. We've got our Martin, our grandson. Wilfred will never be lost to us . . . !'

'Happen tha's right, lass,' he said, 'at least, till Georgina comes home.'

They walked along in silence for a couple of hundred yards, both thinking about Martin, and Georgina. Emily missed not having Georgina around; she seemed to have struck up a stronger relationship with her than with either of her own two daughters. Of course it would be different when the two girls were married and started families, though she had resigned herself to them travelling far away with their husbands. She was heartily sick of Liz's American affectations – she'd even begun to speak, it seemed to Emily, with an American accent picked up from the cinema, and to use American expressions Emily couldn't understand, though she guessed the girl got them from the current spate of popular songs that everybody was singing on the noisy wireless. She cursed the day Reuben had bought the wireless; she had to chuckle, sometimes, at the comic programmes they put on, though she couldn't understand half of them. And she did like to hear Gracie Fields singing, and George Formby, though she couldn't stand that Vera Lynn. Hopefully Georgina, as Wilfred's widow, would live in the house with them once she came out of the WRNs. That way, they'd keep Martin! Her heart ached to think that one day Georgina might marry again and take Martin away to her new home and husband. She felt a shiver of apprehension at the thought that Georgina, a widow in Washington DC, America – wherever that might be – might meet some American over there and not come back, except to take Martin to a foreign land.

'We'd better make t' most of it, Reuben,' she said, not

realizing she was speaking thoughts Reuben wouldn't understand.

'Most of what, lass?' he asked.

'Most of our Martin being with us.'

He didn't understand what she meant, but said, 'Happen tha's right,' to placate her obvious anxiety.

He was still seeing faces; they hadn't left him since the Tocketts. He was walking along, seeing Arthur's face, seeing Wilfred telling him by that well known gesture to go, then seeing the rope he'd thrown, and the looks on the faces of the other lads as he'd towed his own lads, and Tockett, through them.

'I'll be getting back down south tomorrow,' he said, 'getting back to work.'

Perhaps down there, in London, he'd forget the faces again, and see only lists of names that didn't mean anything to him . . . !

'Your stuff's all ready,' she said, 'except I've got your clean socks hanging to dry. I'll need to run t' iron over them!'

CHAPTER THIRTEEN

A number of US troops had moved into camp on the moors, and many of them came into the village of Ravenswyke, attracted by its old world charm. They brought cameras with them and photographed all the buildings. They brought jeeps and parked them by the boats at the top of the Slip, carried their cigarettes in cartons, and bottles of spirits in their pockets. They flowed over all the streets of Old Quaytown, looking innocently in through the windows, accepting invitations to 'come inside, lad, but wipe thy feet!' with alacrity. Once inside they produced packets of gum, talked often in words and ways the locals couldn't understand, but were disciplined and well-behaved.

At first they refused the food they were offered, since they knew rationing, that autumn of 1944, was tight but then, tempted by the appetising odour of home-made stews cooking in old pots by the fireside, they'd succumb and accept a plateful. Mostly the meat was scrag-end, bones, pigs' feet, tripe bits, cowheel, but this was the fare that had fattened generations of thrifty Yorkshire folk, and the housewives knew how to cook it to perfection. And they never went into too much detail when asked what it was! From the first spoonful, friendships started to develop, and soon almost every family in Old Quaytown seemed to have adopted at least a couple of 'Yanks', as they called them. Even Connie Cathcart, forgetting her perpetual illnesses, had adopted a couple. There were the inevitable scandals, of course. Phil

Mountjoy's wife, it was said, was giving her two 'Yanks' rather more than stew while her husband was away in the Navy. Betty Johnson, the grocer's daughter, was reportedly seen on the scaurs at night-time low-tide on a warm September evening, and reports had it she wasn't studying marine biology with her companion, an American negro.

The once a week socials in the Chapel Rooms became a sell-out, with girls coming into Ravenswyke from all the surrounding villages, and queues of American soldiers outside trying to get past Captain Walham who, despite his advanced years, stood guard on the door like a Beefeater.

'No pass-outs,' he said. 'Once you're in, you stay in!'

Many people used to come early, meet up with a companion for the evening, and then take a stroll through the village streets out on to the scaurs if the tide happened to be low. Many brought a bottle with them, and used to lace the lemonade, Tizer, dandelion and burdock drinks Captain Walham served, with something a little more stimulating to their girl companions. It didn't take long for Captain Walham to realize why young girls would arrive sober, drink Tizer all evening, and leave on the arm of a soldier in a state of intoxication.

He was sitting in his house in Grinklegate one evening in January, 1945, when he heard a knock at the door. He opened it to admit an American officer.

'Major Bernstein,' the officer said. 'I was looking for Captain Wal-ham's residence.'

The officer had jet black skin.

'You've found him, Major,' Captain Walham said, 'but my name's Walham pronounced Wallam, not Walham pronounced Wall-ham. You'd better come inside – you don't want lessons in English pronunciation on the doorstep.'

Major Bernstein whistled as he walked around. The Captain's home was maintained with the same loving care he'd always lavished on the vessels under his command, with every piece of brass burnished bright, every wooden surface gleaming with polish.

'My, what a lovely home you have, Captain,' he said in admiration and respect.

'I'm glad you like it; a bachelor like myself can soon let himself go if he's not careful. What'll you take to drink . . . ?'

'Not that dandelion and burdock,' Major Bernstein said, smiling.

'I wasn't offering dandelion and burdock. That's amply strong enough for young lasses, but not much use to grown men. I'm taking a pink gin myself.'

'I'll have the same . . . '

'Good. I was afraid you were going to ask me for one of those cocktails. Apart from a Planter's Punch I learned when we were loading cargo in Trinidad, and a gin sling they taught me in Singapore, I haven't much in the way of a cocktail repertoire.' He mixed two pink gins, brought a chair closer to the window, and invited his guest to sit down, looking out over the scaurs. It was middle tide, and soon the water would be all the way out. Already couples were walking on the slate shelves, bending over to look into pools formed between the stones at the vast variety of crabs and mussels, limpets, waving fronds of marine life. The Captain chuckled.

'Many a lass has lost her virginity, I'll be bound, by starting to show your lads the marine life for which this little spot is rightly famous. When I walked out the other morning before the tide came back in, I must have passed a dozen French letters! I'm too old now; ten years ago I'd have been out there with my shotgun, but now I realise it's as natural as the changing seasons.'

'You don't resent it?' Major Bernstein asked. 'Americans coming in here to deflower the prime of English womanhood?'

'I don't resent it at all. Up until 1939 I read the Bible every day, said my prayers, threatened everyone with fire and brimstone if they transgressed. Now I think I've become a lot more tolerant. If you knew the number of them who climb my wall looking for solitude, and hear me barking at them like an old seal!'

'If I may say so, Captain, you seem a very tolerant kind of man.'

Captain Walham chuckled. 'Don't let anyone in Ravenswyke hear you say that. You'll ruin my reputation in the Chapel. All my life I've been a Bible thumper, a hell-fire-and-brimstone preacher, and now in the evening of my life I seem to have run out of brimstone. We're sending lads away to foreign parts to fight and die; we're breaking up families, separating loved ones. In the face of all that, Major, how can I begrudge the young ones a bit of human contact, a bit of loving? And if the only way they know how to make contact is to copulate like animals in the field, well, we're all animals before we become human beings, aren't we? Anyway, you haven't called on me to hear the ramblings of a dissolute old man, a reformed preacher who's finally found a little human compassion . . . '

'I'm glad to hear that, Captain. The bit about compassion. I had thought we'd have a problem together but I guess we're going to get along just fine! My job in the camp is sort-of Welfare Officer. What I'm going to tell you is strictly under wraps, if that's okay by you?'

'If you mean you want to consult me about a matter that must remain confidential, then it is – okay by me – as you say.' Captain Walham's chuckle took away any suggestion of condescension. 'I presume it concerns one of your men?'

'Yes, Captain, it does. And one of your girls . . . '

'*My* girls. Come, I can hardly lay claim to proprietorial rights on them. Not in my bachelor condition!'

'I mean, one of the girls of the village.'

'Let's get down to cases, shall we?' Captain Walham's manner had become impersonal and brisk; he half suspected what was coming.

'I hardly know if I can . . . '

'Come on, Major,' Captain Walham said impatiently. 'You have my word it shall go no further.'

'Do you know a girl called Anne Godson?'

'Yes, I do.' Captain Walham's face showed none of the astonishment he felt. Anne Godson . . . ! Reuben Godson's daughter!

'Anne Godson has just told one of my men, Don Meaney, that she's pregnant. She says he is the only man who's ever had relations with her.'

'You can believe that, one hundred per cent,' Captain Walham said immediately. 'I've known the family ever since I came here to Grinklegate. They're one of the oldest families in Old Quaytown. Her father is the leader of the fishing community, a fine man who's earned a Military Medal with bar. They've just awarded his son, Wilfred, a posthumous Military Cross. The girl is not a wanton.'

'God forbid anyone is suggesting that, Captain. I just didn't know the girl. If she'd been some kind of tart, well, I wouldn't be concerned. I wouldn't be talking to you right now. Look, let me lay the cards on the table. Don Meaney's a good guy, and he knows he's done wrong. Seems he was spiking the girl's drink with whisky and she never cottoned on. When he went outside with her, the fresh air and the booze hit her, and they came down here on the – what do you call it . . . ?'

'The scaurs.'

'The scaurs. Well, Captain, he's a full-blooded young guy, one thing led to another, and she wasn't resisting . . . '

'And he raped her . . . ?'

'Well, let's not get into legal definitions, eh, Captain?

He took her. Now, he knows what he did was wrong. He told me they had a good thing going, and she told him about her fiancé who's in the US Army in Europe, and he feels kind-of lousy because he knocked up a decent girl who's the sweetheart of a brother soldier.'

'And so he should!' Captain Walham said. 'That's a pretty rotten story you've just told me. Oh, I know earlier that I implied a certain loosening of sexual morality, but I can't condone the deliberate use of alcohol or force as a means of seduction. By any standards, that is a heathenous, disgraceful act. I hope there are means to punish this young rotter?'

'My thoughts are with the girl, Captain,' Major Bernstein said mildly. 'Apparently, she hasn't seen her boy-friend since April of 1944. She talked to Don Meaney about killing herself! That's why I came at once to see you. I figured she needs help. Punishing the bastard who did it is something we can talk about later, it seems to me.'

Captain Walham wiped his hand over his face. 'Sorry, Major,' he said. 'My age and choler are showing. As one gets older, one tends to forget the need for priority. You're quite right, of course. The girl comes first.'

'You'll go to see her . . . ?'

'I'll work out what is the best thing to do in the circumstances, and make my decision accordingly . . . ?'

'That's all I can ask,' Major Bernstein said. 'I see you're on the phone here. May I call you, Captain?'

'Give me a ring tomorrow,' Captain Walham said.

When the Major had left, Captain Walham sat by the window, thinking about Anne Godson, realizing what a personal hell she must be going through. He was also thinking about himself and his changed attitudes. It had been all too easy to accept a laissez-faire attitude about the changes in personal morality the war had brought about with its separations, its lonelinesses, its increased mobility meaning people were not in one place for very long and not, therefore, accountable to the community. This American boy would doubtless be drafted to fight in Europe very soon and be lost among the many hundreds of thousands of men who'd passed through England, whereas Anne Godson had to live here, to face people with a bastard in a pram. Certainly, if there was any risk of her killing herself, he ought to see her as soon as possible, to let her know she had at least one friend she could turn to.

Possibly that sister of hers, now calling herself Liz, could help? Though he recognised her as a flighty young thing, of no great emotional or intellectual depth.

He knew the knowledge of his daughter's pregnancy would hurt Reuben badly. In his present condition, in and out of hospital, it could possibly flip Reuben on to the other side of reason. Emily, of course, would accept the situation with her usual stoicism, Captain Walham knew, doing her best for Anne in her moment of trouble.

John. John Godson. Perhaps *he* could help Captain Walham?

But, having given his word, did he have the right to disclose Anne's secret to her brother? He quickly decided he didn't have that right, not without seeing the girl first.

Ah, he knew how to do it. He knew a way. He elaborated on his scheme as he pulled on his boots, his pea-jacket, and his woollen hat, and left the warmth of his home to climb the icy cobbles into Old Quaytown.

Emily Godson opened the door of their cottage to him and exclaimed in surprise.

'Captain Walham,' she said, 'what on earth brings you out on a night like this?'

'An old man's whim,' he said as he stepped past her into the warm living-room. John, sitting in his chair by the fire reading the *Gazette*, got up when he saw the Captain.

'Nay, this is no night for you to be out, Captain,' he said. 'Come and sit by the fire.'

Anne and Liz were sitting at the table, playing a game of ludo, and Emily had obviously set her knitting down to answer the door. She helped him out of his jacket and hung it behind the door with his hat. He smoothed the few strands of silver hair across his head and accepted the chair John had offered, pressing his hands towards the fire. The girls had said a 'good-evening' to him as he'd come in, but it was hardly likely he had come to see them.

'Will you take anything,' John asked. 'A glass of whisky?'

'Nay, lad, whisky's hard to come by these days. Save it for yourselves . . . '

John smiled. 'I've a bit put by,' he said, tapping the side of his nose. 'The Godsons aren't an old smuggling family for nowt!'

'Nay, John, whatever will the Captain think!' Emily protested. 'Happen he'd prefer a cup of tea?'

'If you were thinking of putting a spoonful of whisky into it, I shouldn't say no,' he said. 'The cold gets into your bones, at my age.'

When Captain Walham had taken his first gulp of the hot, steaming, and fortified liquid and the cherry-red colour had returned to his cheeks, he glanced at the two girls playing ludo at the table before turning back to Emily.

'The reason I've come,' he said, 'is an old man's whim. I've got a few things down there I'd like sorting out. Papers, photographs, souvenirs, that sort of thing. Well, I started on them myself and have got them into a dreadful muddle. I was wondering if your Anne would give me an hour of her time to help me get back to rights again . . . ?'

Anne was sitting listlessly at the table and seemed not to have heard the Captain's words.

'The Captain's talking about *you*, our Anne,' Liz said, giving her sister's arm a shove. 'You got cloth ears or summat?'

'Eh?' Anne said, 'what's that?'

'I've never known anybody as dozy as thee!' Liz said. 'Captain Walham wants you to help him with his papers . . . '

'Papers? What papers . . . '

Emily spoke sharply across the room. 'Anne, don't be so discourteous to the Captain. He's walked all the way up the street in this weather to ask you to help him sort some papers. The least you could do is pay attention. You'll have to excuse her, Captain,' she added. 'I think she spends her time day-dreaming about that chap of hers.'

'It's hard for the young ones, being separated . . .' he said, kindly.

'It's hard for us older ones, too, but we don't go mooning about the place!' Emily retorted. The Captain looked at her – he'd never known Emily be so snappy, so much on edge, especially with her family.

'If it wouldn't be too much trouble for you, my dear,' Captain Walham said to Anne. 'You'd be doing me a great service.'

'I'd be happy to . . . ' Anne said. 'When do you want me . . . ?'

'Could you possibly manage right away? I've spread everything out, and it's such a mess I can't get round it.'

'Shall I come, as well?' Liz asked, happy to have any kind of diversion.

'That's very kind of you, my dear, but I don't think there'd be the room for *three* of us. We'd be treading on each other's toes all the time.'

'Oh, all right. I think I'll go up and listen to the wireless, anyway,' she said. 'It's ITMA tonight.' Tommy Handley's radio show, It's That Man Again, had gained instant popularity among young and old alike, though Liz preferred Jack Benny, or Starlight Ballroom, from America.

Captain Walham and Anne walked down the street in silence through the cold evening air laden with heavy sea-mist. Anne pointed her torch at the ground so that the Captain could see the path ahead, her arm linked in his. He, who'd always been able to talk to anybody at any time, found himself tongue-tied and couldn't think of anything to say that mightn't lead to the premature disclosure of his knowledge of her pregnancy. He'd been so relieved to hear Major Bernstein's account of how it had all happened, to know that Anne was free of guilt in the matter. If this American rotter had spiked her drinks without her knowing, then she was hardly to blame, was she? The next day, he resolved, he'd ring his solicitor in Whitby. Thrummell should be able to tell him if a civil action could be brought against the chap. He was afraid, however, that the Americans would do what he'd done a couple of times with his chaps in the Navy. He'd put them on the first train for another port when they'd got into trouble, to avoid the possibility of a police prosecution.

'What's happened to all the papers?' Anne asked in surprise when they entered his sitting room. 'I thought you said they were spread all over the place?'

They'd taken off their coats in the lobby; Captain Walham poked the fire into brighter flames then turned to look at the girl. 'That was just my way of getting you out of the house,' he said. 'I want you to sit down while we have a little talk together.'

She sat down, completely baffled but prepared to humour him. She'd known him all her life; he wasn't like other men in Ravenswyke. Somehow he had the refinement of the people, or some of the people, at the top of the Bank, but none of their airs and graces. She'd always thought of him as some sort of perennial grandfather.

He looked at her, seeing a pretty girl of twenty-two, well, a young woman really! She was wearing plain brown shoes, a brown tweed skirt, and a rayon blouse with long sleeves over which she'd put a fawn cardigan. Her hair looked soft and well cared for, and she'd obviously dashed a touch of lipstick on her lips before they came out. Only her eyes revealed to him the troubled nature of her thoughts; they were dark shadowed, as if she hadn't been getting enough sleep. Her hands twitched nervously, restless in her lap. He sat down to make himself a less imposing, less frightening figure.

'Anne,' he said firmly, 'I want you to listen to me and not interrupt me until I finish. Will you do that?'

'Of course,' she said, still thinking in terms of papers, mementoes, souvenirs. Was he going to tell her a story of some part of his life? Reveal something about himself he didn't want others to know? If so, why had he chosen her? She knew he'd always had a soft spot for her over Liz, had always given her toffees from his pocket when he'd met her by the Slip, or a mint humbug. But it was nothing more than he did to many of the young people of Old Quaytown . . . His first words, therefore, were all the more shocking since they were so totally unexpected.

'Anne, I know what has happened between that American, Don Meaney, and yourself. I know you have reason to believe you're going to bear his baby. But I also know the circumstances of *how* it happened, and I think you have nothing with which to reproach yourself. Except, perhaps, foolish naivety!'

She looked at him, stony-faced. How could he possibly know. How could *he*, of all people, possibly know?

'How do *you* know?' she asked, the question bursting rudely from her lips.

'I know,' he said, 'because Mr Meaney apparently did

the decent thing and went to talk with his Welfare Officer, to see if anything could be done. His Welfare Officer very sensibly came to see me, knowing my connection with the Chapel and the Socials. Now, I want to ask you a couple of questions which may be embarrassing for you, but I need to know the answers to clear my own mind. Firstly, do you want me to help you?'

'Oh yes, oh yes!' Anne said impulsively, near to tears but managing to hold them back. 'It'd be a great relief to have somebody to turn to.'

'Good. Now, secondly, will you promise me you won't do anything foolish . . . '

'Oh, that,' she said. 'He took me too seriously when I said I feel like killing myself! I didn't mean it like that, but he thought I did. He was dreadfully worried . . . '

'And quite right he should be,' the Captain said crisply. 'I shall get on to him later. Next question, and this might be the one that embarrasses you. The Major who came to see me implied that you didn't know what was going on at the time. He says that this young chap put something in your drink to make you drunk, some sort of whisky in the Tizer you were drinking. Think about it very carefully,' he said. 'A lot may depend on what you say.'

Anne looked down into her lap, watching her hands twist and untwist themselves.

'Did he put something in your drink, when you weren't looking, Anne?' Captain Walham asked.

Anne couldn't speak.

'Did he?' Captain Walham persisted.

She nodded.

He sat back and sighed with satisfaction. In that case, it couldn't be the girl's fault, could it? That devil of an American had made her drunk, and then had taken advantage of her.

'Good,' he said, 'that's that. Now we can start to think

about the practicalities. And for that, we shall need the advice of Thrummell.'

Anne looked up quickly. 'You're not going to tell Mr Thrummell?' she asked fearfully. 'He knows our Aunt Eleanor.'

'Don't you worry, my dear. Talking to a solicitor is the same as talking to your doctor. Neither of them is permitted to disclose conversations; their professional codes of ethics are very clear about that.'

'I can't see why we have to talk to a solicitor . . . '

'Anne, I think the law will show that the American *raped* you. It's an offence at law to get your own way by deception or trickery, by the use of drugs like alcohol. I'm not exactly certain of the law, and that's why we need Mr Thrummell. But, first of all, we need to see a doctor.'

'Oh, Captain Walham, I couldn't . . . !'

'I'm afraid you *must*, Anne. Before we can proceed any further, we must establish one fact – that you are medically pregnant!'

For once Liz was the first ready for work.

'Come on, our Anne,' she said, 'if you don't get a move on we're going to miss the bus! And I want to get my sweet ration while he still has chocolate!'

'You go on first, then,' Anne said. 'I'll catch you up.'

Emily looked at both her daughters through narrowed eyes. Anne had been dithering about ever since she got up. When Liz had left the house, she took her opportunity of being alone with Anne, since John was already out and Martin was still in bed.

'Anne,' she said, 'there's nowt wrong, is there? You know, if there's owt wrong, you only have to come to me . . . '

'Nay, Mam, there's nowt wrong. I just can't find my bag . . . '

'It's on t' sideboard, where you put it when you came

downstairs!' She held her daughter's arm and looked into her face. 'You know you could come to me, if owt was wrong, don't you . . . ?'

Anne turned her eyes away. 'Nay, Mam, don't keep going on about nothing. I'm all right. Stomach's a bit upset – I don't know why. I suppose it's the lousy food in the canteen. I think I'll go up to the surgery tonight when I come home from work.'

'Yes, why don't you do that,' Emily said drily. 'I heard you being sick this morning . . . '

'It's all them baked beans they give us that don't agree with me . . . '

'You want to be careful. It could be something much worse. Anyway, go and see Doctor Thwaite – he'll know what's wrong with you . . . '

She wanted to add, and so do I, but the girl would have to tell her, sooner or later. Sooner or later, everybody would have to know!

Sgt-Major Smitherson pushed open the door of the Saloon bar and went in, bringing Reuben Godson in with him.

'I think you'll like this place,' he said, 'they keep a good pint of beer here, I've always found.'

When Reuben had returned from leave, Smitherson had greeted him with the news that there was a spare room in the house in which he was lodging, in Warwick Gardens. It was near enough for them to be able to walk to the office and back home when the buses weren't running, as sometimes happened during air-raids. Reuben accepted the offer; he hadn't looked forward to going back to the Cypriot's house, with its perpetual brood of kids and relations making noises. The room Smitherson had found for him, on the fifth floor and very quiet, was larger than the room he'd had at the Cypriot's, and cleaner. The landlady of the boarding house, a spinster of sixty or so, worked part-time at Liberty's shop in Regent Street. The rent included a hot breakfast which they took in the back room of the basement overlooking the gardens, and a hot dinner.

'Just plain English cooking, Sgt-Major,' she'd said. He was grateful to change from the Cypriot's fare with its constant oil, moussaka, bits of salad things, chicken burned one side and smeared with tomato on the other. 'My husband was a military gentleman in peace-time,' the landlady, Mrs Posson, said. 'I know what soldiers like . . . '

Smitherson had winked at Reuben and joked. 'Shame on you, Mrs Posson. Know what soldiers like, do you . . . '

He'd told Reuben that she was a decent old stick. 'You can pull her leg,' he'd said, 'because she's got a nice sense of humour!'

She'd tapped him lightly on the arm. 'I don't think we're talking about the same thing, Sgt-Major,' she'd said, laughing.

'*I'm* talking about food, Mrs Posson,' he'd replied seriously. 'I don't know what *you* might have had in mind . . . !'

Reuben had felt instantly at home – most of the other lodgers turned out to be military, one way and another, most working in some branch of the War Office and boarding out. Since he'd received the telegrams, Smitherson and he had struck up a warmer relationship, both in the office and out, and had taken to spending their off-duty evenings together. Smitherson was married, with two surviving daughters, both in the ATS. His wife was working in a hospital canteen in Bristol and he travelled down there on every possible leave or week-end pass.

'I can't stand these buggers,' he said to Reuben when they were sitting with their pints in the corner of the Saloon Bar in the pub at the end of Warrington Crescent. He indicated three RASC men sitting against the far wall with three ATS girls. One of the men was wearing a thick gold wedding band and the girl he was cuddling was young enough to be his daughter. 'Probably got good wives back home and yet they mess about with the young ones!' Smitherson said.

'Aye, it's not seemly,' Reuben said, though Smitherson could tell his attention was elsewhere. He knew Reuben was an intensely private person, and had no wish to spoil a friendship he was coming to value by being too intrusive. He knew how much the loss of his two lads had upset Reuben and then, one evening, a week after he'd come back, Reuben had told him about the eyes.

'Bloody hell,' he'd said, 'that must be rotten to live with, day and night. I never knew you had anything like that bothering you.' Since then he'd tried several times to introduce into the conversation the subject of an NCO's responsibilities to the men under him, trying to console Reuben with the knowledge that often a man who leads other men must watch them die, must abandon them to their fate in order to protect the majority of his men. 'That's what most people don't realize,' he said. 'When you have a company, they're yours. You have charge of them. Of course, the company commander and the officers lead them, but it takes a good Sgt-Major to get them through. And I reckon with that boat of yours, both at Dieppe and Dunkirk, from what you've told me you did your best! And no man can do more than that.'

It had been a hard task to console Reuben, to cajole him out of the trough of black despair into which he so often sank.

'I don't know why you bother with me, Smithy,' Reuben had said a couple of times. 'I must be rotten company for you.'

Smitherson didn't mind; he was a quiet man who didn't crave the companionship of wildly extraverted people; he couldn't stand the constant jokes, the high jinks, the wild gaiety that so many people seemed to plunge into in London when they were off duty. Of course, he could understand how a man on leave, with nowhere else but London and a room in a Transit Camp hotel, would be out on the town every night, off to the Hammersmith Palais or the Lyceum to try to pick up a girl, but men who lived and worked in London, he felt, ought to behave a bit more quietly. For many people the war in London was one mammoth non-stop party, a round of gaiety that no amount of bombs and air-raids could stop. Eat, drink, and be merry for tomorrow we may be dead! Smitherson intended to live. The war was an interruption of his life, which would start again when peace was declared and he could go home to his missis.

'I'd rather have you for company, old lad, than a bunch of idiots like that lot over there . . . ' He pointed to the party of six who were now half drunk, laughing outrageously at the end of every story they were telling in sequence. All, from the sound of the sniggering laughter of the girls, dirty stories.

One of the girls got up and came across the room to go to the lavatory. The buttons of her shirt were undone and she was revealing a pink, civilian, brassiere beneath her army shirt. Her hat was askew on the back of her head, and she had the out-of-focus look of someone well on the way to drunkenness.

She fumbled with the knob of the door of the ladies before she could get it open.

'One of my girls looked like that,' Smitherson said, 'I'd tan her backside.'

Reuben had looked at the girl crossing the room and his face had clouded again. 'You have a couple of girls, haven't you, Reuben?' Smitherson asked.

Reuben nodded.

'Then you'll know what I mean.'

The girl came out of the lavatory, fumbled the door

closed and turned, overbalancing and cannoning into their table.

'Get away from here, you damned slut!' Reuben said savagely. Smitherson looked at him in surprise – he'd never heard Reuben talk like that before.

'Go back inside, miss,' Smitherson said to the girl, though his voice was kindly. 'You've got sick all down your tunic . . . '

One of the RASC soldiers had heard Reuben's loud exclamation and came rapidly across the room.

'Who the fuck do you think you're talking to, you civvy git!' he asked Reuben. 'Some of you fucking civvies, skiving out of the forces . . . '

'Hold it, Private,' Smitherson said, his voice sharp enough to cut a plank. 'We're sergeant-majors, both of us. One more word, and I'll have you straight inside so fast your feet won't touch . . . '

'Sergeant-majors!' the lad said, too drunk for caution. 'I've shit bigger and better than both of you!' He moved closer to the heavy cast-iron table and put his knee under it, lifting it so that the beer in the pint mugs spilled into their laps. He didn't see Reuben's arm move; Reuben grabbed his hair and smashed his face down on the table's marble top, squashing his nose. The man's two mates let out a roar and dashed across the room, pushing the few people in the bar aside. Most of them moved quickly away, not wanting any part of the fight.

The landlord was shouting. 'Now, gentlemen, no fighting, please,' but everyone ignored him as Reuben pushed the cast-iron table and the soldier aside as if they were featherweights and came up off the bench seat in one smooth movement. Given the time and the chance, the two RASC men would have stopped and gone quietly away, but it was too late. Reuben reached both hands forward, clasped them at the back of the neck and crashed their faces together like a pair of cymbals.

'Reuben, for God's sake,' Smitherson shouted and came forward past the table, putting his hand on Reuben's shoulder. Reuben spun round and would have chopped Smitherson's neck if he hadn't recognised him in time.

'Let's get out of here,' Smitherson said, 'before you do any more damage.'

Two minutes, and Reuben, as savagely and as viciously as Smitherson had ever seen, had smashed the faces of three soldiers. All three, he was certain, had broken noses, broken teeth.

'Bloody hell, Reuben,' he said as they went out, leaving the wreckage of three men and screaming girls behind them, 'you didn't need to take on so! We could have talked him out of a fight. There was no need to smash his face for him . . . '

Reuben was walking along the street like a man possessed.

'Steady on, Reuben,' Smitherson said, recognising his agitation, but he realised the other man couldn't hear him, was lost in some mad, violent world of his own creation. Smitherson slowed down and, as he'd guessed, Reuben went on, striding out, unaware that Smitherson had left him. When Reuben was fifty feet ahead, Smitherson started again, walking behind him, keeping a constant distance far enough away that he wouldn't impose himself on Reuben's thoughts, but near enough to be able to intervene should anything else happen. They walked for miles in that way through the streets of Maida Hill and Maida Vale, up into St John's Wood, Golders Green, and Hampstead. Reuben finally stopped near the pond by Hampstead Heath and Smitherson caught up with him.

'Come on, old lad,' he said, 'we both have to be at work in the morning. Let's get home and get to bed.'

They walked slowly back down the hill towards Swiss Cottage. On the way down a taxi dropped an American and a girl outside a small block of flats.

'Are you going towards the West End?' the driver said to Smitherson, no doubt hoping for a fare to get him back.

'No, we're out for a walk,' Smitherson said.

Once the taxi had gone, Reuben began to talk. 'I've got a girl, same age as that one in the pub, I reckon,' he said. 'I've got two girls, one a year older than the other. Liz, that's the oldest, and Anne. I had a letter from my Emily today. Seeing the sick on that girl's tunic put me in mind of what she'd said in the letter.'

Smitherson didn't interrupt, but continued walking by Reuben's side, waiting.

'Two girls, different as chalk from cheese. Liz, the older one, is a harum-scarum. Allus off to t' pictures. Reads the picture magazines. Got herself a Yank for her fiancé. I've never thought she'd amount to much, too much self in her. The other now, Anne, she was different. Head on her shoulders. Bright as a button. Kept herself very nice, always. She's got herself a Canadian for a fiancé – I'm not supposed to know but they hang t' rings round their necks. I haven't said yes. I want them to sit the war out, see if they feel the same way about it when they see t' lads in civvies.'

'And then, you'll say yes . . . ?'

Reuben stopped dead and turned towards Smitherson. 'There'll be no question of that, now,' he said. 'Emily wrote me. She had her suspicions when she heard her being sick in t' bathroom in t' mornings. Now she's been to t' doctor and it's confirmed. She's going to have a baby . . . '

'Liz . . . ?'

'No. My Anne! A slut, just like t' rest. After the way I've brought 'em both up . . . '

'Well surely, Reuben, her fiancé will put it right . . . ?'

'It's him I'm sorry for,' Reuben said. 'Poor bugger's been away for over a year. It's somebody local! Emily says it isn't her fault. She had too much to drink. But, you and me, we're old enough to know how it is – a girl doesn't drink if she'd a mind to keep herself to herself . . . '

Smitherson didn't know what to say. 'I'm sorry you had bad news like that, Reuben,' he said. 'If there's anything I can do to help . . . Like, you'll be going home this week-end . . . ?' Privately, he hoped Reuben wouldn't! If he was capable of such sudden violence with the three soldiers what might he not do to his daughter and the man who'd made her pregnant?

'No,' Reuben said. 'Emily said there was no need for me to go home just yet. Seems like there's some sort of a case on. She says it'd be better to save my entitlement, and go up then.'

'I'd say that was sensible, Reuben,' Smitherson said, 'I'd say that was a good idea.' Anything that prevented Reuben killing anybody must surely be a good idea. If he could smash the face of an innocent man, what would he do to the guilty one?

Eleanor Godson looked out under the vine at the hillside and the shelled village which still clung precariously to the rocks, reminding her so much of the way Old Quaytown clung to its own hillside. Old Quaytown seemed so near and yet so far away. The evening was mild and they'd driven out from Florence through the rolling hills of Italy. Philip Masterton had brought a bottle of wine, a strong rich Tuscany from a stock preserved as carefully as gold-dust by Luigi Ponticelli in whose house he lived. They'd brought salami with them, and olives, a handful of cheese from the milk of Luigi's miraculously saved ewe. The house behind them belonged to Luigi; it had been his summer retreat but now would need almost complete rebuilding. The Madonna that graced the terrace on which they were sitting had lost one arm and shrapnel had pocked the carved folds of its draperies.

'I would miss all this terribly, now,' Eleanor said to Philip.

He seized his cue immediately. 'That's what I've been telling you, Eleanor,' he said. 'You *would* miss it, and you have no need to! There is a great need for you, here. Working with me!'

It had been a tantalising prospect. Philip, five years older than her at fifty-one, worked for the Fine Arts Commission of the Allied Military Government of Occupied Territories. He had a whole team at his disposal, of men who'd worked in Fine Arts. They were trying to salvage the few treasures of Italy that remained after the German looting and bombardment, to restore them to their rightful places, to repair them when possible. There was so much work to be done, she knew. She had come into it when Philip had needed more transport and it had been arranged that he could have the use of an ambulance and driver, since the vehicle was better sprung than a conventional army lorry. From the first meeting, he and Eleanor had been attracted to each other by a common love of art, of fine things, and a common desire to restore and preserve them. Now Eleanor's detachment of the VAD was being transferred back to England, possibly to the battlefields of Northern Europe. Philip's face fell when she went to tell him.

'Somehow, I'd begun to think of you as a member of our little team,' he'd said. 'An *indispensable* member,' he'd added.

'No one is indispensable!' she'd replied with a light laugh that concealed her thoughts.

Philip Masterton came from Boston; like Eleanor he had been married a long time ago but his wife had died of meningitis two years after their wedding. Since then he had known no other woman – his work in various art galleries throughout America had absorbed him completely. He had the equivalent rank of Major in the

American Army, had been sent to Italy specifically to do his present job of trying to locate the many works of art pillaged from Italian art institutions, to track them down, and if possible retrieve them. It was a mammoth task that could last for years after the war had ended and he had already decided he would continue to live in Italy to do it. With a private income from his wealthy family's investments and trust funds, he could afford to do as he wished.

Eleanor envied his independence, his distinguished good-looking masculinity, his light, easy manner that concealed a wealth of knowledge of his subject, Italian art.

'Eleanor,' he said. 'It would be very easy for me to arrange that you be posted from the VAD on permanent attachment to our unit. You don't have to go back with the others. We could carry on exactly as we are . . . '

She looked at him, reading his finely-chiselled features, the expression in his eyes, much more clearly than he realised.

'I don't think that is strictly true, Philip,' she said. 'I don't think we could carry on exactly as we are. Whether you accept it or not, our relationship has reached a point of crisis . . . '

At first, she had worked with the unit just like any other driver of the hotch-potch of vehicles they had acquired. They were all highly mobile; many works of art had been taken from cities and hidden in country places and often the man who'd secreted them had been killed in the fighting, with only rumour and memory as a guide to the location of the hiding place. Eleanor remembered the thrill that had run through the unit when they'd heard of the Leonardo said to be hidden in the village of Bussano Vecchio, and the dreadful disappointment when they'd finally located the picture which turned out to be a nineteenth-century copy of a Leonardo work. More and more, Eleanor and Philip had travelled together to remote and distant places. Many times they'd had to camp out, for want of better accommodation, in the back of the ambulance. Always they had observed the proprieties; at first Philip had insisted on sleeping in the ambulance's cab, but since there were two stretchers in the back, Eleanor had finally succeeded in persuading him to use one of them. Nothing he'd done or said had in any way offended her modesty; he'd been scrupulous about waiting outside the ambulance until she was safely tucked up in her bed, had turned his face to the wall when she'd come out of bed the following morning.

On the last expedition, however, she'd gone to sleep with her hand in his, since only inches separated the two cots.

'I can't deny that,' he said, and coloured slightly as he looked at her. 'I can't deny I have mixed motives in trying to persuade you to stay. You must have realised, Eleanor, that I have conceived a great affection for you during the time we've been together . . . '

'I have realised that, Philip,' she said, gravely.

'I have even hoped that one day we might begin to think about our personal relationship . . .'

Her heart felt warm towards him. He was a man of such delicate sensibilities, so – what was the word? – refined. She couldn't imagine he'd ever harboured a coarse thought, a mean or selfish motive.

'I would like us to consider a personal relationship . . .' he said, strongly. 'We have so much in common. We fit so well together. We share so many interests.'

Now she laughed. 'Oh, how can you say that, Philip? You're a man of such learning and knowledge. I'm just a Yorkshire lass, who never even had an education to speak of . . . '

'Neither one of us is a child,' he said, firmly. 'Surely, by now, we know what's in our minds . . . ?'

'You may do,' she said, 'but I don't. Until today, I thought there was nothing I'd like better than to continue with my, our, present work. And, I have to admit it, to be with you in doing it, in the professional and the personal way . . . But, you see, my *dear* Philip, I don't know my mind in the clear way you know yours. When I looked across at that village just now, I felt a deep nostalgia for my home village . . . '

'That letter I brought for you today . . . ? I have no wish to pry, you understand?'

She nodded. 'Suddenly, it brought it all back.'

'Not bad news, I hope . . . ?'

She laughed ruefully. 'It depends on which point of view you take,' she said. 'The village I come from is a small community, in which everybody knows everything about everybody else. I have a dreadful confession to make to you. I started my baby, the one who died, before I was married . . . '

'But you were married subsequently. Eleanor, many people have found themselves in that situation. It used to be that people didn't get married until they knew they could conceive a child together . . . !'

'My niece Anne, my favourite niece, is in the same position. But she'd engaged herself to a Canadian boy who's now fighting in Europe. And he, apparently, isn't the baby's father . . . '

He was shaking his head. 'We can't make subjective value judgements about other people, Eleanor,' he said gravely. 'We don't have that right . . . '

'You Americans,' she said in exasperation, 'and your use of the English language! What on earth is a "subjective value judgement"?'

'It means, we can't be judge and jury of other people's faults. We can't judge them by our *own* standards. We can't say that what somebody else does with their lives is wrong. We can say, it is against the accepted moral code, but let's face it, what is the accepted moral code? Merely a set of rules some of us compose to make life easier for ourselves!'

'I'm not saying that what she did is *wrong*!' she said passionately. 'Merely unfortunate in its outcome! Apparently, there are legal complications and there's going to be some sort of Court case. No, I'm not saying any of it is wrong – how could I when I don't know the circumstances . . . ?'

'What you are saying, I think,' Philip said, 'is that you wish you were there, to help your niece, isn't that it? You wish you were there, with the family, doing whatever you could to help them . . . ?'

'I suppose that's what it is,' Eleanor said. 'We forget we have roots. We think we can take ourselves anywhere and settle down in peace. But we can't ignore our origins, we can't break that bond of involvement with our relations, our families. I used to work for the man who will be handling the case if it comes to Court . . . '

'And you'd like to be there now?' Philip asked quietly. His personal code of conduct wouldn't permit him to try to dissuade her though, more than anything he could remember, he wanted to keep Eleanor by his side. He'd realised these past few weeks that the work he was doing would mean infinitely less to him if he had to do it alone. Half the thrill of the discoveries and the chases came from having Eleanor by his side. No, he told himself, *more* than half the thrill – he couldn't quantify it.

'If you wanted to come back . . . ' he said, but they both realised that would never happen. If Eleanor went, she would say goodbye to him. She wasn't one to retrace old footsteps. They were sad and silent as they packed up their picnic; as if, symbolically, the sun had gone in and the day had become chill.

'I believe that among the many powers that come with my rank,' he said, 'I have the ability to send you on immediate compassionate leave. I hate like hell to see you go, Eleanor, but if that's what you want.'

'You are a good, wonderfully kind and understanding man,' she said. 'I'll never forget you.'

'I hope one day you'll forgive me,' he said, 'for not carrying you away to one of these Italian mountain fortresses, and holding you prisoner there until you agreed to marry me! As it is, I'm putting you in charge of that consignment of manuscripts we think might be Vivaldi's. I think they ought to be hand carried to the Bodleian for inspection, and I'm putting them in your charge. You'll get authorisation to travel on the plane leaving Rome tomorrow.'

'I meant it, Philip,' she said. 'I'll never forget you...'

'But blood is thicker, even than the nectar of love, eh?'

'I suppose it is. I suppose it must be . . . '

Sam Toser stepped out of the blackness of the public lavatory by the Slip, a moving shadow in the moonless night.

The short length of anchor chain gleamed in his hand, reflecting starlight.

'Bloody Yanks,' he said, 'coming down here messing about wi' our lasses.'

He swung the anchor chain. Wilbur Shoesmith lifted his arms to protect his head and face and felt the bone snap under the chain's impact. There was an explosion of pain in his knee-cap and he knew he'd been kicked. He bent down, cowering back, as Sam Toser bore in, swinging the chain around the neck and head of the defenceless man, who was beaten down to his knees.

'Chuck him off t' Slip,' he dimly heard a voice say and then he was picked up by several hands and carried across the concrete of the Slip top. He felt himself being swung in the air, then sailing through the air, and then the icy shock as his body hit the cold water; he struck out but cried in pain when he used his broken arm.

Sam Toser watched the American flailing in the water. 'That'll teach t' buggers,' he said. 'Us'll do t' same to any other bugger we catch down here!'

Major Bernstein carried the results of the inquest down to Captain Walham's house in Grinklegate, and invited him to read them. Captain Walham adjusted his glasses as he sat down, and perused the words carefully.

No evidence of alcohol in the man's bloodstream.

Death by drowning. Subject clearly alive when entered water.

Mass of bruises on arms, shoulders, lesions on neck, cheeks, not commensurate with having been washed ashore, but *indicating* – the pathologist at the American Military Hospital had underlined the word carefully – that the subject had been the victim of an assault. Marks on the subject *indicated* that the weapon used *may* have been a length of chain with individual links two inches long and one-and-a-half inches across, of metal five-sixteenths in diameter.

'That report is being kept under wraps, Captain Walham,' Major Bernstein said. 'Shoesmith gets a "death by accidental drowning" verdict from the Coroner's Office.'

'But that's *monstrous*!' Captain Walham protested. 'Whoever did this dreadful thing should be found, and prosecuted with the full vigour of the law.'

'We think we know who's responsible,' Major Bernstein said. 'Well, at least, I've worked out who it could be.'

'Are you going to tell me . . . ?'

'No, Captain. I don't want you getting involved. I've only shown you the report to let you know the true state of affairs. Look, Captain, little as we like it, a state of war exists between your village and our camp. So far we thought it hadn't come out into the open but Shoesmith's death makes us realise differently.'

'I still think it is atrocious that you are making no attempts to apprehend the blackguard who did this . . . I would like to see him prosecuted with full vigour . . . '

'It's out of my hands, Captain. The whole business has been handled higher up the totem pole, and instructions have come down. Believe me, I'm just as sore as you are about it. But we can't go against the Brass, and they don't want the relationship between the local population and our guys upset any more. That's why Meaney is going to be charged in the camp. They won't release him for civil trial – but they are going to permit the civilians to be represented. And any decision will be as binding as if it was reached in your own Courts.'

'I can see the political wisdom of that, though I don't like to see civil offences entrusted to the Military . . . '

'Just one more thing, Captain. I figured I'd tell you myself, before you found out and thought I'd turned traitor to our mutual friendship . . . '

'And what's that, Major . . . ?'

'I'm the one who's going to defend Meaney . . . '

Captain Walham smiled. 'I guessed that,' he said, 'ever since you told me you were qualified in Law. I'm happy to see you do that. At least, I know he'll get the good defence to which I believe all men are entitled. Even the guilty . . . And, don't worry, Major Bernstein. You will still be welcome to come here and sip my pink gins of an evening – so long as the angostura bitters holds out . . .!'

They raised their glasses in a salute of mutual respect.

'There's one question I've never asked you, Major Bernstein, or the girl Anne Godson. I'd like to ask it now, if I may . . . ?'

'Sure, Captain, fire away.'

'Don Meaney – what colour is *his* skin?'

'A dark shade, Captain . . . '

'Oh . . . '

'A dark shade of pink . . . '

'Sam Toser, isn't it?' Major Bernstein asked quietly.

Sam paused on his way along the side of the Cut to look at the American. 'What's it to do with you, you black bastard? I don't talk to Yanks.'

'So I understand. You hit them, with chains, don't you?'

Sam looked about him. Bloody hell, the nigger was twice his size, and broad across t' shoulders.

'I've got nowt to say to thee,' he said defiantly. 'Except tha' can't come down here, chucking thy weight about . . . '

'I'm not the one chucking my weight about,' Bernstein said. 'You're the one doing that. And your foul tongue, too! Like the rest of your kind, the rest of you cowardly bullies, you're all right when you have a few mates with you, and a piece of anchor chain in your hand.'

'You can't prove nowt . . . '

'Ah, Sam, that's where you're wrong, I *have* proved it. And I've made a dossier of it. I've found witnesses and taken statements from them, not witnesses you know, but other people you didn't realise were watching what you, Hefford and Poynter were doing . . . '

'Tha' seems to know all t' names . . . '

'Yes, I do, and I have sworn statements . . . '

Sam started forward wildly, his arm upraised.

'Go on,' Bernstein said, 'come at me. If you dare. I'll break your arm off for you!' Sam knew he would, too.

'All right,' he said, 'what's tha' going to do about it, eh?'

'Me? I'm going to do nothing. The American Army is going to do nothing because we're under orders not to create any disturbance here. *We're under orders*, Sam, and if we weren't, I'd break every bone in your body. Well, you murdered that lad, because you'd seen him talking innocently with a girl you fancied was your girl. And, do you know what, I've just come from talking to that girl, and I've left her a copy of the evidence I've gathered. You've lost that young lady's affections, Sam. And soon, you'll have lost everything else. That young lady of yours, Sam, at this very moment, is on her way to the police-station with that copy of the evidence. I reckon that, in about ten minutes, the local – don't you call him a bobby? – will be knocking on your door. So, you'd better start running, Sam Toser, and God knows when you'll be able to stop. Because, wherever you go, they'll catch you!'

'Tha's joking,' Sam Toser said aghast.

'Joking, am I? Just you try going home, and see what you'll find . . . '

'Bloody hell, tha's done for me . . . '

'Not yet, I haven't!' Bernstein moved like a panther, whirled to the side of Sam Toser, grasped his arm, twisted it in a lock, and heaved. Sam went helter-skelter over the edge of the Cut, to fall flat on his face in the silted wet mud below.

'Now I've finished with you,' Bernstein said, as he turned on his heel and walked away.

'Have you had enough to eat then, lad?' Mrs Marsh asked. She'd watched amazed while John Godson had put away the best part of half a rabbit pie, with a mountain of potatoes and carrots; he'd brought the rabbit the day before and given it to her – she didn't begrudge him eating the major part of it since she and Grace both had small appetites. 'By gow,' she thought, 'his missis will need a lot of housekeeping to feed *him*!

'Yes, Mrs Marsh, and it was smashing. I can see you're a dab hand wi' pies.'

'Aye, my husband, God rest his Soul in Heaven, always liked my pastry . . . Are you off to t' pictures tonight?'

John didn't care too much for pictures; he didn't like the stuffiness of the atmosphere of the 'flea-pit' as he called it. 'No, I reckon we'll be going for a bit of a stroll!'

Mrs Marsh sat there at the table, embarrassed. How she wished she had a man about the place to do certain things for her. She'd sent Grace into the scullery with the pots to do the washing-up. Now she and John were sitting at table over a cup of tea and a home-made bun. She'd told Grace not to come back in until she called for her. But the words were difficult to find.

'You and our Grace seem to get on well together,' she said tentatively.

'Aye, I reckon we do,' he said.

'I mean, you see a lot of each other . . . '

'Aye, I reckon we do, when t' tide permits.' He sat there, looking into the fire. She twiddled her fingers nervously. How would her late husband have said it? She didn't know – the girls had been too young for him to play the part of the enquiring father.

'I reckon the fishing brings in good money?' she said.

'Not bad. Course, there's good days and bad. Sometimes, it doesn't fetch enough to sole a pair of boots.'

'Yes, but, I mean, over the whole year, taking good times wi' bad, it must give you a good living . . . ?'

'Better than some, I reckon, but then worse than others. It's up and down. And diesel's getting that expensive – well, so is everything. You ought to see what they're asking in Whitby for rope. Mind you, it's new stuff, and a lot better than t' old stuff. More breaking strain, if you see what I mean . . . '

She knew if she wasn't careful she'd lose whatever slender thread she'd established between them in a lecture on the problems of fishing.

'I mean, it'd be enough to keep two on? To get married on . . . ?'

'Aye, I reckon it would, just about. If you could find somebody careful wi' t' brass.'

Now she had her opening. 'Our Grace is saving up, you know, for when she gets married. She's already got a tidy bit put by for her bottom drawer, from her wages. She hardly ever spends a penny on herself, you know. I let her do t' shopping for me – she allus seems to do better wi' Fewster than I do. See her peel a potato, peelings are that thin you can practically see through them. And she's wonderful wi' t' left-overs. She can make a shepherd's pie out of nowt, out of stuff as other folks would chuck away. All her clothes is hand-made, you know. Sewing, knitting, crocheting, mending, putting buttons on – she's got a hand for it like I never had. I see you've got a button missing off that jacket sleeve. You ought to give that to our Grace; she'd have it back on in a wink. No, though I say so as shouldn't since I'm her mam, whoever our Grace sets her heart to will get a right bargain . . . '

'Nay, Mrs Marsh,' he said, 'don't say that. There's no bargains to be had, one way or t' other. Lads and lasses come together because that's how they want it, without looking for bargains either side . . . '

'Well, somebody will snap her up, and soon at that!' she said desperately.

'What are you talking about, Missis?' he asked. 'She's snapped up already! By me . . . '

Good. Now she had him. 'But not *engaged*,' she said, 'there's no ring on her finger to show folk she's spoken for . . . '

'Ring on her finger? Is that what she wants? I thought you said she was careful wi' money? There's nowt careful about spending five pounds on a bit of a twinkle, now is there?' He was having her on, teasing her, but she couldn't see it.

'It's once in a lifetime. Anybody can have a ring put on their finger, once in a lifetime. It's a sign, isn't it, that they're loved and wanted, that somebody has bespoken them . . . Nay, John, thy mam must have taught thee that much . . . I hear tell your two lasses wear rings on bits of string round their necks. I wouldn't want our Grace caught like that . . . Or in any other way, either,' she added, thinking of Anne.

'Aye, well, what kind of a ring were you thinking about, Mrs Marsh?' he asked.

'Oh, owt does. It doesn't have to be fancy. Though it should look a bit of summat, not like you picked it up in Woolworths.'

He reached into his waistcoat pocket and took out a small old leather-covered box. When he opened it the diamond on the ring inside it flashed light at her. She reached out .her hand eagerly, holding the box and watching the flash of coloured light in the stone.

'My, John,' she breathed, 'that's lovely. *Lovely*, that is!' She leaned forward and whispered to him. 'Don't tell me that's for our Grace . . . ?'

He leaned forward. 'Well, much as you merit it, I'm not about to slip it on your finger, am I?'

'That's it, then. You're getting engaged . . . '

He smiled wickedly at her. 'We'd have been engaged half an hour ago, if tha'd gone out there to do t' washing up!' he said. 'Why else did you think I brought yon rabbit. *And* three bottles of stout!'

CHAPTER FOURTEEN

The American Headquarters were situated in what, before the war, had been a private school. The house had formerly belonged to the Earl of Skelsdale who died without issue in 1934. William Morrisson had been granted the tenancy of the property by the executors when the Countess decided to live in Bermuda; he paid a nominal rent and a fund had been set aside, in the Will, for the restoration and maintenance of the buildings. In the immediate pre-war days the school had prospered by taking in the sons of wealthy local businessmen and tradesmen, and attempting to make gentlemen of them. Morrisson, who had been Secretary to the Earl for a number of years, was a total snob; he'd taught his pupils first and foremost to be mannered and formal, if not academic; since most of them would be taking over family businesses, their intellectual attainments mattered little.

When war was imminent, Iphegenia, Countess Skelsdale wrote to Mr Morrisson. 'You will find the preservation of Skelsdale far too troublesome in wartime,' she wrote. 'I can offer you a post here should you decide to close the school for the duration of hostilities.' William Morrisson, never a brave man, wanted nothing better than to get out of Europe to the safety of Bermuda, and September 1939 saw the school already occupied by a branch of Headquarters, Northern Command. A succession of military used it until the Americans began arriving in force and took it over as one of their Unit Headquarters.

The Court had been set up in the Great Hall; after much consultation between the Legal Department of the American Forces in Europe in London, the Lord Chancellor's Department, and Colonel Aubrey Sampson, who was to be President of the Court, it was decided that Pfc Meaney would be charged with 'administering a noxious substance, to whit, alcohol, to Miss Anne Godson of Ravenswyke in the County of Yorkshire, with intent to cause her bodily harm.'

Ezra Thrummell had engaged Mr Thomas Villiers, KC, to sit in the Court and represent the interests of his client, Anne Godson.

Pfc Meaney would be represented by Major Bernstein.

Major Siddons, of the USAAF's Legal Section, would prosecute.

The Court was convened for 2 March 1945, but Colonel Sampson called a meeting in Skelsdale Hall the previous evening, in what had been the morning-room. They sat informally round the fire in deep armchairs; Ezra Thrummell and Thomas Villiers were on one side, Major Bernstein and Major Siddons on the other, with Colonel Sampson in a chair directly facing the fire, getting the full benefit of its warmth.

'How people used to live in houses like these I'll never know,' he said, rubbing his hands as the Mess waiter helped them all to a drink. 'We'll help ourselves now, Jones,' he said, 'and we don't want to be disturbed, okay?'

'Okay, Colonel.'

He waited until the warming glow of the bourbon hit him, shrugged his shoulders as if trying to shake off a chill, then looked round the room.

'I thought we all ought to meet here informally,' he said, 'to talk over the guide-lines for tomorrow. One thing we have to remember. What we're about to do is a public relations exercise and shouldn't be confused with a trial.'

He could see that Villiers looked uncomfortable and added, 'A public relations exercise with a double purpose, Mr Villiers. We want to clear that girl's name, and we want the people of your country to see that we are prepared to punish our soldiers when they step out of line!'

'So long as it is made quite clear that my client was in no way a willing or consenting party, so long as my client emerges from the trial with her reputation unbesmirched and is shown to have been the victim of what is, after all, a rape, no matter what we may care to call it, then I believe my client will be satisfied. If that is not done, if *any* attempt is made to impugn the reputation of my client, then I shall feel an obligation to my brief to pursue the matter with all the vigour at my command. I hope I make my position quite clear . . . '

'Clear as crystal, Mr Villiers,' Colonel Sampson said. 'Whatever your client may or may not have done in the past, she'll emerge from this trial pure as virgin snow – well, that was hardly an apt expression – pure as driven snow!'

'And there will be a financial consideration . . . ?'

'The Court will see to that, Mr Villiers. We'll put Meaney in hock for the rest of his life . . . '

'And an immediate recompense . . . ?'

'That's one of the subjects we might profitably discuss, to fix an appropriate amount which will be paid out of military funds and debited to Meaney . . . '

'And costs . . . '

'The Court recognises, Mr Villiers, that neither you nor Mr Thrummell is a charitable organisation. Your fees and costs will be met by the Court.'

Villiers sat back, happy with the first exchange.

Colonel Sampson looked at him over the rim of his glass. He hoped Villiers wasn't going to be a pain in the ass during the hearing. Not another guy intent on burnishing his own reputation at the expense of the Americans. Colonel Sampson hated this kind of game-playing – privately he thought they ought to have thrown this guy Meaney to the wolves, let the civilians have him and charge him with any goddam thing they could make stick. But he was all too aware that the years of Isolationism had started them off in Europe at a disadvantage; the British figured they'd borne the brunt of the war alone and that the Americans had come in to cream off the victory. The feuds between the top generals, even between the two governments, were public knowledge; Mark Clark in Italy, Ike in France, were doing nothing to help a feeling of togetherness. So, if one little public relations exercise up here in this godforsaken frozen north of England could help, the sooner he got it over with the faster he could get back to his heated apartment in Hill Street.

'I reckon two days should see us through, wouldn't you agree?' he asked Major Siddons and Major Bernstein.

Siddons nodded.

Bernstein looked doubtful. God, not another trouble-maker, the Colonel thought. Between him and Villiers . . .

'I had figured on three days, Colonel,' Bernstein said. 'I was thinking of offering *some* evidence in the way of mitigation . . . '

'Meaney will plead guilty, right?'

'Under duress, Colonel.' Oh, Christ, not the duress bit.

'Not *duress*, Major. He was given good advice! Surely we're not going over that ground again tomorrow. Look, Major, nobody's trying to railroad the guy. He told the Investigating Officers that he put booze in that girl's drink when she wasn't looking . . . '

'I wasn't there, Colonel, when that interrogation took place!'

'It wasn't an *interrogation*, Major! They were merely talking with him informally and he told them. You were there when he was charged, and you've had ample opportunity to talk with him since. Major, the Court doesn't mind what you say the day after tomorrow to make Meaney look as good as you can . . . '

'Provided that doesn't blacken the reputation of my client,' Villiers interjected. 'We don't want any "but Brutus is an honourable man . . . " speeches made about my client . . . '

'There will not be, Mr Villiers. You have my word on that. Look, gentlemen, this is the way I see it. In the morning we will have the prosecution's evidence, showing that Meaney *was* at the dance, that he *was* in the company of Miss Godson, that he *did* put alcohol in her drink – I hope no-one is going to require proof that the stuff in the bottle marked whisky contained alcohol . . . ?'

'It *should* be established,' Bernstein said, fighting desperately. 'Look, Colonel, there's a lot of bootleg liquor about . . . Some of the stuff the guys are buying *and* selling never got near to alcohol. I can *prove* that it's possible to buy cold *tea*, bottled up as whisky, at the back door of some of the lousier pubs around . . . '

'Meaney was drinking it, Major Bernstein,' the Colonel said patiently. 'Do you think, do you honestly believe, he would have admitted to a charge of administering alcohol if the bottle he was drinking out of contained *tea*?'

'Interesting legal point, that,' Villiers said blandly, obviously enjoying himself in the dispute between the two Americans. 'Had a case once, man thought he was administering arsenic to his wife, but the chemist had made a mistake and had given him the wrong stuff. Charged him with attempted murder, and got a conviction. It's written up in the Law Journal; if you'd care to see an extract I could get my clerk to pop up with it?'

'No, Mr Villiers, neither Major Bernstein nor I would

care to see an extract, though we're grateful for the offer. The fact is, that Meaney has *admitted* he fed liquor to the girl with the intention of making her seduction easier. It's open and shut. That admission, Major Bernstein, tomorrow will be translated into a plea of guilty. We'll go through the motions so that we don't get any upset on appeal. We'll wrap it up in all the trimmings. All your client will have to do, Mr Villiers, is to go into the witness box on the second day and tell us she didn't know, didn't realise, what was in her drink. We don't need to talk about anything else in Court, is that understood? The fact that he made her pregnant is neither here nor there . . . '

'I object,' Villiers said immediately. 'It's entirely relevant to the assessment of damages to which my client is entitled. We must reveal the extent to which her reputation, her prospects of marriage, her physical well-being have been damaged . . . '

'Mr Villiers, I'm sure you won't object if I suggest you are possibly being naïve. One of the reasons for this informal discussion is to assess exactly the amount of damages to which your client may or may not be entitled, but which, *a priori*, she will receive. Now, gentlemen, what do we think about the following? Two hundred pounds immediately, two hundred pounds when the baby is born, three quarters of the weekly allowance for wedded spouses, and all her legal and out of pocket costs . . . '

'Three, three, seven eighths, and her legals and out of pockets . . . ' Villiers said immediately.

'Okay, gentlemen, let's start horse-trading,' Colonel Sampson said. 'But first, help yourselves to another drink. And this, Major Bernstein, is *not* cold tea!'

On the principle that Justice must not only be done, but must be seen to be done, the Americans had issued fifty tickets for the general public to attend the trial, which took place in the Great Room of Skelsdale Hall.

A number of rostra had been installed at one end; Colonel Sampson, with deference to his dignity, sat in the centre of the highest rostrum, with two American officers, one each side of him, Colonel Laxton and Colonel Minetta, both from the Supply Corps. In recognition of the civilian involvement, the Mayor of Whitby was seated below Colonel Sampson, with Mrs Probert, the leader of the Ravenswyke Parish Council and the Reverend Michael Roberts. Captain Walham had been offered a seat on the lower Bench, but had declined – he was afraid his feelings would reveal themselves all too clearly on his face and knew no-one wanted to look at him scowling at the accused.

Major Bernstein and Pfc Meaney sat at a table on the right. The witness *box* was a chair on a rostrum to the left.

The *Whitby Gazette* sent a reporter, but no photographer was allowed. Two stringers were covering the story for the national dailies and the Sundays, and all the Press were seated on a rostrum above the accused where they could not see the accused's face, but could hear the witnesses. When they complained, Colonel Sampson instructed that they could sit among the general public, if they preferred.

The Godsons were given seats in the front row to the left; Reuben had taken leave and was sitting next to Anne, with Emily on the other side of her. Eleanor sat next to Emily. John sat next to Reuben, with Liz and Grace next to him. Martin had been left at home in the care of Sophie Mountjoy.

John looked around the room when they'd taken their seats and were waiting for the proceedings to begin. The legal people were huddled round the President's table in some sort of discussion, and everyone else waited. It was ten o'clock and the Great Room was freezing cold, though John noticed a number of electric fires had been placed strategically pointed at the top rostrum. Columns of air rose from the enormous radiators that lined the room, but the effect of the heat they gave out was negligible. Light beams coming down from the top windows gave the place the appearance of a chapel; the curtains on the windows had remained drawn, doubtless so that no-one would be distracted by the normal life going on outside. John was amused, rather than awed, by the solemnity of it all. Of course, it was right that this fellow Meaney should be tried, sentenced and punished. It was right that Anne should get some sort of compensation for the damage he'd done her, though Reuben had already said she mustn't accept it – it smacked too much of charity for Reuben and it had never been the Godson way to accept *that*! John knew it was all concerned with looking after Anne's good name, to show she wasn't like the rest of the girls who hung around the Americans, looking for favours and not caring what they gave in exchange, how drunk they became, how badly they behaved.

It was sadly true that the American Forces had attracted the worst kind of English girl along with the good ones. Many of the girls were perfectly sincere – life had brought them into contact with new and exciting people and they'd seen a possibility of a new kind of life in a far away country. Of course, many of the Americans were only messing about with the girls out of loneliness; many had wives and families back in America and would eventually return to them. From what John had seen at the dances in Whitby and Scarborough that he and Grace had been to, there was no difference in this respect between Americans and soldiers of other nationalities posted away from home – it seemed they were all intent on grabbing a girl for themselves and having a good time. Well, this trial was supposed to show them that Anne wasn't a 'good-time girl', anybody's for the asking. That she was an honest, hard-working, moral girl who came from a good family with a local reputation for respectability.

But, to John, it seemed like casting a giant net to catch tiddlers . . . !

He looked at the watch he could see on his dad's wrist. Ten-past ten and they were still arguing up there, with the black man taking the brunt of it. If he hadn't been up here, they'd have been off at half-past nine. Only three boats now – the rest of them were away in the forces. Himself, Mountjoy with the *Rose*, and Bredford with the *Nelson.* He wanted to look round at them, give them a wink, but this wasn't the time or place . . . He looked sideways at his dad; Reuben was sitting like a sgt-major, wearing his uniform with his medal ribbon and bar as Villiers had suggested. That Villiers, John thought, was not much of a man. A sniff-nosed nit-picker. Tall and thin, with hands like a bunch of sticks he kept knotting in cat's cradles as he spoke. Long spiky legs and a habit of crossing one over the other and winding them round, with one toe behind the other heel. Gaunt cheeks, like he'd never eaten a square meal in his life, and yellow skin that had never felt the blow of a wind. Now he was sitting there like a berk, wearing a schoolmaster's gown and with that damned silly grey wig on his head – the only man in the room to wear one.

Reuben felt John looking at him and turned. His face was like granite and John, who knew his dad's every expression, recognised the suffering that lay behind his eyes. His dad was taking the whole thing badly, too badly, John thought. Of course, he'd been astounded when they'd had the family conference and had all learned that Anne had a bun in t'oven – nobody more surprised than Liz.

'You never told us,' she kept on saying to Anne, 'you never told us!'

When they'd all been sitting round the table, and Reuben had told them, it seemed as if Anne was going to say something but one look at her dad's face had told her to keep her mouth shut. They'd all seen he was on the edge of something terrible, though they didn't know exactly what it could be. They'd been surprised when Sgt-Major Smitherson had come home with him, had stayed only for one meal, and had then left, saying he had to get back to London. John wondered why Smitherson had bothered to come all that way with his dad – did he think he was a young bairn who needed lifting on to and off t' pot? Of course, their mam had already known. It was all a mystery to John how his mam always knew everything in advance of telling – it seemed as if she was so closely tuned to them all that she could read them without words, without question and answer.

Best of all, though, had been Auntie Eleanor. She'd sat at the far end of the table, next to Anne, and it was she rather than Reuben who ran it. Of course she was the oldest member of the Godson family, and in a way it was more to do with women than men, John realised, but she'd been champion. By gow, how she'd changed since she'd been away in t' VAD. She'd really become a – well, there was no other word for it, John thought, but Lady. She was talking different, looking different. She had a sparkle in her eyes very different from the spinster look she'd carried away with her. And she now had a sort of, presence, that was it. Before, you'd never been aware she was there. She'd sat in a corner of the room and you'd never heard nowt from her. She'd read her books, done her embroidery, then gathered it all up and sort of drifted away to her own rooms. John knew she'd only sat with them from a sense of obligation to mam, after she'd cooked a meal for her. She hadn't wanted to eat and then leave at once. Now she was a more positive person. She spoke strongly.

'I *like* your Grace Marsh,' she'd said to John, her whole face alive. 'She has a very nice sense of humour! And she'll look after you. *I like her.*' Well, whenever had Auntie Eleanor ever come out with it like that, bold as brass, and said she liked – or for that matter, she *disliked* a person. She'd always been sort of wishy-washy, never giving her opinions out loud to the family, squirming in agony if anyone insisted she tell them what she thought.

'How do you like my new coat, Eleanor?' Emily would ask.

'Yes, well, that colour suits you . . . '

'But do you *like* it? What about these buttons – you don't think they're too big?'

'Well, perhaps they *might* have been a *bit* smaller.'

The first thing she'd said when she'd arrived home was, 'You've changed that awful tablecloth! I like this one much better!'

'You know, John,' she'd said one day, 'after the war, I want you to do something for me . . . '

'What's that, Auntie?'

'I want you to teach me all about fishing . . . '

'Nay, Auntie, tha'll never be strong enough to lift fifty fathoms of line . . . '

'I know that, you dummy! I don't want to *do* it. I just want to know all about how it's done!'

Another thing she'd said that had surprised him. 'When you get married, you and Grace can have my place if you like. I'm going to find a cottage for myself, so that you won't have to put up with me all the time . . . '

'Nay, Auntie,' he'd protested, 'Grace and me'll never put you out!'

It was accepted, of course, with tragic clarity that John would one day take over the Godson family responsibility, with Wilfred and Arthur both gone. The name on the beam, carved to follow Reuben's name, would be John Godson, not Wilfred . . . He reached out to Reuben's hand, resting formally on his knee, and went to squeeze the back. Reuben turned his hand over and grasped John's fiercely, establishing a strong bond between them for that moment in that place where neither of them wanted to be sitting.

The men withdrew from the President's table, and resumed their own seats. Bernstein leaned sideways to whisper to Meaney. The contrast between the large round face of the big negro, and the thin features of Meaney, with his straw coloured hair, could not have been greater. Meaney came from Montana; his ancestors were northern European though he was a third generation American. Bernstein came from Alabama, but had come north with his parents and had worked his way through college and then through Law School. He knew he could never have succeeded in doing that in his native Alabama.

Colonel Sampson tapped the table with his gavel to still the quiet murmur of conversation that had sounded uneasily throughout the Great Room while they had been conferring.

'I must ask your pardon,' he said. 'If it had been possible, we would have retired to Chambers for such a discussion, but here . . . ' He shrugged. 'Master at Arms,' he said, 'I think we can begin.'

All through the opening ceremonies John, standing beside his father, watched Villiers. The man couldn't keep still, twitching constantly. 'God,' John thought, 'if this nervous nellie was defending me . . . ?'

When Meaney had been charged the prosecution began its case by bringing in Master-Sergeant Rainer Horst, a big man whose American was hard for the British people sitting there to understand.

After he had established the witness's identity Major Siddons lost no time. 'Did you attend the social function held in the Chapel Rooms, Old Quaytown, Ravenswyke, on the night of November 25th last year?'

'Yes, Major, I did.'

'Can you see any other American serviceman in this room who attended that same social function?'

'Yes, Major, I can.' To John, it sounded as if the sergeant had said something like 'Uz, maje, ucayn.'

Villiers leaped to his feet. 'I crave the indulgence of the Court,' he said, 'but some of us are not as familar with the richer sounds of the American tongue as we might be. I wonder if some method could be devised to make this witness's doubtless colourful speech more comprehensible to the rest of us . . . ?'

Sampson leaned forward. 'What my learned colleague is trying to say, Sergeant, is could you speak more clearly! I don't think we need bother with the question again . . .'

'Yerz, Maje, u daid see him,' he said, pointing in the direction of Meaney.

'Will the accused please rise,' the Master at Arms intoned. Meaney got to his feet.

'Yes, he was there,' the Master-Sergeant said in his colourful but irreproducable speech.

'Did you speak with the accused?'

'Yes, I did. I told him that if I caught him pouring any more of that danged whisky into his girl's drink, I'd send him back to camp under armed guard and into the stockade.'

'Did you see the accused tip part of the contents of a bottle he was carrying into a glass?'

'Yes, I did.'

'Did you see him subsequently hand that glass to his companion?'

'Yes, I did.'

Villiers rose languorously to his feet. 'Does the Court require me to say that the prosecution is leading the witness? Or is such questioning permitted under the American Legal System?'

'It will be permitted in this court, Mr Villiers, in the interests of time saving and your comprehension . . . '

Villiers sat down, a pained look on his face, sour as lemon juice, as if asking what on earth he could be doing in such a barbaric situation.

'Did you see his companion drink from that glass?'

'Yes, I did, I sure as hell did!'

'Could you identify his companion for us?'

'Yes, I sure can. It's that sweet little miss over there expecting a baby!'

Villiers leaped to his feet, his languor gone. 'May I remind the Court . . . '

Sampson was already holding up his hand. 'No need, Mr Villiers . . . ' He leaned over the table and looked directly at the witness. 'When you are asked a question you can answer with a yes, or a no, please answer that question with a yes, or a no, whichever is appropriate. Do not add such phrases as "like hell I did," or refer in any way to the physical characteristics or personal appearance or present condition of anyone in this Court-room. Is that quite clear, Sergeant?'

'Yes, Colonel, it sure as hell is!'

Sampson shrugged his shoulders, looking at Villiers. 'Does that satisfy you, Mr Villiers?'

Villiers nodded and shrugged *his* shoulders.

Major Siddons called three witnesses, each as incomprehensible as the other to the English people in the Court; each one attested that he had seen Meaney in the company of the girl, Anne Godson; that Meaney was carrying a bottle of whisky, and using it furtively to top up his own and the girl's drinks. Bernstein waited until the last witness had given his evidence before rising to cross-examine.

'When you attended these social functions, did you find alcoholic refreshment being supplied?' he asked quietly.

'No, Sir, there were no alcoholic refreshments. Only soft drinks . . . '

'And that's why, if you wanted to drink something stronger, you took your own.'

'Yes, Sir.'

'Did you take a bottle with you?'

'I shared a bottle with my friend.'

'And did *you* and your friend supply some of the contents of that bottle to your companions . . . ?'

'Objection,' Major Siddons said quickly. 'This witness is not on trial.'

'Objection over-ruled,' Sampson said sternly. 'I can see where Counsel is heading. The witness may answer.'

'Waal, like, everybody does it, huh? Dancing ain't much fun without a little snort to warm your blood, is it?'

The Court erupted in laughter, which Sampson quickly gavelled into silence.

'So, you would say it was no uncommon thing to provide your *companion* with a little something stronger than soft drinks . . . '

'No, Sir, everybody did it . . . '

'But the organisers of the dance didn't approve . . . ?'

'No, Sir, they didn't. They kept the dances dry as a revival meeting . . . '

Again there was laughter which quickly faded under Sampson's glare.

'So, in order to provide *refreshment* for your *companions* you had to do it clandestinely . . . ?'

'How's that, Major?'

'In secret . . . ?'

'Oh yes, *Sir*! Anybody saw what you was doing, and you was out on your . . . kicked out of the Hall, muy pronto . . . '

'And you would say it was perfectly normal for any man

to conceal the fact that he was putting alcohol into his *companion's* drink, to avoid being turned out?'

'That's the way it was done, Major, that's the way it was done.'

Bernstein turned to Siddons. 'I've no more questions to ask this witness,' he said.

Sampson intervened quickly. 'The witness may step down,' he said. 'And I think this may be a good time to adjourn for lunch. The Court will reconvene at three o'clock.'

Reuben had arranged for two taxis from Whitby to take them to and from the US Camp, preferring not to accept the meal the Americans had offered them. The women folk rode in one taxi; he and John sat in the other. Neither spoke until they arrived at the top of the Slip, when John said, 'Fancy a half of bitter, Dad?'

Reuben grunted approval and they went inside. Though the Snug was half full and everyone knew where they had been, no-one asked any questions. They knew Reuben would tell them when he was ready. They took their half pints and sat in the corner away from the others.

'It's hard to know what they're getting at, most of the time,' Reuben said. 'It seems as if they have to have everything said over and over again! It all seems as plain as the nose on your face, to me!'

'Aye,' John said, 'they have to do things their way. I wish I could earn my brass as easy as yon fellow, Villiers.'

'They're paid for what they know,' Reuben said, 'not what they do!'

'So what happens next?' John asked.

'Thrummell was telling me that this afternoon they'll deal with the question of whether our Anne knew or not that he was putting whisky in her drink. She'll tell 'em she didn't, of course. Tomorrow will be worse for her. She'll have to tell them tomorrow about him taking her outside, down on t' scaurs, the bloody swine, and say as she didn't remember nowt about it. One thing, they'll be able to see what state he's got her into – her belly will speak for itself! Poor bloody lass!'

It was the first time John had heard Reuben give a word of sympathy for Anne. All the time his dad had been home, he'd preserved a stony silence to Anne. John thought his dad ought to have been a bit more, well, affectionate. He ought to do as John had done and put his arm round her, saying how sorry he was that such a dreadful thing had happened to her. After all, it doesn't cost owt to say a word, he'd said to Grace. He'd accused his dad of being hard-hearted but Grace had chided him.

'We don't know what he's thinking,' she said, reproving him. 'It must have been a terrible shock to him, to any man to have that happen to his lass . . . '

'If owt like that ever happened to thee,' John had vowed, 'I'd kill t' bugger responsible, I would, even though they might hang me for it!'

'Aye, well, happen that's why your dad is keeping a tight hold on himself,' Grace had said. 'You mustn't judge him.'

John was glum; the household had been a mess since all this happened, with Thrummell coming and asking questions, with Liz sulking because she'd not been told, even his mam, looking at Anne and crying quietly in the kitchen when she thought nobody was looking. The only ray of light had come from Aunt Eleanor, who'd taken over when she returned, had seen all the callers to the house, had taken Anne into Whitby to the lawyer's office to meet Villiers, to make statements that were typed out and signed in front of witnesses. Others had been approached. Captain Walham had sworn a statement that he had known Anne all her life, and had never seen her take an intoxicating drink.

Thrummell's clerk had been to each of the pubs in

Ravenswyke and had obtained a sworn statement that Anne Godson was not a regular drinker in any one of them, and that the most they'd ever seen her drink was lemonade shandy. Both Liz and Anne would have got a braying from Reuben, if ever he'd discovered them drinking anything stronger than shandy in a pub!

John had tried hard to be protective towards Anne, to sit with her and talk to her when, as so often happened, she was staring off into space, lost in her thoughts. He and Grace had stayed at home more than they usually did, to offer her a game of rummy or Monopoly. But she seemed to have no interest in games. Everybody seemed to have had the same idea at Christmas, and the pillow case each of them traditionally hung at the bottom of the bed in anticipation of gifts was filled, for Anne, with things to do and things to read. John had bought her a boxed weaving loom, that could be assembled easily and on which you could weave table mats twelve inches square. He'd paid all of three pounds for it and had been upset when she never even put it together. He'd assembled it one evening to try to stimulate her interest, but had found stringing the pins fiddly work. Which was surprising, since he was such a dab hand at tying hooks and baiting lines . . .

Emily, practical as ever, had bought a packet of needles, and skeins of white knitting wool. They, too, had been ignored.

Reuben hadn't been able to get leave, or so he'd said, for Christmas. It was either him, or Smitherson, and since Smitherson had done him so many kindnesses, he'd volunteered to man the office during the holiday break, but hadn't told his family. He felt that he owed it to Smitherson but, anyway, hadn't wanted to be home during that time, with its sentimentality, its associations with birth. He also felt an enormous burden of guilt at the violence that had erupted from him when he'd received Emily's letter and hadn't understood all the facts. That was one reason why he hadn't found it easy to talk to Anne when he'd eventually come home. He was appalled that he could so easily have thought her a slut, knowing that in his mind he hadn't given her the benefit of the doubt but had immediately assumed the worst. As the evidence had unfolded during the pre-trial investigation, he'd felt worse and worse. Dammit, the lass was his own daughter; all her life she'd behaved herself and never given him or her mam worries the way other lasses had. If it had been Liz he could have understood – Liz's head had always been full of romanticised notions even to the extent that, when she'd been fourteen/fifteen, she'd become a chronic liar! He'd soon put a stop to that by skelping her a time or two.

But it was one thing to skelp the lasses for simple trangressions, and another to half kill three lads in London because a letter had upset him! It added further to his doubts about himself, the doubts that had begun with the eyes. Was he going mad? Raving mad? Was he losing control of himself? It was a fear that never left him these days, causing him to withdraw, keep a tight rein on his feelings and his words, in case he should give summat away of his inner turmoil. And he knew the way he was behaving was affecting the lad, John.

'Aye, poor bloody lass!' he repeated to John as he downed his half of bitter. 'Come on, let's be getting home. Mam'll have t' dinner on and we'd best make haste if we're going back to t' Court.'

He nodded to Ephraim on the way out, and Ephraim nodded back, knowing they'd pay for the drinks next time they came in, or the time after. He didn't even bother to get out the slate; John, he knew, had a perfect remembrance of his financial obligations and the Godson credit was safe as a bank deposit.

They were sitting round the table when Reuben arrived, waiting for him. This last time, he'd taken to eating with the family again. He sat at one end of the table, with Emily at the other, easy for the pots and pans. Eleanor sat half way down one side, facing the door, with John across from her. The stew had been on the stove all morning and was thick with meat and vegetables, savoury with onions.

'My, that tastes grand, lass,' Reuben said as he took the first spoonful. 'There's nowt like home cooking . . . '

'Aye, it were no problem to put it together,' Emily said, pleased that for once he'd praised her cooking. 'Though I don't imagine it's much for you, Eleanor, with all that fancy foreign food you were telling us about?'

Eleanor had talked about anything and everything to divert their minds during the pre-trial days. Italy, of course, was a fruitful source of anecdotes, though she knew they didn't understand the difference between a spaghetti and a Botticelli.

'You'd be astounded, Emily, how much you come to long for solid, well-cooked, tasty home-cooking, when you're eating abroad. I used to long for the sight of a potato . . . '

'Get away!' Emily said, 'there's nowt much about taties . . . '

'Yes, and some of our John's fish! Cooked the way you do it, either in milk, or in batter, without a bunch of herbs taking away the taste!' Eleanor was lying furiously, but knew they wouldn't know. She was remembering one evening in a village on the coast south of Genoa, where they'd gone to seek a suspected Bernini marble. They hadn't found the marble, but they had found a fisherman who'd brought in a dorado and whose wife had cooked it for them over a slow fire, rubbing it with salt, fennel, and thyme . . . Sometimes, often in fact, her heart ached to be back with Philip, but she thrust such thoughts resolutely aside, knowing her place was here, with her family.

In the silence which followed Eleanor's remark,

Reuben cleared his throat, his usual preliminary, these days, to speaking.

'Aye, lass,' he said, addressing Anne. 'It's going to be bad for thee this afternoon, when tha' has to go into t' witness box and speak up in front of all of them. But, tha' knows, we'll be with thee, all of us. We'll be with thee, just remember that.'

There were tears in Emily's eyes, of gratitude to Reuben for finally speaking out and giving Anne that bit of encouragement she sorely needed. Anne herself sat there stony-faced, as if all the fight had been crushed out of her by these events over which she had no control.

'Aye,' John said, 'we're all with thee. The whole family.'

Anne could only nod her head.

'And that includes Grace, here, too, doesn't it, Grace?'

'Well, I'm practically family, aren't I, with grandma Godson's diamond ring on my finger!'

'It looks well on you,' Eleanor said. 'Young girls should always wear diamonds. They look so much better on a young girl than an older woman . . . '

'I like sapphires myself,' Liz said. 'Nothing nicer than a sapphire, set in pearls. Did you see that ring Mrs Probert was wearing in the Court. That's where all their profits go, I'll be bound. On buying jewels for Mrs Probert!'

Reuben wanted to say, stop your chattering, lass, but realised her mindless prattle was serving a useful purpose in letting them all think their own thoughts. It was going to be a trying afternoon for all of them, but especially for Anne, sitting up there on the witness chair. As he looked down the table at her he felt a surge of pity for her, and love. He'd been a fortunate man, he knew, and could love all his children, each in a different way. Even prattling Liz, who was going on about some brooch or other she'd seen.

'Eat a bit of dinner, Anne,' he said. 'Tha' needs thy food, wi' two mouths to feed!'

He meant the remark well, but it must have hit Anne in a way he didn't intend. She choked, bursting into tears and sobs, and got up from the table. Eleanor got up with her and followed her out of the room, and they all heard the sound of retching coming from the bathroom John had installed upstairs.

'I meant no harm,' Reuben said. 'I meant the lass no harm!'

'We know you didn't, Reuben,' Emily said. 'It's just that the lass is sensitive about t' baby, that's all.'

They were walking down the street towards the Slip, where the taxis would be waiting to take them back to Court, when they met Elsie Tockett coming up, out of breath from hurrying.

'I hoped I hadn't missed you!' she said. She put her arms round Anne and kissed her on the cheek; Anne looked uncomfortable but accepted the embrace.

'How did it go this morning?' Elsie asked Reuben.

'Aye, well, this morning it were just him, and witnesses explaining what he'd done to put drink into her Tizer...'

Elsie had tried to get someone else to take her hospital duty that morning, but hadn't been able to find anyone. Ezra had explained to her that the morning would be taken up with witnesses, that Anne herself wouldn't appear on the witness stand until the afternoon.

'Come in the car with us,' Emily suggested, 'and our Liz can travel with her dad and Grace.'

Liz pouted; she wanted to be next to Elsie, with her fine clothes and her expensive perfume and jewellery, though Elsie was only wearing her three rings, and a string of pearls over her cashmere jumper. Liz envied Elsie; she had achieved everything that Liz would have liked for herself – a big house, a rich husband, and all the trappings to go with it. Why, they said Elsie had a fur coat worth five hundred pounds. Five hundred pounds for a coat! To Liz, that was living!

The Great Hall was filled with sunshine when they returned, the air filled with rising dust-motes. The heating radiators had begun to take effect, and the atmosphere was comfortable with after-lunch euphoria, much less tense than at the start of the day. Now it had been established beyond doubt that Meaney *had* put the alcohol in the drink he'd given Anne, though Bernstein had successfully made the point that such a thing was normal, that Meaney was no worse than any other GI at the dances. Somehow Bernstein had managed to imply that all the soldiers who went to the dances had the same purpose in mind, to find a girl, give her a few drinks, and then take her down on to the scaurs, or up into the moorland. He'd contrived to make it all sound natural, a part of life itself, of being human rather than criminal.

Now they were going to hear the answer to the vital questions: did Anne know she was being given drink, did she know what was happening to her, was she a willing, a consenting party? If she *were* then the 'with intent to cause her bodily harm' part of the indictment would not stand up. And without that, there was no case, since it wasn't a crime to give another person alcohol.

Villiers had asked Colonel Sampson for a meeting after lunch; they'd all sat together in the library before the trial started again.

'It must be obvious to all of us that certain fundamental rules of procedure are being ignored in the course of this hearing,' he'd said pompously. 'I'm aware that a certain informality is permitted in the American Courts of Justice, and here we are observing American rather than British standards of conduct!'

Sampson had nodded impatiently. 'We're trying an American on American territory, Mr Villiers,' he'd said.

'We're using American procedures. I can't see the harm in that.'

'The victim is an English girl . . . ' Villiers said.

'We're aware of that fact . . . '

'I just would like to make it quite clear that if I feel the girl is receiving less than English standards of justice, I shall feel obliged to intervene, irrespective of the definition that has arbitrarily been placed on the nature of these proceedings . . . '

Sampson's temper, carefully controlled up to this moment, flared. 'Mr Villiers,' he said, 'I'm the President of that Court. I, and I alone, will decide if the girl is receiving justice! Now, let's get back in there, and get the show on the road!'

'*I object* . . . ' Villiers said, but the sound of his voice was lost in the shuffling of feet as they filed out of the room.

'Your name is Anne Godson?' Major Siddons asked, his voice low and kindly.

'Yes, Anne Godson.'

'You live in the village of Old Quaytown, in Ravenswyke, in the county of Yorkshire?'

'Yes, I do . . . '

'And you are a spinster, aged twenty-two . . . ?'

'Yes, I am.'

Though her voice was faint, it was clear enough to be heard across the silent room.

'Miss Godson, what is your normal daily consumption of alcohol . . . ?'

'I object,' Villiers said.

'Objection over-ruled,' Sampson said immediately.

'How much alcohol, in the form of drinks, do you normally drink each day?'

Anne looked bewildered. 'I don't,' she said, 'I don't drink every day.'

Siddons looked satisfied. 'Well then, Miss Godson,' he

asked urbanely, 'let me ask you how much you drink each *week*.'

'Objection . . . ,' Villiers said.

'Over-ruled,' Sampson replied without even looking at him.

'How much would you estimate you normally drink each week?'

'I don't,' Anne said, still bewildered. 'I go out perhaps once a week, but to the pictures, or to a dance, and I drink Tizer or lemonade.'

'So, you are not in the habit of drinking alcoholic drinks, such as whisky, gin, rum, brandy, liqueurs . . . ?'

Anne shook her head. 'No,' she said, 'my dad would skelp me if he found me drinking strong stuff . . . '

A ripple of quiet laughter ran round the Court; Mrs Probert and the Rev Michael Roberts looked at each other and smiled.

'It isn't usual, then, for a well-brought up girl in Yorkshire to drink strong drinks . . . ?'

'I don't know about others, but we don't, in our family . . . '

Siddons nodded approvingly. Now the Court had heard, from the girl's own lips, that she wasn't a habitual drinker. Later he would be submitting evidence in support of that contention, but for the moment he was trying to sketch the girl's personality with a few simple strokes.

'These – socials, I think you call them, these dances, are they held very often in the Chapel Rooms?'

'Most every week . . . '

'And you usually go . . . ?'

'If I'm not working . . . '

'It's a good opportunity to meet Americans, to get yourself a boy-friend?' The question was deftly, laconically asked and, as he'd hoped, aroused an instant reaction. The trouble, Siddons felt, was that the bloody fool, Villiers, wouldn't let his client demonstrate her feelings for herself.

'I strongly object to that last question,' Villiers shouted, taking the Court's attention away from the girl's outraged face.

'And I, equally strongly, object to you raising your voice in this Court, Mr Villiers,' Sampson snapped. 'Objection over-ruled.'

'I've got a boy-friend,' Anne replied. 'I mean, I don't go to the socials . . . it's, like, just because, it's the Chapel, isn't it, and we've always gone to t' Chapel socials . . . '

'It is customary for the girls of Old Quaytown to attend the social functions held in the Chapel, is that what you're saying, Miss Godson?'

Even Sampson smiled at that. 'You really mustn't put words into the witness's mouth, Major,' he said, his voice gently reproving.

'We always go. We used to go before the war, before there were any Americans.'

'Thank you, Miss Godson.'

Grace squeezed John's hand. 'She's doing all right,' she whispered in his ear. John hadn't understood the drift of Siddon's questions, and had felt anger when Siddons had slipped in the bit about going to the socials to get American boy-friends. Now he realised what had been done; clearly it had been established from Anne's own mouth and her facial expressions, that she had no intention of picking up Americans at the socials, that she'd gone there because she always went there . . . He shook his head wonderingly – the ways of lawyers and Courts was a mystery to him. Why had they gone into all this guff? Why hadn't they asked her, straight out, did you know he was giving you whisky . . . ?

'You like dancing, do you?' Siddons was asking.

'Yes, I do.'

'You can do them all? Waltz, slow-foxtrot, quickstep, veleta . . . ?'

'Yes, we used to have dancing classes when we were younger . . . '

'Since you *can* do them all, would you say you dance frequently?'

'Well, I go there to dance . . . '

'You go there to dance, so you dance as many dances as you can? Do you receive many invitations to dance?'

'I suppose so . . . '

'And when you dance, you get hot, and when you get hot, you get thirsty . . . ?'

'Is that a question, Major Siddons?' Sampson asked. 'Would you care to rephrase it before Mr Villiers spends our time on another objection . . . ?'

Villiers appeared to have given up. His legs were wound together like the tendrils of a vine; his fingers had formed into a cat's cradle in his lap, and his chin had sunk to his chest.

'Do you find that dancing frequently, as frequently as you appear to do, increases your thirst, Miss Godson?'

'I suppose it does . . . '

'Do you find, Miss Godson, that when you are more thirsty than usual, you drink more copiously than usual?'

'I suppose I do . . . '

'Don't *suppose*, Miss Godson. Tell us, do you, or don't you, drink more copiously when you are thirsty?'

'I do . . . '

'Thank you.' Siddons paused to let the implications of that remark sink in. If the girl danced vigorously, she'd drink more than usual. If Meaney was putting alcohol in her drink, she'd imbibe more alcohol, she'd become more drunk. And less likely to be able to resist what had happened to her on the scaurs. He could already begin to formulate his winding up statement. Here we have a young lady supporting her local Chapel, a young lady with an ability to dance, happily doing what she had done so many times before, dancing, laughing, drinking refreshing cordials to quench the thirst of her happy occupation. Little did she know that each refreshing drink she took had been debased, poisoned . . .

'What were you drinking on that occasion, Miss Godson?' he asked casually.

'Well, we know . . . '

'I'll rephrase that question,' he said quickly. 'What did you *think* you were drinking?'

The Court waited, watching Anne's face. This was the critical question, the vital moment. She looked across the Court at Meaney, her eyes catching his for the first time during that entire hearing. The look on his face was one of pure misery. He was half-turned towards Major Bernstein, his arms awkwardly placed beside him. He was wearing full uniform, with all the symbols and emblems of the US Army in position. His hair had been carefully combed but still sprang from his head.

Anne looked pityingly at him, biting her lower lip.

'What did you *think* you were drinking on that occasion, Miss Godson?' Major Siddons repeated loudly, as if trying to command her attention, to pull her eyes back from that forlorn figure sitting across the Court-room.

Anne tilted her head slightly to one side and then shook it gently as she spoke. The curls of her hair moved gently beside her oval face. 'I thought . . . I thought . . . that I was drinking . . . Tizer . . . ' she whispered.

The court seemed to sigh with relief.

There it was. She thought she was drinking harmless Tizer.

And it had been established that she was drinking whisky and Tizer.

Siddons waited for a short heart-beat pause, then moved quickly back in again, pounding the message home. 'You thought you were drinking Tizer. You were dancing, you were thirsty because you were dancing and you were taking deep gulps of the refreshment you'd asked for, and you thought was Tizer . . . '

'That's not a question, Major Siddons,' Colonel Sampson said, 'but I don't hear anyone objecting.'

'I thought it was Tizer,' Anne said. 'Honest, I thought it was . . . '

The rest of the questioning was anti-climactic; the Court had heard what it wanted to hear, that Anne Godson had not known that Meaney was giving her whisky to drink. There was, however, a shiver of expectation when Bernstein rose to begin his cross-questioning, and even Villiers seemed to waken, as he uncurled his limbs and sat erect, his beak-like nose pointing like a gun dog's across the room.

'I believe you said you like to dance, Miss Godson,' he said, 'and that you receive many invitations to go out on the floor. Do you accept all the invitations that come your way – to dance, I mean?'

His manner managed to suggest that perhaps she received other invitations of a different sort . . .

'Well, no, I mean, yes, I mean, if people ask me to dance . . . ' Anne stopped, lost in confusion. After all, if a fellow was nice enough to ask for a dance, you didn't want to make him look a fool by turning him down, leaving him standing there, did you?

'Do you mean, you'll dance with anybody who asks you . . . ?' he snapped, his voice full of contempt.

'No,' she said, agitated, 'I didn't mean that!'

'Then what *did* you mean, *Miss* Godson?'

Sampson smiled inwardly. He liked it when lawyers had a go, when they used all their skill and artifice to impugn the standing of a witness. It was an old court-room trick, but he liked its gutsiness.

'I meant, well, the fellows are all right. You don't get the rough ones in the Chapel socials, like you do in the dances in Whitby . . . '

'So, you *do* dance with just about anyone . . . ?'

Anne looked despairingly at Sampson, who smiled benevolently back at her. It was one of Sampson's maxims that you had to earn what you received. Villiers had screwed them out of more money than they'd wanted to pay in damages – now let the girl earn it! Let her show she was worth the six hundred pounds they'd reluctantly settled on, with the seven-eighths of the normal marriage allowance.

'You must answer more precisely, Miss Godson,' he said. 'You mustn't be vague in your answers or we shall all misunderstand you.'

Bernstein had made his point. Now he'd try to make another one. 'Do you know what whisky tastes like?' he asked.

'Yes, of course . . . '.

'Why *of course*, Miss Godson. You have testified that you're not in the habit of drinking it.'

'I have tasted it.'

'When, Miss Godson?'

'Sometimes, when I've had a bad cold, my mam has given it to me in lemonade.'

'Ah! In lemonade. You've *tasted* whisky in lemonade, even though you've had a bad cold when presumably your taste-buds are impaired. Then can you explain to the Court, *Miss* Godson, why it is that, with your taste-buds presumably unimpaired on the night of this dance, you were unable to *taste* the whisky in the *Tizer?*'

The room buzzed with interest. It was a good question! Why *hadn't* she tasted the whisky in the Tizer?

She looked at Bernstein like a trapped animal, then at Villiers. He shrugged his shoulders. It was a perfectly valid legitimate question. He'd known that somebody was going to ask it in the course of the hearing, and had even warned the girl. Silly little chit, to bring in that business about the whisky in the lemonade – she'd given Bernstein a perfect basis on which to ask his question. When he'd asked her the same question – why hadn't she tasted the whisky in this Tizer drink, she'd said she thought it tasted a bit funny but all the drinks were tasting different in wartime when they couldn't get the right things to make them out of . . . He'd instructed her not to say that in Court, but to stick to a straight denial – no, she hadn't tasted the whisky in her drink. And now she'd given Bernstein the perfect opening, and he'd seized it.

'Answer the question, Miss Godson,' Bernstein said.

'I didn't taste the whisky . . . '

'That's not the question I asked . . . '

She shook her head helplessly and he bored in. 'I asked you why, if you are capable of detecting whisky in lemonade when you have a cold, you can't detect it in Tizer when you don't have a cold.'

Villiers looked at her across the Court, trying to *will* her to make the only answer possible in the circumstances.

'*Why* didn't you detect the whisky, Miss Godson . . . ?'

'I don't know why, but I didn't . . . '

Villiers breathed a sigh of relief. It wasn't a good answer but it was the only legitimate one open to her. That devil, Bernstein! He had to admire his technique, even though he deplored his motive.

'You talked with the other girls at the social, Miss Godson, I presume?'

'Yes, of course.'

'They were all happy . . . ?'

'I suppose so . . . '

'We aren't interested in suppositions, Miss Godson. Were the other girls happy?'

'Some were, some weren't . . . '

'Why, do you know why, some girls were not happy?'

'Well, Maisie Faulkner was sick. She wasn't happy...'

'Maisie Faulkner was sick, she wasn't happy,' Bernstein intoned. 'Miss Godson, did you see any other girls being sick . . . ?'

'A girl from Whitby, I don't know her name, I saw her in the lavatory . . . '

'Being sick . . . ?'

'I didn't actually see it . . . '

'Miss Godson, you were at a social. A number of girls were being sick. Do you expect this Court to believe you didn't realise the girls were being sick because they were drinking *alcoholic drinks*. Do you expect this Court to believe that you didn't realise *that you, yourself, were drinking whisky*!'

Siddons and Villiers both leaped to their feet, saying, Objection. Sampson looked in amusement from one to the other. Then he looked elaborately at his watch.

'Gentlemen,' he said, 'I think the time has come to adjourn this hearing for today. I take it under notice that both of you have raised objections to the last question of Major Bernstein. I think it might be as well if we all study a transcript of the question before I give my ruling!' He stood up; the Master at Arms rapped his gavel on his table and called, 'Will you all please rise.'

Anne was sitting on the chair on the witness stand, already crying when Eleanor got to her.

'That brute,' Eleanor said, 'that wretched brute . . . '

Bernstein had left the Court by then. All in all, he was quite pleased with himself. It had been a good afternoon's work! The law said, beyond any reasonable doubt. That was how he intended to force Siddons to make his case. Beyond any reasonable doubt. Only then could Bernstein's conscience be eased; only then could he believe that justice, no matter how hurtful it might be to innocent parties, had truly been done!

Eleanor and Emily rode home in the taxi with Anne, leaving the rest of the Godson family to crowd into the other vehicle with Reuben. Just before the taxi pulled away, Emily beckoned to Elsie Tockett.

'Ride in here, with us, Elsie,' she asked. 'Explain it all to her, Elsie,' Emily pleaded as the taxi pulled away. 'Mark Tockett sits on t' Bench. You've been there . . . '

Mark Tockett had, indeed, been a local Justice of the Peace, and had sat on the Bench in Whitby Magistrate's Court. Elsie, as always interested in everything her husband did, had attended to watch him with pride as he dispensed justice to petty offenders, or referred more serious cases to higher Courts.

'It must be hard to understand, Anne,' Elsie started. 'It's not like being at home, or being up in front of the Headmaster at school. The Court has to be *sure*, you see. They have to be sure. That's why they ask all sorts of questions you might think are irrelevant. They don't know what sort of person you are; they don't know anything about Old Quaytown, and how the lasses behave themselves, not like the lasses in Newquay Town, or the top of the Bank. So, they have to go on probing, probing. It's like a doctor, when you've got a bit of glass in your hand, and he pokes about until he finds it and pulls it out. But he's not sure if he's left another bit in, another bit he can't see and so he goes on probing, probing, until he's certain he's got it all out.'

Anne had stopped crying and was looking straight ahead in abject misery.

'Elsie knows what she's talking about, love,' Emily said. 'She's seen it all, with Mr Tockett. On t' Bench!'

Eleanor squeezed Anne's hand. 'After tomorrow,' she said, 'it'll all fade away like a nightmare.'

Elsie had come with a suggestion. 'My husband knows people in the War Office,' she said. 'We've been talking about you . . . '

'Everybody's talking about me . . . ,' Anne said flatly.

'Aye, but not that way,' Elsie said. 'My husband thinks it might be possible to have your fiancé posted back to England. Then you could get married . . . You are engaged, aren't you?'

'Unofficially, yes they are,' Emily said. 'I'm sure Reuben would give his consent.'

Eleanor was shaking her head. 'Why're you doing that?' Emily asked.

'It's up to Anne and Hugh Dubiel when they get married,' she said. 'It's not something that they can be rushed into . . . '

'He might not want to go ahead with it,' Anne said, her voice listless, 'with me with a baby. Damaged goods. He might not want me . . . '

'Nay, lass, if he loves you . . . ' Emily protested. To her the issue was simple. If this Dubiel said he loved Anne, then he loved her, and would want to help her through this trouble. He'd take the baby in, just as many a lad in Ravenswyke had taken in another's baby to get the girl he'd set his heart on! It didn't seem to be happening so much nowadays, but when she'd been a lass, time and again the bride had gone to t' chapel altar with her dress bulging. *And* the father of the baby not the one waiting for her at the altar!

'You ought to write to him,' Eleanor said. 'At least, you ought to give him the choice . . . ' She'd been surprised to learn, when she came home, that Anne hadn't written to Hugh Dubiel since the trouble, and had expressly forbidden Liz to mention the matter in her letters to Pete Dodds. The two men were serving in different parts of Europe, but Anne was afraid they might have maintained contact. Or might meet if ever they got leave in London.

'I'll write to him,' Anne said, 'when this is all over.'

'Won't you come up and have a cup of tea?' Emily

asked Elsie when the taxi arrived at the top of the Slip, but Elsie shook her head.

'I'd love to,' she said, 'but Mark's coming back from London today and I want to make certain everything's ready for him.'

It had been arranged that the taxi would take her up to Tockett House before returning to Cliff Top where it was garaged. Emily soon had brewed a pot of tea for them all, and had taken a tin of cakes from the cupboard.

'It'll keep us going,' she said, 'while I get t' supper on.'

Reuben sat on the sofa next to Anne, holding her hand awkwardly in his. He'd never been a demonstrative man, and the Godson family was not one much for touching and embracing.

He patted the back of her hand with his other one, saying, 'Now then, lass, tha' did champion today. It's going to be all right, I tell thee, it's going to be all right, take my word for it.' Then he placed her limp hand in her lap, handling it as if it were fragile porcelain.

'It's going to be all right,' he said.

John and Grace looked at each other, not knowing what to say. 'Are you stopping for supper?' he asked quietly. She nodded. 'All right if Grace stops for supper, Mam?' he asked.

'Of course, no need to ask . . . ' Emily smiled at Grace with true warmth; it would be a relief to have somebody non-family at the table.

Liz was playing with Martin, dandling him on her knee. 'You been a good lad while we've been out?' she asked him.

'Yes. We went for walkies . . . '

'That's good . . . '

'She made me have a sleep . . . '

'That's good . . . ' Liz's mind was elsewhere. She'd known they were putting whisky into the drinks at the socials. All the girls had talked about it. How funny, come to think about it, that Anne hadn't realised. Still, Anne always had been a bit dozy . . . Wouldn't catch anybody getting Liz drunk. She remembered the night of the social only vaguely. Three of them had met the three American boys – she couldn't even remember their names. They'd left the social and gone up the Bank to the Hotel. She'd had two port-and-lemons. On the way back down the Bank, the American she was with had tried to get fresh, but she'd slapped his hand away, told him she was already engaged and what kind of a girl did he think she was anyway? She'd been home by eleven. It had been quarter past by the time Anne came in, and she was already in bed and dozy with sleep . . . But funny that Anne hadn't known about the drinks . . .

'I'm going out for a walk,' Anne said suddenly.

'Good. I'll come with you,' Liz said.

'I want to be on my own,' Anne said stubbornly.

They all looked at Reuben. 'Let the lass go out on her own,' he said. 'She's had enough of folks today.'

Anne went upstairs, came down again with her thicker coat. 'That's right, love,' Emily said, 'tha' mun dress warm. Dinner'll be in half an hour . . . '

'If I'm not back, put mine on a plate,' Anne said. Emily started to protest but Reuben cut across her.

'Aye, lass, we'll keep summat warm for thee,' he said firmly.

Anne went out, leaving them sitting silently around the room, not looking at each other, not wishing to speak. It was Eleanor who broke the silence by deliberately introducing a subject she knew would be controversial.

'I've had a word with Mrs Burroughs,' she said. 'I can have the cottage.'

'The one Elsie lived in . . . ?'

'Yes. I was wondering if you'd come up with me before you go back? Give me a bit of advice as to how to fix it up. I shall want a bathroom and a lavatory fixing inside, and I don't believe it's been wired for electric.'

'You know I'm opposed to it,' Reuben said. 'Godsons have always lived here.' He glanced up at the beam which bore his name, following that of his father Silas. 'Our dad wouldn't countenance it, I can tell you. He'd say your proper place, so long as you've breath in your body, is here.'

Eleanor tried to laugh but it came out as a shrill sound. 'Oh, la, Reuben! It's 1945 now. No harm will befall me up there. I shall come and see you, often. You'll come and see me . . . '

'Folks'll reckon we've rowed,' Emily said anxiously.

'It's not folks I'm thinking about,' Reuben said. 'It's us. The Godsons. It's keeping t' family together, the way we've always been. I don't want t' family breaking up. There's plenty of room for our John and Grace in Wilfred's room, until I'm gone. Then they'll have t' big room. There's no call for you to move out of your place. I built it special for you because I know how you like to be by yourself a bit, and have your own stuff about you, and I can respect that. Nobody likes having folks on top of them all the time. But, to live under a different roof...'

'We'd be very happy in Wilfred's room, Auntie,' Grace said. 'We don't want to turn you out of your place.'

'That's right, Auntie Eleanor,' John said, and they all laughed when Martin mimicked him, 'yeth, that's right, Auntie Eleanor . . . '

When the laugh had finished, Eleanor said, quietly, 'I've made up my mind, Reuben. You and I are of an age. I'm not going to get married. Slowly, but surely, the two of us are going to become older, more set in our ways. We'd be getting on each other's nerves, and we don't want that. I want to be here in Old Quaytown because, after all, I'm a Godson, but I want my independence in a place of my own. I've a bit put by, and Mrs Burroughs is only asking two hundred for the cottage which I can find out of my own pocket . . . '

'It's expensive. It can't have cost more than a hundred to build.'

'Prices are going up, Reuben. This is 1945, not 1935...'

'Then you'll have the cost of fixing it up.'

'Wilton says it should come to £50, or thereabouts.'

'Aye, well, if Wilton does it, it'll be done right.'

'I'll give you a hand wi' curtains, Eleanor, if you've a mind . . . ' Emily said.

'So will I,' Grace volunteered. 'I can use Mam's sewing machine.'

Soon they were lost in talk of what could be done. Reuben knew the cottage well, and had often visited it when Elsie Tockett, Milner as she then was, had lived there. John knew it; one of the Burroughs lads had been a fisherman until he drowned in the bad storms of '37. Only Reuben didn't join in with enthusiasm, preoccupied with the knowledge this would be yet another division in the family. In all likelihood, the two girls would marry their fiancés, and go off to America. Martin would doubtless be taken from them. There'd be only him and Emily, John and Grace, and whatever bairns they might have, to keep the Godson name going. He was unaccountably depressed by the thought of the future, by the changes he could foresee not only in the Godson family, but also in the Old Quaytown way of life.

'Tha' mun make up thy own mind, Eleanor,' he said. 'I'll not stand in your way!'

He stood up and took his coat from the peg behind the door. 'I'm just off to t' pub for half an hour,' he said, looking at John.

'I think I'll stop at home, Dad,' John said. He could see

his dad wanted to be on his own or he'd have invited his son to come.

'Keep an eye out for Anne,' Emily said. 'I don't like her to be out on her own of an evening.'

'Nowt will befall her,' Reuben growled. 'Tha' have to learn to stop worrying!'

When he had gone, Eleanor, Liz, John and Grace settled down to a game of Monopoly. Emily, who had no head for games, brought out her basket of mending; socks, shirts, pullovers all needing her endless attention. She sat by the fire thinking of the day's events, suffering once again as she'd suffered all through the hearing, for her daughter. Poor Anne – whatever had she done to deserve such a thing? She could have understood it more had it been Liz, who was thoughtless and careless. She'd be very happy when Liz was married and protected by a strong husband, which this Pete Dodds undoubtedly would be. But Anne had always been thoughtful, careful, always restrained in her life, and had never given Emily a moment's worry. Of course, she was no angel; Emily could see herself so often in Anne and she'd done many things as a young lass she blushed now to recall. But there was a world of difference between making a young lass's mistakes and being a wrong 'un! Emily longed in her own inarticulate way to find something positive that she could do, some way she could fight *actively* for her daughter, instead of merely being there in a supporting role. She'd have liked to stand on her hind legs that afternoon and tell that Bernstein a thing or two, waggle her fist at him and tell him firmly to stop talking to her daughter in that way. She could understand how some men could become violent with anger; if she'd been a man she'd have been sorely tried not to go up to him and punch him on the nose! How any man could take it out of a young girl like that . . . Making all those suggestions . . .

'Our Anne's a long time,' she said at half-past nine.

She said it again at ten o'clock, to John, but he di
nothing.

'Nay, Mam, I've just got a hotel on Mayfair,' he said
She'd no idea what he meant, but she'd never playe
Monopoly.

It was quarter-past ten when Reuben came home and
unusually, Emily could tell he'd had a few.

'Isn't our lass home yet, then?' he said.

'No,' Emily said, 'and I'm that worried.'

'Nay, tha' worries too much, lass,' he said.

At half-past ten the game ended.

'Now will you take a walk round, and look for ou
Anne?' Emily asked, exasperated.

John dragged on his coat. 'Come on, Grace,' he said
'I'll take you home.'

'And don't stay half the night, courting,' Emily pleade
with him. 'I want our lass home, and in bed.'

Something of his mam's worry communicated itself t
John, and he bundled Grace inside her door with only
quick goodnight kiss and a muttered 'see thee in t' morn
and don't forget, I love thee!' It could have taken te
minutes for Grace to demonstrate her answer to that, bu
he pushed her inside, where he knew her mam would b
waiting with a cup of tea for news of the day's hearing
He walked rapidly round the few streets of Ol
Quaytown, to all the places Anne might possibly be o
such a cold night. Of course, she might be sitting huddle
on the bench seat they'd put by the Cockpit for th
pensioners, looking out to sea. Courting couples some
times sat there on late summer evenings because you
couldn't be seen in detail from the houses nearby, bu
Anne wasn't there.

'By gow,' he thought, 'it's a cold night to be out thi
late.' He tried to rack his brain for people she might b
visiting, but he knew it was doubtful she'd have gone t
see anyone in Old Quaytown tonight. And, if she had, th

Old Quaytowners were early-to-bed folks, and they'd have hinted at her to be on her way long afore now.

He walked down the street again to the Snug, which was closed, though one light burned inside over the bar where Ephraim would be washing up the glasses before locking the door, something he'd never done prior to the war. John knocked and tried the door; it was on the latch and he was able to open it and go inside. Ephraim had just finished, and was hanging the wet cloth over the beer pumps.

'Nay, John,' he said, 'what are you after at this time of night? Your dad's long gone.'

'Nay, I were wondering, have you seen owt of our Anne?'

'Your *Anne*? This evening? I'd have thought she was long abed by this time, with the Court an' all . . . '

'She hasn't been in . . . ?'

'Anne? In here? Haven't seen sight nor sound of her, and wouldn't expect to! Is she missing, or summat?'

'No. She's gone out. I fully imagine she'll be with Betty. You know how they talk, the lasses, when they get together. But I just thought . . . as I was passing . . . I'd give her a walk home . . . ' It sounded lame and they both knew it. The Snug was the end of the world in Old Quaytown. You could never happen to be 'just passing'.

'Here, John, is owt wrong?' Ephraim asked.

'It's our Anne,' John said. 'She went for a walk and hasn't come back.'

'I hope nowt's happened . . . ?' Ephraim said, voicing a fear John had not yet dared to admit to himself. Both of them knew there was nowhere Anne could sensibly be at this time of night in Old Quaytown, if everything was all right with her. And if she'd been in anybody's house, staying that late because she wasn't feeling very well, they'd have been bound to send somebody to the Godson home to tell them. It had happened a time or two, as John could remember.

'Your Liz was feeling a bit dizzy and Mam's put her in the spare room . . . '

'Arthur's helping dad fix t' wireless and happen they'll be at it a bit late . . . '

'Eleanor says to tell you the meeting's going on a bit longer and not to worry because Arthur Helliwell will see her home, after.'

It was a tight-knit community with communication passing backwards and forwards all the time. John decided to hurry back up home and, when he arrived, he found Reuben sitting with his outdoor coat on.

'So, lad . . . ?' he asked.

'Can't see owt of her,' John said. 'Our Liz, do *you* know where she might be at this time of night . . . ?'

Liz was shaking her head. 'Nay, she wouldn't go see Heather Springfield at ten o'clock . . . ' Heather Springfield was Anne's closest personal friend who also worked in the rubber factory with them. But Heather would surely be asleep and in bed by this time of night . . . ?

'I'll pop up there,' John said. 'Just to make sure.'

The Springfields were cousins of Sam Gainer, who was a fisherman; they'd taken his cottage and Springfield meant to take out Sam's boat when he got out of the Navy. They had three daughters, two of whom were away in the WRNS. Springfield had been in the D-Day fighting. His wife had a hare-lip. They went to the Chapel . . .

'I'll bet she's with Captain Walham,' John said, as if light had suddenly dawned. 'That's where she'll be, I'll be bound.'

Without waiting for an answer to his guess, he hurried out and back down the street, to Grinklegate. He had to cross the new bridge across the mouth of the Cut that had been constructed when the Cut silted up in 1939, following the path Grace always took to the Gas Works Office, then turn right past Tockett's Boatyard towards the start of

Grinklegate. The moon was out in force but few people still showed lights in their windows at half-past eleven at night.

There were no lights in the back of Captain Walham's house, but there seldom were. The Captain liked to sit in the room on the other side which overlooked the ocean – the two of them, John guessed, would be sitting there talking, looking out across the moon-washed scaurs. He knocked on the solid door, using the brass knocker shaped whimsically in the form of a mermaid. He waited a minute or two and then knocked again, this time louder. They might have the wireless on . . . He knew Captain Walham had a big set and used to twiddle the knobs on the receiver, bringing in foreign stations. It was said he'd even got America once . . .

Still no reply.

John walked down the side of the house to go round it. Happen they were wearing the headphones the Captain used sometimes and couldn't hear the door. He'd reached the corner of the house and felt the cold blast of the air coming off the sea when, behind him, he heard the door open with a clatter of bolts, and the voice of Captain Walham.

'Now, who the devil can that be, disturbing a man's rest at this time of night . . . '

He hurried back. 'It's me, Captain Walham, John Godson . . . '

'Oh, aye, John, well you'd better come inside, I'm frozen to the marrow here on the step.' Captain Walham was wearing a heavy, piped dressing-gown over his flannelette night-shirt, and a woollen cap on his head with a pom-pom on it. He'd slipped his feet into rubber boots. They went inside and he slammed the great door.

'What's amiss, John?' he asked, leading the way into the sitting room with its large window overlooking the ocean. 'I've been abed this past two hours . . . '

'It's our Anne,' John said. 'She's not wi' you, then?'
Captain Walham turned to look at him. 'Wi' me, lad? At this time o' night, and dressed like this . . . ?'

John looked confused. 'I didn't mean it like that, Captain,' he said. 'She went out for a walk after supper, no, it was before supper, and she hasn't come back in yet. We wondered, like, if she was here with you, talking about the case . . . '

'No, lad, she isn't. Nor has been,' the Captain said thoughtfully. 'I've had Major Bernstein with me this evening. He's been telling me what happened up there today.'

It seemed treacherous of the Captain to be conferring with Major Bernstein, after the grilling he'd given Anne, but John was too worried about his sister to think more about that.

'You've checked all around?' the Captain said.

'Aye, all the likely places . . . '

'Then we'll have to think of a few unlikely places,' the Captain said. 'Now, you'll know this better than me. Is there anywhere special young folks go when they want to be on their own, you know what I mean, to do a bit of cuddling . . . ?'

'There's Willie's barn up on t' Cliff Top . . . '

'Have you been up there . . . ?'

'No, I haven't.'

'Then you'd better get up there right away. I'll get dressed . . . '

'Nay, Captain Walham, it's too cold for you to be out at this time of night . . . tramping about . . . '

'I'm not going tramping about, young John,' Captain Walham said grimly, 'I'm going up to the police station.'

By dawn, Old Quaytown was seething with activity, and there had been the flashes of torches all the way along the cliff tops and the scaurs beneath. Fortunately, the tide had been out and people had walked along the scaurs for half a mile each way, but found nothing. John had moved tirelessly from group to group, up on the cliffs one minute, down by the Slip the next. Somebody had telephoned to Mark Tockett and he had come down with Elsie to help take part in the search. The Snug had been opened, and Ephraim's wife, Peggy, was making cups of tea for everybody, using up the Hotel's ration. The police constable, Etheridge, had spread a large contour map of the district on one of the tables, and was marking each place as it was searched. The copse at Barn Top, the small fold above Cliff Top, the sides of the Cut, the tunnel called Smugglers' Run, the tunnel called The Bolts, up which smugglers used to 'bolt for the moors' when the revenue men chased them.

Grace Marsh and her mam had come down, bundled in thick coats. Emily was at home with Liz and Martin, but Eleanor was in the Snug with Reuben whose gaunt, haggard features grew more and more grey as the night wore on. It was Grace, finally, who told John where she thought he'd find Anne.

She'd taken him on one side and they were standing at the top of the Slip looking out over the sea, at the tide that was rising to full as the dawn came up in its spectacular display that, this day, found few interested observers.

'John,' Grace said, putting her hand in his, 'promise you won't be mad?'

'I won't be mad, love,' he said, disinterestedly. He thought she was going to confess some foolish girlish thing, to try to take his mind off Anne.

'I think I might know . . . where . . . your Anne is . . . '

He turned instantly. 'Where, love, where?'

'Mind you, I don't *know*, not for *sure*, but . . . like, I'm only guessing . . . '

'Where is she, Grace?' he asked her.

She looked round, verifying they couldn't be overheard. A large group was standing by the door of the Snug, waiting for instructions; a small knot of people conversed in low tones by the tractor used for hauling the boats. A couple, carrying a rope and a grappling hook, were leaning against the *Hope*. Gulls, no doubt disturbed by the nocturnal activity, wheeled overhead, cawking loudly, protesting. A dog barked, somewhere along Grinklegate. John looked at Grace's face, searching her tired, guilty eyes.

'What do you know, Gracie, love?' he asked, his voice softening. 'Come on, you'll have to tell us, sooner or later.'

'I don't *know*, John,' she said in misery, 'It's just a feeling . . . She might be at Old Sally Fieldings . . . '

He gave a groan. 'Of course,' he said, 'why didn't I *think* of *that*? Come on, let's get Auntie Eleanor . . . '

He popped his head inside the Snug door. Eleanor was poring over the map with the constable, shaking her head. They'd looked everywhere . . . She saw John's face, read his almost imperceptible shake of the head, and came outside.

'Come on up home,' he said in a normal voice. 'It's time you had summat to eat.'

She looked hard at him. 'Right,' she said, and they set off up the back lanes after she'd called into the Snug to say she was going for a bite to eat.

Once they were out of reach of the people at the bottom she turned to him.

'Right, where is she?' she said, thinking John had found his sister and needed her help.

'I don't know,' he said grimly, 'I don't know for sure, but Grace thinks she might have gone to see Old Sally Fieldings . . . '

Eleanor stood still, closed her eyes and swayed. 'Of course,' she said hoarsely, 'why didn't *I* think of that?' They went swiftly up the cobbled lane, beneath the arch at the entrance to Wally's Close, across Wesley Square named after the preacher had delivered a sermon there, to Beckview, a small knot of cottages that hung high over the edge of the cliff, looking down the bank to the sea below. Over the years the cottages that comprised Beckview one by one had slipped down into the ocean as erosion had eaten away the cliff; now the county council was talking about building a massive breakwater that would contain the hill-side, but the cost was estimated at millions and the scheme had often been shelved. Three cottages remained; two had lost their roofs as the walls had crumbled when the foundations went. The other, barely habitable and condemned by the Council these last twenty years, was occupied by Old Sally Fieldings.

Old Sally had taken over the mantle of herbalist, midwife, cure-all. Believed by most people to be slightly, if harmlessly, mad, she spent her days wandering in the hedgerows, picking plants and berries, with which to make her concoctions. They used to say Old Sally could cure a cough or a cold faster than any doctor, any chemist. They used to say her goose-grease, made each Christmas in her own special way, and stinking to high heaven for the rest of the year, was the best cure ever for lumbago, sciatica, rheumatism, arthritis. Her herb tea could move your bowels even if they'd been blocked by concrete. And her rose-madder water certainly cured pimples and boils.

Since the war, Old Sally's income had derived from one principal source.

She was the neighbourhood abortionist.

Anne was lying on an old door across one end of the tiny sitting room.

The lower half of her body was covered in blood. Old Sally had tried to staunch the flow with towels, all of which were filthy.

'You'd better get out of here,' Eleanor said to John.

'Nay, Auntie Eleanor, I shall stay. You might need me.'

Anne was unconscious. 'What have you done to her, you wicked old woman!' Eleanor said, slapping Old Sally across the cheeks to bring her to consciousness as she sat by the door-table, her eyes closed. Eleanor turned to Grace. 'See if you can find any water anywhere,' she said. 'John, you run up to the doctor's. Run, John. And tell him there'll be need of an ambulance and two strong men with a stretcher.'

John left at once, and Eleanor slapped Old Sally ruthlessly, jerking her back to full consciousness. 'What have you done to her, you wicked old woman?' she said. She turned to Grace who'd come in with a bucket of water. 'Is it clean?' she asked, but Grace shook her head.

'There's nothing clean in the place,' she said despairingly.

'It weren't me!' Old Sally suddenly said, screeching. 'She done it herself.'

'What do you mean, you evil woman, that it wasn't you . . . '

'Look,' Old Sally said. She fumbled about in the dross that lay with Anne, the towels soaked with blood, Anne's coat, her underclothes, and from them she produced a knitting needle. Eleanor immediately recognised the stop at the end of it – one of the pair Emily had bought for Anne's Christmas present, it had a ruby red counting device.

'She done it herself,' Old Sally Fielding screeched, 'then she come to me. As if I can do miracles. Half dead when she came in here. "Sal," she said, "you've got to help me. I've stuck a knitting needle up myself like they say, and nowt's happened." It were too late. No sooner had I got her on the truckle, than it all started. I've never touched her, never give her nowt, God's honest truth. Sure as God is my Judge, Eleanor Godson, I never touched her; the poor bairn done it to herself, wi' a knitting needle!'

The ambulance came mercifully quickly, and the two attendants, with John to help them, raced the stretcher through the twisted cobbled streets of Old Quaytown, the doctor hurrying beside them. When they took Anne into the emergency station in the Whitby hospital, she was barely alive. They laboured hours over her, giving her blood transfusions and massive injections to keep down the effects of the blood-poisoning. They cleaned away the remains of Anne's miscarriage and washed her body. Dr Thwaite never left her side during the remainder of that morning. Mr Forbes, the specialist gynaecologist, came in at seven and exclaimed in horror at what he found. At noon it was all over and they knew that, barring complications, Anne would live, though they'd have a struggle to hold back the acute sepsis that raged through her body and her bloodstream. Dr Thwaite knew that without the new drugs that had been developed as a result of the war, the sulphanilamides, they would never have pulled her through. As it was, it had been touch-and-go, and only the girl's healthy out-of-doors constitution had enabled her finally to survive.

Reuben and Eleanor spent all day at the hospital, Reuben mostly sitting in the waiting room with his head in his hands, sorrowing. Eleanor had told Emily to stay at home since there was nothing she could do at the hospital; when Dr Thwaite came out of the Emergency Room at mid-day, and told her Anne was going to survive, she telephoned immediately to the Raven Hotel, and Ephraim promised to send somebody immediately with the message.

'Come on, Reuben,' Eleanor said, 'it's time to take you home.' The strain of the night and the morning showed on his face – she had never seen him looking so downbeaten.

She found a taxi outside the hospital and they rode home in it, side by side, she holding his hand to comfort him but not speaking. Truth to tell, she too was exhausted.

Emily took one look at him when he arrived home and sent him straight upstairs to bed – she'd placed an earthenware hot water bottle in the bed in anticipation of his arrival and had kept the kettle near boiling on the hob. 'Help your dad upstairs, John,' she said, but he thrust his son aside. 'Nay, I'm not a baby,' he said, 'I can manage on my own.'

'You'd better get off to bed, too, Eleanor,' Emily said. 'You look done in.

'What about you, Emily? I don't suppose you've had any sleep . . . '

'I've been sitting down dozing in t' chair by t' fire. That'll do me until night-time. Any road, I can never drop off during t' day.' She bustled around Eleanor, fixing her a cup of tea, taking her coat and hanging it for her, despatching Liz for Eleanor's slippers. 'When did the pair of you last eat?' she asked.

'No, Emily, I couldn't manage anything . . . '

Emily ignored her and brought a plate of stew with a couple of slices of bread cut thin the way she knew Eleanor liked them, and Eleanor suddenly discovered what an appetite she had. She watched Emily bustle about as she ate and it came to her yet again what a tremendous power of strength her sister-in-law had always been. When she'd finished, and had wiped her lips with her napkin, she caught Emily's hand as she was about to take the plate away.

'Emily,' she said, 'I've never said this before. I've never given you the credit for it before. But you're the one who holds this family together. You're the Godson out of the lot of us . . . '

Emily flushed with pleasure though she tried to laugh

it off. 'By gow, tha'd better not let Reuben hear you say that,' she said.

'It's true, Emily. And I never realised it until now...'

'Well, a body does what she has to, Eleanor. Can't say nowt more than that in this life! We come on this earth wi' nowt, to toil and strive for what's best. Aye, and then we leave it all behind.'

'The Godson men have always been lucky in the women they've chosen,' Eleanor said sombrely. 'My mother, before her my grandmother, and now you, Emily. The women the Godsons bring into the family have always been the family strength. That's why the women *born* Godson have never amounted to much!'

'Nay, Eleanor, tha' munt say that,' Emily reproached her, embarrassed. 'Tha's given us a thing or two to think about; tha's lifted some of our eyes above t' Cliff Top out into t' world! And that, in itself, is no small thing to have done!'

It was a week before they permitted Anne to receive visitors and Emily was the first. She went into the bright ward with a carrier bag of flowers and fruits she'd scoured Whitby to find, including a bunch of grapes Elsie had given her from the Tockett vine. This late in the season they were shrivelled and small but it was a miracle they were still on the vine anyway.

'I'd have brought chocolate, but I didn't know if they'd allow it,' she said. 'Anyroad, I've brought you a bit of pasty and some shortcake as I made myself, so tha'll not starve!'

She sat by the bed and looked at her daughter, catching her eyes for the first time. 'Tha's made a right muck of it, lass!' she said, 'Hasn't tha'?'

There were tears in Anne's eyes but she brushed them away defiantly. 'What have they done with the Court case?' she asked.

'Oh, they stopped that mullarkey! I heard they were sending t' lad overseas. He'll not be sorry to go!'

'They've dropped the charge . . . ?'

'Yes, they dropped it. What you did was wrong, you know that. You'll have t' police in here, now you're getting better, and you'll have to answer for it, I warn you, so you'd better set your mind to it. Some things we do, we have to pay for! There's no getting round it. You'll have to brace yourself, my girl, that you'll have to pay for what you've done . . . ' Emily spoke hard words, but kindly and with infinite understanding, as if explaining a simple lesson to a child. Emily's world consisted of simple lessons. You did wrong and were caught, you had to pay, one way or the other. And it was as well that Anne learned that lesson immediately. 'There's no point in beating around the bush, love,' she said. 'You'll have to answer for it. But you know we'll always be behind you, we'll always be there when you need us, just as our John, by the Grace of God, was there when you needed him!'

'How's my dad?' Anne asked quietly.

'Your dad's back in t' hospital. He had another breakdown. And I may as well say it straight out, so's you know what's on my mind – you have to bear the responsibility for that, too. Owt happens to your dad as a result of what you did to yourself and you'll have to carry the burden of that all your life. If it's any consolation to you, Suddaby's looking after your dad, and he says he thinks he'll be all right. It just came as such a shock to him, on t' top of Wilfred and Arthur, and being out on that boat all those nights wi' dead bodies about him. Your dad's a very sick man, Anne, and I don't think we know the half of it. Nor ever will. Any road, what's done is done, and we've got to get on, haven't we? Is there owt you need, before I let our Liz come in? They said you can only have one person at a time, and then only for five minutes.'

She stood up to go, then bent down over her daughter,

slipped her arm round Anne's shoulders and kissed her cheek. 'Tha' were a very silly lass,' she said, 'but it's all over with now. Just get yourself better and we'll see how soon we can get you home again.'

'I'm sorry, Mam!' Anne said.

'And so you ought to be, lass!' Emily said firmly. 'And now, there's an end to it.'

It was left to Captain Walham to ask the one question, why?

Anne, thanks to her strong constitution, had made a wonderful recovery and Dr Thwaite had said she could go home on the Saturday, provided she took it easy for a few days when she got there. He'd insisted that, when the time came, she'd be carried up the cobbled street in a chair from the Slip, to avoid having to walk up the steep slope.

Captain Walham arrived at the hospital on the Thursday, after supper, having ascertained that the rest of the family would have been for the mid-day visiting session. He was wearing his sombre navy-blue suit, with a waistcoat over a snowy-white linen shirt, with a silver-flecked bow tie. He carried his bowler hat in his hand, and a walking stick with a silver top.

'My, don't you look dapper, Captain Walham?' Anne said with a lightness she didn't feel. She had dreaded seeing him again, realising that more than any one else, she had betrayed him. He had worked so hard to see justice done, had pressed Ezra Thrummell and Villiers to get on with matters.

He'd brought flowers, and a box of liqueur chocolates to add to the pounds she had already received. He sat beside her bed, his body erect, his pink-scrubbed cheeks glistening, his silver hair strands carefully arranged across his scalp, the picture of correctness, neatness and order, as precise in his personal appearance as she knew him to be in his dealings with others.

'Why did you do it, Anne?' he asked baldly, bluntly. 'Major Bernstein told me that evening that you had the case all wrapped up, neat and tidy. The Court would have cleared your reputation; you would have been able to walk through Old Quaytown with your head held high!'

She sat up in bed with her hands crossed on the counterpane, dry-eyed but with her head hung down. He was totally out of his depth but determined to press ahead with the question. It seemed to him such a terrible breach of faith, such an act of betrayal. He'd relied on her helping him make absolutely clear to the Americans that they couldn't come into the village and behave as they wished. He had realised how wrong he'd been in his first conversations with Major Bernstein, how foolish to suggest that he could accept lowered moral standards. This girl, this victim, had shown him what happens inevitably when standards are lowered. He'd pressed the case against the American as a signpost to show that moral standards must remain high, and that transgressors must be punished. Of course, the moralities he'd been preaching in his Bible-thumping days had been all right for the already converted, but had had little reality for young girls such as Anne, caught in the dilemma of her time and place, facing events so new that no-one could anticipate what would happen. *Of course* she'd always attended the socials, as she'd said in Court, because she'd been brought up to support the Chapel in whatever way she could. It didn't matter that she didn't attend worship in the Chapel – it was a starter that she could be brought to attend the other functions. *Of course* she'd expected to be *safe* – no-one could have anticipated that an invading horde would arrive with strong drink as their weapon of assault! And he knew that he had failed to recognise the danger, failed to do anything adequate to protect the girls whom loyalty to the Chapel had brought in as sitting ducks for the raiders.

'I feel very strongly for you, my dear,' he said, 'as if you were my own daughter. But why, why, did you do it?'

She looked up at him, and swallowed hard, determined to speak. This loving, kindly man deserved better than her silence. 'I know you'll be shocked and hate me and think the worst of me, Captain Walham, but I can't have it on my conscience any longer. I don't know how or why it happened but that evening, at the social, I knew what was happening and I didn't care . . . '

'You *knew* there was whisky in the drink,' he whispered.

She nodded.

'And you drank it . . . ?'

She nodded again. 'I was so miserable that evening, Captain Walham,' she said brokenly. 'I know it's no excuse, now. I'd had a rotten day at work with a foreman who kept on picking at me. I'd been thinking all day about our Wilfred and our Arthur, both killed, and my dad, in and out of hospital all the time. When Liz and me came to the social I was feeling really bad, and then Liz started rowing with me, and Don Meaney gave me a drink, and I drank it. It made me feel better, made me forget how miserable I'd been – I knew there was something in it but I didn't care. And then I had another, and another . . . '

'You knew . . . everything?'

'It was like there was two of me. One of me was miserable and said, go on, cheer up, why not? That part of me said, your two brothers are dead, you'll probably never see Hugh again, your dad's going mad, so go on, have a good time, why not . . . ?'

'I can't listen to you any more, Anne,' Captain Walham said, agitated.

'You've got to listen, Captain Walham,' she whispered. 'You've got to listen, to help me . . . Else I'll be the next one to go mad! I was split in two, and one part of me was watching the other part of me but couldn't do anything about it, anything to stop it. I mean . . . ' Her voice tailed off and he had to lean forward to hear her. 'I knew what he was doing, all the time, but I had no will-power to say no. He never forced me; he just, did it. And I didn't have the will-power to stop him. Not even . . . at the end . . . when I knew . . . he was making me . . . a baby.'

'Anne,' he said, 'stop, Anne, please stop . . . '

'When I looked at him, across the Court, I could read it in his eyes. He was prepared to take the blame, for something he didn't really do. He was prepared to be done down, to pay all that money, to lose his reputation, rather than see me shamed! He was a good man, Captain Walham, and me, and that baby we'd made together, we were ruining his life for him. And that's why I had to get rid of that baby, even if it killed me . . . '

CHAPTER FIFTEEN

When Reuben came home, they all knew he'd come home for good. He'd lost three stones in weight and his cheeks were sunken. There was a lost look in his eyes, and his hair had turned white. His fingers were stained yellow with tobacco and his once strong hands were like the bones of a skeleton. His back stooped; he was already, at forty-six, an old man.

Emily had done all her crying long ago, seeing his deterioration in the Mental Hospital outside Leeds into which the Army finally, and reluctantly, had placed him. They'd all visited him every week, turn and turn about, but he'd shown no interest in them, other than to recognise them as his family, to talk with them about the hospital and the other inmates in his lack-lustre voice.

John came home from the sea and found his dad sitting in his armchair by the fire. 'Right, Dad, tha's back,' he said. 'Now we can get on wi' t' fishing again!'

'We've been listening to t' wireless,' Emily said. 'Hitler's dead!'

'Well, I never,' John said. 'So the bloody war is all over?.

'All bar t' shouting!'

'So, Dad, it's all over, eh? Now we can get back to t' fishing.'

He'd brought the book in which he wrote the day's catch, handing the carbon copy page to Walter Craggs for the record. He gave the book to Reuben, who looked at it lying in his hands without opening it.

'Open it, Dad,' John said, 'have a look what I got today. Three boxes of haddock! How do you like that, eh? Three boxes of haddock . . . '

'You've done well, lad,' Reuben said. 'You've done well for April.'

'Don't bother your dad,' Emily said, 'and get up to t' bathroom and get yourself clean before I dish up your supper.'

'Have you seen the new bathroom, Dad? No more washing in t' tub before t' fire, eh? Have you seen the warm towel rail I've put in, to hang my clothes on . . . ?'

'He's seen nowt, yet,' Emily said. 'I've nobbut just got him home.'

'Well, now you're home, Dad, we can make plans for t' wedding. I wasn't going to be married without you here . . . ' John was looking into Reuben's face, trying in vain to spark interest in his eyes.

Emily grabbed his arm, shaking her head. 'Get upstairs, lad,' she said, 'and get yourself washed. It's been a long journey home for your dad. Leave him be for a minute or two.'

Eleanor had been assigned to a VAD section in Whitby and came home each day when she was off shift. Liz still worked at the rubber factory and Anne had got a job helping Mrs Probert in the Post Office. It didn't pay as much as the rubber factory, but it was close at hand and she was able to help Emily about the house. She also spent part of each day at Captain Walham's, tidying his place for him.

Grace still worked in the Gas Office but intended to give up her job when she and John were married.

They all gathered round the table at seven o'clock. Fewster had made a present, for Reuben's homecoming, of a leg of pork. He'd wanted to give her a piece of beef but Emily had asked for the pork instead. 'I don't think he'll be up to carving beef just yet,' she'd said, knowing it would shame Reuben if John had to carve the joint for him. As it was, he could hack away at the leg of pork and it wouldn't matter what shape the chunks came off . . . John had brought bottles of stout from the Raven, and a quart of beer for Reuben and himself and the meal took on a festive appearance, especially since Emily got out the best plates and the bone-handled cutlery that had been a family heirloom of the Ducketts.

'Come on, Grace, tha' mun have a bit more pork than that!' Emily said, looking at the tiny piece she had on her plate. 'Reuben, can you manage another slice for our Grace . . . ?'

'I can that!' he said, and broke into a bit of a laugh as he attacked the leg vigorously again. John looked up at his dad. By gow, he was laughing! Aye, they'd soon have him better, now that he was back home again. He felt wonderfully relaxed – Hitler bloody-well dead, dad back home, the date for his wedding to Grace fixed for a month hence, and three boxes of haddock in t' book!

'A toast,' he said, lifting his glass of beer. 'a toast to all of us, with our dad back at the helm again!'

They all scrambled to get hold of their glasses, even Martin, who'd been given a glass of milk with a table-spoonful of the stout in it. They all drank deep, each with his or her own reason to be thankful. Even Liz who, that day, had received a letter from Pete, telling her he was on his way back to England.

When they'd finished dinner and the girls were washing up, Emily nudged John. 'Why don't you take your dad down to t' Snug for half an hour?' she said. 'They'd like to see him now that he's back.'

'Hey, Dad, what about it?' John said. 'Half an hour in t' Snug. I'll lick thee at dominoes . . . '

Emily's heart was bursting with happiness as the two of them set out together. Reuben was back home. She'd soon feed him up again. He'd been laughing during dinner, obviously glad to be back with his own folks again. Oh yes, everything was going to be all right. She'd soon have everything back into shape again!

John and Grace were married in the church at the top of the Cliff, with the Reverend Michael Roberts officiating. Grace had chosen Liz and Anne as her bridesmaids – they all wore gowns of white taffeta that rustled as they came down the aisle, where John waited nervously with Francis Bredford, who was taking out the *Nelson* these days.

'I'd rather be out there in a force ten,' John whispered as he heard them coming, and Jenny Naseby started to play the Mendelssohn Wedding March on the church organ. Aunt Eleanor had said they must have the Mendelssohn; John had been doubtful but he had to admit it made a grand noise that filled the church to the rafters.

'I've forgotten t' ring,' Francis whispered in John's ear.

'Getaway,' John whispered back, 'pull t' other!'

It was the traditional local joke, part of the ritual of being a best man, like offering to stand in on the honeymoon if the groom felt inadequate. It had been a grand morning, taken all together. The night before, John had held his stag party in the Snug, and didn't remember Reuben bringing him home and putting him to bed, as was right and proper. Any lad who didn't get himself legless on his last night of *liberty* didn't deserve to be married! His mam had brought him a pot of tea to bed, and a couple of aspirins; he'd needed both to get himself downstairs.

'Tha's not changing thy mind, and taking t' *Hope* out on t' tide, then?' his mam had joked when she saw him.

He'd sat in the chair after breakfast and had gone over the fish accounts with Reuben, in a sense accounting to him for the years of work while Reuben had been away.

'Aye, your mam and me's been talking,' Reuben said

when they'd finished, 'and what we've decided is, that since you kept it all going during the war, you're entitled to half of it.'

'Nay, Dad,' he'd said, 'I've had my fair share, week and week about.'

'Now, don't argue with me, lad,' Reuben had said. 'We want to see you get started on your own, so you're getting half, and that's an end to it.'

His mam had smiled and laid her hand on his shoulder. 'We want to see you start out in t' right way, John,' she said. 'Now that you're getting married, you ought to have a bit of your own behind you, a bit of independence.'

By gow, his share had come to over two thousand pounds! If you took off the thousand he'd already had, it meant he still had another thousand! He was wealthy!

'It'll go in your bank account when I go in tomorrow,' Reuben said, 'yours to do as you like with. Though I pray you won't squander it . . . '

It was an unnecessary fatherly warning and they all knew it – if anything, John had shown himself to be tight with money. His mother had chided him when he'd come home with his wedding suit, for which he'd only paid two pounds. 'Nay,' she'd said, 'you ought to have bought yourself summat a bit better than that!'

'Two pounds is enough for summat I'm only going to wear once,' he'd said. 'Now, if it had been a set of new oilskins . . . '

He felt awkward in his new suit as he and the best man stepped towards the altar where the Reverend Roberts waited, the Common Prayer Book open in his hands. John would have preferred a civil ceremony in the Whitby Registry Office and had said so, but the womenfolk of the two families had been scandalised.

'What!' Emily had said, 'will you shame t' lass? She's a right to walk up to t' altar, aye, and wearing white, I'll be bound!'

He'd coloured beneath his sea-tan. If his mam knew how many times they'd been on the edge of it . . .

'She has that right, Mam, never fear,' he'd said proudly. 'She's nowt to be ashamed of . . . '

'Then let her walk up t' aisle to thee, lad. Let folks see her, in her moment of pride!'

He looked at Grace when she was standing beside him with the veil thrown back from her face. By gow, he were a lucky man to claim such a wife! He'd always thought she looked smashing, but never more so than at this moment. She was surely the pick of the bunch.

He couldn't restrain himself. 'I love thee!' he said quietly, so that only she and the Parson heard. The Parson glanced up from the Prayer Book, reproving him for disturbing the sequence of events, but John smiled cheekily back. Bugger it, whose wedding was it, anyway?

The bells of the Church pealed as they stepped out into Spring sunshine, and people began to throw confetti over them. They'd decided to hold the reception in the Royal Hotel at the top of the Bank and, though it was within easy walking distance, Aunt Eleanor, who'd arbitrated all the arrangements, had told him he and his bride ought to drive there in a wedding car. He smiled at Thurston, standing beside the back door of the big Austin, holding it open, wearing the chauffeur's cap he'd borrowed from Elsie Tockett that was at least two sizes too big for him.

'Ain't got far to go, lad,' he said as he stood aside to let them help Grace in.

As he climbed in beside her she said: 'Don't sit on my dress!' but he was too happy to hear and felt her give him a shove. 'Get off my dress, you great lummox!' she said, and dragged its folds from beneath him.

'Aye, you look grand,' he said, his heart bursting with pleasure, 'you look grand, Mrs Godson.'

'Well, if that's the case, give us a kiss then!' she said, smiling at him through tears of happiness.

The kiss lasted from start to finish of the car ride, and left both of them flushed.

'You'd better come up for air,' Thurston said, 'we've arrived!'

Grace held his hand as Thurston sprang out of the driving seat to open the door for them.

'You'll not get too drunk, will you, John?' she asked nervously.

'No, lass,' he said. 'You can rely on me for that!'

Grace's mam had brought her going-away outfit in a suitcase to the Royal, and John had booked a room for her to change in. The horseshoe table was set when they came into the dining-room; it looked a treat with its snowy-white cloths, the glasses, knives and forks, the plates all ready.

'I'm not having a stand-up do,' John had insisted. 'When I get wed, I want folks to sit down and have a proper meal, not bits of stuff on sticks. It'll be a bowl of soup and, aye, let's have chicken!' There was something very posh about the idea of chicken, but Eleanor had suggested he add an alternative.

'You can order t' meal, Auntie Eleanor,' he'd said, 'just so long as I have a plate of hot chicken in front of me!' Eleanor had added braised beef, with carrots and potatoes, knowing how appetites swell when people are eating a free meal. She'd ordered beer to be put on the table in glasses, not bottles or mugs and, as an alternative for any who wanted it, French wine. She'd chosen the wine herself in Arkwrights in Whitby, an old-established family firm. They'd recommended an Amontillado sherry, to start with, a dryish Graves to drink during the meal, and a Ruby port to finish off with.

'No champagne?' Elsie had asked.

Eleanor had shaken her head. 'It wouldn't be fitting,'

she said. 'I know that both our John and Grace would be embarrassed by it.'

'No brandy . . . ?'

'No,' Eleanor had said firmly. 'If anybody wants to drink brandy, Reuben will take them into the bar after John and Grace have left, and they can drink themselves under the table if they wish. I know our John and Grace, Elsie. They're very simple folk, and all the better for it. Neither one of them has any time for pretence, for impressing folks, for showing off. John will be happy with a glass of beer, and Grace, mark my words, will drink shandy . . . '

What Eleanor had predicted came true. 'Aren't you going to have any of that French wine, missis?' John asked when they were seated at the head of the horseshoe. 'It should be good if Eleanor picked it . . . '

'I think I'll just stay with shandy, John,' Grace said shyly. 'I'm not one much for French wine . . . '

The wedding cake had been baked by Soames in the Old Quaytown bakery. It had three tiers on pillars. Soames wheeled it in on a trolley and everyone gasped with pleasure and admiration of the decorations he had created on it in icing sugar of white, blue, pink, and silver. He stood behind John and handed him the cake-carving knife.

'Don't damage the pillars,' he said, 'they're hard to get these days and I'd like 'em back! But you can eat the roses!'

John laughed for sheer joy as he and Grace stood up behind the cake; she held the knife to it and he pressed his hand on hers. There was a flash as Bill Bradley fired the flare for his plate camera, and then Mrs Soames stepped in to cut the cake into distributable pieces.

'Grace,' John said, 'tha'll never know, lass, how happy you've made me this day . . . '

* * *

Reuben had paid for a double room in Scarborough for the two nights of their honeymoon. Neither wanted to be away longer than that. Thurston drove them over in his smaller taxi, free of charge, as his wedding present to them.

Their room overlooked the sea and had a high ceiling, with its own grand bathroom.

'Have you ever seen owt like that?' John asked, looking at the size of the tub, the marble facing on the walls, the enormous silver-coloured taps from which the hot water gushed rusty at first but then clear and clean.

'I never did,' Grace said.

She unpacked her suitcase and hung some of her things in the wardrobe. Others she refolded and put in the drawer of the vast dressing-table.

'Hey, shall we go down to t' dining-room for supper?' John asked her.

'It'll cost a lot . . . '

'Never you mind. I've plenty of cash in my pocket.'

They walked down the grand staircase, too over-awed to use the lift, stepping side by side, hand in hand, until they reached the vast lobby. Across from them they could see the dining-room, with a black-suited man standing in the doorway with an armful of menu cards, fluttering his hands at each new patron.

John looked at Grace; she patted her hair nervously, apprehensively. 'Do I look all right?' she asked. A lady walking past them wafted perfume.

'You look smashing . . . ' he said, listening to the orchestral trio playing.

'Yes, I know that, but do I look *all right*?' She glanced in a mirrored pillar.

'You look grand, *and* all right,' he said. 'I'd take you anywhere.'

'Do you mean that . . . ?' she asked. 'Do you really mean that?'

'Yes, I do!'

'Then take us round t' corner to t' fish-and-chip shop,' she said. 'My stomach's that nervous, I'd be bound to do summat daft if we went in there.'

'Right, tha's on, lass,' he said, and tucked her arm under his, his mouth already salivating at the thought of a plate of fresh-fried fish, with chips, tea, bread and butter . . .

Mark Adam Tockett used his influence in the War Office, and was one of the first officers to be relieved from active service. They were pleased to see him relinquish his rank since they knew they'd have too many officers with a prior claim to an Establishment as Lieutenant-Colonel, and would have had to reduce him in rank, most probably back to War Substantive Captain.

He came immediately to Yorkshire, to spend a few carefree days with Elsie, freed from the knowledge that he would soon have to leave again. 'I'm fed up with travelling,' he said. 'I never want to see the interior of a train again!'

It was the opportunity she needed. 'I want to talk to you about that, Mark,' she said one evening after supper, when they were sitting in the drawing-room by the fire. She'd put Thomas early to bed – he seemed to be sniffling a bit and was probably sickening for a cold, though she knew he was such a healthy child, spending most of his day out of doors with Jack Prendergast, who adored him, that he'd quickly throw it off. She was not one to mollycoddle her son; even though they were wealthy people, she wanted him to become used to a *strong* life before he went away, as inevitably he would, to boarding school.

Mark was wearing a pair of cords, a woollen shirt, and a comfortable hacking jacket. He'd asked her permission not to dress for dinner and she'd readily accepted. Anyway, his Savile-Row-cut jacket would have served any other man as dress wear, so impeccably did it fit him.

'Do you mind if we talk a bit about the future, Mark?' she asked when he'd given her a cup of coffee and she'd refused a brandy.

He'd lighted a cigar and was sitting back in his armchair, obviously enjoying it, his cup of coffee, and his glass of brandy by the warmth and peace of his own fireside.

'What would you like to talk about?' he said. 'The future of the business? The future of our personal lives?'

'Everything, in a way. But, you understand, I don't want to interfere in things that don't concern me . . . '

'When a lady says that,' he said, smiling contentedly, 'it usually means just the reverse. What do you want to say, my love? Come on, get it out . . . If we're going to have a life with equal shares for each of us, you'll have to learn to speak your mind, won't you? That's the one thing of Old Quaytown that still clings to you, you know . . . ' He wasn't criticising her. He'd never referred to her past in any derogatory way and, she knew, never would. 'We're partners in marriage,' he said, 'and that means something to me . . . '

'If only your father could hear you saying that . . . '

'My father was one of the last of the Victorians, Elsie, and he died before he saw the changes that would have hurt him. I've been giving a lot of thought to the future while I've been away. Life is going to change, you mark my words. The relationship of capital to labour is going to change. Quite apart from anything else, we're going to be in very difficult circumstances as a nation. We're going to be short of the capital we'll need to get our industries going, to switch from wartime to peace-time production. We're going to have to export far more than we've been doing, and compete in a foreign market. We're going to have to go out and borrow a lot of money from somewhere, most probably from America, and in the face of an enormous national debt. And, as if that wasn't a big enough problem, we're going to have to pay more for our labour. Men who've been away serving their country will no longer be content to touch the forelock for a few shillings every Friday. I've got to start thinking very strongly about the Tockett money. Mercifully, it's safe at the moment, and we've done well financially these past few years. But life is going to be a lot harder, and anyone who lacks the capital to survive will have to go to the wall. God willing, that won't be us, not in my lifetime, anyway.'

'I can see the sense of what you're saying, Mark,' Elsie began, 'but I reduce it all to more personal terms. I was wondering, now you're approaching fifty, if perhaps we couldn't change our lives a bit. Instead of you going off to London all the time, couldn't we perhaps pull in our horns again? Couldn't you think a bit more about what happens round here . . . ?'

'In Ravenswyke, do you mean?'

'Yes. It strikes me there are going to be a lot of men coming back from the war out of work. It's going to be a poverty-stricken area if the men don't find jobs. They can go up to Middlesbrough, or into the West Riding, but that'll mean breaking up families, families moving far away. If, on the other hand, you were to apply all your energies to, let's say, the boat-yard . . . '

'But the Cut has silted. The boat-yard's not worth a twopenny damn now . . . '

'The Cut could be dredged, at least enough to give a harbour for launching the boats from the boat-yard. That bit of a bridge could either be knocked down, or turned into a swing bridge on a pontoon . . . '

He looked at her and laughed. 'Who've you been talking with, Elsie?' he asked. 'What do *you* know about dredging, and swing bridges on pontoons . . . ?'

Silas Redfern, whose ill health had kept him out of the Forces, had occupied himself during the war in studying the future of Ravenswyke. The two ideas came from the dossier he had compiled, a copy of which he'd given her to read. He'd done a thorough job, consulting many professionals in Whitby, soliciting their knowledge. Only one thing, she thought, marred his dossier, his ideas. He was proposing that a Co-operative of local people take over the boat-yard and run it as a Socialist enterprise. She knew she daren't show the dossier to Mark Adam – not if she wanted his support.

'Oh, people have been talking, here and there,' she said airily. 'I use my ears . . . '

'I don't suppose that, here and there, people mentioned what the cost was likely to be?' he said, amused by her ideas.

'Oh, not much,' she said, 'using the new dredger they've got in Whitby, around ten thousand pounds.'

He'd heard about the new Whitby dredger though he hadn't actually seen it. 'And the swing bridge?'

'Another ten thousand . . . '

'So, we're talking about an investment of twenty thousand pounds before we even start putting the Works in order. I had thought of selling the Works as it is, taking my losses, and getting out of Ravenswyke altogether. I thought you and I might live in London. Brook Street is near the Park. When everything settles down again, we could do a bit of travelling, if you've a mind, once the lad gets into school? I had thought we might go and look at the West Indies, Bermuda, Jamaica, places like that. We could build ourselves a place in the sun. I could pull out of some of my less productive Holdings, perhaps invest in America. The dollar is going to be the strongest currency in the world from now on, and I've been talking with tax accountants about ways of pulling out of the pound . . . '

He saw the pain on Elsie's face. 'I feel a sense of loss when you talk about the pound and the dollar like that,' she said wistfully, 'and of getting out of Ravenswyke. Oh, I don't know how to say this, Mark, but there's always been a Tockett here in Ravenswyke. There've always been Tocketts, just as there've always been Gainers and Godsons, Fewsters and Clewsons, Bredfords and Mountjoys . . . '

'An' Uncle Tom Cobley an' all!' he said good-naturedly. 'Elsie, I have no sense of history, as you have. Tockett House has always, to me, been a cold and draughty place. I didn't enjoy my childhood here, with my father, feeling all the time that I was competing with my brother Rupert, wondering what sort of mood my father would be in when next I saw him, what sort of impossible standards he would have arbitrarily set for me. I *was* happy here for a while with Hester, I can't deny that, but not for long. It didn't take long for me to prefer to be back in London. I don't know, now, here with you. I'm happy just to be with you, but the war hasn't yet permitted us to be fully together. One of the reasons I wanted to take you to London is that I didn't want it to happen again, that I felt happy when that damned train pulled out of York going south, and miserable when it pulled out of King's Cross, coming north. I'm happy with you, Elsie, don't misunderstand me, happier than I've ever been. But, as yet, we haven't had a chance to test that happiness. I don't want, I haven't wanted, Tockett House to be an influencing factor.'

She held out her hand to him. 'Poor Mark,' she said, 'if only I'd realised all those years ago how unhappy you were. If only I'd realised how much we could come to mean to each other . . . '

'I don't know if it would have worked, then,' he said thoughtfully. 'Perhaps I'm a man who needs to go through fire, first!'

She looked round the room; she had to admit it looked much more elegant now that she'd taken out most of the heavy furniture, had changed the curtains and the lamps. She tried to imagine it again as it had been when she first came here, dark and gloomy. She remembered Mark's father, James Henry Tockett, as if it was only yesterday, sitting behind his desk which he kept across the carpet at an angle so that he could look at the fire while he was doing his accounts. Folks always said, no doubt unkindly and untruthfully, that he kept his desk angled that way so that, when he was interviewing them, he got the benefit of the warmth and not them, so that they had no tendency to linger with their petitions. She couldn't see Mark sitting there while the villagers touched their forelocks to him to ask him to forgive them the rent, or pay them a pound or two compensation for the death of a relative.

'This can be a happy place,' she said. 'When I first came here to work as parlourmaid, I was very happy here. Of course there was a lot of unnecessary work and the place was gloomy, but I was still happy, even though I was carting buckets of coal from the coal cellar away at the back of the house. I do wish you'd try to see it my way, Mark, and not surrender too easily to it. I wish you'd let us – oh, how can I put it – bend this house to our will, instead of letting it beat us and drive us away. And I wish you'd think about opening the Works again, if only to provide employment for the lads who'll be coming back to Old Quaytown, with nothing to do. If you could think of it this way, it could be a memorial to the lads who are never coming back, the Godsons, Bredford, Gainer, Fewster, and now Mountjoy . . . '

'He died, then?'

'He spent two months, I heard, in a pit lined with bamboo. If I'd had my way, I'd have dropped that atom bomb on Tokyo. At least, he came home to die, though you could have put what was left of him in a baby's pram!'

She looked up at him with tears forming in the corners of her eyes. 'We can't forget that, Mark. We've got to do something for them . . . for the lads who got back, safe and sound, like you did. It'd only be a way of thanking God for a safe deliverance . . . '

He turned away and stared into the fire. 'Elsie,' he said, 'I know what you're saying but I've got to speak my mind. We can't be a charity, Elsie, we can't.'

'They gave their *lives*, Mark! That was a charity . . . '

'I *offered* my life, Elsie,' he said firmly. 'I can't give away our fortune and our future! The Tockett money is not *mine*. I'm only the steward of it for my lifetime. The Tockett money belongs as much to Thomas as it does to me. I have a *duty*, Elsie, to husband that money until the time comes to hand it on. That's one side of being wealthy!'

'You wouldn't say these things, Mark, if you'd been in that hospital today, and seen them bring in young Mountjoy. Then you wouldn't have been talking about *charity*, and being *wealthy*.'

He turned quickly back to her. 'And you wouldn't say a thing like that to *me*, Elsie, if you'd been with *me* and watched my own men being killed by Germans. You wouldn't reproach me if you'd had to stand and watch your precious Arthur Godson being chopped down by German bullets, and watched Wilfred needlessly throw himself away on his worthless brother!'

She stared at him. 'Worthless brother, a Godson . . . '

'Well, I never meant to say that, in Ravenswyke, but it's true. Arthur Godson as good as killed his own brother, his brother that was worth ten of him, by his stupidity. Why do you think I recommended Wilfred for the Military Cross and buried his brother in the field without honour?'

'I didn't know . . . '

'Of course you didn't know. Elsie, I will not, I cannot,

squander our money on a charitable scheme. I can, and will, give away specific sums of money for purely charitable purposes – if anybody is in need, I'll not see them suffer. But the boat-works is a business, not a charity. I'll look at it from a businessman's point of view and, if it can be made to work, I'll give it the benefit of the doubt and try it. But I will not run it for one second longer than I want to, and I will not run it at a loss, merely to keep men in work, or to keep Old Quaytown together.'

'Forgive me, Mark,' she said. 'I've made you angry. I've spoiled our evening together. I didn't mean what I said about Mountjoy, and charity . . . '

He moved beside her and put his arms around her. 'I know you didn't, my dear. It must have been an awful thing for you to see . . . we forget, these days, that those of us who've been away have experienced all these things and become hardened to them . . . But please understand that what I'm saying doesn't alter my attitude about the boat-yard. If you want to stay here for a few years, to try to make it work economically, I'm game to try it. Anyway, I'm bored with London, bored with making money for its own sake. It'd be a welcome diversion to make boats, for a change . . . '

The news travelled round Ravenswyke with the speed of gossip – Tockett's opening the Yard again to give the lads jobs when they come back from the Army. As usual, the simple facts were embroidered. 'He's going to give preference to ex-Servicemen – he's going to give the lads the same rank they had in the forces – the sergeants will be the chargehands, the rest will be workers.'

One man, however, was not content with rumour and gossip. He called a meeting of a few cronies in the back room of the Laurel pub. A man came from Whitby and talked fiercely, passionately, with them. Jenkins, who'd taken over the Laurel in 1939 and had kept it going all during the war despite the shortages, went into the room on the pretext of making up the fire, but silence descended as he went in, and persisted until he went out.

'I don't like it,' he said to his wife Myra. 'That devil Silas Redfern is up to something in there. The lad they've brought from Whitby is the same one behind all that trouble in the Whitby Docks – mark my words, that one is a Bolshevik, and Redfern is no better!'

That made two rumours, chasing each other round the streets of Newquay Town. Tockett's opening the Yard, and Redfern is bringing in the Bolsheviks.

Mark Tockett drove to the Yard one afternoon in January, 1946, and opened the gates for the first time since they'd been closed before the war. He went inside and walked across the flat paving to the stone-built offices. He noted the windows that had broken in storms, the tiles that had lifted from a corner of the roof. The offices were dank and stank of rat-droppings. Inside the woodworking shed the machines had all rusted, and some of the belts had decayed and hung down, festooning the overhead power wheels like strips of rotted skin. He became thoroughly dispirited as he tramped around, remembering the works as they had been in his father's time and his own childhood, busily producing boats, smelling of newly worked oak and elm. God knows where they'd get oak now, though he saw the stacks he'd bought when, briefly, he'd run the Works on his own. That had ended when Dobbs had pulled the men out on strike and the atmosphere in the Yard had soured. Mark had thought over those days many times, eventually coming to realise how much of it had been his own fault.

Though his father had been a grim man with a reputation for hard dealing, he'd been able to talk to the men in their own language and they had respected him for it. He'd been a hard unbending Master, but the men had seen his innate fairness. Mark, somehow, had never been able to win the men's confidence to the same extent. They'd always been suspicious of him and his motives and had erected a barrier between them and him that he had never learned to climb. This time, if he opened the Yard, if it seemed to be feasible when he got the figures back from the accountants, he knew he must try to start clean, with no such suspicions. He knew that Elsie would help; the fact that he'd married an Old Quaytown girl would surely stand to his credit.

It would also help that his daughter by Hester, Felicity Mildred, whom he'd sent away to America at the outbreak of war, had married over there and was so busy producing children that, as she said in her letters, she couldn't see her way clear to returning to England for a number of years. He had his son, Thomas, by Elsie and the people would surely now accept him perhaps not as one of them, but as someone prepared to be with them, to fight for them, to look after them. 'I'll send Thomas to the local school for a bit,' he thought. 'That should help!'

The thought buoyed his flagging spirits and he looked round the Yard again with renewed interest. That woodworking machinery was old, anyway, and should be ripped out and sold off as scrap. The idea of overhead power by belting was archaic – he'd install new machines each with its own electric motor, the most modern saws, planers, shapers, he could find. As for wood, well, he'd see what he could get from abroad for the time being, and he'd plant oak, elm and pine on the moor-edge where he owned a thousand acres. He'd put the thousand acres to the plough then plant it with quick growing spruce, the slower growing oak and elm. Part of his legacy to Thomas would be his own supply of the most valuable raw material, wood! His mind bounded ahead. Very well; pull down the offices – they were gloomy early-Victorian buildings and held too many memories. Build something new and light. A few stories high. And put a beacon on top. Dredge the Cut as far as the Yard and build a good berthing dock.

He stopped suddenly. Of course, of course, that was the way to ingratiate himself with the local people, to weld them all together into a single unit.

He'd build a long row of sheds, like big garages. The backs would open on to the Yard; the fronts would open on to the dock. He'd install winches. Then the fishermen could bring in their boats and store them under shelter. He could rent the sheds economically to the fishermen and, as a bonus, he'd get all the repair work . . . They could have beneficial terms from his rigging shop. He could deal in engines. Engage a mechanic for engine repairs. Have a shop that sold parts and fittings. That way, the fishing industry would be part and parcel of the boat-yard, an integrated community!

'A lot of human sweat's gone into making that rust, Mr Tockett,' a voice said.

He turned and saw Silas Redfern, the schoolteacher.

'Ah, Mr Redfern, I didn't catch what you said . . . '

'I said, *Mister* Tockett, that a lot of human sweat has gone into the rusting of those machines . . . '

'Well, yes, I suppose it has . . . I'm pleased to see you. I was just thinking – it's only a thought at the moment and I haven't yet had time to think it over properly, nor talk it over with Mrs Tockett – but what would you say to having our boy, Thomas, in your school?'

Redfern's reaction was instant. 'Mercy me, Mr Tockett, our poor school isn't for the likes of a high and mighty Tockett. We should all have to look to our manners then, wouldn't we?'

Tockett was taken aback – this wasn't the reaction he'd anticipated. He'd thought Redfern would have been pleased to be entrusted with Thomas's education. 'I thought you'd welcome the chance to bring him on . . . '

'For boarding school and University? I've far and away too much to do to get my poor flock prepared for the rigours of the factories and the mines . . . '

Tockett stopped the angry retort that came to his lips – it wouldn't do his future plans any good to cross verbal swords with the schoolmaster. 'Ah well,' he said, aiming for a lightness of tone, a disarming ease. 'It's no matter if you can't accommodate him.'

'I'm afraid the school has to give priority to the children of people who can't afford, because they're underpaid, to send their children for exclusive education. Anyway, Tockett,' Redfern added slyly, 'I may not be concerned with the school much longer. I've been suggested for a much more important post . . . '

'I can't think there's anything more important in life than educating the young ones,' Tockett said.

'Yes, there is, Mr Tockett. Educating the old ones so that people can no longer take advantage of them, can no longer exploit their labour for pittances, can no longer make capital profit from the sweat of a man's honest toil without giving back some of that profit where it rightfully belongs. You see, Mr Tockett, in peace-time we're going to strive for a world in which we can *all* send our sons to boarding schools and Universities, if we're so minded!'

'Ah, you're going to run the Workers' Education Classes. I've always thought they were a good thing, like the free libraries . . . '

'They were a sop to Victorian consciences, Mr Tockett. A way in which the capitalists of another generation could salve their consciences. We're having no more of that. I've been suggested as District Union Organiser. We shall strike where the fire is hottest, on the factory floors, at the mine face, yes, and on the boat-yard benches. I hope, when you were doing your calculations about opening up the Yard again, you weren't counting on finding a plentiful supply of cheap labour to exploit the way your father, and his father before him, did? Cheap labour, Mr Tockett, is a thing of the past. Grace and favour jobs, depending on the whim of the Master, are a thing of the past. In the future, Mr Tockett, you'll be negotiating not with a number of individuals you can play one against the other for the available jobs, but with one organiser, one man who'll negotiate wages and conditions for every man in the place. You're going to be unionised, Mr Tockett, like it or not . . . '

Mark looked at him, noting the fire in Redfern's eyes, the passionate conviction. Very well, he told himself, you half expected this, but not so soon. Hadn't he been saying to Elsie only a few evenings ago, that people would no longer be prepared to sell their labour cheaply, that men who'd risked their lives for their country would no longer be willing to throw those lives away in unsanitary conditions of back-breaking labour! But he was damned if he'd take the words of Redfern without some kind of fight.

'Mr Redfern,' he said, 'I find your ideas interesting, but this is neither the time nor the place to discuss them. Do you see that gate? On this side of that gate, you're trespassing. You're trespassing at this very moment. The next time you walk through that gate, it will be by appointment, understand me? By appointment. If ever you achieve a position of responsibility in which I have to negotiate with you, then I'll negotiate. By appointment only.'

'You'll change your tune, Mark Tockett!'

'Mister Tockett to you, Redfern, now and for ever more!'

Mark Tockett, imbued with a new determination to make the Yard work *despite* Redfern's threats, went to see Reuben Godson. When Emily went to answer the knock she stepped back in amazement. 'Reuben,' she called, 'it's Mr Tockett. Come to see you.'

Mark heard Reuben's voice from within. 'Then let him come inside, woman. He can't see me standing on t' step, can he?'

Emily was in a dither and Mark regretted the impulse which had brought him unannounced. 'If it's not a convenient time . . . ?' he said.

'Nay, Mr Tockett, tha' mun come in!' Never let it be said that Emily had turned a Tockett from her doorstep! She could see the curtains fluttering along the street and Connie Cathcart had already opened her door so she could look out. It'd be round the place in a second if Tockett went away again!

Reuben was sitting by the fire; he got up and said, 'Sit yourself down, Colonel. Emily, fetch t' whisky.'

'I'd rather a cup of tea if you have one going,' Mark said, noting the mug by Reuben's chair.

'Tea?' Emily asked. 'How do you take it?'

'Milk and sugar, like everybody else.'

Reuben indicated the chair across from the fireplace that was nominally Emily's.

Mark went to sit in it but Emily exclaimed. She'd left her knitting in it when she'd gone to answer the door. 'Nay, you don't want them sticking in you,' she said, pulling the needles and the wool out of the chair.

He sat down, extended his hands to the fire and rubbed them together. 'Nothing like a fire,' he said, 'especially weather like this!' He noted Reuben was wearing his fisherman's sweater and his smock was hanging over the oven door, no doubt warming for when he would put it on to go out. The tide would be up in a couple of hours; a few of them, including John Godson, had been working on the boats as he started up the street.

'I want to put an idea to you,' he said. 'It's only an idea

at the moment, but I thought I'd like to discuss it with you while it's still in embryo.'

'Right,' Reuben said, 'discuss away, Colonel.'

Emily gave him his tea, in a cup and saucer he noticed, with a biscuit popped into the saucer alongside the spoon.

'We've got to do something about the Cut,' he said. 'It seems to me that if the Cut was cleared again, as it used to be in the old days, you could sail right into it with your boats in all weathers. You'd have fair and foul weather mooring.'

'I can remember when you could take a boat all the way up to the bridge,' Reuben said. 'The old bridge into Newquay Town, not this bit of a bridge we've got now.'

'Yes, well, it wouldn't take much dredging to get that silt out. I've been talking with them in Whitby and they reckon we could do it in two months or so.'

'You'd have to shift a powerful lot of muck . . . '

'They could do it, with the new dredger.'

'I reckon they could. But who'd pay? And who'd reap the benefit?'

'I'd pay,' Tockett said, 'and we'd all reap the benefit.' He told Reuben in detail his idea for sheds for the fishing boats, for increasing the size of the fishing fleet by providing easier handling. He told him about opening the Yard again, and giving the fishermen preferential rates for supplies in the new chandlery. About building cobles, selling them to new fishermen on deferred payments. When he was half-way through, John came in. Reuben motioned his son to sit down and listen without interrupting, and Mark carried on, swept away by his own enthusiasm.

'It would bring life back to that corner,' he said, 'to have an active boat-yard, to have the fishermen coming and going more easily – I've talked with the people in Whitby and they reckon that if we cut a fifteen foot draught at the entrance to the Cut, you'd have two hours when you could come and go, an hour on each side of the high tide. You could sail your boats into the cradles we'd build, let into the side of the quay, and when the tide went out, they'd settle and stand neatly on the bottom, to float again on the next tide's coming.'

The same thing happened in parts of Whitby harbour, they knew. When the tide went out the boats bottomed into the muddy silt, then floated again when the tide came back in. They wouldn't need to haul the boats out of the water every time they came in, and launch them again when they went out. They'd just float them away, over the bar of the entrance to the Cut. The back of each boat bay would be sloped, so that each boat, effectively, would have its own Slip.

Reuben listened intently until Mark Tockett had finished. 'What do you think, Reuben?' Mark asked. 'What do you think? I'd like to hear your opinion.'

Reuben looked at John who, he could see, was bursting to speak but wouldn't until his dad said he could.

'It's a revolutionary proposal,' Reuben finally said. 'It'd take a lot of figuring out. And it's going to cost a penny or two, by gow!'

'Over the years,' Mark said, 'it would pay for itself in rents. I wouldn't want much. A pound a week would do it.'

'And you'd have the swing bridge on a pontoon. Who'd look after that?'

'I'd have a man to do that. Hydraulic pressure. When you were ready to go out, the man would walk down, work the bridge, and leave it open until you were all out. He'd be standing by when you came in again.'

'And, if the bridge didn't work? If it broke down...?'

'It wouldn't. We'd make sure it didn't break down, that it always worked.'

'You've a greater faith in machinery, Colonel, than I have . . . '

If the machine broke down and the swing bridge couldn't be opened, they could be stuck outside, possibly in a gale. As it was now they could run up the present Slip. It was difficult and dangerous but they'd all mastered it even in the worst storms. If they installed a pontoon and a swing bridge, they'd have to destroy the present Slip by the Raven to put in the footings.

'What do you think, our John?' he asked.

John shook his head. 'They won't do it,' he said. 'In the past there's been many an attempt to get them to use the side of the Cut, even when it were fully open, but they never would. You see, Mr Tockett, it's bred into the fishermen to stay on this side, in Old Quaytown. If the sheds an' all were being built *this* side, the scheme might stand a chance, but as it is now, I can't see the fishermen giving up hundreds of years of tradition. We allus go up the Slip to the Raven. We've got t' Snug there, we've got t' Slip Top, and Old Millie Harrison's shed. We're accustomed to sitting there, in t' boats, working on 'em. We'd feel wrong, somehow, on t' other side of t' Cut!'

'Nay, John,' Reuben said, 'we've got to move along with the times.'

'We've got to try to preserve a fishing industry,' Mark Tockett said despairingly. 'More men would take out boats if they had an easy launching, and a safer all-weather homecoming. It'd make life easier . . . '

John had a stubborn smile on his face. 'Fishermen don't look to make life easier for themselves, Mr Tockett,' he said, 'else why would they do it in the first place? And I reckon that any fisherman who started thinking of the easy way of life would soon lose his interest, and his boat. Aye, I'm not one much for this kind of talk, and happen dad could put it better but, somehow, it's all the problems and the difficulties that gives us a challenge, and makes us want to go on doing it. I've got a feeling that if there wasn't a challenge to it, us'd go off our heads just pulling in a bit of line, wi' hooks and fishes hanging off it. I mean, when you come to think of it, there's not a lot of pleasure to be gained, just chucking bits of line over the side, then going back an hour later to pick 'em up. Especially if you're wet through and frozen to t' marrow, and you know that one slip, one moment's lack of concentration could have you over t' side into t' water! So, you can forget about making life easier for t' fishermen, that's my opinion.'

Mark Tockett looked to Reuben for repudiation of John's prejudices, but Reuben could only reaffirm them. 'There's a lot in what the lad says, Colonel. Fishermen don't count much on an easy life – they've never expected it and have begun to suspect it. And as for giving up the Slip so that a pontoon bridge could be built – I'm afraid they're that wedded to the Snug and the Slip top on the northern side of the Cut, and so opposed to anything that smacks of locating in Newquay Town, that I don't reckon they'd countenance it, somehow.'

'If I can get the boat-yard working, I can give employment to all the lads coming home,' Tockett insisted. 'I can find work for all of them . . . '

'Aye, well, it's nowt to do with us, you know, Colonel, but I hear there's been talk of a union. Are you sure you can *afford* the men these days? They'll not go back to the bad old times, when you and me stood face to face across that yard . . . '

'That's all in the past, Reuben. I know Redfern is talking a lot of hot air about Unions and Closed Shops . . . '

'It isn't *all* hot air, Colonel,' Reuben quietly insisted. 'Fair wage for a fair day's work has been on people's minds ever since the Industrial Revolution started by depriving men of their dignity. The Factories Acts, the

Mines Acts, the Acts to prevent the employment of children, were all necessary . . . '

'You sound as if you've been swallowing Redfern's propaganda, Reuben,' Mark Tockett said, disappointed, but Reuben smiled. He was not a man to take quick offence.

'The only thing I got from Redfern was a good education for my two lads,' he said. 'God bless 'em both, and him for that. It's right enough I've been to listen to him and in my opinion he's a self-interested windbag. What little I know about these matters, and I'll grant you it's little enough, has come to me from a bit of reading. Aye, and a lot of thinking . . . Afore the war it was enough to give a man a job, any job, that paid him a living wage. The employers have gotten away wi' murder sometimes. Now that working men have travelled further afield, and have been valued for the strength of their arms, they're asking a bit more than a working wage that keeps 'em just above the breadline. They're asking for *opportunities*; opportunities to educate their kids, to take their missus on holidays, to have some free time about the house, to make something of themselves. And any employer who doesn't realise that, it seems to me, would be asking for trouble.

'You're going to have to come up wi' summat original, Colonel, if you're hoping to get by Redfern, because a lot of 'em are spellbound by him, and will bend to his will. Well, I understand you sent him on his way t' other day wi' a flea in his ear, so it's going to be a personal battle between you and him. I wish you both well! There, I've stated my position! I wish you *both* well. I hope he gets good terms and conditions for his lads, and that you get a good work-force at a price you can afford, to show a bit of a profit for *your* labours. And, if I might add a personal note, Colonel, and you mustn't think I'm speaking out of turn in any way – I'm right happy, personally, that you're having a go. That boat-yard has been an eyesore long enough and, if you can get it back again as it was, you'll have my support and the support of my family, eh, John!'

'That's right, Mr Tockett, and you'll be able to start by building us a new *Hope*. My dad and me, we're going into partnership wi' a new boat!'

Emily read the long letter twice and saw her worst fears had been realised. Reuben saw her face as she sat in her chair opposite from him, and put down his paper.

'What's lass got to say, Emily,' he asked. 'Not bad news? Tha's got a face as long as a fiddle.'

'Well, I always knew it,' Emily said. 'She's not coming home. Not just yet. She's met this fellow and she wants to get wed with him. She'll be out of the WRNS next month and they'll let her take her demobilisation over there. She's asking if we'll send on her marriage lines, and our Wilfred's death certificate. So's she can . . . get . . . wed . . . again . . . ' She struggled to hold back her tears but it was a forlorn hope.

Reuben reached out his hand and took the letter from her. 'Nay, lass, don't take on so,' he said. 'You've said yourself, times beyond recall, that it would happen.'

'Yes, Reuben, but our Wilfred's wife . . . '

'His *widow*, Emily. She's a right to a life of her own. She were good to him throughout his days. She gave him a grand bairn. She's never said or done any single thing to let him down. And it's been a while, now.'

He came to the paragraph in which Georgina told them about Martin.

I know it will come as a wrench to you, Mam, but I couldn't be happy if I didn't have my lad with me. I know I'm being selfish and that he means a lot to you, but I've talked about him with Elmer, and I've shown him the pictures you've sent over in your letters, and he says he would like to bring the lad up. Mam, he's a very kind man, and I know he'll be a good dad for our Martin . . .

'So, that's it,' Reuben said. 'Well, Emily, I never set much store by our keeping the lad. I'll be sorry to see him go, because I know how much you'll miss him.'

'Don't say as you won't miss him . . . '

'Of course I shall miss him, you muggins.'

'He's our flesh and blood. What's he want with a Yankee for a dad?'

'He's Georgina's flesh and blood, Emily, not ours, and we moan't forget it. He's Georgina's son, and she has a right to him. And, what's more, Martin has a right to be brought up by his own mam.'

'Oh, I shall miss him so, Reuben. I shall miss the poor little mite so . . . '

'You never wrote,' Hugh Dubiel said. 'I didn't know what to think. You got my letters?'

'Yes, Hugh, I got 'em.'

'But you never replied. If it hadn't been for your John, and then Grace . . . '

'What do you mean?'

Hugh Dubiel smiled. 'I've been keeping in touch with you, via Grace. I wrote to her care of her mother, and she wrote back to me. I know all about you . . . About your new job with Mrs Probyn, about you being in hospital and very ill with pneumonia . . . '

'Pneumonia?'

'Sure. I nearly sent you a cable, with flowers, but Grace had told me not to. I used to wait for Grace's letters. Your brother John wasn't a great correspondent. Anne is well, mam is well, I caught three boxes of haddock, submarine got the *Marguerite*, we caught another mine, hoping this finds you as it leaves me . . . '

Anne had to laugh, for the first time since she'd seen him. Liz had been agog when she'd come home and had found Hugh sitting at the table in the living room. 'Where's Pete?' she'd shrieked, and Hugh had said he didn't know, that Pete had been separated from him in a camp in Lubeck, but he hoped he'd be here, soon. 'How did *you* get here so quick?' Liz had demanded, and Hugh had smiled. 'I caught a ride on an Air Force Transport,' he said. He didn't tell them he'd had to bribe his way on board with a German Luger, an officer's swastika badge, and a Gestapo armband.

He'd arrived in Ravenswyke by train from Whitby and had walked down the cliff in trepidation, asking himself if he was being a mug. Jesus, he'd told himself, the girl hasn't written to you, not once. She's likely met another guy. Only the fact that Grace had said Anne hadn't been out with anybody else had persuaded him to try his chances. He blessed Grace for keeping up the correspondence – all the time he'd been away, Anne had been on his mind, and he'd never looked at anyone else, in London, or recently on leave in Paris.

He'd walked up to the door through the barrage of eyes and twitching curtains. One door had opened and the girl he remembered as Jenny Bideford, now a very pregnant woman, had said, half-mocking, 'I see the Yanks are back.'

He'd knocked on the Godson door and, as he and Pete used to do, turned round and thumbed his nose to Connie Cathcart who, sure enough, was still in position behind *her* curtain. He'd had his thumb to his nose when Anne opened the door.

'Why didn't you write, Anne?' he asked gently. 'I've missed you so. Can I ask you, are you still carrying my ring?'

Without speaking, she opened the top button of her blouse and drew out the thin silver chain she'd bought herself to replace the leather thongs she and Liz had first used, all those months ago.

'Does that mean what I pray to God it means?' he asked.

'We've got a lot to talk about, Hugh,' she said, 'an awful lot. Don't ask me any more questions. Not yet. Can you give me a little time? Can you? Just give me a little time, now you're back, so that I can get my thoughts together.'

'That ring around your neck, Anne, so far as I'm concerned – and I haven't changed – still means what it meant when I gave it to you. That you have all the time in the world . . . '

CHAPTER SIXTEEN

'What do you reckon to this bonus scheme of Tockett's, Dad?' John asked. 'Do you reckon it'll work?'

'Well, the lads seem to like it – there's none of 'em taking home less than three pounds a week, without overtime, and with the stoppages.'

'I can't see how Tockett can pay that much wages, and still stay in business. It's a lot of money to find . . . '

'Aye, well, I reckon he's running at a loss, and will likely do so for a year or two, while he's paying for the new machinery and the buildings. It's all had to come out of his capital, you know! That's what lads like Redfern seem to forget.'

'We shan't be having Sly Silas around much longer. I hear he's been offered a very grand job, up in Newcastle, with a car of his own and a house ready to move into . . .'

'They look after their own,' Reuben said. 'Any road, it's grand to see t' boat-yard running again. I reckon as they'll have t' *Hope* ready for trials next week. Then we'll have to look sharp to get the motor in, and the rigging done.'

'Stainless steel, eh? Won't that look summat!'

'And don't forget your idea for t' deck winches. There'll be no more heavy hand hauling.'

John looked around the present *Hope*, sitting in the stern with his dad, eating the snap Mam had put up for them. It was good to have a bit of crispy bacon in the sandwiches again and sugar in the tea, though there'd been talk that bread rationing would come, even now, after the war.

They had a little galley on the new boat of John's own basic design and additional suggestions from Grace and Mam. They'd be able to cook themselves a hot meal, if they'd a mind! And make fresh tea any time they wanted it. That *would* be a luxury!

'Us'll have to be careful with yon galley,' Reuben said as if reading his thoughts. 'I'm not very keen on having that bottled gas on board. We'll have to make quite sure all the connections are tight and can't spring in a storm.'

'If they can carry petrol for some of the engines, I don't see why we shouldn't carry a bottle of gas,' John said complacently. 'And right now, it'd be good to have a pot of hot tea brewing. This is right brass monkey weather!'

The day had gradually turned colder while they had been out and the waves had started to pound, lifting a spume of spray that kept them as drenched as a full dousing. Everything they touched seemed to be slimed over with it and their fingers froze to the bone. Visibility was gradually going down, too, and soon they wouldn't be able to see Tockett Top as their weather guide. They paid the adverse conditions no heed; hardened by their years of fishing, they accepted days like this along with all the other, good days as part of the inevitable changing of the ever moving sea. The day had promised good; the sea had a productive feel to them both that many would have thought fanciful. John had often noticed that he did well when the surface of the sea seemed tacky, oily, when it seemed to clem to the side of the boat and his skin. When the light went down, he supposed, the fish came nearer the surface – certainly he'd found that days like this, the catch tended to be heavier, and the fish bigger.

'How does this bonus thing of Tockett's work exactly, Dad?' John asked.

'It's summat he's worked out hisself, give him credit for

that. But, of course, like all such schemes, in the long run it's designed to get the men to give him a better day's work. You'll never see a Master giving summat for nowt, at least not during my lifetime. Old habits die too hard! He simply takes what the things cost to make, and works out how much per cent of that goes on labour. If the men work hard enough that the labour cost drops below a certain per cent, they get the balance to divide among them. The way they've worked it out, him and Bramham, the men's representative, the lads could get as much as £50 each for Christmas this year, and that'd be like another pound a week on their wages.' He chuckled as he remembered Silas Redfern's face when he learned what Bramham had got for the men, who were pledged to join no Union. Redfern had just been making a lot of noise about getting a standard wage for the Union lads of two pounds, seventeen and sixpence a week, for a forty-eight-hour week. The lads working in Tockett's were getting more than that for a forty-six-hour week, with the chance of a big bonus in their hands at the end of the year.

Redfern had sneered when he'd heard. 'You haven't seen the actual size of the bonus, yet,' he'd said. 'It could be a handshake, and "better luck next year, lads". He wouldn't be the first capitalist to lie and cheat to get men to work more, for less . . . '

With the opening of the Tockett boat-yard, Newquay Town had taken on a new lease of life. Tockett had had no difficulty renting the cottages, and had even bought back a couple that had gone to infrequent holiday-makers from Leeds, to rent them to his own workers. Redfern had sneered at that, too.

'Tied cottages,' he'd said, 'one of the tools of capitalism since the beginning of the eighteenth century, a way to blackmail you into staying on the job lest you lose your home!'

The men who returned from the war, finding house

prices had soared, had been happy to find roofs over their head. Tockett had engaged a work force of over one hundred and fifty, and all had been accommodated in Newquay Town or up on the top of the Bank. He'd given priority to Ravenswyke folks, right enough, and they respected him for that. They respected him, also, for having found employment for a few of the injured men who'd imagined they'd be thrown on the scrap-heap when they came home. Young Walter Mountjoy, who'd been blinded by a land-mine in North Africa, was sent at Tockett's own expense to the Blind School near Brighton and had been taught to work a telephone switchboard; Alf Clegg, who'd lost the use of both legs and was condemned to spend the rest of his life in a wheelchair, had been given a job in the stores where he could scoot up and down the aisles in his chair with its basket on the front, fetching the small parts men constantly used in boat-building.

Tockett himself spent all of each working day in the boat-yard, looking at everything. At first the men resented it; there was still the pre-war legacy of Mark Tockett not being like his father. Gradually, it seemed, he was earning the men's confidence, even their respect.

'Do you think they'll get their fifty pounds at the end of the year?' John asked.

Reuben chuckled. 'It's a good point,' he said, 'but at least the idea is one up for Mark Tockett. The men are going to work hard all year, to see if they do get it. So, afore he starts, he gets the promise of a year's hard work out of 'em, doesn't he?' He stood up. 'Looks about right for a pull,' he said.

John looked over the side; anything they were going to catch was already on the hook, he reckoned. If they left it any longer, their fish would be preyed on by predators.

'Right,' he said, and kicked in the motor. The new battery they'd had installed worked a treat; the flywheel started to turn and then, as it built up speed, the cut-out dropped the compression lever. The familiar thump, thump, began at once, and a puff of dark smoke came out of the exhaust.

He let the engine settle for long enough, in his opinion, then kicked in the clutch to start the boat forward.

'Not so fast, young 'un,' Reuben shouted. 'You've got to give it more time to warm up else you'll pull t' guts out of it! Tha's too impatient.'

'Can't hang about all day,' John said. Aye, his dad was right, he did tend to rush things a bit. The habit had crept over him during the years he had been taking the boat out alone. He knew it was a bad failing in himself, but he couldn't bear to hang about. And it seemed to him that, since his dad had come out fishing again, he'd got slower, much too slow for John's eager blood. For example, he would have lifted the lines ten – fifteen minutes ago . . .

Reuben came to the stern after he'd cleared the foot of the mast and had placed the baskets ready to receive the line.

'Tha's got the front basket a bit far forward, Dad,' John said.

'Aye, well, you want to keep it well away, else one of the hooks might kick back at you. I allus reckon it as a full arm's length myself . . . '

'Your arm's a bit longer than mine . . . '

Reuben looked at his son as he settled at the tiller. It wasn't like John to be so picky. All the time they'd been out the lad had been carping at him about one thing or another. And then gabby while they were having snap.

'You got owt on your mind, lad?' he asked.

'Nay, nowt more than usual.'

'Aye, well, you know where to come to, I reckon.'

'It's nowt,' John said, 'except Grace is expecting . . . '

Reuben's face cracked into a smile. 'Tha's been quick!' he said delightedly.

'Aye, happen a bit too quick. We were going to wait a bit. Enjoy ourselves.'

'Nay lad, some things won't wait. And it's best news you could have given your mam. How she's pined since Martin was taken away. She was only saying t' other day how pleased she was, thinking about your bairn . . . '

'T' other day . . . You mean, you knew . . . ?'

Reuben smiled again. 'You can't keep such things from women,' he said. 'Your mam's known a while. She was wondering when you were going to speak about it. Of course, I wouldn't say nowt until you'd broached the subject, but now I can tell you that I'm right glad, right happy for your sake and for Grace's. Nay, wedded couple without any bairns is a terrible waste, to my way of reckoning. It's like slinging your hook without any bait on it!'

John had cheered a little. 'I suppose it's not so bad,' he said, 'though we had talked it over to wait a bit. I mean, what wi' going shares on t' new boat, and all. There'll not be much left over!'

'There won't be any left over, lad, if you don't start picking up them lines . . . '

Reuben was happy to have cleared the air between them. Once or twice recently he'd wondered if it was going to be a good thing for them to fish together, since they were both so different in their styles. John had developed a way of fishing on his own, taking risks, that Reuben didn't approve too well. He, himself, was a more conservative fisherman, who'd rather take his time, be as careful as possible, but yet still bring in a catch. That didn't mean he never took risks – fishermen take risks all the time, but some are calculated, some are foolish.

And right now, he told himself, John was taking what he would call a foolish risk. He was standing in the gunwales, heaving the line, flicking it with his right hand into a neat circle in the basket, the twist he put on the coil settling the line neatly round the basket's rim. He'd developed a good technique and could lay a line with the best, but he was standing wrong in Reuben's estimation, too much abeam. That meant he was casting the line almost behind him past his body. Now, all right, he had a neat cast so long as the line came up smooth, but it sometimes happened that a dangler turned round and round on a hook, which could put a twisted kink into ten or more fathoms. As soon as that section of line came in, as soon as it passed from the tension of the left hand to the freedom of the right hand, it twisted uncontrollably and could wind itself round a man, round his arm, his head, his neck. Thatterthwaite had been caught like that, they said. The twisted line, released from his right hand, curled up and around his neck in an instant. The boat was moving forward, of course, under power. He couldn't free the line fast enough and the weight of line still in the water had pulled him overboard and strangled him.

But it was one of their oldest traditions that the helmsman didn't talk to the man lifting the lines while he was working, didn't disturb his concentration for even a flick of a second. It was Reuben's sole job to keep that boat on a dead-straight path along the line of the floats, to keep a constant speed so that the puller didn't have to bear the burden of the entire fifty fathoms lying in the water. It took co-ordination and understanding, and needed no jabbering. But he'd dearly like to see the lad standing a bit better, keeping his head back, his body turned a bit more fore-and-aft, his arm casting further from himself.

Would he provoke another row if he spoke? Once or twice, he knew, the lad had been choked off with the suggestions he'd made. 'Dad, I've been fishing all the war,' he'd said again and again. 'You're not going to start to teach me now?' The suggestion had been that Reuben was in no position to teach him, and maybe that was true.

Maybe Reuben had lost his edge during those terrible wartime days when all he could think about were the eyes. Those dreadful months in the mental hospital, among the loonies, telling himself, as they all were, that at least *he* was sane, he wasn't crazy like the rest of them. And then coming back wasted away, with the humiliation, the first time he'd come out on the boat with John, of not being able to get the line up, just not having the sheer physical strength to do it until Emily had built him up again. He'd never let any of the family know how he'd gone up into the woods beyond Beck Top where he'd found a fallen log and, day after day, when they thought he was out walking, he'd lifted that log, over and over again, at one end, until he could get if off the ground. Then lifting it five times, ten times, twenty, building up the muscle fibre again so's not to be shamed next time he went out.

He groaned when he saw the cast from John's right hand twist in the air like a coiled watch-spring suddenly let go. John ducked and turned to his dad, knowing what he'd be thinking. Already he was drawing the next section of line and he grinned cheekily, as if to say, you thought that'd get me!

It was because of his bent position that the next section of line, when he attempted to flip it on to the coil in the basket, reared back at him as if it had life of its own, and double looped itself over his head and round his throat.

Reuben instantly finger-touched the throttle to send them forwards to take the weight of the line away from the lad, who was struggling to get his right arm up and under it, the knife in his hand ready to cut if he could. His left arm held the tension of the fathoms that were still down and he tried for the post on the gunwale, where he could lash the line to take the strain off his neck. His left hand couldn't reach, since he'd been caught standing in the wrong position.

Reuben started forward, hoping to grab the line from

John's left hand to snag it round the gunwale post. Then they could slash the line that was round John's throat. He was half-way forward and in that split second, the bow of the boat lifted on the next wave, heaving high into the air. The effect was momentarily to check the boat in the wave trough, but to increase the tension in the line hanging in the water below the vagaries of waves. Reuben saw the line snap tight, saw John trying to hold it with his hand, but no power in a man's arm could have held the full weight of the boat which lay dead on that line. John went overboard.

Reuben didn't think; he raced back and kicked out the clutch, tied a rope round his waist and went over the side. He struck out and found the coil of line that, he knew, would be snaking out of the basket above. Thank God they hadn't yet pulled as far as the hooks. He jerked the line towards himself slowly, knowing that somewhere along its length John was hanging, possibly fighting for breath trying to unkink the line from around his neck, perhaps knocked unconscious by the fall from the boat. Reuben's breath pounded in his lungs as he pulled the line, moving himself along it as fast as he could until he saw the shape of his son in the water, his legs kicking futilely as he tried to rise to the surface. Reuben reached in with his line-cutters and snipped the nylon round John's throat, freeing him. The line cleared instantly under its own weight and now Reuben used the rope round his waist, secured to the post at the stern, to haul them back up. He had no time for anything other than progressing through the water as fast as he could. Already he could feel the flash behind his eyes as he ran out of breath. He knew he'd never make it on the one lungful, but happen he'd be near enough . . .

The haul seemed to go on for ever and the pain in his chest and his head was unbelievable by the time he saw the hull of the *Hope* and dragged on the rope to hoist himself and his burden. He ran out of breath just before he reached the surface and took a half-lungful of sea-water before the air went down after it, bubbling the water back out of his mouth with a foetid odour that hit his nostrils. He was pushing the lad's body over the stern, hanging on to the rope, and then, when John flopped into the *Hope*, he pulled himself over the transom and lay beside him, trying to breathe, trying to clear that foul stuff out of his nostrils and his mouth.

He bent over John, straightening him out. It seemed as if John had stopped breathing. He picked him up and hung him face down over the stern thwart, pressing on his lungs. He saw the water gush out of John's mouth and his nose, relaxed the pressure, then pressed down again. Again, water came out, and with it a bile such as Reuben himself had lost.

He was dreadfully cold and knew John must be, too. Luckily, they kept a couple of blankets on board behind the engine box where they stayed warm. It was a great comfort to come home sometimes, on a freezing night, with a warm blanket wrapped around you. He steadied John on the thwart and got the blankets from the box, wrapping them round John, swaddling him in their warmth. The boy's face was a sort of grey-green colour, almost khaki. Reuben pressed again on his chest, and now he heard a rattle in John's throat. Press, relax, press, relax, press, relax. The boat was bucketing now, swinging wildly to every wave, turning and twisting since the line had run out again and was held amidships. He knew he had to cut the line, which must have knotted itself in its twist below the water so that John had been caught on a loop. Now the *Hope* was being held amidships, being brought across the waves. Already she was shipping water over the starboard side.

He left John, went amidships and slashed the line free.

He rushed back to the stern and cast out the sheet anchor. It was already roped alongside the gunwales to the bow post; it would hold the bows into the wind, ten degrees across the waves, where they'd do no damage.

Press, relax, press, relax. Again, that rattle in John's throat, as if something were trying to come up. He pounded John's back, hung his head down a bit further, pounded again. Then press, relax, press, relax.

He knew instantly when the breathing started of its own volition. He'd been giving John artificial respiration for at least five minutes, it seemed to him, when suddenly he heard the rattle end half-way through in a sigh. He pressed more gently and when he relaxed the sigh became audible over the pounding of the waves. He bent down and looked up into John's face, holding his hand on John's back. The lad had taken one breath. Now he took another. And another.

Reuben pulled John over and squatted in the boat holding John's head in his arms, tears rolling down his face. He couldn't speak. He rocked himself to try to get warm, to try to restore some feeling in his soaked frozen body, but he hugged the lad close to his chest and rocked.

'Thank God,' he said out loud. 'Thank God he's given the lad back to me!'

They sat that way for upwards of fifteen minutes, hugging the engine box for its heat, Reuben pushing his warmth into his son wrapped in the blankets. When John stirred, Reuben looked down into his face, used his free arm to get his sopping handkerchief out of his smock pocket, and wiped the bile and snot from it, as John's eyes slowly opened.

They gazed up into the leaden sky, and Reuben rubbed the side of the lad's face with the handkerchief, cleansing it, stroking it.

'Tha's all right, lad,' he said. 'Tha' went for a bit of a swim, that's all.'

John tried to move his body but couldn't because of the tightness of the blankets.

'Keep still,' Reuben said, 'let thy warmth spread through thee.'

John's eyes focused, lifted upwards to look into his father's.

Reuben was instantly reminded once again, of all the eyes looking at him, pleading, despairing, hating, and suddenly, they were all blotted out by the sight of his own son's eyes, the look in them, the gratitude he couldn't yet put into words.

'Looks like tha's been swimming, as well,' John said.

'Aye, happen I have,' Reuben said, 'but I brought thee back in wi' me. This is no time of year for swimming, lad. I taught thee better than that . . . '

John was all right; his dad's warmth, the blankets, and the engines, had helped him survive.

Reuben was shivering when he finally berthed the boat, and went straight to bed when he arrived in the cottage. In the middle of the night John, totally recovered, went to the Bank and brought Dr Thwaite, who diagnosed pneumonia. That night was unseasonably cold; Dr Thwaite knew it would kill Reuben to have to be carried down that cobbled street, through the knife-edged wind to the ambulance. He stayed with Reuben all night as Reuben lay on the big bed fighting the fluid that was forming inside him. Dr Thwaite had been up the previous two nights with two difficult births in succession. Shortly after six o'clock, he had to confess himself totally beat and they put him to bed in the girls' room, empty since Anne and Liz had married, and gone to live in New Jersey.

Emily sat beside the bed as daylight broke, heard her husband wheezing.

His eyes opened once or twice, and the third time, he spoke. 'Am I going, then, lass?' he asked faintly, but she shook her head at him.

'No, tha's bloody-well not,' she said. It was the first time during their life together that he'd heard her swear. 'Tha's going to get better, if I've owt to do wi' it.'